Pr

MRS

'A giddy, outrageous, passic e. *Mrs Hopkins* is a subversive, dark delight.'

'Shirley Barrett was a vibrant storyteller on screen and on the page. *Mrs Hopkins* is bursting with life, telling a tale of tough young women and kids, mistreated, damaged, but full of swagger, and the blundering individuals who are supposed to care for them. I was gripped from the first chapter, and every time I thought I knew where this shocking, funny, moving story was going, Barrett would surprise me in the most satisfying ways.' **Debra Oswald**

'Shirley's wonderfully nuanced and complicated Mrs Hopkins is immediately engaging, original, and of course full of her trademark curiosity and wit. Her ability to build a simultaneously heightened yet relatable world is unmatched, and her intriguing characters, both questioning and courageous, make for a truly experiential journey. In a profoundly insightful and moving final act, I didn't want it to end.' **Asher Keddie**

Praise for

THE BUS ON THURSDAY

'Shockingly funny and satisfying . . . I was hooked from the opening pages. It's laugh-out-loud horrible and perfectly nuts—you'll never find anything like it again.' ***The Guardian***

'Shirley Barrett takes liberally from horror film classics, twisting the genre's conventions with verve . . . *The Bus on Thursday* is a fun ride.' ***The Saturday Paper***

'Undeniably entertaining, highly visual and cinematic.' ***Sydney Morning Herald***

'A surreal, unnerving romp . . . Shirley Barrett knows how to draw a reader into a psychological conundrum exploring the dark undercurrents of rural Australia, isolation and unfulfilled desires. Recommended for readers who prefer their stories fast paced and unpredictable.' ***Books + Publishing***

'This wise, witty and rather demented novel occupies a strange, and possibly unique, space between screwball comedy, murder mystery and magical realism.' ***Daily Mail*** (UK)

Praise for

RUSH OH!

'Barrett's vivid prose gives savour to a highly enjoyable and unusual yarn.' ***Sydney Morning Herald***

'Expertly balancing light and dark . . . poignant, funny and original.' ***Canberra Weekly***

'A rollicking seaborne ride . . . humorous, imaginative and tender.' ***The Independent***

Shirley Barrett was born in Melbourne in 1961 and is best known for her work as a screenwriter and director. Her first film, *Love Serenade,* won the Camera d'Or at the Cannes Film Festival in 1996. It was followed by *Walk The Talk* (2000) and *South Solitary* (2010). She also had a distinguished career writing and directing for television, including *Heartbreak High, Love Child, Love My Way* and *Offspring.* Shirley's first novel, *Rush Oh!,* was published in 2015, and her second novel, *The Bus on Thursday,* in 2018. Shirley died in Sydney in August 2022 after a long illness. She was adding the final touches to *Mrs Hopkins* at the time of her death.

Shirley Barrett

MRS HOPKINS

ALLEN&UNWIN
SYDNEY • MELBOURNE • AUCKLAND • LONDON

This is a work of fiction. Names, characters, places and incidents are sometimes based on historical events, but are used fictitiously.

First published in 2024

Allen & Unwin
Cammeraygal Country
83 Alexander Street
Crows Nest NSW 2065
Australia
Phone: (61 2) 8425 0100
Email: info@allenandunwin.com
Web: www.allenandunwin.com

Allen & Unwin acknowledges the Traditional Owners of the Country on which we live and work. We pay our respects to all Aboriginal and Torres Strait Islander Elders, past and present.

NATIONAL LIBRARY OF AUSTRALIA

A catalogue record for this book is available from the National Library of Australia

ISBN 978 1 76106 852 2

Set in 13.2/19 pt Adobe Jenson Pro by Bookhouse, Sydney
Printed and bound in Australia by the Opus Group

10 9 8 7 6 5 4 3 2 1

MIX
Paper | Supporting responsible forestry
FSC® C001695
FSC www.fsc.org

The paper in this book is FSC® certified. FSC® promotes environmentally responsible, socially beneficial and economically viable management of the world's forests.

For Chris

In Sydney Harbor thar's an isle
A place that's dull and drear
With nary tree upon its site
It looks pertickler queer
It aint at all the sort of isle
Whar lovers bill and coo—
Its character is raly vile—
Folks call it 'Cockatoo'.
As Cockatoo is known to Fame—
Known also to each Peeler,
But lately they have changed its name
An' called it 'Biloela'.
It's now the home of rowdy gals—
A naughty sisterhood—
Who, prison'd on that rocky isle
Are larning to be good!
But 'taint no use—they'll never larn—
These gals air reglar squealers
An' horrid yarns the folks do tell
About them Biloelas . . .

Sydney Punch, 1871

'They are very peculiar children. There are two things they never lose: wit and courage.'

—Frederick Cane, Biloela Industrial School For Girls.
Commission Into Public Charities, 1871

A small thin woman, hollow-eyed, sat clutching her Gladstone bag as the steamer *Emu* lurched fitfully over the waters. Rather than choosing to sit in the warm saloon as had most passengers given the inclement weather, she had elected instead to sit on one of the hard wooden benches on the front deck, and for this decision she was enduring a regular splattering of spray as the bow of the steamer lifted and fell upon the swell. Emerging from the cabin, the ticket collector eyed her balefully, for her unusual seating preference meant that he would now be forced to skate across the slick deck and receive his dousing, too.

'Lover of Nature, are you?' he asked in ill humour, propping himself against the railing to inspect the ticket she had offered him.

'I don't often go on boats,' she responded, as if this was quite enough of an explanation.

The woman turned her face to him then with a wan smile, and he was surprised to see that in spite of the thinness of her features and the dark circles under her eyes, she was—with the dewy spray upon her cheeks, at least—quite moderately attractive.

'What's your business on Cockatoo Island?' he asked as he handed her ticket back. 'Nothing to do with Biloela, I hope?'

'Why, yes, I'm the new School-Mistress there.'

The boat pitched forward heavily as if to offer its own dramatic punctuation to this pronouncement, and the ticket collector lost his footing altogether, falling clumsily onto the bench seat in front of her.

'Then let me give you some advice,' he said, once he had recovered himself. 'Don't get off. Stay on board. We do a round trip back to King Street, and I'll see that you get back through the turnstiles.'

She cocked her head at an angle in faint reproval, though the smile remained upon her lips.

'I'm not having you on,' he said earnestly, clutching onto his cap for the breeze had picked up. 'They're most of them whores, the very rakings and scrapings of the streets and the gutters. I should know, for they're always escaping. And when they do, they get on this boat and lift up their skirts and offer me anything in lieu of payment. As bold as you like! Some of them as young as twelve!'

The thin woman stopped smiling now, and her expression drew grave.

'And the language they use when they realise that we've tipped off the Water Police!' continued the ticket collector, raising his voice now to be heard above the wind. 'I've served in the Merchant Navy, but what comes out of their mouths shocks even me, and I was a bleedin' stoker, beg yer pardon! And the songs they sing, especially when they're working up a riot—we can hear them from the wharf! Oh no, I'm deadly serious—it's no place for a lady such as yourself.'

'On the contrary,' said the thin woman, 'everything you have told me makes me feel that it is exactly the sort of place where I can prove myself most useful.'

She said all of this in a low voice, and most of it blew away on the wind. The ticket collector heard only the word 'useful', but caught the general gist from her demeanour. A church woman, he thought to himself. A do-gooder. Most likely a spinster. Well, she will learn her lesson soon enough.

'Come and sit inside in the warmth at least,' he urged. 'It's only ten minutes, and you'll be thoroughly drenched if you stay out here.'

'Thank you,' she said, 'but I like to feel the wind and the spray.'

Somewhat touched in the head as well, concluded the ticket collector. And not at all attractive really, now that he looked at her properly, with her hair plastered on her bony forehead like two dank curtains.

'There it is anyway,' he said, rising to his feet, for the boat had veered suddenly and the island now loomed into view. He lurched back towards the comfort of the cabin, clutching onto the railings to avoid another slip, leaving the do-gooder to gaze up at the grim, unwelcoming visage of her new home.

Cockatoo Island was not especially large, but it had about it a look both brooding and battle-scarred. Near its short wharf, which the *Emu* was now approaching, a capacious dry dock had been excavated, in which was currently suspended a battered-looking man-of-war. Beyond the three great masts of the marooned vessel rose a rockface of immense size, its precipice marked with sporadic bursts of plant life. Atop this escarpment, dimly discernible in the fading light, sat a cluster of squat and ugly sandstone buildings, built in haste thirty years ago to serve as convict barracks. In recent times, given the general unruliness of these inmates and the fact that one of them (Frederick Ward, in fact, alias 'Captain Thunderbolt') had proved capable of swimming the distance to Sydney, even while sporting leg-irons, the convicts had been moved to other accommodation. In their place had been installed eighty or so young girls, aged from eighteen months to eighteen years, rounded up off the streets where they had been found wandering, vagrant and destitute, unkempt and apparently uncared-for. It was these lost girls that the thin lady had come to instruct.

As the ticket officer opened the door of the saloon, he glanced back at the woman and saw her brace her shoulders stiffly against the movement of the boat. In fact, she was trying to summon within herself some courage, for doubt and fear had assailed her at the sight of what lay before her.

There had been no one there to meet Mrs Hopkins when she disembarked, so after waiting for fifteen minutes, glancing about anxiously in the hope of someone coming to fetch her, she finally left the chest containing all of her possessions in the care of a large, simple-looking man who was hanging about the wharf and apparently belonged somehow to the island. Then she set off up the steep incline to the barracks, carrying only her late husband's Gladstone bag. It was not a long walk, but it was a difficult one, for all along the way in the undergrowth, seagulls lurked in their scrappy nests. They charged at Mrs Hopkins, beaks agape and wings outstretched. 'Go away go away go away!' they seemed to cry. In response, she swung her Gladstone bag violently at them: 'Shoo! Shoo!'

It was by now almost six o'clock, and the sky was darkening. Heavy drops of rain began to fall. There seemed to be some kind of rumpus emanating from the Biloela buildings—shouting, in girlish voices, and snatches of rollicking song. Mrs Hopkins strained to hear the words of the song, for she feared they might be working up another riot—hadn't the ticket collector mentioned something of the sort? But as far as she could tell (for the seagulls were still screaming), the song seemed chiefly to concern the amorous escapades of a young lass named Millie, possessed of a pair of lily-white thighs. It was sung with great gusto and even some attempts at harmony.

They like to sing, Mrs Hopkins thought to herself. That's a good thing. I can make use of that.

It was raining in earnest by the time Mrs Hopkins reached the gate, and she pulled hard at the bell-rope to be heard above the din. No one seemed to hear it—the raucous singing continued. She pulled again, even more strenuously this time, and peered through the metal bars.

'I will pull your liver out, Connelly, you fat cunt, and stuff it down your throat, so I will!' This was followed by a cackle of laughter.

Mrs Hopkins drew back sharply from the bars. She had an impulse to hide, but it was too late. A tall red-haired girl of about fifteen, apparently the same girl who had just threatened Connelly—whoever Connelly was—appeared before her and shrieked in fright.

'Jesus God, I thought you were a ghost, so I did!' cried the girl, after much vigorous thumping of her chest, apparently in an attempt to have her heart renew its beating. 'What are you doing hanging about at the gate?'

'I am trying to be let in,' said Mrs Hopkins, aware of how feeble that sounded. She had hoped to make a strong impression from the outset. 'I've rung the bell several times.'

'Who are you, though?' asked the girl. 'We can't let in just anyone, can we?'

'I am the new School-Mistress,' said Mrs Hopkins.

'Christ Almighty!' exclaimed the girl, cheerfully. 'We only just got rid of the last one!'

'Will you let me in please?'

'I can't, we're not allowed. If we could let people in, we'd let ourselves out, wouldn't we? Hang about and I'll try and find old Crabface.' And she took off, running across the quadrangle to escape the rain.

How short her skirts are, thought Mrs Hopkins, as she glimpsed the girl's thin calves. And why was she barefoot?

Mrs Hopkins gazed at the grim sandstone walls of the old convict barracks. High up on these walls, narrow apertures had been spaced at intervals for the purposes of ventilation. Within these apertures, she could just make out the movement of dark shapes. There seemed to be a jockeying for position going on, one figure would be yanked down, and replaced with another; torrents of shrill abuse streamed forth. It reminded Mrs Hopkins of the squabbling that goes on in trees in the evening when birds try to find the most favourable roost.

Soon a male voice could be heard above the ruckus. 'Now girls, settle down please, if you will. Where is Eliza? Has anyone seen Eliza? Why is not Eliza here?

'Well, then, what is the point of this muster if the girls do not come to be mustered?

'Get down from those windows, Margaret—what is your name then? Mary-Ann, I beg your pardon. Please hop down from there at once, Mary-Ann. I do not care if Mr Baker-Hunt permitted it—I do not permit it. It is dangerous in the extreme—'

And now the red-haired girl's voice sung out clearly from behind the bars. 'But Mr Crabback, there is the new School-Mistress standing in the rain!'

There ensued a flurry of interest and excitement amongst the shapes in the windows. Those girls lucky enough to have a perch with view of the gate shared their impressions with those less fortunate.

'By Christ, she's a miserable-looking thing!'

'A dreary, dried up old prune, by the looks of her.'

'What an awful old ulster she's wearing!'

'Hey, Missus, have you ever sucked a man's cock till his eyes bulged?'

Mrs Hopkins feigned not to hear any of this, and yet the words stung her. This was her problem, always had been: she was too sensitive. She was not a dreary, dried-up old prune, she felt like telling them, but she could not help her appearance: she had never regained condition since surviving the same flu that had taken her little daughter. And yes, she agreed entirely: it *was* an awful old ulster, she despised the overcoat as much as they did, but it was all she had. And as for the last obscenity, well (she told herself), she had been warned by many, not just the ticket collector of the *Emu*, as to what she was letting herself in for: she must toughen up and learn how to take such remarks in her stride, and not let on how much they distressed her.

But now a large, black umbrella was moving haphazardly towards her across the quadrangle. Beneath it was harried-looking man sporting a fine set of side-whiskers and carrying an enormous set of keys.

'Come in, come in, out of the rain! Have you no umbrella? Here, let me—' Folding his umbrella, he poked it through the bars of the gate for her. And now, standing in the drenching rain, the man sorted through the keys, trying one after another in the lock. 'My intention was to meet you at the wharf! But oh, we are having a difficult time of it. And now, of course it is time to lock them up for the night—can you believe it? At six o'clock! Mark my words, I will change all of that in due course, but for the moment I thought it best to go along with their usual routine.' He threw the gate open at last. 'Is that all you brought with you?' he asked in astonishment at the sight of her Gladstone bag.

'No. I left my chest with a fellow at the wharf.'

'Oh dear. Not with Henry, I hope? Half-witted fellow? Oh no, that won't do! From all reports, he is just as likely to toss it into the water—'

Swinging around, he sighted a cluster of girls who had gathered in the shelter of a doorway to gawk at them. 'Sarah! Eliza! Come here, please, if you will.'

Two strapping young women, one of whom Mrs Hopkins recognised as the foul-mouthed redhead of her first acquaintance, galloped like colts across the quadrangle towards them.

'Kindly run down to the wharf at once and fetch Mrs Hopkins' trunk,' he instructed.

However, the two girls did not run down to the wharf at once but instead stood about, arms akimbo, surveying him dubiously. 'What's it worth then?' said the redhead.

'What do you mean?' asked Mr Crabback.

'Well, it's raining, isn't it? We'll catch our bloody death.'

'You have to make it worth our while,' added her friend. 'That's the system. Normally we get rewards for our good deeds.'

'Oh, for goodness' sake!' exclaimed the harried-looking man. 'Listen. Do as I ask, and I'll see that . . . I'll see that there is something in it for the both of you. Now hurry. And when you bring the chest back, place it in Mrs Day's old quarters, then report back to me and I shall let you back into your dormitory.'

The girls took off out the gate and down the hill, happy to be liberated from their confines. At the sight of this, their comrades within the dormitories issued a roar of protest, for they wished to be running down the hill to the wharf also, rain or no rain.

A sharp-faced woman materialised within the doorway of the barracks. 'Well, do you wish me to lock them up or not then?' she cried.

'Yes, yes—forgive me, Mrs Dunstable—lock them up, by all means. I shall be round for inspection at lights out.' The gentleman then turned to Mrs Hopkins. 'I do beg your pardon for this confusion. I am just learning the ropes, as it were. The Assistant Matrons get very cross with me, but they seem to expect me to know everything at once! I have been here barely fourteen days!'

What a nice face he has, thought Mrs Hopkins; almost handsome, were it not for the fact that his eyes were a little small. She had never seen him up close before, and he put her in mind of a kindly marsupial.

'Come with me to my quarters for a moment to warm yourself while we wait for your chest to be brought up,' he continued. 'Oh, and forgive me—I haven't even introduced myself! My name is Charles Crabback. I am the new Superintendent.'

'I know all about you, Mr Crabback,' said Mrs Hopkins warmly. 'I am a great admirer of your work. I have read all your tracts and heard you speak several times at the Domain. In fact, you are the very reason why I applied for the position of School-Mistress.'

He beamed at her. 'Well! I am quite taken aback. And may I say, also delighted—you see, I am as susceptible to flattery as the next man!'

'Oh no, I am not attempting to flatter you,' said Mrs Hopkins, concerned that he might judge her the sort of woman who would resort to such wiles. 'I am simply speaking the truth.'

What a pity her teeth are so bad, thought Mr Crabback. And so thin, much too thin! If she were to fatten up a little, she might be altogether quite comely.

'In any case, we must get you out of this weather,' he said. 'Here, give me your bag. Take my arm—there are a great many potholes, some of them I swear a foot deep!'

So Mrs Hopkins took his arm and, closing the gate behind them, they walked a short distance along the west wall of the institution till they reached the Superintendent's quarters, a pleasant-looking house of two storeys. There in his parlour, she took off her awful ulster, and Mr Crabback hung it over a chair to dry. He poked at the fire to get it going again and threw some extra wood upon it. Then he warmed up some turnip soup for their supper. All the while, Mrs Hopkins petted his small spaniel, Tippet, who leaned companionably against her mourning skirts. The dog seemed to be of a melancholy disposition, and as Mrs Hopkins gently fondled its ears, it gazed up at her with soft, sorrowful eyes.

'Here we are then,' said Mr Crabback, placing two bowls of soup upon the table. There was a loaf of good bread as well, and a pat of butter. As if not wanting to waste further time, he clasped her hand in his, and launched into grace. 'Bless us, oh Lord, for these thy gifts that we are about to receive from thy bounty through Christ our Lord, Amen.'

It rather surprised Mrs Hopkins that grace was so short and brisk; the truth was that the Superintendent did not wish the soup to get cold.

'I'll tell you my secret: I add a dash of cream and a grating of nutmeg,' he informed her when she complimented him on the soup. 'I have had to learn to cook for myself. My wife has scant interest in domestic duties.'

Mrs Hopkins had scant interest in domestic duties herself, so she let this comment pass unremarked upon. The fact was, she thought to herself with a note of self-righteousness, should she herself be married to Mr Crabback, she would take considerably greater interest in such things and perhaps prove to be a very fine cook indeed.

'Where is your wife?' enquired Mrs Hopkins delicately. She had read in the newspaper that Mrs Crabback had accepted the position of Matron at Biloela, to work alongside her husband. And yet there was no sign of her.

'Well, she is back in Newtown, at the Haven of Hope. There has been some trouble in the press recently—a lot of nonsense about the book-keeping and so forth—also this business with the lass from Orange, and her brother making such a fuss about it. Suffice to say, it is demanding her full attention. Nevertheless, she hopes to join me within a week or two.' He sighed then and gazed down at his soup.

Mr Crabback suddenly looked enormously troubled, and Mrs Hopkins felt a wave of compassion for him. She had an urge to reach out and put her hand on his—some small gesture of comfort and support—but propriety of course forbade such intimacy.

In any case, he soon rallied and looked up at her with a smile. 'And in the meantime, you and I shall have everything shipshape!'

'When you say "shipshape", I hope you don't mean like that battered old ship that's in the dry dock,' said Mrs Hopkins. She was not normally one to venture humorous remarks, but she felt an urge to assist in keeping up his spirits.

He laughed dutifully. 'Oh yes! Yes, indeed. Shipwreck, more like!' he responded jovially.

'On a more serious note,' said Mrs Hopkins. 'It troubles me that the school is situated so close to a place which of necessity is frequented by sailors.'

Mr Crabback pulled out a handkerchief and wiped his brow—the heat emanating from the fire had caused a light sweat to break out upon him. 'Oh, I couldn't agree more. Absolute lunacy! The girls are yoo-hooing at sailors all day long, and so for that matter are the Assistant Matrons. Oh goodness,' he said suddenly. 'Those two ought to be back by now, oughtn't they? Did I do the wrong thing in sending them down to the wharf like that, at this hour?'

'It is good for the girls to be given responsibility,' said Mrs Hopkins. 'Also, the very fact that you entrusted them with an important task grows their self-esteem.'

In truth, she had been somewhat alarmed at his readiness to place her personal possessions in the hands of two such obviously untrustworthy girls. But then, once she had thought about it, she admired the philosophy that she considered was behind the move.

'Perhaps in time we can encourage them to perform these chores without having to resort to bribery,' she added, gently.

He beamed at her across his soup. 'I am very glad you are here,' he said softly. 'I feel you will be a tremendous helpmeet in the work that we have to do together here.'

Mrs Hopkins' pale cheeks pinkened, and to hide her blush, she leaned down to pat Tippet. 'I would be honoured,' she murmured.

Mr Crabback then launched into a potted history of the recent events at Biloela. As mentioned, he had been here less than a fortnight, brought in at short notice after the recent riots. The previous administration—Mr Baker-Hunt and his wife—though well-intentioned, had proved too lenient in their management of the street waifs and delinquents in their charge, and the girls had ridden roughshod over them. They wore their dresses indecently short and roamed all over the island. They were inclined to swim in their underclothes when the weather was fine and pleasure boats filled with young men had taken to cruising around the island, hopeful of a glimpse of feminine flesh, for which they were frequently rewarded. When sent to pump water at the force-pump, the girls would call out to the sailors and workmen at the dry dock below, and thus enticed and encouraged—perhaps believing the place to be a brothel—a posse of foreign sailors had attempted to break into the institution one night. The incursion was quickly quelled, the men duly dealt with by their superiors. Mr Baker-Hunt had put several girls in the cells on bread and water for their part in encouraging the sailors. Believing this to be an injustice, the other girls had risen up in fierce rebellion, setting fire to their bedding and breaking every windowpane in the institution. The little girls had assisted the older girls, gathering rocks and stones for them to use as ammunition. Word had reached Sydney of the uprising; the Colonial Secretary himself, who lived across the water at Birchgrove, had complained of the 'intolerable racket' issuing from Biloela. The Water Police were despatched to the island and were themselves pelted with stones; straitjackets and gags had had to be utilised to control the worst of the offenders. A government enquiry ensued, resulting in the dismissal of Mr and Mrs Baker-Hunt. After careful consideration, the Colonial Secretary had appointed Mr and Mrs Crabback, well-known in Sydney for their tireless work amongst the destitute, to replace them.

'I warn you now that I intend to make a great many changes,' said Mr Crabback, dabbing at his moustache with his handkerchief. 'I daresay these changes will not be popular with the Assistant Matrons. But I have a great objection to this massing of children in barracks, simply for the convenience of those who manage them. Indeed, the poor girls must consider themselves fortunate if the Matrons so much as know their names—' He broke off and rose to his feet, shaking his head in despair. The flicker of flames played across his brow.

'There is overall a want of love,' said Mrs Hopkins quietly.

'Why, yes,' said Mr Crabback, turning to her. 'With a woman's simplicity, you have put your finger upon it. *There is a want of love.* For I believe that even the most depraved and vicious of children has a soft spot somewhere in its heart, through which—with a little patience and sympathy—it may be reclaimed.'

His voice trembled slightly as he spoke, and Mrs Hopkins saw that tears had sprung to his eyes. She was reminded of the first time she had seen Mr Crabback speak at one of his regular open-air gatherings in the Domain. The readiness with which he would dissolve into helpless tears as he talked of the foot-weary men and women roaming hungry in the streets was, in great part, a reason why his Night Refuge for the Homeless, and indeed Mrs Crabback's Haven of Hope for Fallen Women, were so well-supported by the general public. It was true that some members of the press had come to refer to him as 'Cry-baby Crabback', as in '*Cry-baby Crabback, professional philanthropist, was on the graft again last Sunday, blubbering on cue before the masses* . . .' But Mrs Hopkins did not read the sort of newspapers in which such things were written, and if she did, she would have been appalled at the cynicism expressed therein. For the sight of Mr Crabback's tears stirred something deep within her, and even now as she gazed up at him, tears of sympathy spilled from her own eyes and rolled down her cheeks.

'Look at us, a fine pair,' said Mr Crabback softly, lifting her chin and dabbing at her tears with his handkerchief. It smelt faintly, but not unpleasantly, of turnip soup. 'I see that you are afflicted with the same condition as myself; that is, we care too deeply—'

Then came all at once a great banging at the front door.

'Ah,' said Mr Crabback, putting his handkerchief hastily in his pocket. 'With any luck, this will be our two young ladies, back with your chest. What is the hour?' He consulted his watch. 'Good heavens! It is after nine!' He flung open the door, and Sarah and Eliza stood before him. 'Where have you been all this time?' he asked.

'Well, sir, it started to bucket down cats and dogs, so one of the sailors from the *Blanche*, he said, "Come in, girls, out of the rain a while", so we sat in his cabin and had a cup of tea, so we did.'

This account was delivered with a straight face by the redhead Eliza, its effect only undermined by her friend's snort of suppressed laughter.

'You went on the boat?'

'Yes, sir. Just to seek shelter from the rain, sir.'

'In the company of sailors?'

'Just one sailor it was, Mr Crabback. Terribly homesick he was for his mother. He said we cheered him up with our girlish gaiety.'

'I'll bet you cheered him up; that is what I was afraid of.'

'Oh no, sir, you have it all wrong! Long grey beard he had, dear old thing: I doubt he could get it up it even if he wanted to.'

More giggles from Sarah; elbowed sharply in the ribs by her friend. 'Guess who else we saw on the boat, sir!'

'Who?'

'Mrs Dunstable. Doing a bit of the old ta-ra-ra-boom-de-ay with the officers. She saw us and went bright red, and she said to us if we didn't say anything, she wouldn't say anything. We thought it disgraceful, sir. She's supposed to be a moral influence, isn't she, sir?'

'Also she threatened us, sir.'

'And she called you a woolly old koala, sir.'

'And she called you something else, sir, but we dare'st not repeat it. We thought it disgraceful, sir, because she's supposed to be a moral influence.'

'Where is Mrs Hopkins' chest?' demanded Mr Crabback. He had reddened somewhat at the koala reference for he had recently been caricatured as such in the *Sydney Punch,* his side-whiskers unfairly exaggerated.

'In Mrs Day's quarters, sir, like you said. Now what will you give us for it? You said you'd give us something if we did what you asked.'

'I do not believe I will give you anything for you have been keeping company with sailors,' said Mr Crabback sternly. 'You know it is strictly against the rules to have any contact with the dry dock. I gave you a simple task to do, an opportunity to demonstrate that you were equal to responsibility, and you have used it as an excuse to revert to your former ways. Now go to your dormitory at once. I shall be over directly.'

'That's not fair, sir!'

'We were just cheering him up!'

'What about Mrs Dunstable, sir? She was the one doing the ta-ra-ra-boom-de-ay—'

He closed the door upon them.

Mrs Hopkins, sitting by the fire in the next room, had heard the whole thing, and was filled with admiration at the quiet authority with which the Superintendent had conducted the conversation. Yet when he came back into the parlour, he seemed distressed.

'What a fool I am, letting them go down to the wharf unattended! Both girls are known to have been "on the town", as it were. Oh yes, they came to this place riddled with disease by all accounts and not yet fifteen years of age. And now, through my own blind stupidity and my willingness to trust in their innate goodness, I have risked any chance of reformation and allowed them to debase themselves yet further—'

Mrs Hopkins rose to her feet swiftly.

'Stop it, Mr Crabback. It is not helpful to admonish yourself so harshly. Certainly, you have made a mistake; what of it? I have no doubt that we will go on to make many. But no mistake, if borne of good intentions, is irredeemable. Could I—may I—might we take this opportunity to say a prayer together?'

And to Mr Crabback's astonishment, she dropped directly to her knees in front of him, her black bombazine skirts billowing out around her. He found he had no choice but to drop to his knees also.

'O dear Lord, we place ourselves in thy hands,' declaimed Mrs Hopkins. 'Let thy light guide us, thy grace enable us in all that we are about to undertake. O Lord, I thank you for the abundance of wisdom and strength with which you have endowed Mr Crabback, and I ask only that you grant me the spiritual courage that I might faithfully and unwaveringly serve him . . .'

On and on in this vein she went, head bowed, eyes closed, fervently murmuring her prayer. Mr Crabback surveyed her curiously through one half-open eye. He was not unused to pious ladies becoming swept up in this sort of enthusiasm for his good work. But there was something about Mrs Hopkins, rocking on her knees before him, all decked out in full mourning, that he could not quite put his finger on.

It was now nine o'clock: time to do the final inspection and extinguish the lights. Taking a lantern, Mr Crabback and Mrs Hopkins ventured out into the cold night (it was no longer raining, at least), and unlocking the gate again, they passed into the quadrangle of Biloela. The old barracks buildings loomed forbiddingly in the darkness, and a great caterwauling came from within. Mrs Hopkins' heart contracted with a feeling of dread; these sounds, to her ears, were scarcely identifiable as human. She felt like hitching up her skirts and running full tilt to the wharf to flag down a passing ship.

'Be strong and of good courage, fear not, nor be afraid of them,' she whispered to herself.

There were four dormitories, constituting three sides of the quadrangle; the fourth side being comprised of the mess-hall, the schoolroom and a small infirmary. The night was moonless yet there were no lights burning save for a solitary lantern in the narrow passageway adjoining each dormitory. The girls sat clustered behind the grated iron doors, seeking what meagre comfort the lantern provided.

Why, they are like monkeys in a cage, thought Mrs Hopkins as she peered at them from the shadows. And yet the girls seemed cheerful enough if the gleeful exchange of profanities was any indication.

'But why do they not have a lantern or two in their dormitories, that they might have ample light to read or crochet?' asked Mrs Hopkins.

'I am told by the Assistant Matrons that the girls are not to be trusted with a lantern. Unfortunately, they have a way of setting fire to things.' Catching her look of dismay, Mr Crabback continued: 'Mrs Hopkins, I am as appalled by this state of affairs as you are. It is one of the very first things I intend to remedy. But for the moment I shall keep the routine as it is, until such time as we devise a better alternative. Goodnight, girls!' he called out, before extinguishing the passageway lantern. 'Go to sleep!'

'But they were not even in their night-dresses!' said Mrs Hopkins, as he ushered her on to the next dormitory.

'I am told they have no night-dresses,' said Mr Crabback. 'They sleep in their chemises. It is generally believed by the Assistant Matrons that the fewer articles of clothing they have to destroy, the better.'

'And does no one put them to bed and tuck them in?'

'I believe not.'

'Not even the little ones?'

'No.'

'And no one sleeps in the room with them? There is no one there to comfort them if they wake up frightened?' Mrs Hopkins felt that she could hardly bear it.

'No. It is very poorly arranged,' said Mr Crabback. 'The Assistant Matrons quarters—well, you'll see for yourself shortly—they are outside the walls of institution.'

By now they had reached Dormitory Four, where Sarah and Eliza slouched against the walls, waiting to gain admittance.

'We didn't realise you was entertaining Mrs Hopkins, sir,' said Eliza, her face the picture of innocence. 'Must be awfully lonely with your missus not here. Nice for you to have female company.'

'Even if it's just a bit of dried-up old codfish,' came a voice from within the dormitory. Hoots of raucous laughter followed.

'That's enough!' declared Mr Crabback. 'I will not have you talk of Mrs Hopkins in that way. She is an excellent woman, a truly excellent Christian woman, and we are very fortunate to have her here. In fact, we have just now been saying a prayer.'

'She was down on her knees then, was she, Charlie?' enquired Eliza.

'Yes, in fact we were both upon our knees,' said Mr Crabback, but this only prompted more merriment amongst the girls.

'I apologise for this,' Mr Crabback said to Mrs Hopkins as he struggled with the lock of the grated iron door. 'You see, I have tried to place the worst girls—the ones who have been on the streets—all together in the one dormitory. I thought that way at least they would have a less corrupting influence upon the younger ones.'

Mrs Hopkins nodded. She was mortified by the girls' remarks, of course, but also furious with herself for being mortified. They were simply possessed of youthful mischievousness, she told herself, or trying to impress their peers with their brashness. In any case, if their talk was lewd or insulting, it was only because they knew no better, and if Mrs Hopkins was going to get upset every time she was compared to a dried-up old codfish, then she would be wise to catch the next steamer back to Sydney.

'Charlie is my darling, my darling, my darling,' the girls were singing. *'Charlie is my darling, my handsome grenadier.'*

In spite of himself, Mrs Hopkins noted that Mr Crabback blushed. It seemed he was quite flattered by the song. But without making any further comment, or remonstrating with the girls for the impudence of the song, he instead concentrated his efforts on unlocking the door. Sarah and Eliza waltzed into the dormitory, swishing their skirts in the brazen manner of music hall entertainers. Mrs Hopkins held up her lantern and peered after them into the dark dormitory. As the singing and laughter petered out, she heard something else: a thin and plaintive keening sound, like a lost kitten calling for its mother. In the furthest corner of the room, Mrs Hopkins could just make out the form of a small child weeping upon her narrow bed.

'Oh dear, is she still carrying on?' said Mr Crabback in a distracted fashion, for he was struggling to lock the padlock again. 'That's a new girl—I've quite forgotten her name. Only been here for a day or two, and not very happy about it either. Her mother runs a notorious bawdy-house, so I thought it best to place her in here with the rest of them.'

'If you would kindly allow me entry, Mr Crabback,' said Mrs Hopkins. 'I would like to see if there is anything I can do for her.'

Mr Crabback hesitated, for he had only just succeeded in getting the padlock secured again. Also, and perhaps Mrs Hopkins did not take this into consideration, it had been an exhausting day for Mr Crabback; he had been on his feet since six in the morning and now he longed for the comfort of his down-filled mattress. But Mrs Hopkins was new and filled with good intentions so it was best not to discourage her. Nor did he wish to appear to be wanting in compassion for the child. He unlocked the padlock with some difficulty and opened the door for her.

'If you don't mind, I will wait out here,' he said.

Before the courage she had summoned could fail her, Mrs Hopkins entered the dormitory and made her way to the narrow bed on which the unhappy child lay. 'Whatever is the matter?' she asked.

The child responded by burying her face into her pillow and thumping her fists in fury.

Oh, how stupid I am, thought Mrs Hopkins bitterly as she gazed down upon the girl. It is quite obvious what the matter is: she has been removed from her family and placed in a hulking prison. She sat herself down on the edge of the bed and patted the child upon the shoulder—a dismal gesture that only made the waif cry harder.

'She's missing her mother, that's what the problem is,' said a girl on the next bed. 'She's bawling her head off every night.'

'Well, that is quite understandable,' said Mrs Hopkins. A vision arose in her mind of the girl's mother in her notorious bawdy-house: reclining against satin cushions in a state of déshabillé perhaps or smoking an opium pipe in the company of a leering Chinaman. Mrs Hopkins had occasionally read about such things in the gutter rags that her peas came wrapped in when she bought them from the barrowman. 'I have an idea,' said Mrs Hopkins to the child. 'Perhaps tomorrow in class we could write a letter to your mother. I will help you if you'd like me to.'

The small child turned her head now and looked up at Mrs Hopkins, her thick lashes wet with tears.

'Would you like that?' asked Mrs Hopkins, smiling down upon her.

And by way of response, the girl jerked back her head and spat at her.

The room erupted. The girls leapt up and down on their beds with glee. The great gob of spit had landed unerringly on the very tip of Mrs Hopkins' nose, from which it dangled precariously until—further humiliation!—it dropped upon her skirt. The wicked child grinned at her in satisfaction, happy at having won the approbation of her peers. Mrs Hopkins reached for the black pocket mourning handkerchief she had tucked into her sleeve and wiped the spittle from her nose and skirt. Then she rose to her feet with as much dignity as she could muster amidst the catcalls and the jeering, and she hurried out of the dormitory, past Mr Crabback, who was staring at her, mouth agape, and into the quadrangle. She had failed, failed hopelessly; shown herself to be unequal to the job, and in front of Mr Crabback of all people. Be strong, she told herself. Be strong and of good courage! But the words felt hollow, a mockery. Her courage had failed her and the scrappy little urchin had humiliated her.

Mr Crabback emerged with his lantern, peering into the darkness of the quadrangle. It was beginning to rain again. 'Mrs Hopkins?' he called.

'Yes, I am here,' she said, causing him to start for she stood closer than he had realised.

'Forgive me, I could not see you in the darkness, what with your black dress—' He broke off for it seemed impolite to draw attention to her mourning garb in this way. And yet it was eerie the way her white face seemed to hover skull-like above her high black collar. 'I will take you to your quarters now,' he said, feeling it best to say nothing of the incident he had just witnessed. 'It is best if you take my arm—the pathway is uneven.'

She took his arm and he led her out of the institution, locking the big gate behind them. Then they walked in silence towards the officers' quarters, the dreadful shouting and carousing growing fainter as they left the institution behind.

Why, she is trembling, thought Mr Crabback. The realisation touched him, although she would need to toughen up if she were to succeed here.

'I am sorry you have had to experience this trouble on your first evening,' he said, when they had reached her doorway.

But Mrs Hopkins' humiliation was such that it prevented her from offering any response.

'In any case, I hope you will be comfortable here,' said Mr Crabback, eying her quarters doubtfully. How mean and shabby these huts were, especially compared to his own commodious accommodation. No wonder the Assistant Matrons seemed perpetually disgruntled.

Mrs Hopkins said nothing. She made no move to enter, but simply stood there on the threshold.

'Well . . . we will talk further in the morrow,' he said. 'Goodnight.'

'Is there a lamp?' she asked abruptly, for it seemed he was about to leave her plunged in the darkness.

'A lamp?' he asked, in a bewildered fashion.

Holding up his own lantern, Mr Crabback peered inside. The quarters contained a narrow bed, a table, a chair, a kitchen cupboard of sorts fashioned from a series of kerosene boxes. It could scarcely be bleaker. There was no lamp to be seen.

'Here, you may take this for now,' he said, placing the lamp upon the table. 'Goodnight, Mrs Hopkins.' Mr Crabback turned and made his way out of the cottage, disappearing into the darkness.

And that is all there is to be said about Mrs Hopkins' first night at Biloela, except that upon examination, she found that the lock of her chest had been broken open and its contents comprehensively rifled through.

Laid out like a corpse on his feather mattress, sleep did not come easily to Mr Crabback. He found himself, quite unexpectedly, troubled by thoughts of Mrs Hopkins. She was an odd one, of course, and yet there was something arousing about the full-throated ardour with which she admired him, *wished to serve him*, rocking passionately upon her knees like that. He remembered with a thrill the moment when he had dabbed at her tears with his handkerchief, and she had gazed up at him so beseechingly. '*We are alike in that we care too deeply*,' he had murmured, or something along those lines anyway. One of his own tears had splashed upon her cheek, and she had closed her eyes and sighed. Had he imagined it or had he not glimpsed at that moment a shiver of something akin to rapture pass through her slight frame? Why, he might almost have leaned down and kissed her! It was just as well that the girls had chosen that moment to come banging at the door.

And in fact, at five minutes past six the next morning, it was Mr Crabback who was banging at Mrs Hopkins' door, the moody spaniel Tippet by his side. She opened the door immediately as if she had been standing directly behind it. She was dressed in black from top to toe, her hair in a long plait that fell across one shoulder.

Why, she looks much older in the daylight, he thought with a stab of disappointment. There were wisps of unruly grey hair poking out around her temples. And yet she pinkened at the sight of him, and lowered her gaze, and his heart thumped inside his chest in spite of himself.

'Good morning,' he said, with a bow of his head. 'I am sorry to rouse you so early. The business of the institution begins at six, and I thought I might perhaps show you around and give you some idea of our daily routine before you commence your classes.'

'Thank you,' said Mrs Hopkins. 'Would you allow me a moment to complete my toilet?'

'Certainly,' said Mr Crabback, bowing again, and she closed the door upon him. When she emerged a few minutes later, he saw that she had wound her plait tightly into a bun at the base of her neck and smoothed down those errant wisps of grey.

'Mr Crabback,' she said, 'before we set off. I want you to know that I composed a letter to you last night, in which, amongst other things, I offered you my resignation. You see, I felt—after the events of the evening—that I had no more right to serve as your helpmeet—yes, your helpmeet, Mr Crabback, for that is the word you yourself used—than the half-witted fellow down at the wharf.'

Good heavens! he thought in alarm. Is she going to carry on like this every time she is spat upon?

'Would you believe I felt anger in my heart towards you?' she continued. 'Yes, anger that you had neither protected nor defended me. For in my wickedness, all I could think of was myself, you see, and the wounding of my own vanity.' Here she shook her head, as if in bitter disbelief.

'Oh dear,' said Mr Crabback. 'I did think later that perhaps I should have—I should have probably said something—'

'No, Mr Crabback. In your wisdom, you chose the correct course which was to behave exactly as if nothing had happened,' she said. 'For to have done otherwise would be to reward and thus reinforce the behaviour.'

And yet how infinitely preferable was this renting of garments, this donning of proverbial sackcloth and ashes, thought Mr Crabback, than the lackadaisical attitude displayed by the other Matrons.

'Mr Crabback,' she said, raising her eyes now to look at him (up to this point she had kept them firmly downcast), 'I prayed into the night, and this morning when I arose, all feelings of anger or self-pity had vanished. Instead, I find myself filled with a renewed sense of courage and purpose. I want you to know that I have torn my letter of resignation into a thousand pieces.' And here she opened up the palms of her hands and revealed to him many, many tiny pieces of torn paper. 'But I say this to you now: if it is your wish that I depart the island, then I will take my leave of you at once;

with sadness, yes, but gladness also, for I will be serving you in so doing.'

Why, she is a hysteric, he thought in wonderment, for he had once read a scholarly article on the subject. Such women (for hysterics were usually women) experienced their emotions in fierce tempests unknown to the average person, and thus were capable of performing tremendous feats. Had not Joan of Arc been a hysteric? By all accounts (the writer of the scholarly article had gone on to suggest), any kind of romantic *liaison* with a hysteric should of necessity be kept brief, and while inadvisable, would prove to be an experience of unparalleled intensity. The danger lay, or so the writer cautioned (he seemed to have some personal experience in the matter), in the hysteric leaving her *inamorato* seriously depleted: complete nervous and physical collapse was not unheard-of. For some reason, although he had read the article several years ago, the description had stayed with Mr Crabback.

'Mrs Hopkins,' he said, and he found that his voice trembled slightly, 'I have no doubt that you will be the finest helpmeet I could ever hope for.'

The thousand torn pieces of letter fell to the ground. Her eyes shone up at him, and in that moment, she appeared to him almost radiantly beautiful. But immediately, as a cloud passes across the sun, Mrs Hopkins lowered her gaze again and busied herself in brushing away the stray scraps of paper that had become caught up in the stiff crepe trimmings of her mourning.

The daily routine for the girls, Mr Crabback explained as they walked to the institution, was as follows:

Roused from their dormitories at six o'clock, the girls were assigned a number of chores to be completed before breakfast. They were to milk the cows; feed the pigs and fowls; pump water for the institution's washing and cooking requirements; scrub the flagstone floors of the dormitories; muck out the earth-closets and sweep the sewing room and schoolroom. Breakfast (cold porridge, made the evening before) was served at half past seven, after which the dishes were to be washed and the mess-hall cleaned and swept. At half past eight, the girls would be called to muster, followed by morning prayers. The younger girls would then proceed to the schoolroom for lessons till twelve noon, while the older girls were sent to the sewing room or to assigned duties in the kitchen and laundry. At half past twelve, it was dinner time (boiled mutton and turnips), after which more water was to be pumped, dishes washed, the mess-hall cleaned and floor scrubbed. The younger girls would then have their allotted time in the sewing room, while the older girls attended the schoolroom for lessons till four o'clock. Thence, the cows were milked once again, and at five o'clock, it was time for tea (brown bread with a scant spread of dripping or suet), followed by a wash, then muster and evening prayers. The girls were then locked away in their dormitories promptly at six o'clock, with the passageway lanterns extinguished at nine.

Mrs Hopkins listened to all this attentively. She was a punctilious person by nature and believed that children thrived if grounded in strict routine. However, the sights that greeted her as Mr Crabback guided her about the institution filled her with dismay, for it seemed that the daily routine, as he had so carefully laid out for her, was adhered to in only the most notional sense. At best it appeared that Mrs Dunstable, the House Matron, and her two Assistant Matrons, Miss Foy and Mrs Baird, viewed the routine as a kind of loose suggestion as to how the day might run. As for the inmates, they mostly disregarded it altogether.

Tossed out of their dormitories, the girls were to be seen slouching about, partially dressed and barefoot. Many wore only their chemises, and their hair hung loose and uncombed. The girls sent to clean the pigsties simply played with the piglets, not caring one hoot about the muck they were wallowing in. Other girls sat about, enjoying the morning sunshine, idly gossiping like so many fishwives. Those who were sent to pump water used the opportunity to yoo-hoo down to the sailors, and when asked by Mr Crabback if they would kindly commence pumping, responded with impertinence.

As for breakfast, well, it was quite simply chaos. Girls wandered in and out of the mess-hall as they wished, and who could blame them for the porridge was grey, cold and covered with a quivering skin. To Mrs Hopkins' consternation, the girls scooped the porridge up with their hands, whereupon it dripped down the front of their filthy pinafores, or else (slightly more decorously) lapped it straight from the battered tin plates on which it was doled out—indeed one small child had gone further and was sharing her porridge with a mange-ridden tabby.

'Get away!' cried Mr Crabback, shooing the cat. This startled both the cat and the child—the cat took off a short distance, and eyed Mr Crabback warily from under the table. The child commenced to cry.

'That is one of the Tunks sisters,' he told Mrs Hopkins, lowering his voice discreetly. 'They were found abandoned in a house in George Street, starving and covered in filth. That one is not quite right in the head, as you can see.'

'But why do none of the girls have utensils with which to eat?' asked Mrs Hopkins, gazing in disbelief at the scene before her.

'I know, I know—it is appalling. But apparently they cannot be trusted with cutlery of any form, and thus they are left to lap their porridge like animals and tear apart their meat with their fingers.'

The cat had returned to share the porridge and the small child stopped her crying. Mr Crabback did not notice though as his attention was taken by Tippet, who, rallying out of his usual melancholy, had taken exception to several piglets, scrounging for scraps under the tables. The dog's barking set the piglets into a frenzy of high-pitched squealing.

'Get out of here, the lot of you!' cried the sharp-faced woman who was doling out the porridge, and she chased the piglets outside, waving her ladle fiercely.

'That is Mrs Dunstable—she is our House Matron, in charge of all the cleaning and laundry and bedding and so forth. Ah, Mrs Dunstable,' said Mr Crabback, as she returned from chasing out the animals, 'allow me to introduce to you Mrs Hopkins, our new School-Mistress.'

'How do you do,' said Mrs Dunstable stiffly.

'How do you do,' said Mrs Hopkins, eyeing the House Matron curiously. She was a thin-lipped, worn-looking woman of some forty-five years. She did not at all look the sort of woman to perform the ta-ra-ra-boom-de-ay for the amusement of sailors.

'I would thank you to control your dog, sir,' said Mrs Dunstable, turning to Mr Crabback. 'I have enough trouble as it is with the pigs and the cats.'

'Oh, Tippet does no harm,' said Mr Crabback, smiling amiably. 'The girls enjoy petting him. But yes, I daresay you are quite right. I shall endeavour to keep him confined to my quarters during mealtimes.'

'Very good, sir,' said Mrs Dunstable.

'Oh, and Mrs Dunstable,' he continued, 'I should like a word with you after prayers, if I may.'

'I'm busy after prayers,' she said. 'I have all the stores to sort out, and whatnot.'

'Nevertheless, you will pay me the courtesy of a few moments of your time,' said Mr Crabback evenly. 'I will not keep you long.'

It was at muster that Mrs Hopkins was introduced to the Assistant Matrons, Mrs Baird and Miss Foy. They were cordial enough in their greetings, yet Mrs Hopkins sensed a certain reserve in their manner, a watchful wariness particularly on the part of Mrs Baird. She was an older woman of some fifty years, who peered at Mrs Hopkins behind thick spectacles; the girls referred to her as 'Betty Four-eyes.' Miss Foy was younger, in fact barely older than some of the girls; plump and jovial in nature.

'Let's hope you last longer than poor old Mrs Day,' said Miss Foy gaily. 'It's not a job for the faint of heart, that's for sure!'

I shall have to watch this one for she is inclined to foolishness, Mrs Hopkins thought to herself. She had little patience for silly young women, giggling all the time. She herself had always been earnest to the point of dreariness, a fact of which she was well aware. She had no sense of humour to speak of. Giddy young woman like Miss Foy, always looking for merriment, grated upon her nerves.

Muster consisted not of a rollcall, as Mrs Hopkins had expected, but simply a headcount, only commenced upon once the girls were persuaded to form approximate lines. And yet any hope of arriving at an accurate number appeared utterly futile as the girls kept changing position, ducking in and out of their line at whim or simply wandering off altogether. Nevertheless, after several attempts, it seemed they were either six or seven girls short of the correct total—no one could be quite sure—and Miss Foy was sent down to the beach where apparently the truants had been sighted, although it was strictly out of bounds.

'Oh, the boot leather I've worn out chasing these girls around the island,' she exclaimed quite cheerfully as she set off.

'*Almighty God, Father of our Lord Jesus Christ, Judge of All Men, Maker of All Things*,' intoned Mr Crabback. He was reading aloud from an ancient copy of the Book of Common Prayer. '*We acknowledge and bewail our manifold sins and wickedness which we, from time to time, most grievously have committed by thought, word and deed, provoking most justly thy wrath and indignation against us. We do earnestly repent and are heartily sorry for our misdeeds. Have mercy upon us, most merciful Father . . .*'

Good heavens, thought Mrs Hopkins, a sense of indignation rising within her as she listened. This prayer would be more suitable for a group of hardened prisoners awaiting execution at Darlinghurst Gaol. What dreadful wickedness, what terrible misdeeds, had these tousle-headed innocents committed, beyond being born into abject poverty? Of course, there were the prostitute girls, she reminded herself, peering through one half-open eye at the older girls, who were mumbling along sullenly with Mr Crabback. How pretty they were, some of them, even in their drab dungaree dresses. And now that she looked, she saw that several of them had tied coloured ribbons in their hair—ribbons that Mrs Hopkins recognised as having been purchased from a haberdasher near the King Street Wharf with her last shilling for the purpose of using them as rewards for good conduct, and which had been subsequently purloined from her chest.

Crossing the quadrangle on her way to the schoolroom, Mrs Hopkins chanced to witness Mr Crabback engaged in an altercation with Mrs Dunstable.

'And you would believe the word of those two over me?' Mrs Dunstable was saying, somewhat loudly and heatedly. 'Why, they could not lie straight in bed, the pair of them!'

Mrs Hopkins realised that Mr Crabback must be taking her to task for having visited the ship last night. However, as she would have expected from him with his sense of decency and decorum, he was speaking very quietly and earnestly so Mrs Hopkins was unable to hear his side of the conversation.

'Let me tell you something, for you'll learn it soon enough,' interjected Mrs Dunstable, her voice ringing clearly across the quadrangle. 'These girls have not the slightest regard for the truth, not a single one of them. And what's more, they delight in setting us against one another, just to amuse themselves—'

That was the last Mrs Hopkins heard of the discussion, for she hastily ushered her young charges into the schoolroom lest they hear any more of Mrs Dunstable's opinion of them.

The schoolroom was situated in close proximity to the earth-closets, and prevailing winds were such that unpleasant odours wafted through the windowpanes still broken from the recent rioting. Fortunately, Mrs Hopkins was in the habit of scenting her pocket handkerchiefs with dried lavender, and she found that if she held one to her nostrils at regular intervals, she could keep the nauseating smells at bay. The children however seemed perfectly used to it and made no comment.

Once they had settled into their seats, Mrs Hopkins noticed amongst their number the girl who had spat upon her the night before. Immediately, she felt a sharp spasm in her belly which she had, from experience, come to identify as an involuntary release of bile. For Mrs Hopkins had a failing of which she was painfully aware: she found it very difficult sometimes to forgive, to properly and fully forgive, when she felt had been wronged in any way or injured.

I believe I will just have a quiet word with her, she thought to herself. Picking up her cane and tucking it under her arm, she approached the sullen child and stood over her.

'What is your name?'

'Josephine.' The girl had sighted the cane and had an idea of what was coming. She lowered her head and hunched her shoulders in readiness.

'Josephine who? I'm assuming you have a surname. Do you have a surname?'

Still hunched, the child just sat there. Come on, give me an answer, thought Mrs Hopkins grimly, remembering the shock she had felt as the gob of spit had landed upon her nose. And perhaps sensing the rising tension in her School-Mistress or seeing the way the cane quivered under her arm, the child gave a small, terrified nod of her head.

'Then what is it?'

'Briars.'

'Louder. I cannot hear you.'

'Briars, Miss.'

'Your name is "Briars Miss"?'

A titter went around the room which caused the child to redden in shame.

'Say, "My name is Josephine Briars, Mrs Hopkins."'

'My name is Josephine Briars, Mrs Hopkins,' mumbled the miserable child.

'Kindly pay me the courtesy of looking at me when you address me.'

The child cast her eyes up at her School-Mistress now and Mrs Hopkins stopped quite still. A wave of shock passed through her. For she saw at once that Josephine's eyes were of different colours: one was hazel, the other green. This minor imperfection would have passed unnoticed by most, but it caused Mrs Hopkins' heart to lurch within her chest. She had once had a little girl of her own with mismatched eyes: her name was Eugenie, and she had died at the age of four.

'How old are you, Josephine?' Mrs Hopkins asked finally.

'Eleven.'

Now a great sigh rose up within Mrs Hopkins' chest. For, had she survived, Eugenie would have turned eleven just the week before last. Mrs Hopkins had marked her birthday, as she always did, by making the long trek to Rookwood Cemetery, an expedition that always plunged her into the greatest misery. For after her death, Eugenie had been 'tossed' (that is how she saw it) into an unmarked paupers' grave, and the ignominy of this filled her with despair, when other children within the cemetery had such beautiful tombstones depicting lambs and cherubs, and bore heart-rending inscriptions such as:

A Little Bud of Love
To Bloom with God Above

'But who else is in there?' she had demanded to know of the gravedigger as she gazed down at the dismal coffins below, barely separated from each other by a thin layer of dirt.

'Well, let me think,' he responded, taking off his cap to wipe his brow. 'There's the Duchess of Windsor, of course, and His Lordship the Crown Prince of Darlinghurst.'

It turned out that the ones that he knew of, directly beneath Eugenie in the deep, dank hole, were an old crone found stiff in a paddock under a piece of sodden cardboard, and a young lass who had died mad with the effects of drink at the Lunatic Reception House. Eugenie was simply the latest to be interred. They had thrown in the clods of dirt on top.

At least they are women, Mrs Hopkins had thought, though she stopped short of calling them 'ladies'. In a fanciful way, she sometimes found herself hoping that the two paupers might somehow take care of the little girl. Perhaps they would comfort her if she was lonely and fearful in that bleak hole.

That was seven years ago. Now, whenever Mrs Hopkins made her pilgrimage, she could not find the grave in the wasteland of Rookwood's pauper allotment. She wandered up and down, trying to summon her memories of that dreadful day, to get her bearings, that she might lay her little bouquet of flowers, pilfered mostly from the Roman Catholic section. But where was Eugenie's grave? Why had Mrs Hopkins not paid closer attention on the day, making note of the closest trees, the nearest pathways, the tombstones of cherubs? The answer to that was simple—she had been awash with grief and scarcely capable of standing. Now, when she visited, the place seemed unrecognisable. There were fresh mounds of earth wherever she looked, for there was no shortage of dead paupers in Sydney. In fact, she thought bitterly, it would not surprise her if they had re-opened Eugenie's grave to cram in yet more bodies. Up and down she paced, with a rising sense of panic. What kind of mother does not know where her child is buried?

Afterwards, exhausted and despairing, she had taken herself off for a cup of tea at Mrs Cruikshank's pie shop. She had once taken Eugenie to the same shop, and the little girl had been such a pet that Mrs Cruikshank gave her a sugar biscuit in a paper bag to take home with her. Eugenie had tried very hard to save it, but all the way home she kept nibbling tiny morsels around the edge of it. By the time they reached home, it was all gone. How she had wept when admonished for her greediness!

'Josephine,' said Mrs Hopkins, and her voice was now much kinder, 'I am very much in need of a good assistant to help the little ones with their work. I would like you to be my classroom monitor. You will pass out all the slates and slate pencils and help the little ones with their lessons. Then at the end of class, you will ensure that the slates are wiped clean and the slate pencils sharpened and then you may put them all away back in their boxes.'

For a moment, Josephine seemed not to comprehend what was being said to her. Or perhaps she thought it was a trick of some sort, for she bit her lip and looked like she might burst into tears.

'You are not in trouble,' said Mrs Hopkins. 'To be a classroom monitor is a privilege.'

'But I can't help the little ones, Miss.'

'Why not?'

'I can't read, Miss, or write.'

'Not a word?'

The girl shook her head in shame, and the colour rose in her cheeks.

'Well, that's all right,' said Mrs Hopkins. 'After all, that is why I have come here. To teach you.'

And taking the girl by the hand, she led her over to where the slate boxes were kept, and Josephine passed out all the slates and slate pencils as she was bid.

Mrs Hopkins soon found that several of the children were quite shockingly ignorant; amongst them the three pathetic Tunks sisters, who had been found abandoned in the house in George Street. Upon their arrival at Biloela, their scalps were discovered to be infested with lice and their hair had had to be cut off completely; only now were their dark curls beginning to reveal themselves. They were sad little children, painfully thin and all of them bandy-legged from rickets. The eldest, Emma, was timid and nervous; Martha, the middle one, was (as Mr Crabback had pointed out in the mess-hall) 'touched in the head', and the youngest, Janie, was inclined to scratch and bite the other children.

'Will you sit with the young ones and help them as best you can?' Mrs Hopkins asked Josephine, and the girl nodded earnestly although she scarcely knew the alphabet herself. And in fact, the gentle attention the older girl gave the three sisters soon had a remarkable effect upon them: Emma and Martha leaned in close on either side of her, while little Janie sat quietly on her lap. The sight of them bent over their slates, lips pursed in concentration as they formed their letters, touched Mrs Hopkins deeply. It gave her a sense of hope that she had made the right decision in coming to Biloela.

'Josephine, you have been a great help to me on my first day,' Mrs Hopkins said when the class was over. She opened up an exercise book in which she had written the children's names and put a tick alongside Josephine's name in the column headed *Conduct*. 'And another thing, Josephine, before you go. I am going to speak to Mrs Dunstable about moving you into a dormitory with the younger children. That way if any of them were to get upset, or frightened in the night, you would be there to comfort them. What do you think?'

The girl nodded. 'Yes, Miss. I should like that.'

'You are a good girl, Josephine,' said Mrs Hopkins. 'We got off to a bad start, but we shall put it behind us.'

And here something quite extraordinary happened: the child turned pink and flung her thin arms around Mrs Hopkins' neck. The School-Mistress stiffened for she had never been comfortable with physical displays of affection. Firmly, but not unkindly, she extricated herself from the embrace and sent the girl out into the quadrangle to join the others. Then Mrs Hopkins proceeded to tidy the schoolroom.

In truth, the hug had unsettled her painfully. For a fleeting moment, she had felt that it was not Josephine but her little lost daughter whose arms were flung around her neck and whose sour porridgey breath fell upon her cheek. But no, she told herself, such thinking was fanciful: Josephine was not her daughter, she was the daughter of a notorious brothel-keeper. And after all, as Mrs Hopkins studied her from this distance, was there really such a resemblance? Before she became ill,

Eugenie had been the sort of child you would see on a chocolate box with golden curls, dimpled knees and apple cheeks. Why, even as a baby in the perambulator, people used to stop in the street to admire her! Josephine was not like that at all: she was pale and scrawny, her hair lank and mouse-coloured. And yet—a new thought occurred to Mrs Hopkins—might not Eugenie's fair hair have grown darker over the years; might not those baby curls have fallen straight as is so often the way? But no, enough of such nonsense! Josephine was not Eugenie. It was coincidence, nothing more, a coincidence of little more than a pair of mismatched eyes and approximately the same year of birth.

The older girls, of course, were considerably less compliant than the younger girls.

At lunchtime, Mrs Hopkins had written upon the blackboard an exercise, in preparation:

Every vice fights against nature.
Folly is never pleased with itself.
What cannot be cured must be endured.
No one of you knows where the shoe pinches.

But as she watched them slope into class on her first afternoon, she realised that she would need to have her wits about her if she were to get anywhere with them.

'Where are the rest of the girls?' Mrs Hopkins asked, for only fourteen of the thirty-seven older girls listed on her roll sat before her.

A large dullish girl, wall-eyed, shrugged her shoulders. 'Laundry, Miss?'

'What is your name?'

'Rosabella.'

'Rosabella who?'

'Rosabella Connelly, Miss.'

'Rosabella, my name is Mrs Hopkins; please address me as such. Only five girls are required in the laundry, and they are accounted for.'

'I don't know then, Miss. 'Aven't seen 'em.'

Mrs Hopkins sighed. She had a fair idea where the missing girls were, for the day was a pleasant one. 'Very well,' she said. 'I am going down to the beach to fetch them.'

And instructing these more dutiful students to copy out the lesson in their best handwriting, she took off down to the beach to find the truants.

The narrow beach, inaccessible to the rest of the island, had been part of the precinct allocated to the original convicts, with the idea that occasional saltwater bathing might have a therapeutic effect on their festering skin conditions. It was a matter of relative ease for the girls to clamber over the rudimentary fence that had been put up since as a deterrent. And one could certainly see why the beach was appealing, given the grim penitentiary walls within which they were forced to spend their days. The soft sand under bare toes; the delicate little shells to collect; the smooth, grey boulders on which to recline and soak up the sun's warmth. Reaching the top of the rocks from which she could look down upon the beach, Mrs Hopkins could count at least twenty of her would-be pupils, many in varying states of undress. How pretty they look in the sunshine, she thought appreciatively. It was a scene such as a painter might depict. *The sea hath its pearls . . .*

'Girls,' she called out, 'have you forgotten? It is time for your lessons. Come at once.'

Mrs Hopkins had a thin voice, and it did not travel well in the outdoors. Perhaps one or two girls heard her and turned their heads towards her; they did not seem to consider it worth their while responding, and simply resumed whatever it was they had been doing. The sound of idle laughter wafted up towards her.

Mrs Hopkins tried again, this time with a couple of brisk hand-claps to herald her call. But the girls just continued to ignore her.

Mrs Hopkins faced something of a dilemma. She had no wish to clamber down the damp rocks to the beach as she could see there was a real danger of slipping. Were she to slip, she would appear ridiculous, and after last night's humiliation in the dormitory, she could ill-afford another. And yet to stand here calling out in this fashion, her words lost on the breeze, was clearly futile.

As she pondered her situation, Mrs Hopkins became aware of distant voices, and looking out to the water, she espied some workmen standing upon a dredge. They appeared to be staring intently at something, and shifting her gaze in that direction, she sighted four girls splashing about in the water. And here Mrs Hopkins froze in horror, for she saw that the girls were completely and utterly naked.

She could scarcely believe what she was seeing. She knew she must act at once, and yet for a moment she stood as mesmerised as were the workmen, for the sight of these girls in all their natural loveliness, glistening and slippery as porpoises, filled her with a kind of awe. She paid such little attention to her own body when undressing that the female form, particularly the *youthful* female form, took her by surprise. Every part of their anatomy seemed more pronounced than she'd realised possible: their breasts more buoyant, their nipples pinker, their bottoms plump and round and adorned with Venusian dimples. Now they were climbing on one another's shoulders and wrestling each other, their long hair streaming down their breasts. They seemed to her a vision of enchantment: nymphs, mermaids, water sprites. When they fell into the water, their laughter pealed like silver bells. The workmen could not tear their eyes away, nor indeed could Mrs Hopkins.

'Girls!' she called out, but still no one paid her any notice. So she took off, slipping and sliding down the rocks in an ungainly fashion, at one point having to creep along sideways on all fours like a crab, till she reached the sand. Then she brushed off her skirts and hurried to the water's edge and called again. 'Girls! Come in at once!'

No response: it was as if they did not hear her.

'Come in at once or there will be serious consequences!'

They all glanced at her now in irritation and a quick conference ensued amongst themselves. Then the girls resumed their wrestling match with renewed vigour. This time they attempted standing on one another's shoulders, their full nudity on display for the benefit of the ogling workmen, who whistled and applauded heartily. Into the water the girls fell again, shrieking with laughter.

Mrs Hopkins stared at them, utterly at a loss. What was she to do? She wanted to wade in, clothes and all, and drag them away from the leering eyes of the dredge men, but this was impossible; Mrs Hopkins could not swim, and the weight of her clothes would surely pull her under. It struck her suddenly that this was a test of some sort, but a test in a language foreign and inexplicable to her. Should she march indignantly back up to the school (more slipping and sliding on the rocks inevitably) and return, red-faced and flustered, with Mr Crabback? No, that would never do; she must manage these crises herself and not be running to him whenever she faced difficulty. And yet to continue standing here with the water washing around her skirts, shouting threats of no consequence, would only make her appear to the girls as comical and ineffectual as a crotchety old spinster in a burlesque show.

She turned to a group of girls who loitered nearby, enjoying the unfolding spectacle. Amongst them were Sarah and Eliza, who she at least knew by name.

'Sarah and Eliza,' she said, 'run up to the classroom for me and tell the other girls to come down and join us here. We will have our lesson on the beach today since it is such pleasant weather.'

Some of the girls clapped their hands in delight at this idea, but Sarah and Eliza stared at her with blank disdain.

'What will you pay us if we do, Miss?'

'Nothing at all,' said Mrs Hopkins. 'For I see that you are already wearing my ribbons. Consider those your payment and we will speak no more of the matter. In time, I hope you will learn to respect other people's property.'

Mrs Hopkins was quite pleased with this short speech and hoped that the girls might have the decency to lower their heads in shame. But instead their faces puckered in puzzlement and hurt.

'Your ribbons, Miss? But these are our ribbons. We got them for Christmas from the Sisters of the Good Shepherd. You can ask anyone.'

'You've falsely accused us, Miss. You've as good as called us thieves.'

'Just because we're Biloela girls, everyone always thinks the worst of us.'

'Everyone thinks we don't deserve nice things!'

'On the contrary,' said Mrs Hopkins, anxious to nip this in the bud for the girls were working themselves up into a state, 'I think you do deserve nice things. And that is why I spent my last shilling at the haberdashery to buy ribbons for you girls as rewards for good conduct. You may earn your ribbons now, if you like, by hurrying up to tell your classmates that we are going to learn a new song on the beach.'

'What song? Not a boring old hymn?' enquired Eliza.

'Not a bit of it. It is a popular song entitled "Love Amongst the Roses", and we are going to learn a pretty little harmony. Now hurry along and fetch the other girls so we can begin.'

And to her pleasant surprise, after conferring with each other briefly, Sarah and Eliza took off up the rocks quite willingly.

'Now where shall we sit?' said Mrs Hopkins to the others. 'The sun is warm, but none of us are wearing hats. Let us preserve our complexions by sitting in the shade near the old wall. Come along now, and we will warm up our voices before the others get here.'

And she took off in that direction at a brisk pace, hoping that if she continued to act in this forthright and decisive fashion, the girls might simply follow along behind her. And once again to her surprise, they did. Perhaps, like the younger ones, they yearned for someone to lead with a firm hand, she mused. When the four girls who had been frolicking naked in the water saw the procession of other girls coming down from the institution with the gleeful air of prisoners on a picnic day, they clambered out of the water themselves to see what was going on. They wrung the water out of their hair and pulled on their petticoats to the accompaniment of whistles and shouts from the dredge men, to which the water sprites responded with rude gestures.

'Sit in the sun a little longer till you warm up,' said Mrs Hopkins, for the girls were shivering. They looked bedraggled now, blotchy and blue-lipped, not at all the enchanted nymphs they had been in the water. 'Kindly pay those men no attention. We do not wish to encourage them.'

And then she commenced to sing.

It was on one Summer's evening,
In the merry month of June,
I beheld a damsel sitting
'Mid flowers' sweet perfume.
She had a novel, reading,
Just as I was passing by,
And as she turned another page,
I saw the brightest eye.
A bewitching smile was on her face.
As charming as the posies;
I felt the smart of Cupid's dart
'Twas love amongst the roses . . .

Now it was a funny thing about the Biloela girls; hardened and streetwise as they were, singing was the chief pleasure in their lives, where pleasures were few and far between. Mrs Hopkins was possessed of a reasonable singing voice, melodious if a little thin, and they listened attentively. The song was new to them, but it was exactly the sort of song they enjoyed most. It had a pleasing melody, and it told a romantic story.

Now I passed her house next evening.
The clock had just struck eight,

And I saw my future happiness—
Standing by the garden gate;
She smiled as I approached her,
And I begged her to excuse.
'May I view those pretty flowers?'
She murmured: 'If you choose.'
I spoke about the violets,
Then finally made proposes.
Thro' the garden we walked, of happiness talked
'Twas love amongst the roses.

How quickly they are picking up the words, Mrs Hopkins marvelled. If they show this sort of aptitude in the classroom, we will do very well together.

She taught them the entire song and a simple harmony as well, and then, because she had no wish to return to the classroom, she had them take turns in playing the roles of the courting couple. This idea of play-acting, which had occurred to her quite out of the blue (she was not normally the sort of School-Mistress who indulged in such things), turned out to be a great success. The girls seemed to delight in acting out their youthful notion of romantic courtship. There was much bowing and tipping of caps on the part of the 'gentlemen', and a great fluttering of imaginary fans on the part of the various damsels.

And to think that many of these girls have worked as prostitutes, thought Mrs Hopkins, as she watched their little plays of courtship. What unspeakable violations had these poor girls endured and were yet capable of dancing about in the sand, feigning 'love amongst the roses'.

'Oh, look, there is old Crabface perving at us,' one of the girls remarked.

Mrs Hopkins looked up and saw that Mr Crabback was standing at the top of the rocks. He seemed to be calling out something and gesticulating wildly, but no one could quite make out what he was on about. Finally, in exasperation, he launched himself scuttling down the rocks, slipping and sliding along sideways just as Mrs Hopkins had done, causing the girls to giggle wickedly at his crabbishness. By the time he reached them, he looked quite red-faced and agitated.

'I see that you are allowing the girls to romp,' he said to Mrs Hopkins, with a brusqueness that surprised her.

'It is a music lesson,' she replied. 'I have taught the girls a new song. Would you like to hear it? The girls sing it very well indeed.'

'Not at this moment, no,' said Mr Crabback. 'It is time for the girls to go up to their chores. Off you go, girls! At once, please!' He clapped his hands several times to hurry them up. Then he turned to Mrs Hopkins. 'I thought I made it clear to you, Mrs Hopkins, that the beach is strictly off-limits,' he declared. 'And now you have allowed the girls to romp about in their under-things in full view of all the passengers and crew of the Parramatta ferry!'

Mrs Hopkins stared at him, indignation rising in her chest. Although some of the girls had moved off, others lingered and regarded the altercation between the Superintendent and the new School-Mistress with frank interest.

'Mr Crabback, if you have something to say to me, then please say it to me privately and not in front of the girls,' Mrs Hopkins said quietly.

'As Superintendent, I'll speak to you whenever and however I choose!' exclaimed Mr Crabback. 'You have a perfectly adequate classroom, and I'll thank you to use it.' And with this, he turned on his heel and began to move off up the rocks.

'But the windowpanes in my classroom are broken, and the smell from the earth-closets abominable,' said Mrs Hopkins, quite loudly this time.

He stopped and turned back to her, an expression of disbelief on his face.

'It is enough that my little ones had to endure it this morning,' she continued, her voice trembling with indignation. 'The older girls will not tolerate it, and I do not blame them.'

At this, the girls erupted into cheers.

'Go to your chores at once, girls!' cried Mr Crabback. And then when they did not move immediately, he shouted, 'At once, I say, you disobedient little sluts!' His hand flew to his mouth in horror at the word that had just passed his lips. His eyes met hers for a brief moment, and a spasm of anguish passed over his face. He turned at once and hurried back up the rocks towards the institution.

Mrs Hopkins stared after him in bewilderment. Something must surely have happened, she thought, to cause him to behave in this fashion.

'Come along, girls,' she said when she had collected herself from the shock. 'Let us go up and do the chores, then we shall have our tea.'

'He shouldn't have called us that word, Miss,' said one of the water sprites. 'It was disrespectful.'

'Indeed it was,' said Mrs Hopkins. 'But even the kindest and wisest of men can make mistakes under duress. Let us not judge him too hastily. He is a good man, a very good man, and I will tell you this now: he has only your best interests at heart.'

Although she had had every intention of setting an example to the girls by joining them for tea in the mess-hall, instead Mrs Hopkins hastened to her own quarters as soon as an opportunity allowed it. The events of the afternoon had been such that she needed a moment of quiet in order to regain her composure. But as she sat and drank her tea, she began to feel that it was a matter of some urgency that she explain herself to Mr Crabback. The sight of the girls twirling about, many still dressed only in their under-garments, must have struck him as debauched, bacchanalian even. Oh, if only she could discuss the matter with him by his fireside, she could make him see that all she had been trying to achieve was . . . what was it exactly she had been trying to achieve? Had she been trying to win the girls over in the hope that they would not spit at her and call her a dried-up old codfish? No, no, surely that had not been her intention! She had simply been endeavouring to win the girls' trust—yes, that was it! The silly romantic song had been a first step towards gaining their sympathy that she might bring to bear, eventually, some kind of moral influence upon them.

In her agitation, Mrs Hopkins rose up from her seat and hurried out of her quarters. Heaving open the heavy gate of the institution, she found the girls standing in the quadrangle, in the midst of their evening prayer. It was Mrs Dunstable who intoned the prayer tonight—there was no sign of Mr Crabback—and she threw Mrs Hopkins a reproving look as the gate squeaked shut behind her.

Chastened, Mrs Hopkins lowered her head at once, and murmured along with the prayer as best she could. '*We acknowledge and bewail our manifold sins and wickedness . . .*' A horrible clarity suddenly descended upon Mrs Hopkins: yes, she must acknowledge and bewail her own wickedness! How quickly she had been led astray! Allowing the girls to cavort in their under-things, on the beach, in full public view! And then, when corrected, had she not spoken impertinently to Mr Crabback? In front of the girls, no less! '*. . . provoking most justly thy wrath and indignation . . .*' How right he was to be angry with her! She had goaded him into using a terrible word: she who had sought to serve as his loyal and devoted helpmeet! If only she could go to him and plead for his mercy and understanding!

'*We do earnestly repent and are heartily sorry for our misdeeds,*' the girls mumbled sullenly, heads bowed. '*Have mercy upon us, most merciful Father.*'

The prayer at last over, Josephine was now tugging at her sleeve. 'Mrs Hopkins? Which dormitory will I sleep in tonight?'

For a moment, Mrs Hopkins gazed at the child in blank confusion. Then she remembered what she had promised her. 'Yes, yes, Josephine, I had not forgotten. Go to your usual dormitory now, and I will speak to Mrs Dunstable on the matter. Then I will come and fetch you. Off you go now, child.'

The girl beamed up at her happily and skipped away. Mrs Dunstable, keys in hand, was on her way to the first dormitory to commence lock-up.

Mrs Hopkins hurried to catch up with her. 'Mrs Dunstable. May I have a word?'

'Make it a quick one. I want to get my tea on.'

'I thought it a good idea if young Josephine Briars, the new girl, could move into this dormitory. It would get her out of Dormitory Four, where all the bigger—what is the expression? The girls who have been "on the town", as it were—'

'Are you the new Matron?' interrupted Mrs Dunstable. They had reached the door of Dormitory One now, and the little children were filing past them inside.

'Am I the new Matron? No, I am the new School-Mistress,' responded Mrs Hopkins.

'Oh, pardon me, I'm sure,' said Mrs Dunstable. 'I thought you must be the new Matron, giving orders like that.'

'I am not giving orders, Mrs Dunstable—'

'Well, it certainly sounded like it. And you been here all of a day!' She heaved shut the heavy iron door. 'Keep it quiet tonight, you lot!' she shouted through the grille as she locked the padlock.

'Mrs Dunstable, I was only trying to make a suggestion—'

'It's the Matron or the Superintendent that decides who sleeps where—maybe me sometimes, if necessary, but then I am the House Matron, so it is perfectly justified in my case—'

'But that is why I am asking you, Mrs Dunstable!'

'I daresay you expect me now to drag in a new bed and run about the place looking for blankets! Never mind I've been on my feet since dawn.'

'Mrs Dunstable, I do not expect you to do anything—'

'There's scarcely a whole blanket in the place—the girls rip them up to make fires—where am I expected to find a fresh one, you tell me that, Mrs Hopkins, since you know so much about the running of this institution?'

'Mrs Dunstable, I was simply making a suggestion, with the welfare of a child in mind. But I will not keep you from your tea any longer, for as you say, you have been on your feet since dawn—I will speak to the Superintendent instead. Good evening.' And she gave a low bow before turning and sweeping out into the quadrangle. Her heart pounded with fury. What was wrong with that woman? How dare she speak to her like that!

The child in question was waiting for her in the quadrangle. 'Is it all right?' she asked hopefully.

'Josephine, I told you to wait for me in your usual dormitory.'

'But did Mrs Dunstable say it was all right for me to sleep there?'

'I am going to talk to Mr Crabback on the matter. Go to your dormitory. I shall be there shortly once I have discussed . . . once I have discussed the matter with the Superintendent.'

And she hurried off towards the Superintendent's quarters. Surely Mr Crabback would see the merit in placing Josephine with the younger girls. Of course, before she dared broach the subject, she had first to beg his forgiveness for her outburst down on the beach. She would drop to the hearth before him and place her head upon his knee. A thrill of excitement ran through her at the prospect. Perhaps he would dab her tears away with his handkerchief as he had done the previous night.

She knocked upon the front door and was rewarded by the sound of Tippet's barking.

'Stop your barking, you wretch of a thing!'

A woman's voice! Mrs Hopkins drew back—she had not expected Mr Crabback to have company. Who could this interloper be? The front door swung open.

'Yes?' demanded a stout lady of formidable bearing, dressed in a handsome grey brocade.

'Is—is Mr Crabback in?'

'Yes.'

'I would like a moment of his time, if you please.'

'Would you indeed? And you are?'

'I am Mrs Hopkins, ma'am, the new School-Mistress.'

'Yes, I thought as much,' said the woman. 'I would be pleased if you could tell me why I should not write to the Colonial Secretary at once to demand your immediate dismissal.'

Mrs Hopkins stared at her. 'Is there—is there something I have done wrong?'

'You were observed encouraging the girls to cavort upon the beach in their under-clothes. I hardly think that is the pathway to reform, do you?'

'It was not—it was not as you think, ma'am.'

'I saw you with my own eyes from the steamer that brought me here,' said the imposing woman. 'Are you saying that I imagined it?'

Mrs Hopkins shook her head meekly. How ludicrous it seemed now, as she stood upon the doorstep, to propose that she had been simply endeavouring to win the girls' trust. How preposterous to declare that allowing them to gamble about in their petticoats was a first step towards gaining moral influence over them.

'Very well. I will write to Mr Massie in the morning. I should warn you that he is likely take a very dim view on this.' And she began to close the door.

'But may I see Mr Crabback, please?' said Mrs Hopkins.

The woman stared at her. 'No. You may not.'

'If I could just have a moment with him, I implore you—'

'Mrs Hopkins, my husband has a very delicate constitution. Your conduct has caused him to take to his bed with a violent headache. Do you see what you have done now, the trouble you have caused?'

And Mrs Crabback closed the door upon Mrs Hopkins, who stood there gasping for air, almost as a fish would, left discarded upon a jetty.

It was true that Mr Crabback had taken to his bed, but it was not true that he had a headache. He had argued with his wife, over Mrs Hopkins' fate, no less, and in his fury at his wife's implacability, her unwillingness to bend, or even to listen to him, he had retreated to his room.

'There, you see, Myra, you have brought on one of my headaches,' he had cried, and although he had not quite slammed the bedroom door, he had certainly pulled it shut more forcefully than was necessary. It was infuriating that she had turned up to the island unexpectedly in this manner: a deliberate move, no doubt, designed to catch him off-guard.

A quiver of excitement had passed over him at the sound of Mrs Hopkins' voice on the doorstep below. As he lay there listening to the to and fro between the women, his hand had slid down the front of his trousers and he commenced to cautiously pleasure himself. He hadn't done so in a good long while, but there was something about Mrs Hopkins' humiliation, unfolding below, that stirred him. How brazen of her to try to see him now, to *insist* upon it, to his own wife, no less. *'If I could just have a moment with him, I implore you!'* Well, she would be in for quite a surprise if she were to walk in on him right now.

He closed his eyes and tried to imagine such a scene. Oh, she would be startled at first, undoubtedly, her pale cheeks flushing—but then, without a word, she would turn and swiftly close the bedroom door behind her. Yes, yes, and then what? Might she not make a pretty little speech in which she once again expressed her willingness to serve him in any capacity he saw fit? And as she made this pretty little speech, might she not move towards the bed and lift her petticoats—*yes, yes!*—to reveal her pretty little drawers?

'My dear Mrs Hopkins,' he protested as she boldly climbed astride him. 'What on earth do you mean by this?'

'Shh!' She placed a fingertip to his lips. Next thing she was throwing her head back, her hair uncoiling wildly as she lost herself in her pleasure. In fact, such a rumpus was Mrs Hopkins making in Mr Crabback's imaginings that he failed to hear the warning creaks of footsteps upon the staircase, nor did he notice the door swing open until it was altogether too late.

Mrs Hopkins was so badly shaken by her exchange with Mrs Crabback that she felt she could neither return to her lonely quarters nor yet the institution. Instead, she took herself down to the beach, where she sat upon a rock and wept bitterly. She wept for herself, at the thought that she would soon be cast out upon the world again; a heartless world of dingy boarding houses reeking of boiled cabbage and mildew. The endless bronchial hacking from behind closed doors, the coughing up and spitting out of phlegm. Mr Feeney, the landlord, leaning over the bannister, extending a yellowed finger, accusing her of yet another imagined misdeed. Unable to bear her dismal room, Mrs Hopkins would walk the streets, looking for work or begging for pennies, seeking shelter in churches just so she could sit a moment and rest her weary feet.

Mrs Hopkins recalled that one day, attracted by the small crowd gathered around him, she had chanced upon Mr Crabback speaking at the Domain. Standing upon an apple crate, he had spoken of friendless young women, many of whom had travelled far from their homes, filled with the hopes and aspirations of a new life in the big city. But alas! Their dreams had been blighted almost as soon as they stepped foot off the train. Lonely and defenceless, they were easy prey to the spielers and schemers of the back slums, and rapidly these young innocents descended into a life of intemperance and vice. *'Don't go into that place; it will bring us disgrace. It will drive your poor parents to the grave.'* Hence the establishment of Mr and Mrs Crabback's Haven of Hope for Fallen Women where, by kindly counsel and the grace of God, such women might be directed to a path of amendment and virtue. It wasn't always easy, by God, for some of these girls were as depraved as you could possibly imagine. But nonetheless, he and Mrs Crabback persisted, and almost every day now they received letters stained with tears of gratitude, such as this one from Millie (here he waved a hand-written letter in the air), once a dead-eyed prostitute, now a Nurse in a crisp white apron at the Sydney Hospital and widely esteemed by all who knew her. One of her patients was a roof tiler who had fallen from a high gable—she nursed him back to health and now they were engaged to be married. The letter concluded with an invitation to their wedding (here Mr Crabback had wiped away a tear) with a postscript asking that the Crabbacks might feign simply to be old friends, for her fiancé knew nothing of her troubled past.

Now Mr Crabback's face grew troubled. The expense of running such an establishment was ruinous, he confessed. Up until now they had been helped out greatly by contributions from good-hearted citizens such as those gathered around him now. Make no mistake, concerted efforts were underway to enlist the support of the Government. But until then, just to fend off the bailiff and though it shamed him to ask, he wondered if his listeners might not dig into their pockets and make a small contribution towards the restitution of these poor, defenceless girls . . .

Here Mr Crabback became so overwhelmed with emotion that he was momentarily unable to continue. He launched tremulously into a hymn as the hat was passed around. Mrs Hopkins wept, too. For after all, what was there to distinguish her from the women he had just described? Youthful? Well, no longer, admittedly. Intemperate? Never. But lonely and defenceless and susceptible to temptation? Yes. She opened her purse and gave what she could, though she was scarcely in a position to do so.

And to think that, only this morning, this same good man had clasped her hands and told her she would be the finest helpmeet he could ever hope for! And yet—already!—she had let him down.

All the time Mrs Hopkins sat upon her rock, she was dimly aware of the sounds, wafting down from the dormitories, of the girls exchanging their customary profanities and jibes. After a while, it dawned upon her that she could now hear them singing, and the song that they were singing was 'Love Amongst The Roses'. They were managing the harmony quite effectively, and the sound of their voices blending so prettily went some way to easing Mrs Hopkins' troubled heart. She took her pocket handkerchief from her sleeve and dried her eyes. Her thoughts turned to Josephine, and she remembered with a rush the moment that the girl had flung her arms around Mrs Hopkins' neck. The child was waiting for her now, in that grim dark dormitory, hoping that Mrs Hopkins would come to rescue her. And what was Mrs Hopkins doing while the poor child anxiously waited? Why, she was wallowing in self-pity on the beach! At once, Mrs Hopkins rose to her feet and commenced to clamber up the rocks—with some difficulty, as it was now getting quite dark.

As she approached the institution, she realised that the girls were singing a hymn which Mrs Hopkins had not heard before. They sang slowly and reverently, and she paused to listen, for she was struck by the beauty of the words.

Shall we meet beyond the river
Where the surges cease to roll?
Where in all the bright forever
Sorrow ne'er shall press the soul?
Shall we meet in that blest harbour
When our stormy voyage is o'er?
Shall we meet and cast the anchor
By the fair, celestial shore?
Shall we meet, shall we meet

Shall we meet beyond the river?
Shall we meet beyond the river
Where the surges cease to roll?

Mrs Hopkins had long been susceptible to waking visions, mostly by night, but occasionally by daylight. One such vision came upon her now. She saw herself, quite vividly, wading into a deep and flowing river, as if in a baptism. On the distant opposite shore, all of those who were dear to her and lost forever, now gathered together in a small group. That shore was Heaven, she understood; the bright forever. She could see her long-dead parents, silver-haired and bandy-legged, waving and smiling and beckoning her over. With them, her older brother Edward who had died of typhus at the age of fourteen. Was that not also her Auntie Mary, arm in arm with her husband Harold; this was surprising in itself for Harold had cruelly deserted Auntie Mary and the children, never to be heard from again—and yet to judge by Mary's fond smile and the way she patted his hand, there were no hard feelings in the hereafter.

But—oh, why had this not yet struck her—where was Eugenie? Where was her blessed little four-year-old? A surge of panic rose within Mrs Hopkins, for she could not see the child at all in this gathering of spirits. *And yet if not with them on that celestial shore, where could she be?*

A small sticky hand slipped into hers and looking down, she saw it was Josephine.

'Were you looking for me?' asked the child with the mismatched eyes.

'Yes! Yes, I was,' cried Mrs Hopkins. She bent down and (quite unlike herself) caught the girl tightly in her arms. And from that moment on, she began to quite unquestioningly believe that Josephine was her daughter Eugenie, brought back to her as a scrawny eleven-year-old girl in a sandstone convict barracks.

It did not strike Mrs Hopkins as odd that there was no sign of her husband amidst the motley gathering of dead folk on the far celestial shore, and that was because he was not dead. Nor, as a matter of fact, had he ever been her husband. Reginald Dodds was one of those 'spielers and schemers of the back slums' as described by Mr Crabback on his apple box, whose modus operandi included but was not confined to the 'View to Matrimony' column in the *Sydney Morning Herald*. There he had advertised himself thus:

> Widower, of the highest principles, seeks refined lady with means, view to above. R.D. GPO, Syd.

After a courtship of barely a fortnight, culminating in a half-hour of fumbling behind the potting sheds of the Botanical Gardens, Reginald had asked her to marry him. Although she experienced certain misgivings, her options were few so she accepted. He told her of a dear little cottage he had seen that was going for a song, a perfect little love-nest for the pair of them; all they needed was a deposit. She floated giddily to the bank and withdrew her life savings of £10. He took off with it in unseemly haste. 'I should be back by tea-time, Carmel,' he said, which was a bad sign as her Christian name was Constance. 'See if you can get your hands on a bit of fish for our supper.' She never heard from him again. All she had to remember him by was his Gladstone bag, which he had thrust upon her as a surety. It was empty, of course, and had some other man's name inscribed inside, *Geo. Hopkins*. Nonetheless, she kept it, and from that point on, referred to herself as Mrs Hopkins, for of course she had found herself *enceinte*.

'Why are we here?' asked Josephine. She stood in the middle of the room, gazing around Mrs Hopkins' dismal accommodation. I need to make this more homely and inviting, thought Mrs Hopkins, noticing the child's dismay. She imagined herself setting things to rights by rustling up some lace curtains where the battered old blind now drooped.

'Well, I thought it might be nice for us to get to know each other better,' said Mrs Hopkins. 'Come and sit down beside me on the bed.' And she patted the moth-eaten blanket encouragingly. But a wariness seemed to have come over the child once the door of Mrs Hopkins' quarters had closed behind her.

'No, thanks,' she said.

'I could brush your hair for you, if you like,' offered Mrs Hopkins.

The girl shook her head sullenly. What a little vagabond she is, thought Mrs Hopkins. Her hair seemed practically alive with eggs and tiny insects. It would probably require several dousings with kerosene, if not to be shorn off altogether.

'You said you were going to put me in the dormitory with the little ones,' said Josephine.

'And so I was. But unfortunately, Mr Crabback is unwell, so I was unable to speak with him. But you may sleep here with me tonight if you like.'

'I don't like,' said the child. Clearly, she was used to associating with the sort of people who spoke in this blunt manner and no doubt thought it clever.

'Then how about a piece of cake?'

'What sort of cake?'

'It is a very nice seed cake.'

'All right then.'

So Mrs Hopkins got up and cut her off quite a large piece, and the child stood in the middle of the room and munched on it, the crumbs falling unheeded to the floor.

'Is that your doll?' she asked. Her eyes had alighted upon the old rag doll, resting against Mrs Hopkins' pillow. It had been Eugenie's doll; Mrs Hopkins had made it herself. It had wool sewn in for hair, and a couple of mismatched buttons for eyes.

'Why yes, that's Miss Minnie!'

Delighted to have a subject with which to break the ice, Mrs Hopkins scooped up the doll and placed it, sitting up like a small person, upon her lap. 'Miss Minnie, where are your manners!' she exclaimed brightly to the doll. 'Please say "How do you do?" to our visitor.'

'How do you do, Our Visitor,' said the doll, in a funny little voice which Mrs Hopkins affected by holding her lips in a certain way.

'Oh no, Miss Minnie,' cried Mrs Hopkins gaily in her normal voice. How easily she was slipping back into the old game! 'Our visitor's name is Josephine. Say "How do you do, Miss Josephine."'

'*How do you do, Miss Josephine*,' parroted the doll.

But Josephine was not impressed. 'I can see your lips moving when you do that,' she said.

'You had better say "How do you do" back,' whispered Mrs Hopkins playfully. 'Otherwise, Miss Minnie is inclined to get cross.'

Josephine said nothing but glanced uneasily at the door.

'*How do you do, Miss Josephine!*' repeated the doll in her funny little voice.

'How do you do,' mumbled Josephine.

'*How do you do, Miss Minnie!*' shrilled the doll.

'I am very sorry,' said Mrs Hopkins. 'But Miss Minnie here wants you to say, "*How do you do, Miss Minnie!*"'

'I won't,' said Josephine, her cheeks darkening. 'I won't say it.'

What was wrong with the child? Why was she being so contrary?

Eugenie would be chortling her little head off by now. 'Come on now, Josephine. Just for fun!'

The girl shook her head. She was starting to get a strange look about her, like she might burst into tears.

'*Josephine!*' cried the doll. (Now Mrs Hopkins was waving it in front of the child's face.) '*Can I tell you a secret?*'

'Stop making the doll talk.'

'You remind me of a little girl I used to know.'

'I don't like it!'

'Her name was Eugenie.'

And suddenly with a mighty swing, Josephine belted the doll clear across the room.

For a long moment, Mrs Hopkins simply stared at the child in shock. Then she stood up, crossed the room and picked the doll up from the floor. When she turned back, she saw that the threatening storm clouds had broken; the girl stood there forlornly in the centre of the room, tears streaming down her face.

'Oh dear!' cried Mrs Hopkins. 'I *am* sorry! I didn't mean to upset you.'

And swooping upon her, she pulled the child up onto the bed and placed her arm around the girl's thin shoulders and gave her one of her pocket handkerchiefs edged with black lace with which to dry her tears. Then she told the girl all about Eugenie and how Miss Minnie had been her special doll, and how Eugenie had loved to play that game where Miss Minnie was always making a fuss about everything.

'And do you know the funny thing? Eugenie had eyes just like yours. One eye was hazel, and one was green.'

'Do I have one eye hazel and one eye green?' asked Josephine.

'Yes,' said Mrs Hopkins. 'Has no one ever told you that?'

'No.'

'Well, it is nothing to be ashamed of. In fact, I think it makes you rather special.'

'Is she dead then, your daughter?' asked Josephine, only mildly interested. She had stopped crying by now and was poking her little finger through the lacework of the pocket handkerchief.

'Yes,' replied Mrs Hopkins. And with a pang, she remembered that strange vision she had just experienced where Eugenie could not be accounted for amongst her dear departed on that fair celestial shore.

'What did she die of?' asked Josephine.

'She had a sickness come over her.'

'What sort of sickness?'

'She wasted. She wasted away.'

'Didn't you feed her?'

'Oh, I tried. But she was a stubborn child. She had made her mind up, you see, that she must join the angels. And so she did.'

But she must have tired of their company, thought Mrs Hopkins, for she has returned to earth in human form, with vermin crawling through her scalp.

'And do you know, she would be eleven years old now, just like you,' said Mrs Hopkins.

'I thought you said she was dead,' said Josephine.

'Yes, she is dead. But if she was alive, I mean. If she was alive, she would be eleven years old. You will destroy that handkerchief if you keep poking holes in it like that.'

And just at that moment, there came a low furtive knock upon the door.

Mrs Hopkins looked up in alarm. 'Who could this be?' she whispered. Putting a finger to her lips to indicate that the child keep quiet, she moved swiftly to the door and opened it just enough to peek out. There upon her porch stood Mr Crabback.

'I had to see you,' he declared in a hoarse voice. 'May I come in?'

'No,' said Mrs Hopkins, through the crack in the door. 'I'm sorry. Now is not—now is not a convenient time.'

'It is a matter of some urgency!'

'Then speak to me. I am listening.'

'I cannot say—what I have to say to you—while standing out here in full view.'

'Nevertheless, you must,' she replied.

How infuriating she was! He longed to push the door open and seize her violently in his arms.

'Very well, if you insist,' he said, endeavouring to keep his voice steady. 'My message to you is this: you need not worry about my wife. Your position here is secure. I have dealt with the matter, and no more will come of it.'

'I see,' said Mrs Hopkins. She had heard a noise behind her and was hoping that the child would not reveal herself.

'I have dealt with the matter,' he repeated, for he felt that she had not grasped the full import of his words. 'And that is the end of it.'

'Yes,' she nodded. 'I heard you the first time.'

'We have had a terrific row,' continued Mr Crabback. 'She is leaving tomorrow on the first steamer.'

'She threatened to report me to the Colonial Secretary,' said Mrs Hopkins, flushing with the memory. 'When I was simply endeavouring, by use of song and dance, to gain the girls' trust.'

'Of course you were. Your efforts were entirely admirable. It grieves me that I lost my temper in that fashion, but she was on at me and on at me from the moment she arrived.'

'Yes, but will she write to the Colonial Secretary? For if she does, I will lose my job.'

'No, no, she will not write to him. I convinced her that your conduct was blameless; granted, your methods more modern than those she is used to.'

Mrs Hopkins felt the hard knot of anxiety begin to release from between her shoulder blades. He had accepted her explanation without argument; further, he considered her methods 'modern'. She had never considered herself in that light, and it pleased her.

'Perhaps I attempted too much too soon,' she conceded.

'She threw an ink-stand at me,' said Mr Crabback. 'Do you see? I have a cut.' He held the lantern up near his face. There was a small cut just above his eyebrow, and a slight swelling. 'It has always been like this: we are not compatible in any way. I have been wretchedly—*wretchedly*—unhappy the entirety of my married life.'

'I regret that I may have inadvertently been the cause of your . . . disharmony,' said Mrs Hopkins, and her voice throbbed appealingly.

'No!' he cried, seizing her hand and pressing it to his cheek. 'You have caused me only—only—'

He longed to tell her the magnificent truth, that she had caused him such arousal that he had achieved his first sexual climax in years. Mrs Hopkins of all people, in her buttoned-up mourning! And here he was surrounded by dozens of comely young maidens, waltzing about half-undressed, as brazen as you like. It was unaccountable! He pressed his lips to each of her fingertips in turn. She closed her eyes and gave a small involuntary shiver—yes, quite unmistakable this time—as if a frisson of physical rapture passed through her.

'My intention is to promote you to the office of Matron,' he declared, scarcely able to believe the words that were tumbling out of his mouth. *Matron?* What on earth was he talking about? His own wife was to be the Matron! How was he ever to explain it to his wife when she inevitably cooled down and returned to the island that he had installed the new School-Mistress in the role? But no matter, no matter, he could see that his words had had the desired result: Mrs Hopkins coloured deeply and she lowered her head in an expression of abject humility.

'I would be honoured to serve you in whatever capacity you believe best,' she murmured.

'Then let me come in, I beg of you,' he urged.

'No—I cannot!'

'Just for a minute!' He pressed his hand against her door. 'Please do not ask me—'

'Do you have someone there with you?' He thought he glimpsed the movement of a shadow on the wall behind her.

'No!' cried Mrs Hopkins. 'It is just that it is best—it is best for the moment that you return to your wife, for if there is any suggestion of improper conduct—'

'Are you suggesting that my intentions in wishing to consult with you privately are not entirely proper and above-board?' A sense of indignation swelled within him.

'No! Of course not. It is only that they may be interpreted as such—by those less honourable than yourself, those who may have cause to wish you ill—'

'Yes,' he acknowledged, for he saw that there was merit in her argument. He glanced around, uncomfortably aware now of the close proximity of Mrs Dunstable's quarters. Her shabby hut sat all in darkness, and yet there was a suspicious gap between the curtains. No doubt the House Matron was lurking within, spying upon them.

'Let us find a moment tomorrow where we might come to one another and speak,' said Mrs Hopkins.

'In privacy?'

'In privacy, yes.'

'Very well. Come to my house first thing—once the six o'clock steamer has departed, of course. For there is a great deal—a great deal I wish to discuss with you,' said Mr Crabback. 'Regarding my thoughts as to the management of the institution and so forth—'

Mrs Hopkins closed the door upon him. And as he withdrew into the darkness (for strangely his lantern had sputtered and extinguished itself at the very moment the door had shut), he found himself in a state of greater agitation than he could conceive possible. The woman was turning him into a raving madman! It was just as the scholarly article had suggested—in her fashion, she was depleting him, not only of his vital juices, but of his senses! What was he doing, trying to force his way into her quarters, in full view of other staff members, with his own wife packing her bags not two hundred yards away? The thought of his wife, and the terrible scene that had unfolded when she had surprised him at the very moment of his ecstasy, caused him to groan out loud. But no matter, she would be gone soon; it was for the best.

His thoughts surged back to Mrs Hopkins, and a spasm of doubt rose to the surface—why had she been so reluctant to allow him entry to her quarters? Was it possible that she had been entertaining a gentleman, an officer from the *Blanche* perhaps? It certainly seemed unlikely (and she had denied it very prettily), but if his short stint at Biloela had taught Mr Crabback anything it was that the female of his species was capable of all manner of duplicitous behaviours.

The child gazed up at Mrs Hopkins curiously as she closed the door. She had heard much of the conversation, and having witnessed many times her own mother sending away those customers, possessed of insufficient funds, who tried to force their way into her bedroom, formed her own idea of what had just transpired between the Superintendent and the School-Mistress. The sight of Mrs Hopkins leaning her slight frame against the door to prevent Mr Crabback's entry aroused her sympathies, and when Mrs Hopkins sat herself down again on the bed, Josephine leaned her head against her in a gesture of solidarity.

'Men!' she said, with a great sigh.

In fact, while Mrs Hopkins was engaged at the door fending off Mr Crabback, Josephine had spent much of her time quietly rummaging through Mrs Hopkins' possessions. Of course, since they had already been systematically rummaged through by others, it had not proved as profitable as she had hoped. Nonetheless, she had secreted at this moment in the bodice of her dress a pair of woollen gloves, a bar of Sunlight soap, a scent-bag filled with dried lavender and a crocheted doyley. Hence her insistence that she remain fully clothed when Mrs Hopkins folded down the sheet and invited her into her bed. She also insisted that Miss Minnie be removed—first to a chair situated at the furthest point possible from the bed, and then, when that proved unsatisfactory, to the inside of Mrs Hopkins' chest, with the lid firmly closed and a heavy pot placed upon it, since the lock was broken.

Mrs Hopkins did not sleep well that night. For one thing, the child was a restless sleeper, tossing about and kicking and making garbled, impassioned speeches in her sleep. For another thing, Mrs Hopkins had become used to sleeping with Miss Minnie, now banished to the chest: her little daughter's beloved doll had long been a comfort to her in her loneliness. But the real reason for Mrs Hopkins' insomnia was that Mr Crabback's visit had greatly unsettled her.

On the one hand, it was an extraordinary and wholly unexpected turn of events that he should send his wife packing and elevate Mrs Hopkins to the position of Matron. But on the other hand, she had been somewhat disturbed by the feverishness of his demeanour. Could it possibly be (and this she barely dared ask herself) that he had developed romantic feelings towards her? But no, she reminded herself sternly, he was a married man, albeit an unhappily married man: it was very wrong of her to entertain such foolish notions about him. Besides, Mrs Hopkins suffered no illusions about her appearance; even in her youth, she had never been one to turn heads, and the ravages of time, poverty, illness and loss had only drawn her lips thinner and heightened the bony prominence of her brow. No, no, she told herself: amidst his troubles, Mr Crabback sought only a tender helpmeet to toil loyally by his side, a steadfast companion offering wisdom and counsel in times of difficulty. If he had expressed himself rather more freely that evening than seemed entirely fitting, could it not be interpreted as simply an indication of his satisfaction in finding these hoped-for qualities in Mrs Hopkins? And with these pleasant thoughts to comfort her, and the memory of his lips upon her fingertips, she finally drifted off to sleep.

Hours later, she was visited upon for the first time by the paupers. In her half-conscious state, she became aware of the smell of pipe tobacco combined with a putrid, nauseating odour of mould and decay. Her belly retched involuntarily. Opening her eyes blearily, she saw a hunchbacked crone seated at the end of her bed, rocking back and forth. An old clay pipe hung from her lip, and she was crooning in a hoarse voice some kind of lullaby, the words of which Mrs Hopkins could not make out. A young girl sat next to her, her face a mess of deep crevices, presumably from the effects of the rotgut alcohol she had imbibed in her short life. She rocked back and forth in unison with the old lady, and it was then that Mrs Hopkins realised that the old woman had Eugenie on her lap.

In some way, it was just as Mrs Hopkins had hoped; that her little girl was being cared for by the other paupers, the ones who had been tossed in the pit before her. And although she sensed that she was most likely dreaming she felt strongly that the two mouldering women, the crone and the ginhead, were not happy with Mrs Hopkins, not happy at all.

Who shall spare a thought for Mrs Crabback in all of this? As dawn broke over Cockatoo Island, she could be seen marching down towards the steamer wharf, a valise in each hand. Her husband was sound asleep with Tippet snuggled at his side; their snores reverberated through the house. She had not woken him to say goodbye. She had no time for him at all. He had behaved disgracefully, and although he had tried to argue that it was her unexpected arrival that had excited him in this manner, she was not deceived. The silly old fool, surrounded as he was by young women of the lowest morals imaginable, had lost his head. Well, let him stew in his own juices a while. She would return to her duties at the Haven of Hope for the time being. He would soon be imploring her to return, for this much she knew: he was incapable of running the institution on his own.

Josephine was the next to rise. While Mrs Hopkins slept on, mouth open, lips parched, exhausted by the emotions of the previous day, the young girl polished off another chunk of seed cake, and enjoying her freedom for the gates to the institution were still locked against her, took herself down to the beach. She was a city child, not used to the water: a trip to the seaside with her mother and her numerous 'aunties' had been a once-a-year event. Holding up her skirts, she let the white foam rush around her ankles; she studied a crab; she ran wildly towards a group of resting seagulls waving a stick. When the steamer carrying Mrs Crabback hove into view on its way back to the city, Josephine gave it a friendly wave. Mrs Crabback, however, already ensconced in the saloon with her back to the island, did not see her.

After a while, Josephine set about burying her new treasures in the sand between the rocks: the woollen gloves, the soap, the scent-bag, the crocheted doyley. They were to be presents for her mother, and there was nowhere else to keep them (certainly not the dormitory) where they would not be promptly purloined by someone else: she had learned that lesson already in the short time she had been at Biloela. She took care to memorise where each of the items was buried, marking each spot with cryptic arrangements of seaweed and shells. It was only when she had finished and was brushing the sand from her dress that she saw that Henry the simpleton was standing watching her, only a few feet away.

'I seen what you did,' he said.

Josephine stared at him. She had heard some of the older girls talking about Henry: he was one of the original convicts of the island, and for some unknown reason had never left. He did odd jobs for the institution, such as bringing up stores from the wharf in the hand-cart or mending pots and pans. Someone who had seen him bathing in the sea described his back as a mass of raised welts, no doubt from all the floggings he had received. One of the girls swore black and blue that she had seen him on the wharf strangling something—a dog or a cat, or possibly even a baby—and then had tossed its small corpse into the water.

'Here, I will give you this handkerchief if you don't say nothing,' said Josephine, and she took from her sleeve the black lace-edged handkerchief belonging to Mrs Hopkins and presented it to Henry.

'I already got one of them,' said Henry. And he pulled from the pocket of his trousers an identical, if grubbier, black lace-edged handkerchief, which he had pilfered from Mrs Hopkins' trunk on the evening of her arrival, along with a bag of milk toffees and a pillow sham.

'Have another one then,' said Josephine, and he duly took the handkerchief she proffered.

'Smell it,' said Josephine. 'It smells nice.'

Henry held the handkerchief to his nose and sniffed.

'It's lavender,' said Josephine. 'I can get you some more if you like.'

'I seen what you did,' reiterated Henry as he pocketed the handkerchief. 'I seen you bury those things.'

'I know. You told me already. Are you hungry? I can bring you some cake too if you don't say nothing. It's got seeds stuck in it but it tastes all right. Or a doll. Do you want a doll? I can get you a doll.'

'Why would I want a stupid fecking doll!' shouted Henry at the top of his voice, and the veins stood out on his neck alarmingly.

'You could sell it maybe,' said Josephine, who was celebrated in her family for the cool head she had on her shoulders. 'You could easily get a few bob for it, and then the world's your oyster. You could take yourself for a ride on the trams. See the world. That's what I'd do if I wasn't stuck in this joint.'

'Josephine!' called Mrs Hopkins, from the top of the rocks. She had awoken to find the child missing and gone searching for her. 'Come up at once!'

Josephine turned and gazed up at her.

'This minute!' cried Mrs Hopkins.

'I got to go,' said Josephine to Henry. 'Remember, don't say nothing. Don't say nothing and I'll bring you stuff.' And with that, she set off scrambling nimbly up the rocks in her bare feet. 'Don't dig it all up either!' she called back to Henry, for the thought had just occurred to her that that was most likely what he would do. She would have to come back at the soonest opportunity, after breakfast maybe, and bury it all somewhere else.

'What were you doing talking to that man?' cried Mrs Hopkins when Josephine had reached the top. 'Don't you realise he is a very dangerous imbecile?'

'He wanted to sell me one of your handkerchiefs,' said Josephine, for it was the first lie that came into her head.

'My handkerchiefs?' repeated Mrs Hopkins in surprise.

'You know, with the black lace. I don't know how he got it.'

'Why, he must have stolen it from my chest when I left it in his charge,' said Mrs Hopkins. 'Very well. I will have a word with him. You go at once to have your wash and do your chores. Off you go now.'

And although the child was filled with misgivings at the idea of Mrs Hopkins discussing with the simpleton the matter of her handkerchiefs, she knew that to protest would only arouse suspicion. So she set off at a gallop back to the institution, the gates of which were now opened for the day.

'Excuse me!' Mrs Hopkins called down to Henry, who was now scratching his foot speculatively around the site of Josephine's burials. 'May I have a word please?'

Henry took off at once. He did not care for the spectral lady in black; she had frightened him badly on the evening of her arrival when she had loomed out of the darkness, her pale and bony face aglow, demanding that he supervise her battered trunk without any mention of payment.

Mrs Hopkins sighed as she watched him go (such an odd syphilitic gait!), but in truth she was relieved that she did not have to confront him. What on earth would she have said? she wondered. Besides, were those gloomy black lace-edged handkerchiefs really of such importance to her?

Perhaps—and this was an entirely new and daring thought—it was time to ease her mourning: she had already observed it for many years longer than required. There were several reasons for this, her poverty looming large amongst them, as she had been in no position financially to replace her attire when the period of official mourning was over. Further, the dull black bombazine was practical in that it did not show up dirt. But was it also possible, she wondered (for there were times when Mrs Hopkins did not shirk from self-examination), that she had come to enjoy the sympathy the tragic aspect of her mourning evoked in others? Yes, there were times when it had proved very useful, providing her with a hot meal or a roof over her head for the evening, perhaps even a few shillings pressed hastily into her palm.

This evening I will remove those awful crepe trimmings from my dress, she told herself. And perhaps in time, if she saved her pennies, she would be able to buy a nice lilac or grey silk brocade and make herself up a couple of new dresses in the modern style. This reminded Mrs Hopkins of the fact that Mr Crabback had promoted her to the position of Matron, which would surely mean an improvement in her wages. Light of heart, she hurried through the gates, ready to commence work.

What Mrs Hopkins had not noticed, as she was imagining herself the picture of refinement in her brocades, was that the normally sure-footed little Josephine had meanwhile 'come a cropper'. One foot had slid between the rocks and become wedged, and she had fallen violently forward, almost as if struck from behind. Her thin little knees were badly grazed, her ankle twisted, but on glancing about and seeing that the accident had not been observed, she simply picked herself up and continued onwards. She had too much pride to be a sook about it.

Mrs Hopkins had not forgotten that Mr Crabback had asked her to come to his quarters once the boat carrying his wife had departed. But given his demeanour the night before, she deemed it best to keep a respectful distance for the time being. Besides, if anyone should chance to see her on his doorstep, it would only provoke the worst sort of speculation. Thus Mr Crabback, all freshly bathed and toileted, side-whiskers combed, waited for her in vain; finally, he gave up and somewhat belatedly went to oversee the morning duties at the school.

'I have an important announcement to make,' said Mr Crabback, as the girls lined up for muster. 'Mrs Crabback has been called back to Sydney on urgent business.'

This prompted a good deal of sniggering amongst the girls, for the swelling above Mr Crabback's right eye was now quite conspicuous.

'Quiet please!' he admonished, to little avail. 'In her absence, I have appointed Mrs Hopkins to the position of Acting Matron. She will continue her duties as School-Mistress concurrently.'

Standing with her class of young charges, Mrs Hopkins was somewhat surprised to hear the term 'Acting Matron': she had understood, when he made his proposal the night before, that the position was to be more permanent. Nor had she realised that he expected her to maintain her position as School-Mistress; surely that could only be for the short term? Nevertheless, the girls let out a boisterous cheer of approval at the announcement, which caused her to blush with pleasure. Perhaps, she dared think, she had made some progress in gaining their trust with all that frolicking to 'Love Amongst The Roses'.

'How is that fair?' Mrs Dunstable's voice rang out. 'By rights, as House Matron, I am the one who should be promoted to Matron. Besides, she has only just got here. She knows nothing about the running of the place.'

The Assistant Matrons, Mrs Baird and Miss Foy, made noises of agreement.

'Mrs Dunstable, if you have something to say to me, you will kindly choose a more appropriate time and place—' began Mr Crabback.

'I've been here three years and virtually run this institution single-handed. And this is the thanks I get!' cried Mrs Dunstable.

'You haven't run this place single-handed,' objected Mrs Baird. 'If anything, we do most of the running around.'

'She has no experience, is my point!'

'Mrs Dunstable,' intervened Mr Crabback, 'if you will calm down, I am happy to explain the reasoning for my decision—'

'Go on then! And while you're at it, explain why you were calling upon her in the middle of the night!'

'Oooh-ahh!' cried the girls, who had been avidly enjoying this entertainment.

Mr Crabback went very red in the face. 'How dare you cast aspersions—' he blustered.

'I saw him with my own eyes on her doorstep, carrying on like a lovesick puppy! No wonder he's copped a walloping from the missus!'

'Oh!' cried Mrs Hopkins, covering her face with her hands. Then she turned and stumbled blindly from the quadrangle. It was all rather theatrical, but better than standing about waiting to hear more.

'There, you see what you have done now?' cried Mr Crabback. 'You have called into question the moral character of one who bears the highest—the highest possible—moral character that any person can possibly bear. Your behaviour disgusts and appals me, Mrs Dunstable. Your services at Biloela are dispensed with forthwith.'

'You can't just sack me!'

'I most certainly can—'

'I shall write to the Colonial Secretary!'

'Then kindly bear in mind the fact that I shall be writing also. Now pack your bags at once—I want you off the island on the one o'clock ferry!'

And with that, he turned and hurried back to his quarters, very red in the face, almost purple, in fact; leaving Mrs Dunstable, awash with tears, to be comforted by Mrs Baird and Miss Foy.

Having taken a few necessary moments to compose herself after the humiliation of the scene in the quadrangle, Mrs Hopkins spent the morning in the schoolroom with her young charges. She paid particular attention to Josephine, for the girl—in spite of her own illiteracy—was determined to prove herself as a good little teacher to the poor addled Tunks sisters. A fierce attachment seemed to have formed between them; the bandy-legged sisters hung off her in the quadrangle, and Josephine doted upon them tenderly. When Mrs Hopkins commended her on her efforts, Josephine's cheeks pinkened and she bit her lip to stop herself from beaming with pride.

'Will you move me into their dormitory like you said you would, Mrs Hopkins?'

'Are you sure you would not rather sleep in my quarters with me?'

'I want to sleep with the little girls!' cried Josephine. 'You said I could!'

'Yes, of course, but first I must speak to Mr Crabback, you understand. It simply may not be possible.'

It was disappointing: Mrs Hopkins had rather hoped that the girl might continue to sleep in her own quarters. Admittedly her bed was a narrow one and could not comfortably sleep two, but perhaps a spare cot could be installed for her. Questions might be asked by the others, of course, but as Matron—even as Acting Matron—she could rightly do as she saw fit. They could 'like it or lump it', as the saying goes.

So preoccupied was she with the morning's lessons that when Mrs Baird knocked on the door of the schoolroom to enquire who was taking charge of the stores now that Mrs Dunstable had been 'given the boot', it came to her as something of a surprise. Nevertheless, she took the news of the House Matron's departure with quiet composure, though she felt a secret pleasure at the thought that Mr Crabback had acted so decisively to defend her honour.

'Why, Mrs Baird, I believe that you should take charge of the stores,' she said simply.

'Me, ma'am?'

'Yes, of course. We will require you to take on the position of House Matron, now that Mrs Dunstable is leaving us,' she said.

'Oh dear,' said Mrs Baird. 'I have an awful lot to do as it is.'

'Obviously, your salary would need to reflect the increased responsibility assigned you,' said Mrs Hopkins. 'I shall talk to Mr Crabback about it at the earliest opportunity.'

This seemed to cheer Mrs Baird inordinately, and she hurried off to sort out the day's supply of meat and bread, which Henry had brought up from the wharf. Mrs Hopkins meanwhile returned to her students. But soon she was interrupted by another knock. It was Mary-Ann, one of the water sprites, a plump, pretty girl with wavy dark hair.

'Mrs Hopkins, I have a message for you,' she said from the doorway.

'Yes?' said Mrs Hopkins. 'What is it?'

But Mary-Ann seemed reluctant to reveal anything further, instead indicating via hand signals and motions of her head that Mrs Hopkins join her in the doorway.

'It's from Mr Crabback,' whispered Mary-Ann, surreptitiously passing Mrs Hopkins a folded note which she plucked from deep within her bodice. 'He says it's of the utmost importance that he sees you tonight after lock-up.'

In spite of herself, Mrs Hopkins blushed.

'He called me out of the sewing room,' continued Mary-Ann eagerly. 'He said, "Mary-Ann, I need you to take this note at once to Mrs Hopkins." I said, "I will, with pleasure, sir." The other girls made a fuss and carried on, but I told them to shut it, Miss. I think it's lovely that he's sweet on you.'

'Oh no, Mr Crabback is not sweet on me,' said Mrs Hopkins. 'His wife has had to leave on urgent business, that's all, and I daresay Mr Crabback needs to discuss things—'

'Aren't you going to read the note, Miss?'

'Not at this moment, no.'

'But he told me he needed an answer, Miss. He said there was a sixpence in it if I hung about till I got one.'

And so Mrs Hopkins had no choice but to unfold the note and read it there and then.

My dear Mrs Hopkins,

I must tell you how desprately sorry I am regarding the unplesantness to wich you were exposd at Muster. Rest ashord I have termnatd Mrs Dunstable's employment forf with. I would be pleasd if you could kindly atend my quawters this evening after Lock-up that in order we may discus privetly your new dutys as Matron and other matters conserning the running of this Institushon.

I have the honnur to be, etc.
CHARLES CRABBACK
Superintendent

It took longer than one would expect for Mrs Hopkins to read the letter as the writing was so bad as to be practically illegible.

'Mary-Ann,' said Mrs Hopkins once she had read it through several times and satisfied herself as to its meaning, 'are you sure that Mr Crabback wrote this note?'

'What do you mean, Miss?'

'Well, did you see him actually write it?'

'No, Miss. But he gave it to me to give to you.'

'He gave it to you?'

'Yes, Miss.'

'This note I have here in my hand?'

'Yes, Miss. His writing's awful, isn't it? I had trouble making sense of it myself.'

'Mary-Ann, if someone gives you a note to deliver to somebody else, you must not read it. A note is a private thing. Do you understand?'

'I just read it quickly through once, Miss.'

'But you mustn't read it at all. Do you follow?'

'Just to make sure it was for you, Miss, that was all. I'd hate to give it to the wrong person. Imagine if I gave it to old Dunny-Can!'

'Please do not call Mrs Dunstable by that.'

'I love that bit where he says how he's desperately sorry,' continued Mary-Ann. 'Oh my word, my heart did a flip when I read that. I wish my Phillipe would write such nice things, Miss.'

Once again, Mrs Hopkins felt her cheeks pinkening in pleasure.

'Don't get me wrong, my boy's a sweetheart,' the girl continued. 'But he doesn't know English that good. Oh! And do you know what else, Miss? Mr Crabback apologised for calling me a slut yesterday. Which I thought on the whole very decent of him.'

'That was certainly very decent of him—'

'He said he lost his head because his wife was at him and he knew in his heart I wasn't a slut, I was a very nice girl with my head screwed on straight, though he couldn't speak for the others. Are you going to write back, Miss? I don't mind waiting. Not at all.'

And so Mrs Hopkins hurried to her desk and wrote a reply.

Sir,

I would be honoured to discuss my new duties as Matron and matters concerning the running of the institution with you this evening after lock-up.

I have the honour to be, Your obedient servant,
Constance E. Hopkins
School-Mistress, Biloela Industrial School for Girls

Then she folded the note carefully several times over and gave it to Mary-Ann, who tucked it down her bodice.

'I just wanted to say also, Miss,' whispered Mary-Ann, 'if you have any messages or love notes for Mr Crabback, just ask me. Don't bother asking the other girls. They're not so discreet, Miss. They'll spread it all over the place. Not me, Miss. Mum's the word with me.'

And she skipped away, singing 'Love Amongst The Roses'.

The next visitor to appear in the doorway of Mrs Hopkins' schoolroom that morning was Mrs Dunstable herself.

Noticing the room had fallen suddenly quiet, Mrs Hopkins glanced up from her work to see that the children were staring dumbstruck at the doorway as if at an apparition. For their normally strait-laced House Matron stood swaying, distraught and dishevelled, one trembling arm outstretched towards their School-Mistress. Some dark substance had been spilt down the front of her blouse, which had itself come askew from her skirt-waist, and her grey frizzled hair was sticking out wildly, having broken free from its various pins and clips. The whole effect was such that Mrs Hopkins was sadly reminded of an illustration she had seen in one of Mr Crabback's tracts, depicting 'The Evils of Drink'.

'Why, Mrs Dunstable, whatever do you want?'

The House Matron's trembling hand now beckoned for Mrs Hopkins to approach her. And somewhat reluctantly, Mrs Hopkins rose from her desk and did as she was bid.

'Oh, Mrs Hopkins!' cried the apparition. 'Would you find it in your heart to forgive me? It was terrible what I said, but I meant no harm, I swear I didn't! I beg of you to let me stay!'

Just as Mrs Hopkins suspected, Mrs Dunstable had been drinking. The fumes of some kind of fortified spirit were redolent upon her breath.

'Why, Mrs Dunstable, it is not up to me,' said Mrs Hopkins. 'It is up to Mr Crabback. Such decisions as these rest entirely in the hands of the Superintendent.'

'Oh no, Mrs Hopkins, I've been to see him already. I went down on my knees—I begged him, I did. I said, "Please Mr Crabback, will you reconsider—I have nowhere to go—I will be destitute upon the streets!"'

'And what did he say?'

'He said if it were left to him, I would go most certainly, but since I carried on so, he would leave the decision up to you, for you were the party most gravely injured by—by the things I said.' Mrs Dunstable clutched hold of her arm now. 'Please, Mrs Hopkins, I implore you! Have pity upon me. I was wrong, I was terribly wrong, but I don't deserve to be—to be—cast out like a piece of rubbish—worse than rubbish, like a piece of shit under your boot—'

'Mrs Dunstable, please—compose yourself! The children can hear you!'

Giving the older woman a shove in order that she move out of the doorway, Mrs Hopkins stepped out of the schoolroom and closed the door behind them.

Mrs Dunstable looked up at her hopefully. 'So will you?'

'What?'

'Will you give me a second chance?'

'You ask a great deal of me, Mrs Dunstable,' said Mrs Hopkins. 'And perhaps I could forgive you on my own account for idle gossip is nothing to me. I have never cared what people say; to me, it is so much water off a duck's back. But I tell you this now, and I will speak plainly: I could never forgive you for the manner in which you have sullied the honour and good standing of Mr Crabback as you did so publicly this morning. That man is kindness and decency incarnate; it is simply an impossibility for him to behave in any way dishonourably. You are correct: he did visit my quarters last night, but only to offer words of reassurance, for his wife had spoken to me with—with quite unnecessary harshness—'

Here she broke off, for the memory of Mrs Crabback's words came back to her afresh. How dare that woman speak to her as she had done, threatening to report her to the Colonial Secretary! And then to throw an ink-stand at her own husband! How Mrs Hopkins longed to press her lips to his battered brow—why had she not done so? Why had she closed the door so abruptly upon him when all he sought was her gentle solicitude?

Meanwhile (although Mrs Hopkins did not notice any of this, so caught up was she with thoughts of Mr Crabback), all the hope that had momentarily illuminated Mrs Dunstable's features ebbed away. In its place, a look of grim resignation had set in.

'Ah well,' she said quietly, 'is it any wonder Mrs Crabback spoke to you harshly? You've cast a spell upon her husband, that's plain to see.'

'Whatever are you talking about?'

'With my own eyes, I saw him fawning all over you.'

'Mrs Dunstable!'

'Pawing and suckling at your fingertips, oh yes, I saw it all. And you lapping it up like a cat with the cream.'

It was at this moment that Mrs Hopkins struck her (for what else could she do to stop her talking?) quite hard across the face with a closed fist. The House Matron reeled back and dropped to the ground. For a long moment she lay motionless, and then—just as Mrs Hopkins began to think she may have knocked the woman unconscious—the House Matron began to mewl, her thin limbs scrabbling as she endeavoured to pull herself upright.

'Don't cast me out, Mrs Hopkins. As one widow to another. I have nothing, I have nobody. I will die out there. I will die upon the streets—'

But Mrs Hopkins simply turned and re-entered the schoolroom, closing the door upon her.

'Get back to your work, girls,' she said, for the children were staring at her agog. They had seen much of what transpired through the broken panes of the schoolroom door. 'Mrs Dunstable is quite drunk. She is no concern of yours or mine.'

And so Mrs Dunstable departed on the one o'clock ferry. Mr Crabback, sitting at his desk composing his weekly report to the Colonial Secretary, glanced out his window and saw her weaving her way to the ferry wharf, carrying a small wicker fancy basket and a battered valise. Ah, he thought to himself, so Mrs Hopkins has not found it in her heart to forgive her. Well, it was for the best. After all, it would be a nuisance having her around the place, spying on them all the time. Now—should circumstances arise which necessitated such a thing—he might visit Mrs Hopkins' quarters unobserved. Nevertheless, he now found himself in a position where he must justify in his weekly report not only the sudden promotion of the School-Mistress to Matron, replacing his own wife, but the abrupt dismissal of the House Matron as well! He rolled his pen between his fingers fretfully. With his weekly reports up to now, he had simply been able to replicate the reports of his predecessor, Mr Baker-Hunt, which had been helpfully copied into the Correspondence Book. To endeavour to explain these staff changes would prove much more taxing, especially given the absence of his wife who could usually be relied upon, somewhat grudgingly, to assist him. Perhaps he could prevail upon Mrs Hopkins to compose such a missive when she visited this evening and explain it as one of her duties as Matron?

And yet—a horrid thought occurred to him—was there not the danger that Mrs Dunstable might get in before him? She had certainly threatened this morning to present her own version of events to the Colonial Secretary. Might she not already have such a letter secreted on her person, ready to drop into a mailbox just as soon as she landed at King Street Wharf? The thought sent a wave of panic through him: he rose at once from his desk and hurried out of his house to catch up with her.

'Mrs Dunstable!' he called out. When she turned, he saw she was sporting a tremendous black eye. Surely that had not been Mrs Hopkins' considered response? To clock her one?

'Please, Mrs Dunstable,' he said, digging into his pockets. He pulled out a few shillings and pressed them into her palm. 'Here. This might help tide you over.'

Mrs Dunstable gazed at the coins a long moment. 'So you would cross my palm with silver,' she said.

'Just a—just a small gift. To tide you over. What—may I ask—what has happened to your eye?' he ventured.

'She did it to me.'

'Who?'

'The witch. Whose spell you have fallen under.'

'Are you talking of Mrs Hopkins?'

'Since you ask your fortune, I will tell it you. She has placed a charm upon you. But you are a fool and cannot see it.'

Now it was Mr Crabback's turn to fall silent. For Mrs Dunstable had given voice to the fear that had kept him twitching in bed the long night previous: the possibility that Mrs Hopkins had exercised some kind of dark magic over him. How else to account for his behaviour since she had landed upon the island: the self-pleasuring, the banging on her door in the dark of night, slobbering over her fingertips! It was all so unaccountable, so unlike him! He had thought her a hysteric, but now that Mrs Dunstable had spoken, he saw that she was something else: she was a witch. Such creatures existed, of this he felt certain. In any case, she had bewitched him—it was plain even to casual observers such as Mrs Dunstable.

'Oh God!' he cried out. 'What am I to do?'

But Mrs Dunstable just stared off out to the water. The *Emu* was now approaching the wharf, blasting its horn.

He clutched hold of her arm. 'How can I—is it possible?—how can I reverse the spell? There must be some way to release myself—surely?'

Mrs Dunstable simply pocketed the coins he had given her.

'Here, do you want more?' And now he reached deep into his pockets and produced more silver which he tried to foist upon her.

But she turned away from him now and broke into a lurching run, anxious not to miss the ferry.

'Please, Mrs Dunstable—if you know of any way!' he cried after her. 'I will give you your job back! I will make you Matron! Write to me, Mrs Dunstable, I beg of you—'

It is possible that she did not hear him.

'From now on, we will no longer say our prayers in the quadrangle,' announced Mrs Hopkins. 'The girls shall say their prayers in their dormitories. It will help them settle for the evening. Come, let us begin our rounds.'

Mrs Baird and Miss Foy stared at her in surprise. The new Matron seemed to be making a great many decisions without any apparent consultation of the Superintendent. And where on earth was Mr Crabback anyway? He had not been sighted all afternoon, except for a brief appearance in the stores when Miss Foy had come upon him rifling through the provisions.

'But those are for the girls,' she protested, as she watched him stash a turnip or two into his coat pockets. 'We barely have enough for them as it is.'

'Quite right, quite right,' said Mr Crabback, untying a bacon hock from where it hung. 'And that is why I am just now writing to the Colonial Secretary. It is disgraceful—absolutely disgraceful—these poor waifs are fed the barest scraps.' And off he scurried with his goodies, Tippet hurrying after him.

So in the absence of the Superintendent this evening, and with Mrs Dunstable having departed so suddenly and acrimoniously, Miss Foy and Mrs Baird thought they might just as well fall in behind Mrs Hopkins and her new methods. It was a pleasant change not to be standing out in the windswept quadrangle, bemoaning the wickedness of their ways while wondering what paltry scraps they might scrape together for their evening meals.

Admittedly, Mrs Hopkins might have waited to consult with Mr Crabback before implementing this new system of prayers. But as he had made no appearance that evening at muster, and as she was anxious to put the new system in place without delay, Mrs Hopkins chose to interpret Mr Crabback's absence as a sign of his expectation that she could make her own decisions and run the institution as she saw fit. Besides which, she would be meeting with him privately after lock-up to discuss her new role, and she felt certain, once she explained the extraordinary experience she had had in the schoolroom earlier today with the older girls, he would whole-heartedly embrace these new measures. For that very afternoon, Mrs Hopkins had forged a profound connection with the girls and she realised that she must act promptly and decisively, if she were to consolidate her advantage.

To her pleasant surprise, almost all of her older girls had turned up to class after lunch, and there they sat at their desks, eyeing her expectantly. (Admittedly, the day was dull and grey and windy; the beach had not been so inviting that afternoon.) Of course, they had wanted to sing 'Love Amongst The Roses' again. However, Mrs Hopkins assured them that, while they would finish their class with a song, they must first settle down to the business of learning. It was important that she ascertain how many of these older girls, in spite of their haphazard early years spent wandering the streets or being tossed in and out of institutions, had managed (somewhat miraculously, it seemed to Mrs Hopkins) to learn to read and write.

The schoolroom had been gifted with a comprehensive set of readers of the Pollards Synthetic Series, from the first to the third level.

Mrs Hopkins decided she might just as well dive in to the third level and hope for the best. She instructed Mary-Ann (her freshly appointed senior classroom monitor) to distribute the books amongst the girls, and browsing through her copy quickly, she asked them to turn to page twenty-two, on which commenced a simple enough story entitled 'Mopsy's Birthday', Mopsy being some kind of little terrier. The girls had a soft spot for dogs, if their enthusiasm for feeding scraps to Tippet was any indication, and this short piece was interspersed with pleasing illustrations. Further, the test was broken up into short, clearly defined paragraphs, so each of the girls might simply read their brief section before moving on to the next girl.

'Remember,' said Mrs Hopkins, 'there is no shame in not being able to read. Just simply say, "I cannot read this, Mrs Hopkins," and we will move on to the next girl.'

And thus they began their lesson, with a fair-headed girl of about fifteen years named Catherine standing up to commence.

Today is my birthday. I am just two years old. This morning my darling little mistress gave me my bath, rubbed me dry, and tied this lovely ribbon around my neck. 'There, little Mopsy, is not that a nice birthday gift? Your own mother would not know you now.'

Mrs Hopkins looked up at her in surprise. The girl had read clearly and fluently, without any hesitation at all.

'Why, that was excellent, Catherine. Next?'

'I cannot read this, Mrs Hopkins,' said Rosabella Connelly, reddening.

'That's quite all right, Rosabella. We will move on. Sarah?'

'I can't read either, Mrs Hopkins,' said Sarah.

'Yes, you can!' cried Eliza, punching her friend fondly in the arm.

'Shut up, I can't,' cried Sarah, now reddening dangerously herself.

Mrs Hopkins immediately saw the problem: Catherine had started off so strongly that everyone else was embarrassed to be compared with her.

'Sarah,' said Mrs Hopkins, 'even if you can only read a little, I am anxious to hear you. Do not be embarrassed or ashamed—that is why I have come here, after all, to teach you all. I promise you that no one will think any less of you for trying, nor laugh or tease. Girls, will we all promise that we will be kind to each other as we read today?'

And to her surprise, the girls—many of them quite ferociously tough-looking in their appearance—nodded solemnly.

'Go on, Sarah,' said Catherine, encouragingly. 'You're a good reader. I've heard you.'

Sarah threw the girl a look that seemed to promise recriminations later, yet she rose to her feet, the book trembling in her hand. '*Then she . . . put me upon . . . the sill, w-where the . . . m-morning sun was . . . sss . . .*'

'Streaming,' prompted Mrs Hopkins gently.

'*Streaming*,' repeated Sarah. A long pause ensued as the girl stared at the page.

'Streaming through,' said Mrs Hopkins.

'*Streaming through . . . the . . .*' Again the girl was unable to continue.

'Streaming through the window,' said Mrs Hopkins.

'*The window . . . "Take a nap, little doggie," she said.*'

Sarah had read slowly and stumblingly but she finished strongly and was warmly commended for her efforts by her classmates. Mrs Hopkins beamed fondly upon them. How easy everything was if you just simply treated the girls with kindness and dignity, instead of the indifference, or worse, cruelty, to which they had sadly grown accustomed.

The reading lesson continued in this fashion—some of the girls declining altogether, others stumbling through as best as they could.

'I . . . sat . . . on . . . the . . . sill . . . and . . . thought . . . back . . . to the . . . time . . . when I . . . lived . . . with . . . my . . . mother . . . out . . . in a . . . barn,' read a wispy wraith of a girl named Hannah.

Each word had to be sounded out with agonising effort—it took all Mrs Hopkins' patience and tact not to intervene too soon with the answer.

'There . . . were . . . three . . . of us . . . little . . . puppies . . . at the . . . time . . . but mother . . . told . . . me . . . that . . . two . . . of my . . .'

'Brothers,' prompted Mrs Hopkins

'Brothers . . . had been . . . taken . . . away . . . from her . . . when I was . . . young.'

The pitiful stiltedness of the girl's delivery seemed to add extra poignancy to these last words, and they hung in the air a long moment. Mrs Hopkins glanced down at her own copy—she had not realised that the story concerned itself with such themes as the forced separation of infants from their mothers. Why on earth had the otherwise excellent Mrs Pollard thought this suitable fare for young minds, especially such young minds as these girls, torn from their families and condemned by the courts to this sandstone prison? With some relief, Mrs Hopkins saw that it was Mary-Ann's turn next—a confident reader (to judge from her facility with

Mr Crabback's note), she was already on her feet, book in hand. She would get through it quickly at least; the words would not linger painfully as Hannah's had done.

'*I think this is what made Mama so nervous and anxious when strangers came to look at us,*' read Mary-Ann. '*She always growled and trembled, and often laid her paw upon my back as if she feared that I might too be snatched away from her.*'

Must the girl read so expressively? thought Mrs Hopkins. Clearly, she had dreams of the stage, for she was adding a good deal of unnecessary emotion.

'*Only think what she must have suffered,*' continued Mary-Ann, her voice throbbing with sorrow. '*Why, if I had five little baby puppies of my own, I should growl as loud as ever I could if any stranger dared to try to take them from me.*'

And now Mrs Hopkins realised that poor dumpy Rosabella Connelly was quietly crying. She sat there slumped in her misery, wiping her eyes with the sleeve of her scratchy dungaree dress.

'Oh dear,' said Mrs Hopkins. 'You mustn't cry, Rosabella. You must remember, this is simply a story; a made-up story about a little dog.'

'It's her brothers, Miss,' said Catherine. 'They got taken away, too, and she don't know where they got sent and no one will tell her anything.'

At this, Rosabella gave in to her sorrow and sobbed.

'I'm sure that wherever they are, Rosabella, they will be very well looked after,' said Mrs Hopkins, horrified at how hollow and unconvincing her words sounded. The truth was, she was utterly at a loss to know what to say that might console poor Rosabella about her lost brothers. So instead, she handed the girl one of her last remaining black lace-edged handkerchiefs. 'Here,' she said quietly. 'Use this to wipe your nose, not your sleeve. You may keep it.'

'Thank you, Miss,' mumbled Rosabella. She did not use it but simply gazed at it forlornly, the snot rolling down her lip unchecked.

Later that afternoon, Mrs Hopkins took herself off to look up Rosabella's history in the Entrance Book, in the hope that it would provide some details on the whereabouts of the missing brothers. The book was kept carefully in Mr Baker-Hunt's methodical script: a newspaper article had been cut from the *Sydney Morning Herald*, and held in place with a pin. The headline was '*Boy Bushrangers*'.

It appeared that her three younger brothers, not one older than thirteen, had been living wild in the bush, robbing hen yards, vineyards and orchards to survive. The police had great difficulty in capturing them, owing to their '*fleetness of foot*' and knowledge of the area. They stole an old breech loader gun and cartridges, and threatened anyone who tried to interfere with them; the oldest one in particular was known to be a good shot. They were at last apprehended when trying to rob a pigsty. '*They are now in custody, charged with larceny, but in the cells are as jolly as ever and amuse themselves with leap frog and other games.*'

A post-script indicated that the boys were incarcerated in the Randwick Asylum for Destitute Children. They had been there now for several years. Rosabella, who had committed no crime but had no place else to go, had been sent to Biloela.

'Should I keep reading, Miss?' asked Mary-Ann.

'Yes, yes, I think it's best—as I say, it is simply a story. And I think we will find that it has a happy ending—these stories usually do. Please continue, Mary-Ann. You are reading very nicely.'

'*Poor Mam would grow so very sad when she talked to me about her lost babies,*' said Mary-Ann, and suddenly her voice caught with genuine emotion. '*What made it so hard for her to bear was the fear that they might not be treated kindly. For that is any mother's fear when her babies are removed from her care.*'

At this, Catherine—who, unnoticed by Mrs Hopkins, had been growing very pale and blotchy in the face—suddenly put her head in her hands and began to weep.

'She's missing her Mammy, Mrs Hopkins,' said Rosabella, her arm wrapped protectively around her friend's shoulders. 'She hasn't heard from her the whole time her since she's bin here. Not one letter or nothing.'

'She has not visited?' asked Mrs Hopkins.

'Oh no, they never let our families visit,' said Mary-Ann.

'Never?'

'They say we don't deserve it.'

'Also, they reckon our families are a bad influence on us,' said Sarah.

'They reckon our families are scum,' sniffed Catherine through her tears.

'Yeah, well, in some cases it's true, they are scum,' drawled a sullen, freckled girl named Annie Laughton, slumped in the back row. This was the first time Mrs Hopkins had ever heard her speak. 'Wasn't it your Mammy what dumped you here in the first place?'

In an instant, Catherine rose up from her seat, flew across the room and had the freckled girl pinned to the floor.

'Take that back, you ugly faggot!' she screamed.

'I won't!'

'At least I got a mother, you fecking whore!'

'Get off me! Get her off me!'

'Girls! Girls! Stop it!' cried Mrs Hopkins in horror.

For now Annie had wrestled Catherine to the ground and appeared to be attempting to strangle her. The other girls all gathered around, shouting encouragement. Smaller spats broke out on the sidelines; one of Annie's friends had Rosabella in a headlock; another girl was being dragged about the floor by her hair. It had all erupted in a flash, and Mrs Hopkins saw that she had utterly lost control.

'Girls!' she cried. 'Think of your mothers! What would your mothers say if they were to see you now? Do you not want to make them proud of you when we have our Special Visiting Day for Mothers?'

Special Visiting Day for Mothers? Where had these words sprung from? Mrs Hopkins did not know, but miraculously they had their effect. Annie stopped throttling Catherine and stared up at Mrs Hopkins in a kind of wonderment.

'You are missing your mothers, of course you are!' cried Mrs Hopkins, realising she must keep talking if she were to keep them from fighting. 'Nothing could be more natural. So that is why the Superintendent and I have decided we are going to have special day when all your mothers come to visit. Yes, yes, and if you don't have a mother, then you will invite your father or your grandmother or your auntie—or yes, Rosabella, your brothers. There will be cake and games and singing—oh, it will be wonderful! Quickly, back to your seats and let us plan it, for we haven't much time before chores.'

To her amazement, the girls did immediately as they were told. It was as if the brawl had never happened. Annie let go of Catherine's throat and helped her to her feet. Others slapped each other on the back, with a cry of 'No hard feelings!' They straightened the benches that had toppled over in the melee, and resumed their seats, gazing up at her expectantly.

Mrs Hopkins stood before them and began to weave from thin air a beautiful vision. In this vision, each of the girls (with careful instruction from Mrs Hopkins) would write a letter to their mothers (or, if unfortunate enough to have no mothers, their fathers or aunties or grandmothers), inviting them to visit on a Sunday afternoon. The mothers would be met at the wharf by the girls, all dressed in their

Sunday best, hair neatly tied in ribbons, their boots polished till they shone. (Do they even have boots? she wondered. So many seem to be barefoot!) Then the girls would lead their mothers (or fathers or aunties or grandmothers) on a tour of inspection of the school: the dormitories would be scrubbed from top to bottom and made to look as nice as possible. (This would not be easy, but perhaps some fresh whitewash might help and some pictures could be acquired to adorn those dreary walls?) Examples of the girls' penmanship and drawing would be laid out in the schoolroom for mothers to examine. (Of course, the shattered windows would need to be repaired beforehand—and something surely must be done about the smell from the earth-closets?) After the tour, there would be games in the quadrangle: hoops and rounders and skipping rope and froggie in the middle, and anyone could join in—mothers or aunties, or yes, Rosabella, little brothers—and meanwhile, as this was going on, the mess-hall tables would be set with simple arrangements of flowers. (Where would they ever find flowers on the rugged, rocky escarpments of Cockatoo Island?) With the assistance of the new House Matron Mrs Baird, the girls would have baked all manner of delicious cakes (sponges filled with jam and cream!), which the girls would now serve to their mothers (or fathers or aunties or grandmothers) alongside giant pots of steaming hot tea. (Where would they get the crockery for this? They certainly couldn't use those dreadful battered tin pannikins.) When afternoon tea was over, the tables would be quickly cleared and the chairs arranged in a semi-circle for a concert, in which the girls would sing 'Love Amongst The Roses' (yes, they could act it out just as they had done on the beach, why not!) and perhaps that lovely hymn she had heard the girls singing the evening before. The day would end with a short, improving talk from Mr Crabback ('Thoughts Upon Dissipation' perhaps), and then all the girls would walk with their mothers (or fathers or aunties or grandmothers) down to the wharf and wave them goodbye until next time. For if it all went as smoothly and successfully as Mrs Hopkins had just described, then perhaps the Special Visiting Day for Mothers could become a regular event to be held several times a year?

'Girls, I will tell you this now,' said Mrs Hopkins, realising she must strike a sobering note for the girls were by now quite giddy with excitement. 'If we are to convince Mr Crabback—and not only Mr Crabback but the Colonial Secretary himself—that you are all deserving of such a privilege, then you must be on your very best behaviour from hereon. There is to be no more going to the beach; no more fighting amongst yourselves; and no more singing of unsuitable songs in the dormitories after lock-up. Further, you must perform all chores assigned to you willingly and without complaint and work diligently at your lessons. Is that understood?'

The girls nodded earnestly. 'Yes, Mrs Hopkins,' they responded eagerly. Then they rose up and hurried from their classroom and launched themselves with such enthusiasm into their chores that Mrs Baird and Miss Foy could scarcely believe what they were witnessing. This new Acting Matron worked the girls a charm!

And now prayers in the dormitories. With the girls kneeling by their beds, eyes closed, hands clasped together fervently, as Mrs Hopkins read aloud—not the usual grim lament from the Book of Common Prayer, but something altogether different which she read from a small book she had produced from the pockets of her mourning skirt.

'*O Lord God, thou knowest all things,*' she murmured in a low and comforting voice. '*Make me thankful for all the mercies I have received this day. Pardon whatever thou hast seen amiss in my temper and help me to correct my imperfections and to perform my duties more fully. Bless and protect my dear family—may they be continually under thy care. Take me under thy protection this night while I am sleeping; let nothing terrifying or destructive befall me. Listen to my prayer, I beseech thee, through my son and our redeemer, Jesus Christ. Our Father, Who Art in Heaven . . .*'

Mr Crabback stood in silent amazement in the doorway, for the grated iron door hung open. It was now getting on for seven o'clock. As wary as he was about the dangers of another encounter with Mrs Hopkins, who had cast her spell upon him, the fear that she had forgotten their appointment altogether and might simply not show up at all had prompted him to don his coat and set off in search of her. And there he found her, kneeling upon the cold flagstones of Dormitory Four alongside all those wild, unruly prostitute girls as they murmured together the Lord's Prayer. He was struck by the beauty of the scene: it brought back to him the words of a poem he had once cherished but long since forgotten:

HUSH! 'tis a holy hour—the quiet room
Seems like a temple, while yon soft lamp sheds
A faint and starry radiance, through the gloom
And the sweet stillness, down on fair young heads,
With all their clustering locks, untouch'd by care
And bow'd, as flowers are bow'd with night, in prayer . . .

The Lord's Prayer concluded, and Mr Crabback hastily ducked out of the doorway and into the quadrangle to await her. There was a full moon this night and the bleak open space glowed eerily in the silvery light. How quiet it was! Instead of the usual caterwauling and singing and clambering up to the window ledges, all was peaceful within the dormitories. What extraordinary transformation had this woman wrought upon these girls, he marvelled, in the space of a single evening. The beauty and blessedness of female piety, as he had just witnessed! How it softened and elevated the natural grace of a woman, so even a plain and homely woman such as Mrs Hopkins—or the brazen, blousy tartlets in her charge—seemed almost kin to angels in that moment.

And yet how hastily he had been prepared to judge her, on the words of that monstrous drunkard, Mrs Dunstable! He winced in shame that he could have allowed himself to have been misled by that appalling woman. A witch? Mrs Hopkins? How could he ever have entertained—even for a moment—such a preposterous notion? From a woman who had spread such vile untruths in front of the girls and the Assistant Matrons, no less! From a woman who could barely stand from the effects of liquor, and it just after half-noon! And yet he had lavished all those shillings upon her—what madness! If there had been a witch upon the island, it was Mrs Dunstable; what a blessing to be rid of her! For Mrs Hopkins . . . if not a saint, she was a form of angel.

He paced restlessly—what on earth was keeping her? Ten minutes passed before he heard the key in the padlock and Mrs Hopkins finally appeared in the quadrangle.

'Mrs Hopkins,' he said, lunging towards her, 'had you forgotten our appointment?'

'Oh, Mr Crabback, forgive me. I have implemented a new system for the saying of evening prayers, and it has taken a good deal longer than I reckoned on. I sent Mrs Baird and Miss Foy to their quarters for they were getting anxious for their tea. But in future, I hope—if we each take a dormitory—the girls will be settled more efficiently.'

'You must also be quite anxious for your tea,' he ventured. 'I have made a very good pea soup with bacon hock, which I have left warming on the fire. Come and partake of it with me and we will discuss your new duties as Matron.'

'Mr Crabback,' said Mrs Hopkins, hesitating, for some of her courage had dissipated in the intervening hour, 'you are not angry with me?'

'Angry with you? Whatever for?'

'For introducing this new system for evening prayers, without first consulting you.'

'Mrs Hopkins,' said Mr Crabback, 'how could I possibly be angry, witnessing what I have just witnessed? For I must tell you, the sight I have just beheld has moved me beyond words.'

Josephine, watching all this from just outside the gate of the institution, was unable to hear any further for the pair of them now lowered their voices and spoke quite softly to each other. Was Mrs Hopkins asking Mr Crabback if Josephine could sleep in Dormitory One with the little girls? Or had she forgotten about her promise once again? A wave of irritation passed over Josephine; she didn't want to spend another night with the horrible big girls, she wanted to fuss over and comfort the poor little Tunks sisters, and meanwhile these two were hanging about making goo-goo eyes at one another.

Now Mr Crabback and Mrs Hopkins were heading briskly towards the gate: Josephine quickly ducked behind the frangipani tree. She watched as the Superintendent locked the gate behind him, then trailed behind them at a short distance as they walked together towards his quarters. Wasn't it old Mr Crabback who had been trying to force his way into Mrs Hopkins' quarters the night before? And now look at her, she was willingly going into his house with him. Well, it was nothing she hadn't seen her own mother do, with any old creep really, if some money or a jug of beer had suddenly appeared.

'Well, that's darned annoying,' Josephine muttered to herself as Mr Crabback ushered Mrs Hopkins inside and closed the front door behind them. For now, since she was locked outside the institution, all Josephine could do was hang around and wait for Mrs Hopkins to emerge again and try to plead her case. The danger, of course, was that she would have to spend another night in Mrs Hopkins' bed, a grim prospect, even with that awful doll locked in the chest.

Still, it occurred to her, since the night was bright, that now would be as good a time as any to go down to the beach and re-bury her stolen treasures. The Tunks girls had demanded her attention all day and she had been unable to get away. With any luck, Henry would not have got to them yet. The full moon made everything so silvery and pretty, it put a skip in the girl's step, and she leapt as nimbly as she could, given her grazed knees, down to the beach.

The pea soup was indeed very good, and Mrs Hopkins had not realised how hungry she was. And how comforting to be in Mr Crabback's warm parlour, the fire blazing, and dear Tippet leaning companionably against her skirts. How things had changed in the space of twenty-four hours—to think that this time yesterday evening she had been crying alone on the beach, convinced that she had lost her job. Now she sat at Mr Crabback's table, describing to him in detail her plans for the Special Visiting Day for Mothers.

'I had not realised that the girls were forbidden visits from their families—it seems to me a measure of the utmost cruelty. And what I soon discovered is that the very possibility of being reunited with their dearest ones, especially their mothers, even for an afternoon, served as a powerful inducement for the girls to improve their conduct,' she explained. 'You saw for yourself how willingly and quietly they said their prayers.'

'Indeed,' said Mr Crabback, beaming at her across the table. 'There is a great deal of merit in the idea. Also it might afford us an opportunity to invite dignitaries and benefactors and members of the press as well. The positive attention, the chance to see these girls rehabilitated, will be useful for us in terms of garnering public subscriptions, of which the school is sorely in need.'

'Yes,' said Mrs Hopkins, pleased that Mr Crabback seemed to be embracing the idea so readily. 'But of course, we would need to spend money first in order to put the idea into fruition. The windows must be repaired and the walls whitewashed. And the girls' dresses are a disgrace. If we could make them a set of new dresses from some decent material—'

'Oh dear, but you do see that the girls will tear off their dresses at the gathers, especially the older girls—they seem to like their dresses scanty—'

'But that is my point, Mr Crabback. Their dresses are ugly and made of the coarsest dungaree. If we were to spend the money on a decent material, perhaps a pleasing print—it need not be too expensive—and thus give them the opportunity to dress respectably, then they might take some pride in their appearance and be less inclined to destroy them.'

Mr Crabback nodded thoughtfully as he buttered his bread.

'And we need pictures upon the walls to brighten the place—nice homely pictures, or perhaps a scene from Scripture—and mats upon the floor so at prayer-time the girls don't have to kneel upon those dreadful cold flagstones, and crockery—nice Delft cups from which to drink their tea, not those awful tin pannikins—'

She broke off for she could see from Mr Crabback's demeanour that he was becoming increasingly uneasy.

'Oh dear,' he said. 'Nice Delft cups from which to drink their tea! How quickly they would be taken down to the beach and smashed upon the rocks.'

'I do not think so, Mr Crabback: not if we teach them to appreciate the value of such things.'

'I must caution you, Mrs Hopkins, that, as much as I applaud your intentions, I fear we will meet with considerable resistance. The Colonial Secretary made it perfectly clear to me that I must somehow reduce the running costs of the institution.'

Mrs Hopkins stared at him in dismay. 'Reduce the running costs? But . . . however are we to do that?'

'Well, one measure that I have put in place effective of today is to have eliminated the position of House Matron. I'm happy to say that will save the institution seventy-three pounds per annum.'

Had Mr Crabback been paying more attention to Mrs Hopkins than he was to his soup, he might have noticed that the colour was rising in her cheeks.

'But of course, that is a role that must be filled,' she said. 'In fact, with your permission, I would like Mrs Baird to take over these duties.'

She dared not mention that she had already, impulsively, elevated Mrs Baird to the position, complete with the promise of an appropriate rise in her wages.

'She may very well take over the duties of House Matron if you feel it necessary, but her wages must remain the same. And of course, she must continue her regular duties, just as you are combining your roles as Acting Matron and School-Mistress. Speaking of such matters, one task we must attend to as a matter of urgency is to write to the Colonial Secretary and advise him of these new changes we have implemented. I think once we explain the considerable savings, he will be well satisfied. Obviously, there is significant wastage in the way the institution is run, and particularly in the matter of staff wages.'

Mr Crabback felt well-pleased with his idea of Mrs Hopkins combining the two roles of Acting Matron and School-Mistress. Not only did it justify his decision to elevate Mrs Hopkins to the role of Matron (Acting) in lieu of his own wife—a decision that might draw unfavourable comment in some quarters, he suspected—but, seen in concert with the abrupt discharge of Mrs Dunstable as House Matron with no view to hiring a replacement, it would earn him the reputation of a man who was not afraid to 'drive a broom' through the place.

'Let me get you a pen and paper; I will dictate a letter immediately,' he said, rising from the table and disappearing in search of the necessary writing tools.

Left alone with Tippet, Mrs Hopkins found herself struggling to retain her composure. This was not at all the outcome she had hoped for. How was she to effectively run the school as Matron, while still being expected to teach the children?

She had assumed, of course—who wouldn't?—that a replacement School-Mistress would be hired. And could it possibly be that Mr Crabback did not mean to remunerate her for all this extra work—after all, he had spoken of the 'tremendous savings' the decision afforded him. How was the school to be run efficiently with just herself and the two Assistant Matrons, at least one of whom must now face considerably more responsibilities and yet no rise in her paltry wages.

And, more importantly, what about the girls? What of their new dresses, new boots, fresh whitewash and the comforting pictures on their dormitory walls? What of the skipping ropes and hoops and rounders sets she had hoped to procure for them; the lanterns for their dormitories that they might read and crochet in the long hours after lock-up? What of the knives and forks and spoons so that they need not eat like animals? She had raised their hopes; was it all to amount to nothing? Mrs Hopkins felt that her very heart was breaking. Tears rolled down her cheeks unchecked.

Mr Crabback, having returned with pen and paper, stared at her in surprise. 'Mrs Hopkins! Why are you crying?'

For a long moment, she was unable to respond, but simply sat and sorrowfully wept.

He sat down beside her, aghast that his words had had this effect upon her. At last, unable to help himself, he took her hand in his. 'Tell me,' he whispered. 'Tell me why you weep.'

'I weep for the girls,' she faltered. 'That they are seen only as a burden upon society. That they must spend their childhood locked up in this dreadful prison—their only crime to be born into poverty—the barest comforts begrudged and withheld from them.'

A deep sense of shame overcame Mr Crabback at these words. He saw with hideous clarity that he had lost his way again and veered from the path to which he had sought to stay true. For Mr Crabback, the welfare of those less fortunate had long been the great mission of his life. It had driven him to set up, at his own initial expense, the Night Refuge for the Homeless, that the poor, hungry, wandering men might have a bed instead of a doorway in which to sleep and a bowl of hot soup to warm them. From there, with the assistance of his wife, he had gone on to establish the Haven of Hope, a lying-in hospital for women who had lost their way. They were both institutions of which Sydney had been desperately in need. His natural skills at public speaking had been such that he had managed to secure, at times, quite sizeable donations from the general public, and yet . . . so often things had not gone as they should, sometimes through his own lapses of judgement, admittedly—those moments of personal weakness to which he was susceptible.

And the press seemed always poised to catch him out! The Haven of Hope, for example: the newspapers had got hold of a story of how quantities of good tea and sugar and biscuits, donated each week by a kindly grocer, never reached the young women for whom they were intended but were enjoyed instead by Mr and Mrs Crabback in their own private quarters. The article caused a great hullabaloo; donations had dried up, there had been follow-up articles about Mr Crabback's book-keeping, or lack thereof, with the implication that perhaps donations were being funnelled away for other purposes than those for which they were intended. He had tried his best to defend himself, but considerable damage had been done. And on top of all this bad press, that lass from Orange had up and died of septicaemia, a bloody foetus wrapped in rags found in the paddock next door.

Had Mr Crabback been better supported by his wife, of course, perhaps he might not have found himself in this scenario. And yet he must only blame himself, for there were many instances in his life when, undoubtedly filled with lofty intentions, he had nonetheless been craven and weak. For here he was, once again, thinking only of his reputation, crafting his own face-saving machinations, and in the process losing sight of his true mission here at Biloela: to offer succour and shelter for neglected children; to provide them with the necessary skills that they might ultimately find work in service, so that their own children might not end up confined within the same grim sandstone walls, the deprivations of poverty perpetually repeating themselves generation after generation.

'Forgive me,' he said finally. 'Forgive me.'

'Mr Crabback, I do not blame you, not for one moment,' Mrs Hopkins responded, wiping away her tears roughly with her hands. 'You are in a thankless and hopeless position, with impossible expectations placed upon you. Of course, you must take every necessary action to satisfy the governors—to do otherwise would be foolhardy—and with our hard work and your expert management, I have no doubt we will find a way—' Once again, she found herself unable to continue.

'We *will* find a way,' he said quietly. 'We will find a way to bring funds into the school and to provide the girls with all they require. Write me a complete list of everything you need, Mrs Hopkins, and leave nothing off it, no matter how trivial it may seem.'

She gazed up at him, her eyes wet. He squeezed her hand gently. What intimacy hung between them in that moment. How easily he could lean forward and kiss those tears from her cheek, and quite likely, given her present vulnerability, she would allow him to do so. And yet, for once, some better, nobler instinct saw him remove his hand and rise to his feet, moving across to the fireplace.

'Dry your tears, Mrs Hopkins,' he said. 'First we will write to the Colonial Secretary, and then we will commence upon your plans for the Special Visiting Day for Mothers.'

Meanwhile, down upon the beach, Josephine had busily set about exhuming the gloves, the scent bag and the crocheted doyley from the damp sand. She was pleased to see that they were all where she had deposited them: her gift to Henry of the black lace-edged handkerchief and her promise of seed cake seemed to have done the trick. And yet as she dug her hands deep within the sand to pull out the bar of soap, she found stashed alongside it a grubby black lace-edged handkerchief wound tightly into a small bundle. Josephine frowned: this must be Henry's doing; he had interfered with her treasures after all. Cautiously, she untied the handkerchief and found to her surprise a small clump of milk toffees, all stuck together in a hard lump. With some effort, she managed to break off a piece. Josephine wiped the sand from it and popped it into her mouth. How good it tasted, so sweet and comforting. Henry wasn't such a bad old galoot after all, she told herself; she would definitely have to bring him some kind of present now! Happily, she stowed the remaining lump of toffees into the pocket of her pinafore: there were just enough to share with the Tunks girls and still enjoy a little more for herself.

Gathering up her treasures, she clambered up amongst the higher rocks for it occurred to her that if she buried her prizes around here, they would be much less likely to be exposed by the tide. And so, with the big full moon providing her its light and the milk toffee melting in her mouth, Josephine set about her work, taking great care to memorise each rock under which she buried her treasures.

Her work complete and feeling well-pleased with her efforts, she climbed back down the rocks again to wash her sandy hands in the shallows. The water rushed up around her ankles; she squealed and pulled her dress up. As the water drained back to the sea again, exposing the smooth wet sand, her eye was caught by something small and round and shiny.

With a whoop of delight, she scooped it up—it was a shilling! A whole shilling. And there—another one, just lying there on the exposed wet sand! In that moment, the sea rushed in again, obscuring the second shilling from view. Desperate not to lose it, she dropped to her knees and scrabbled blindly about for it—and by some miracle, the sea drained away and there it lay, exactly where she had last seen it! She scooped it up quickly—what a night this was turning out to be! Had anyone in the world ever been so lucky? And there, further out, what was that? Another shilling unmistakably! Jumping to her feet, she pulled up her wet skirts and rushed towards it—she must reach it before the water returned! But this time the wave came too quickly, and before she knew it, she was almost waist deep for the sandy bottom plunged sharply at that point. The sea pulled back again now, dragging at her skirts as if intent on carrying her away. And here came another wave, a big wave this time, knocking her clean off her feet as it rushed towards the shoreline. Vainly she floundered, trying to keep her head above water, for she knew that if she were to go under (her mother had warned her) then she would swallow water and choke and drown. Another wave followed hard upon the first, bringing with it something large and heavy which knocked against her so violently that she went under. 'Keep your mouth shut, keep your mouth shut!' she told herself as she thrashed about in the darkness. She mustn't drown—it would break her mother's heart! And yet still she tumbled under the water, her feet unable to find footing. Again, something shoved against her, very forceful and deliberate as if meaning to push her out of its path. Reaching out wildly, she found herself grasping onto something—it was a boot, a woman's boot, for she felt its elastic sides and buttons. Another wave pushed the boot forward and carried Josephine with it. Her feet touched the sandy bottom: at last, she was able to stand upright. She staggered forward a step or two, then gave a shriek of terror. For the lady's boot was attached to a lady's body, which lurched forward and pushed her under again.

This time it happened so quickly she swallowed a lungful of sea water. With frantic effort, she pulled herself upright, and tugging her skirts up around her waist, she waded out of the foul water till she reached the sand. There she fell to her knees and vomited a great plume of sea water, but terrified lest the horrible corpse in the boots be right behind her, she lurched to her feet at once and staggered across the damp sand and up the rocks and all the way to Mr Crabback's house, slipping and sliding and whimpering all the way.

And so the quiet scene of letter-writing in Mr Crabback's parlour had been disrupted by the frantic pummelling of small fists upon the front door. Mr Crabback and Mrs Hopkins had stopped and stared at each other; then came the awful sound of a child wailing. Flinging the door open, such a pitiful sight greeted them: poor exhausted Josephine, thin and bedraggled in her wet rags; so weak they could barely make out what it was she was saying.

'Mrs Dunstable . . . Mrs Dunstable . . . She is drownded . . .'

Of course, Mrs Hopkins had immediately scooped the child up in her arms and carried her into the warm parlour, kneeling with her before the fire. She instructed Mr Crabback to find dry clothes—a nightshirt, any blankets he could spare, for the child was shivering violently, her lips quite blue. This he did, and then donning his own coat, Mr Crabback picked up a lantern.

'I must go and see for myself,' he said.

He had hoped that the child was inventing things, but he knew as he saw the dark shape dragging in the shallows, that of course it was Mrs Dunstable, come back to make trouble in her spiteful way. He stood and contemplated her a moment. This was not a good development, not good at all. After all, how would it look? First, he sacks her, then she goes and drowns herself: the press would have a field day with it.

He had to do something. He could not leave the corpse exposed upon the beach. If he could push it into deeper water, he pondered, surely there was a chance that the sea currents might carry her away. Eventually, she might sink to the sandy bottom in some lonesome inlet, never to be heard from again. It seemed peaceful in its way. He almost envied her. Pulling off his boots and rolling up his trousers, he waded resolutely in.

Grasping hold of one stiff arm and pulling the body in this fashion, he waded out till the water was almost up to his neck. He could certainly go no further: he would have to send her off from here. 'Godspeed,' he said, for he felt there was a need to say something. He gave the body a final mighty shove to set it on its course. 'And God bless.'

But immediately, as if to mock his efforts, a wave collected the corpse and sent it back to him, pulling up its skirts to reveal its drab, pathetic drawers, a watery scene from a burlesque show. Oh, but it was a sight he had no wish to see. Crying out in horror, he turned and waded frantically in the direction of the shore, and yet the corpse seemed intent on embracing him, entangling him in its petticoats, fondling him roughly with its ghastly stiff limbs. Tearing himself free at last, he staggered up onto the sand. The frightful remains of Mrs Dunstable washed towards him, nudged into the shallows by the tide. She had no intention of departing, he realised. She meant to get him, that was clear.

There was nothing for it. As Superintendent of the institution, he must act, and act accordingly. So he set off at once to wake Henry, for the imbecile must be charged with the task of rowing across to Balmain and alerting the Water Police.

'There will be a sizeable reward in it for you,' he told the simpleton, who stood before him bleary and confused. He had been roused from his slumber moments earlier by Mr Crabback's frantic beating upon his door. 'Quickly, make haste! Tell the Water Police to come at once. It is a matter of the greatest urgency. Do you follow?'

Infuriatingly, the man just stood there, gazing at Mr Crabback blankly. He seemed not to comprehend. Mr Crabback felt a powerful urge to strike him. But of course, that would not end well—Henry was a good deal taller than Mr Crabback, and powerfully built.

He found himself with no choice but to resort to threats. 'If you don't do as I say this instant, Henry, I'm afraid that I have no other choice than to put you down in the cells,' said Mr Crabback. 'Do you understand what I'm saying to you? I am talking about the blackholes.'

With a cry, Henry took off at once, lumbering along jerkily down to the boat shed where the small rowboat was stored. Mr Crabback followed a short distance behind, not entirely confident that the man was up to the job. But what other recourse did he have?

'The Water Police, do you follow?' he called after Henry as he dragged the boat into the water. 'You will find them in Darling Street, not far from the wharf. Tell them they must come at once to Biloela! As a matter of the utmost urgency!'

Clambering now into the boat, Henry bent to the oars and commenced to row. Mr Crabback turned and hurried back to his quarters. He did not look back towards the beach where the pitiful corpse of Mrs Dunstable now scraped against the sand.

Meanwhile, Mrs Hopkins had pulled off Josephine's wet clothes, dressed her in Mr Crabback's nightshirt and covered her in blankets. The girl seemed to be half-demented from shock. There had been a great struggle between them when it came to removing her wet pinafore, and as Mrs Hopkins finally managed to pull it over the girl's head, the child had clutched hold of it, searching wildly through its pockets before throwing it down in despair. Then she commenced to weep, for she realised, even in her wretched state, that she had lost her two shillings and the milk toffees to the sea.

Mrs Hopkins held the child tightly to her, rocking her in her arms. The poor girl finally stopped her weeping and drifted off into a deep sleep, her face crushed against Mrs Hopkins' breast. How lovely it felt, thought Mrs Hopkins, as she gazed tenderly down at her, to hold this sweet, bedraggled waif in her arms; to provide her at this terrible time with the love and comfort she had probably never known from her own mother, the infamous bawdy-house proprietor. A few gruff words would likely be the best she could have hoped for, if not a clip over the ears and an exhortation to 'stop yer bawling'. Mrs Hopkins hugged the little girl tighter and pressed a kiss upon her forehead. What on earth had happened out there, she wondered. Why was the girl half-drowned?

At last, she heard the front door open and Mr Crabback hurried in, dripping wet.

'It is all true,' he said. 'It is Mrs Dunstable, all right, washed up on the beach.'

With a finger to her lips, Mrs Hopkins motioned for him to speak quietly, lest he wake the child. 'Dead?' she whispered.

'Oh yes. Quite dead,' said Mr Crabback, thinking that a strange question in light of what he had just told her. 'There can be no doubt about it.'

Mrs Hopkins nodded.

'I have sent Henry to summon the Water Police,' he continued, pulling off his wet coat and draping it over a chair. 'I imagine they will be here in an hour or two. Then I shall be in for it.'

She stared at him. 'But why should you be in for it?' she asked. 'You have done nothing wrong.'

'Well, dismissing her the way I did. And then she goes and jumps off the boat or whatever it is that she's done.'

A deep colour rose in Mrs Hopkins' cheeks. 'You had no choice but to dismiss her, given the terrible accusations that she made about us, and in front of the entire school.'

'Yes, yes, but it looks bad, don't you see? My giving her the sack like that. A tad hasty perhaps. I daresay the Colonial Secretary will have a strong view on the matter, given that I'm supposed to consult him and what-have-you.'

'She was quite drunk,' said Mrs Hopkins. 'I will testify to that, for she reeked of liquor when she came to ask my forgiveness.'

'Yes,' said Mr Crabback. 'That is true.'

'Then there's the business of the black eye,' he said after a moment.

'A black eye?' said Mrs Hopkins.

'Oh yes, she was sporting quite the bruiser. That will prompt questions, undoubtedly.'

'Her body has been tossed about in the water for some time,' said Mrs Hopkins. 'I imagine that is how she has incurred the injury.' Then, after a moment or two of thought, she added, 'Possibly a boat hit her. It is a busy harbour, after all. It is a wonder she did not incur more injuries.'

Mr Crabback gazed at her a long moment and said nothing. The boat story seemed plausible, after all, and was certainly better than saying anything about Mrs Hopkins having struck her.

'In any case, you have explained the reasons behind your decision to the Colonial Secretary admirably in the letter you dictated to me,' said Mrs Hopkins. 'I expect, once considered, your reasoning will satisfy him entirely.'

In fact, Mrs Hopkins had been somewhat alarmed by Mr Crabback's reasoning. He had declaimed at length, citing all sorts of minor slights and differences between he and Mrs Dunstable. He had even included her scolding of

Tippet during breakfast the previous morning, stating quite untruthfully that Mrs Dunstable had raised her hand and struck the dog. Mrs Hopkins had thought it best to take advantage of Mr Crabback's illiteracy by presenting the recent changes in the simplest, most straightforward terms in order to justify them.

Sir,

I have the honour to state for the information of the Hon. Colonial Secretary that the conduct of Mrs Ernestine Dunstable, House Matron of Biloela Industrial School For Girls, has been such as to warrant the immediate termination of her duties. She has not only repudiated my authority and responded to my orders with contempt, but she has also besmirched the reputation of the School-Mistress Mrs Hopkins, a woman entirely incapable of dishonourable conduct. Further, I regret to inform the Hon. Colonial Secretary that it has been reported to me that Mrs Dunstable had been consorting with sailors on the dry dock, and on the morning of her termination, appeared before the inmates and staff while under the influence of liquor.

Since it is quite improbable under the circumstances that any good could come from her continuing in the position, I found myself with no other choice but to terminate her position effective immediately.

'Mr Crabback, with the greatest respect, sir,' Mrs Hopkins had said, her pen poised, 'ought not we advise the Colonial Secretary of the fact that I have taken on the role of Matron?'

Mr Crabback hesitated; he was beginning to suffer doubts as to the wisdom of his rash proposal on her doorstep. The more he thought about it, the more unlikely he felt it was that his wife would accept the matter graciously. He had also completely failed to consider the question of her wages: his wife was to receive ninety-eight pounds per annum for her duties as Matron at Biloela, a very welcome windfall indeed. Oh, he had not thought this through at all! And yet, with Mrs Hopkins gazing up at him, he had not the courage to retract his proposal.

'Yes, I daresay. I only hesitate for to advise them of too many changes at once may alarm them unnecessarily,' he had said. 'But yes, perhaps it is for the best that we let them know that you have had to step in as Acting Matron.'

Mrs Hopkins felt her heart sink: she was to be Acting Matron only. Her hopes of emerging from her mourning attire into a smart new dress of grey brocade faded a little.

'What reason should I give?' she asked.

'Reason?'

'Yes, for me stepping in for Mrs Crabback.'

'Oh, I don't know! You think of something. She threw an ink-stand at me, will that do?' He seemed rather annoyed all of a sudden, so Mrs Hopkins did not persist; instead, she added the following:

Further, I have tasked Mrs Hopkins, the School-Mistress, to step in as Acting Matron, as my wife is currently unavoidably detained by urgent matters at the Haven of Hope. I have utter confidence that Mrs Hopkins will fill the role admirably.

I have the honour to be, Sir, Your most obedient servant.
Charles Crabback
Superintendent, Biloela Industrial School For Girls

After proffering the pen to Mr Crabback, he leaned over to sign his name, and thence had come the terrible pummelling on the door and the wailing, and poor little Josephine collapsed on the doorstep.

Now, as Mrs Hopkins knelt by the fire and nursed the child, Mr Crabback seemed to grow increasingly agitated. He paced the room. He picked up her letter, stared at it a moment, and put it down again. Then he pulled out his watch, frowned and tapped at its case. 'I thought perhaps it had stopped,' he said as Mrs Hopkins looked at him queryingly. 'It happens sometimes, does it not, at times of great personal shock?'

'I have heard of such things,' said Mrs Hopkins. At this, Josephine stirred in her arms and mumbled something. Mrs Hopkins pulled the blankets up around her more securely.

'Good heavens!' cried Mr Crabback. 'We have quite forgotten lights out!' He pulled out his watch again. 'And look, it is ten minutes after eleven! The girls will be working up a riot by now!'

And donning his coat again and re-lighting his lantern, he hurried out into the night. But instead of making his way to the institution, he veered down the rocks towards the beach where Mrs Dunstable's body now lay marooned upon the wet sand. Dropping to his knees, he ran his hands into the various pockets and folds of her skirt. Unable to find anything, he dug his hands into the bodice, pushing them beneath her tight stays, for he felt he must make certain that there was no letter hidden upon her person, addressed to the Colonial Secretary and plainly stating her side of the story. With a shock, his hands discovered her breasts, icy cold, quite covered in wet sand, yet still oddly pleasing in their firmness—how odd, he thought as he groped them greedily, that he had never noticed Mrs Dunstable's fine bosom before. How curious that even grim, unappealing women such as Mrs Dunstable had such delights hidden away under their stays. Only then, as he leaned over her person, did he glance down upon her face and realise that, with her one good eye (the other was swollen shut, presumably from where Mrs Hopkins had struck her) she gazed up at him in the cold moonlight, a vile pinkish foam oozing steadily from between her pale lips.

With a groan, Mr Crabback lurched away and vomited into the sand. He vomited again and again, in a bid to dispel not just the pea soup but his self-loathing, his sorry wretchedness at the unmistakable foulness of the act he had just committed. Finally, for it took some time to regain his strength, he covered up his mess and made his way back up to his quarters, leaving the corpse he had just defiled to wait for her attendants.

The Water Police arrived just before dawn and after a good bit of standing around and staring queasily at the corpse, finally gathered themselves to ask Mr Crabback for a sheet in which to wind the body, and thence carried it over the sand and into their five-oared skiff. Thus the mortal remains of Mrs Dunstable were conveyed to the dead house at Circular Quay. This procession was watched from the top of the rocks by the full assembly of girls, and indeed by Mrs Baird and Miss Foy, for once the girls were released from their dormitories, word had spread quickly of the matters down on the beach. Miss Foy was quite friendly with Constable Glassington, and she nipped down for a quick word. He confirmed what they all suspected: it was their former House Matron; she had likely leapt from the steamer; the body was quite 'banged up'.

Miss Foy clambered back up the rocks to report this news to Mrs Baird, who at once dissolved into tears. She had had her differences with Mrs Dunstable over the years, but no one deserved to wash up ashore like a bit of old kelp. Many of the younger girls began to weep also, for there were many instances they could recall where Mrs Dunstable had not been unkind to them.

Mrs Hopkins had long since carried Josephine back to her quarters where she put her into her bed and covered her with as many coats and blankets as she could find, for the child would not stop shivering. She lit a fire and made a pot of tea, and this she sweetened with ration sugar. Then she sat the girl up in her arms and tried to get her to drink it. But the child did not want to drink—she turned her head away. Her skin felt clammy to the touch; her cheeks were unnaturally flushed. Laying the child carefully back down again, she sponged her brow with a little vinegar and water. She had done the same for Eugenie in her fever, and it had seemed to provide her with some relief. She dropped to her knees and prayed for the child's recovery. 'Please Lord, don't let her die,' she murmured. 'Let this one survive, I beg of you.' Then she pulled up a chair beside the bed, intending to watch over the little girl till it was six o'clock and time to unlock the dormitories; instead, she had fallen into a heavy dreamless sleep, her head slumped upon her chest. She did not stir at all until after seven, when Josephine commenced calling fitfully for her mother.

'I'm here, Eugenie,' Mrs Hopkins said at once, sitting upright, quite groggy from her sleep. 'I'm here.'

But Josephine had recoiled as Mrs Hopkins reached out to smooth away the sweaty strands of hair from her brow. Then she started to cry, that awful keening that Mrs Hopkins had heard on that first night, the night she had insisted on going in to comfort her, the night that Josephine had spat upon her. The girl was pining for her mother. There was nothing Mrs Hopkins could say to make it better. It was hopeless.

So she left the child and hurried into the institution, mortified to realise that on her first full day as Acting Matron she had overslept. The quadrangle seemed curiously empty; there were only the Tunks girls, playing in the dirt. Nor was there any sign of activity in the mess-hall—in fact, it was completely empty. Where was everybody? She hurried to the kitchen to see how breakfast was progressing. But the kitchen too was quite deserted; the big iron copper that should have boiled the porridge sat cold and empty. There was no sign of any breakfast at all.

'Mrs Baird!' she called out, as if expecting the newly appointed House Matron to materialise instantaneously. Surely, the preparation of breakfast fell under her duties? She called out her name several times, with increasing volume and irritation. She felt she might bite the woman's head off if she actually dared show herself. But just at that moment Catherine, the girl who had read so well in class the previous day, appeared in the doorway, panting heavily. She had just lugged a big sack of oatmeal up the steps from the stores beneath the kitchen.

'They're all on the rocks, Mrs Hopkins,' said Catherine. 'Did you hear about poor Mrs Dunstable?'

'Yes, I did,' said Mrs Hopkins briskly. 'But I am more concerned at this moment that you girls have your breakfast.'

'That's what I thought, Miss. So I thought maybe I should get started since nobody else was.'

'That's very considerate of you, Catherine, and your behaviour will not go unrewarded. Now, will you kindly run down to the rocks and tell Mrs Baird that I am waiting upon her in the kitchen?'

And beaming with pleasure at the compliment bestowed upon her, Catherine took off down to the rocks. Mrs Hopkins looked around for some kind of implement with which to open the sack of oatmeal, and finally found a blunt old knife with which she tore a ragged hole in it. Then, with some difficulty owing to its great weight, she hoisted the bag to her shoulder and dumped its contents into the copper. A cloud of rancid oatmeal dust flew up in her face. She gazed down at the oats in dismay—they were mouldy.

The enormous stress of the last twelve hours—now culminating in a dead House Matron and a child sick with fever—threatened to overwhelm her in that moment. She longed to throw herself onto the flagstones and beat her fists and weep. But she did not. For there was no time for such nonsense—she must make the girls porridge, and to do that she needed water, which meant she needed some girls to go and man the force-pump immediately. She peered out into the quadrangle, hoping to see some of the older girls. But all she could find were the poor little Tunks girls, sitting about in the dirt. Even the eldest and biggest of the sisters was too thin and weak to manage the unwieldy force-pump, let alone carry the weight of the bucket on her poor little rickety legs. What she needed—what all the Tunks girls needed—were regular doses of cod liver oil, and Mrs Hopkins made a note to herself to add it to her list of requirements. But in the meantime, what the Tunks girls needed—what everybody needed—was breakfast.

'Yes, Mrs Hopkins, you wanted me?' said Mrs Baird.

Mrs Hopkins turned to find her standing in the doorway, her eyes red and swollen behind her spectacles.

'Yes, indeed I want you! Yesterday I elevated you to the position of House Matron. And now I find to my dismay that not only do the girls not have their breakfast but indeed there is no sign of any preparation whatsoever!'

'Why, it's not House Matron's business, ma'am, nor any of the kitchen duties.'

'Indeed, Mrs Baird? Then pray, whose business is it?'

'Why, I believed it to be yours, Mrs Hopkins. As Matron, I thought you would take charge of it. The House Matron is all about the cleaning, Mrs Hopkins. It's all about the cleaning and the stores and the sewing.'

Mrs Hopkins stared at her. Was it possible that Mrs Baird was telling the truth? But had she not seen Mrs Dunstable herself doling out the breakfast in the mess-hall that first morning?

'Are you quite sure of this?'

'Yes, indeed, Mrs Hopkins. If you read the regulations—'

'Regulations or not, I should think the Matron of an institution such as this has quite enough on her plate without being charged with the preparation of the food, Mrs Baird.'

'Well, you're quite right there, Mrs Hopkins. But ever since our last Cook walked out, some months ago now, they've not bothered to replace her. Mrs Baker-Hunt managed it for a while, but when she left, Mrs Dunstable had to step in. She did her best, God bless her—not that she was any cook, not by any means—but she did what she could because who else was going to do it? She couldn't just let the girls go hungry.' And here Mrs Baird began to weep afresh, her voice rising in pitch. 'And if I'd had any brains, I should have done the same. But I thought you would take charge, I did, since you're our new Matron now!'

By now, Miss Foy and Rosabella and Catherine, and several of the younger children, had joined them in the kitchen and were standing around staring at Mrs Hopkins in a kind of awe. Her face and throat were quite covered in white dust from the rancid oatmeal, and against the black of her mourning, she struck an eerie sight.

'You know she's dead, don't you, Mrs Hopkins?' continued Mrs Baird, and Mrs Hopkins felt her tone carried a note of accusation. 'Her poor old body's just now washed up upon the beach. She couldn't leave the girls, you see. Even in her sorrow, she came back to the girls!'

And here some of the little ones started to weep, too.

'We will pray for her,' said Mrs Hopkins briskly. 'We will say a special prayer for her at muster.'

'You shouldn't have hit her,' said a small voice. It was one of the weeping little ones, scowling amidst her tears.

'I didn't hit her,' said Mrs Hopkins. It was the first thing that came out of her mouth, a flat denial.

'You struck her to the ground with your closed fist,' said the child. Mrs Hopkins didn't even know her name, but she stood there in her dirty bare feet quite determined to have her say. 'If that's not the God's honest truth, may I drop down dead this minute!'

'Is this true what Bridget says?' asked Mrs Baird, her voice trembling dangerously.

'You know yourself these girls cannot be trusted,' said Mrs Hopkins in a low voice. 'They try to set us against each other. That is how they operate.'

'We all saw you!' cried the girl, and her little heart-shaped face pinkened in outrage.

'You did not see it,' said Mrs Hopkins, gazing at the child steadily. 'For it happened outside the classroom. Yes, she fell to the ground, I grant you that, but that was because she was drunk.'

'How dare you speak ill of the dead and her not able to defend herself,' cried Mrs Baird.

'She *was* drunk, Mrs Baird,' said Catherine. 'We saw her from the washing line, didn't we, Rosabella? She was staggering all over the place, falling down and getting up again.'

'It's true,' agreed Miss Foy. 'I went over to say goodbye when she was packing her bags. She was swigging straight from the bottle—'

But Mrs Baird did not wish to hear any more; she turned and swept out of the kitchen.

Mrs Hopkins found herself standing in an uncomfortable silence with Miss Foy and the girls.

Bridget stared at her, steely-eyed. 'You struck her hard,' she said, 'with your closed fist. I saw it with my own eyes.'

'Shut your mouth, Bridget, or I will smash your teeth in,' said Rosabella.

'I'll not shut my mouth. I'll speak the truth to anyone who asks me,' said Bridget. She must have been barely nine years old, yet she stood to her full height and her voice shook with emotion. 'You shall never conquer me if I am steeped to my neck in blood. For I am a Socialist and always will be.'

'Good heavens!' cried Mrs Hopkins. 'There is no need for such talk. Quickly, let us get started on our breakfast! We will make just the nicest breakfast we can because everybody is quite shaken up.'

But the young Socialist and her friends would not be bought with promises of a nice breakfast; they departed in high dudgeon.

So Mrs Hopkins had Rosabella and Catherine to man the force-pump as hard as they could (what good and willing girls they were proving to be, not requiring anything by way of enticements or threats), while Miss Foy set about lighting the fires beneath the coppers. Then Mrs Hopkins hurried down to the stores to see what provisions might enliven the girls' breakfast. Flour, suet, raisins, the coarsest ration sugar you could ever imagine—but there, her eyes lit upon a large tin of black treacle. Surely a generous dollop or two might disguise the mouldiness of the oats, about which she could do nothing? And what about milk? Were the little ones to have some milk?

'Miss Foy,' she said, as she returned to the kitchen with the treacle, 'who should be milking the cows?'

'There's only one girl in the whole place who knows how to milk,' said Miss Foy. 'And that's Rosabella.'

'Oh dear,' said Mrs Hopkins. 'Then let us call her from the force-pump at once and set her to milking. Then I need you to go to the rocks and get all the girls back here immediately.'

But instead of setting off at once as instructed, Miss Foy started to giggle. She kept glancing up at Mrs Hopkins, then turning away again and giggling helplessly behind her hand, apparently quite unable to stop herself. It was completely infuriating. The woman was a fool, thought Mrs Hopkins.

'Do you find something amusing, Miss Foy?' she asked.

'Oh, you do look a sight, Mrs Hopkins. I'm sorry! But you're all covered in white dust like a ghost, you do have me in stitches! If you could see yourself! You'd frighten the dead from the grave, oh my word!'

And although Mrs Hopkins could cheerfully have struck Miss Foy to the ground with her closed fist at this moment, instead she gathered what remaining shreds of dignity she had left. 'I see. Well, I am pleased that I have been able to provide you with a moment of levity, given the gravity of the situation in which we find ourselves. I wonder that you are capable of laughter at all, for try as I might, given the recent tragic passing of Mrs Dunstable, I find myself quite unable to find any cause for merriment, let alone any reason for such an outburst of foolish tittering as I have just witnessed. But clearly my appearance is humorous enough to warrant it, so there you have it. I shall speak to the Superintendent on the subject, for I find your lack of respect and overall conduct quite improper, given my position as Matron.'

She did not say 'Acting Matron'.

Chastened and ashamed of herself, Miss Foy mumbled her abject apologies and set off at once to summon the girls.

Then Mrs Hopkins did her best, while she had a moment of privacy in the kitchen, to brush off the awful-smelling oatmeal dust which was all through her hair and over her face, extending halfway down her bodice. She burned with humiliation at the thought of how she must have presented herself before them all, like a ghost in a pantomime, even as she tried to establish her authority as Matron. The only comfort she could draw was that at least Mr Crabback had not seen her in that state, for even in her dismal mourning, Mrs Hopkins had her pride. As soon as Catherine returned, staggering in with the first buckets of water, Mrs Hopkins dipped her handkerchief in one and cleaned her face as best she could.

'I wanted to say something,' whispered Catherine, as she tipped the other bucket into the copper, 'but I didn't want to embarrass you.'

What a dear girl, thought Mrs Hopkins, and that small expression of kindness and concern on the part of the girl did much to restore her spirits. Soon the porridge was on, and much improved by the treacle, for Mrs Hopkins and Catherine felt they needed to be generous this morning and ended up using the entire tin.

The old coppers took an eternity to boil so it was well after ten o'clock before the girls had eaten their breakfast. There was now the business of muster and prayers. Mrs Hopkins had hoped that Mr Crabback would perhaps take over at this point, for if ever the girls and the Assistant Matrons needed their Superintendent to offer words of hope and consolation, it was surely on this terrible morning. But there was no sign of him at all. Once the Water Police had departed with the corpse of Mrs Dunstable, Mr Crabback had seized the opportunity to take himself off to bed for a short nap. He felt it was warranted after such a harrowing night. He was right at this moment sound asleep with Tippet curled up on the bed beside him.

So it was left to Mrs Hopkins to offer, at the very least, a prayer for Mrs Dunstable, just as she had promised. Leaving Miss Foy to gather the girls in the quadrangle, she hurried back to her quarters to find her prayer book. There lay poor Josephine, entangled in Mr Crabback's nightshirt, the bedclothes tossed upon the floor. Her brow was hot to the touch and she tossed her head from side to side, as if in the grip of a nightmare. Mrs Hopkins stared down at her, a feeling of hopelessness welling within her.

'It is all right, Josephine, Mother's here,' said Mrs Hopkins, for that was the only comfort she could think of to offer the child. And then, realising that she probably sounded quite different to the child's actual mother, she attempted a gruffer voice that she imagined might befit the proprietor of a notorious bawdy-house. 'Mammy's 'ere, loov. Roight beside yer, oi am.'

It was not very convincing. Even in her half-conscious state, Josephine frowned. She seemed perplexed that someone was mocking her mother.

But Mrs Hopkins had no time to minister further to the sick child for she could hear the inmates assembling noisily for muster. So she straightened the girl's nightshirt and restored the fallen bedclothes and then rummaged in her chest as quietly as she could for one of her prayer books. The first one she found was the Book of Private Devotion. In haste, she cast her eyes down its table of contents: happily, it seemed to have several prayers pertaining to the subject of death. In fact, the very book itself smelt of death. She had come into possession of it only recently, having prised it from the cold dead hands of Aggie Miller, the old woman who dwelled in the top attic of the boarding house at which Mrs Hopkins had formerly resided. She had been a dreadful hag, foul-mouthed and mean-spirited. She would lean over the bannister, accusing

Mrs Hopkins of all sorts of preposterous things; of entertaining sea captains or stealing her teapot or smoking opium in the company of Chinamen, her spittle all the while raining down upon Mrs Hopkins. And yet, when they broke down Aggie's door and found her dead body (some days after her death, for it was the terrible smell that prompted them to do so), the old lady had been clutching onto this prayer book! How surprising people were. 'You might as well have it if it's of use to you,' said the landlady, for she was helping herself to everything else.

Well, perhaps the prayer book would be of use to her now. Tucking it into her pocket and casting a last anxious glance towards the sickbed, Mrs Hopkins tiptoed from the room, closing the door quietly behind her. Then she hurried back to the quadrangle where the girls were now forming haphazard lines.

'Catherine! Rosabella!' cried Mrs Hopkins. They were the only two girls who could be relied upon. 'Will you take a bowl of porridge to my quarters? You will find the girl Josephine there—overnight she has taken ill. Will you try to encourage her to eat something? Or drink some tea? And will you sponge her with some cool water and try to see that she is comfortable?'

'Yes, Mrs Hopkins,' said Rosabella, nodding earnestly.

'We'll look after her just as if she was our own sister,' added Catherine.

'And if you feel she is worsening, come and fetch me at once. If not, I shall come at dinnertime as soon as I can get away.'

And so the two girls, filled with pride and self-importance at the responsibility with which they were charged, hurried first to the kitchen to fetch the tea and porridge and then to Mrs Hopkins' quarters to minister to the invalid.

Now Mrs Hopkins turned her attention to the inmates gathered before her in the quadrangle. The older girls, still on their best behaviour after yesterday's promise of a Special Visiting Day for Mothers, stood in neat rows, quiet and expectant. Even the normally rambunctious Sarah and Eliza seemed subdued, perhaps aware of the gravity of the occasion. Many of the smaller children were still weeping and comforting one another forlornly. Little Bridget stood at the front, her arms folded in an expression of defiance. Miss Foy wrung her handkerchief between her fingers. Off to one side, a short distance from the others, Mrs Baird stood quite alone. She seemed unable to bring herself to even look at Mrs Hopkins, but instead stared angrily at the ground before her.

'On the Loss of Beloved Friends' was the title of the prayer that seemed to Mrs Hopkins the most appropriate for the occasion. And so, without preamble, she held the book before her and commenced, in as commanding a voice as she could summon. '*We love the creature too well.*' The creature? She thought, with a moment's pause: what an odd choice of words. And so she started again. '*We loved Mrs Dunstable too well. We put her above our God, and this is the way He casts her from her throne. He suffers the reed we lean upon to pierce us as it breaks. And then our eyes are open, our misery brings us to ourselves. We turn from our broken idols and withered gourds and we ask ourselves, Why do I cling so closely to those which death may tear from me in an hour—'*

She stopped abruptly. This was going very badly. Changing 'the creature' to 'Mrs Dunstable' had not improved things; she could hear the sound of weeping. She dared not look up, but she suspected it was Mrs Baird. Perhaps these words resonated with the newly appointed House Matron: perhaps Mrs Baird had loved Mrs Dunstable too well, placing her before God, and hence He had cast Mrs Dunstable from her throne as a withered gourd. It seemed unlikely, but these days one never knew. In any case, Mrs Hopkins did not like to continue in this vein, for it seemed to offer little comfort. So she turned to the next prayer, entitled 'On Death'.

'*We were born and we must die,*' it began in a matter of fact fashion. '*The time allotted to us is short indeed. If we listen with attention, we seem to hear the labour of Him who is preparing our grave—*'

Again Mrs Hopkins broke off. If the girls 'listened with attention', they could hear the cursing of the sailors at the dry dock; several of the girls glanced at one another and smirked. Mrs Hopkins closed the book and cast a desperate glance in the direction of the gate, in the hope that Mr Crabback might materialise. How she wished that she possessed some small measure of his powers of oratory at this moment.

'Mrs Baird, Miss Foy, girls. I wish I could offer you some comfort for the loss of Mrs Dunstable,' she began, 'but I cannot seem to find the right prayers with which to do so. I am very sorry that she has died. I only learned from Mrs Baird this morning that she had taken on the role of Cook, as well as her other duties, in order to ensure that you girls would be fed. That speaks of her sense of duty and of her compassion. I can see from your tears that many of you were very fond of her. I hope that we will all remember her for her kindness and the great efforts that she made on your behalf—'

And in that moment, a wave of emotion hit Mrs Hopkins. It suddenly seemed dreadful to her, the awful fate of Mrs Dunstable. Of course, she had deserved to be promoted to Matron, given the efforts she had made to keep the institution running and the girls fed, with no Matron and no Cook. If she was occasionally bad-tempered, who could blame her? The difficulties of preparing breakfast that morning had given Mrs Hopkins an insight into how endless and exhausting it all was, with limited provisions and mouldy oatmeal and stale bread—and that was just breakfast! Oh, it was small wonder that Mrs Dunstable had been angered by Mrs Hopkins' entirely unwarranted promotion. Yes, she had sullied Mrs Hopkins' honour—in front of the girls, no less—but was there not some truth to her accusations? Mr Crabback *had* been fawning over her, and in her vanity, Mrs Hopkins had permitted him to do so. Like the cat that ate the cream, was that not how Mrs Dunstable had described her? And when Mrs Dunstable had come to Mrs Hopkins, desperate and pleading for a second chance, she had responded by speechifying self-righteously and striking her to the ground!

'Girls,' she said, and her voice trembled, 'the other night I heard you sing a beautiful hymn. I cannot quite recall the words . . .'

'Shall We Meet Beyond The River,' volunteered someone.

'That's the one! Will you girls sing it for us now, just as nicely as you can, in memory of Mrs Dunstable?'

And so, gathered there in the windswept quadrangle, the girls commenced to sing.

Shall we meet beyond the river
Where the surges cease to roll?
Where in all the bright forever
Sorrow ne'er shall press the soul?

They had begun shyly and tentatively, but as they gained confidence, the pure sweetness of their young voices—the innocent trill of the little ones, the honeyed tones of the older girls—combined to fill the air as if they were a choir of bedraggled angels.

Shall we meet in that blest harbour
When our stormy voyage is o'er?
Shall we meet and cast the anchor
By that fair, celestial shore?

They sung with great solemnity and feeling; it was impossible to hear them and not be moved. Who are they thinking of, wondered Mrs Hopkins; what loved and longed-for mother or father or sister or brother did they hope to reunite with in that blest harbour?

Shall we meet, shall we meet
Shall we meet beyond the river?
Shall we meet beyond the river
Where the surges cease to roll?

'Shall we keep going, Miss?' asked Sarah, for they had reached the end of the chorus.

'Oh yes, please. Don't stop. You are singing so beautifully!' cried Mrs Hopkins, clasping her hands together. And so, after exchanging a few doubtful looks between themselves, the girls continued.

Shall we meet at the Lord Nelson
For a glass of Falcon Gin?
If you buy another round, dear
I might let you poke it in.

Shall we meet at the Rag and Famish
For a pint of half and half?
If buy another round, dear
You can take me up the arse—

'Stop!' cried Ms Baird suddenly, for the girls had continued to sing so solemnly that it had taken time for her to notice the unexpected turn to lewdness that the song had taken.

Miss Foy had noticed, of course, having heard the girls sing it before, and was wondering if they would get so far as the particularly filthy verse concerning the pint of Seppelts Rum. Mrs Hopkins, dazed and exhausted after her long night, had failed to notice at all. She was shocked to see Mrs Baird suddenly all red in the face and screaming at the girls.

'How dare you? How dare you? Vagabonds! Worthless filthy vagabonds, every last one of you!'

'Mrs Baird!' cried Mrs Hopkins, completely bewildered by this outburst. 'Please, do not speak to the girls in that way—'

'She told us to keep going!' declared Sarah, pointing to Mrs Hopkins.

'I know, I heard her,' cried Mrs Baird, turning on Mrs Hopkins now. 'Oh, how I wish you'd never come here. She knew you were trouble, Mrs Dunstable did! She told me so the minute she laid eyes upon you. "You watch her, Betty," that's what she said to me. "There's something odd about her, I cannot put my finger upon it. But keep a close eye upon her for I fancy she is some kind of witch!"'

The girls gasped out loud in astonishment; some of them even clapped their hands over their mouths. The little ones began to wail afresh. Mrs Hopkins was rendered speechless. She had no idea what had brought on this attack, but it seemed entirely unfair—and hurtful, terribly hurtful—that people would view her in this way—for no reason—for she could not help the way she looked.

'She tried to warn me, she did,' Mrs Baird continued. 'And look—if any of you doubt what I say—look at what has become of Mrs Dunstable for all her trouble! Washed up on the beach like a piece of old cuttlefish. A piece of old cuttlefish you might place in the bottom of a bird cage!'

It was at this point, or shortly after, that several of the girls started up the chant of '*Witch! Witch! Witch!*'

'I am not a witch!' cried Mrs Hopkins.

Someone flung a rock, hitting her hard in the middle of her forehead. She swayed a moment, then fell to the ground. She felt suddenly terribly tired, like she might sleep for a hundred years.

'I am not a witch,' she repeated limply.

'Well, she would say that,' she heard one of the girls say. 'Of course, no one's going to say, "Oh yes, I'm a witch." They're going to deny it, aren't they?'

When she opened her eyes again some time later, she was still lying on the ground in the dusty quadrangle. Everyone seemed to have departed. The muster was over, but who had given permission for the girls to disperse? And what was to happen next? Was something required of her? The dinner meal, of course—the mutton must be boiled. And Josephine—what about poor Josephine? Oh, and were there not the little ones to teach? She rose blearily to her feet and dusted down her dress. She felt her forehead gingerly. A lump the size of a walnut had formed upon her forehead.

She made her way to the kitchen and found Miss Foy in there with Hannah and several other girls; they had the mutton in the coppers already and were scraping potatoes and gossiping idly. They stopped their chatter the moment that she entered.

'Oh, very good. I see that you have the meat on,' said Mrs Hopkins, gazing at the chunks of grey meat stewing away. It smelt bad, like the meat was on the turn. 'Is that meat all right, do you think?' she asked.

But they all ignored her, as if she had not spoken.

'It smells to me like it might be off,' she persisted.

This time Miss Foy sniffed petulantly, as though Mrs Hopkins had insulted her cooking. 'Perhaps it is off because your sorcery has made it so,' said the younger woman.

'Don't speak foolishly,' said Mrs Hopkins. 'The meat is old and has been left in the sun.'

'It only started to smell bad when you walked in here,' said Miss Foy defiantly. 'You have probably cast a spell upon it.'

It was useless to try to reason with her, so Mrs Hopkins simply turned and left.

She made her way to the schoolroom, but only the three little Tunks sisters awaited her. They sat huddled together on their narrow bench, eyeing her warily. What huge eyes they have in their sunken faces, thought Mrs Hopkins. And yet the prospect of having some children to teach, even if only the Tunks sisters, was somehow bolstering in that it gave her a sense of purpose.

'Oh, girls, this is wonderful,' she cried. It took all her effort to try to sound cheerful. 'I have wanted to have some special time with you. Shall we spend this morning on the alphabet?'

Emma, the eldest, bit her lip. The younger two remained mute; Martha, the most defective, was trembling and the little one seemed about to cry.

Really, it was too ridiculous; all Mrs Hopkins could do was proceed with the lesson and hope that they would snap out of it. 'A is for axe,' she said, picking up a piece of chalk. 'And B is—'

Turning to the blackboard, she froze. Her heart thudded; her chalk fell to the ground. For there, filling almost the entire board, was a crudely rendered drawing of a hideous crone mounted upon a broomstick. She was quite naked—her breasts pendulous, her belly sagging, her bare backside rising upwards to the sky. Scrawled in giant letters, a single word: *WICH.*

Mr Crabback woke, dry-mouthed. Tippet was whining at the bedroom door, needing to get out. The bedroom was horribly light: what time was it? Mr Crabback grasped for his watch and stared at it in disbelief: it was after eleven. At once, the memory of the whole ghastly night descended upon him: Mrs Dunstable drifting in the shallows, the ghastly thrill of her cold dead breasts; the dull thump as the young constables from the Water Police heaved her body into the bottom of the boat. And all the while the imbecile Henry hanging about and staring at him, till Mr Crabback lost his temper and shouted at him to go away!

But what else? There was something else lurking in his subconscious, something that Constable Glassington had said as a parting shot as he leapt into the rowboat. What was it? He recalled that he had pressed the letter he had dictated to Mrs Hopkins upon the Constable and asked that he get it to the Colonial Secretary as a matter of urgency: it seemed imperative somehow that his representation of events reach the authorities before any nonsense that Mrs Dunstable may have concocted. Oh God, yes. That was it! Tucking the letter into his pocket, the Constable had mentioned, quite in passing, that Mr Noyes, the Water Police Magistrate, would undoubtedly make a visit later that very day. Mr Noyes was known to be conscientious to a fault; he would not suffer any delay in investigating the matter. For all Mr Crabback knew, the man could be snooping about the island now.

The one comfort that Mr Crabback drew upon, as he washed and shaved and dressed, and then made himself a pot of tea and warmed some soup for his dinner, was the thought that the excellent Mrs Hopkins, in her new role of Acting Matron, would have everything well in hand. He smiled at the memory of the beautiful scene in the dormitory the previous evening; all those young *nymphs du pave*, heads bowed in quiet devotion. Once Mr Noyes witnessed the calm and capable manner in which Mrs Hopkins was able to manage these soiled doves, he would see that Mr Crabback had not been acting rashly and impulsively in elevating her to this new position, but instead taking decisive action out of urgent necessity, and if Mrs Dunstable got her nose out of joint and was so unstable as to . . . as to . . . But he did not like to think too much about Mrs Dunstable, so he finished his soup and then washed his few dishes and dried them and put them away, and then he and Tippet proceeded to the institution.

Almost immediately he realised something was terribly wrong. For down below on the beach, most of the older girls seemed to be idling about, many in their customary state of semi-undress. He hesitated a moment at the top of the rocks: ought he not summon them back inside the barracks? But no, best leave that sort of thing to Mrs Hopkins; most likely she had some scheme afoot. 'Though this be madness, yet there is method in it,' he told himself, though he felt a twinge of doubt. In any case, he would need to alert her as to the Magistrate's impending visit. Now was not the time to be engaging in fanciful new educational practices.

But on entering the gates of the institution, he found yet further cause for concern. For the quadrangle was a scene of mayhem; all the younger girls squealing and carrying on, playing chasey or leapfrog or knucklebones in the dirt. They could not have looked more slovenly and unkempt. Not one of them appeared to have had a wash; their hair was uncombed and tangled, their bare feet filthy. A small brawl ensued right in front of him; the youngest Tunks sister, Janie, bit another small child on the arm, whereupon the other girl howled and slapped Janie so hard she ended up flat on her back. Now she too commenced to howl, so loudly that Mr Crabback was forced to stick his fingers into his ears. What a racket these little ones made! Where were the Assistant Matrons to deal with such things? Where indeed was Mrs Hopkins? Why were these children not in class?

He checked his watch. It was well past noon by now; time for the dinner meal, and no doubt it was late as usual. He proceeded to the kitchen, and there at last he discovered Mrs Hopkins, quite on her own, surrounded by foul-smelling chunks of boiled mutton. These she had lifted from the copper with the aid of a wooden paddle and placed on the bench in order to inspect them. Now she was shaking her head and whimpering to herself; she seemed on the verge of tears.

'Oh, Mr Crabback,' she cried in a desperate fashion when she saw him. 'I cannot serve the girls this meat! It is rotten! What on earth are we to do?'

'Is it rotten?' he asked, although the terrible smell would seem to confirm it. 'Perhaps it is just on the turn?'

'It is rancid!' she declared.

He did not care for the defiant tone in her voice. 'Please, Mrs Hopkins, there is no need to raise your voice in that fashion. If we cannot serve the meat, what else are we to offer them?'

'There is nothing! Stale bread and boiled turnips!' And she indicated the copper filled with soggy boiled vegetables.

'Then we must simply serve them the meat.'

'It will make them sick!'

'If they do not like it, they need not eat it. But in truth, Mrs Hopkins, these matters are your concern, not mine. I am expecting a visit from Mr Noyes, the Water Police Magistrate—for all I know, he may well turn up on the one o'clock steamer.'

'But why—what is he coming for?'

'Why, regarding Mrs Dunstable, of course. He will be making a report of some sort and I imagine he has every intention of going through the place with a fine-toothed comb.

Do you understand the seriousness of the situation in which we find ourselves?'

And here, Mrs Hopkins leaned heavily against the bench as if she might fall if she did not support herself. Flies were now congregating upon the spoiled meat. She waved them away feebly. 'Yes,' she responded.

'What is that on your head?' he asked, indicating her forehead.

Gingerly, she reached up and touched it. 'Someone threw a rock at me.' She did not like to mention the witch business.

Mr Crabback sighed. He was simply too tired for this sort of nonsense. 'Well, this is very disappointing. I leave the school in your charge for a morning, and it has fallen into chaos. However, I do not have the time to deal with your problems at this moment. I need you to leave what you are doing and accompany me.'

'Right now?' asked Mrs Hopkins. She had been hoping to get to her quarters to see how Josephine was faring. There had been no sign of Catherine and Rosabella, which would seem to indicate that at least the girl's condition had not worsened.

'Yes, immediately. We need to conduct an urgent inspection and set this place to rights before he gets here,' said Mr Crabback. And rather enjoying the masterful way in which he was talking, he strode out of the kitchen and into the quadrangle, where he sighted Mrs Baird, coming through the gates of the institution.

'We are expecting a visit from the Magistrate,' Mr Crabback informed her. 'I need everything shipshape. So as soon as you can serve the dinner meal and clean it all up, the better. I would like to see the mess-hall thoroughly mopped out before he shows himself.'

Mrs Baird nodded, refusing to even look at Mrs Hopkins.

'Will you get the Burke girl out of the cell, Mr Crabback? She's been shouting and carrying on, and it's stirring all the girls up. She might make a bit of unpleasantness, that's all, with the Magistrate coming.'

'Oh, good heavens, we can't have that. How long has she been in there now?'

'Four days now, sir.'

'And what did I say at the time?'

'You said seven days, I believe, sir.'

'Very well, yes, I suppose it might be best to get her out, even if just while the Magistrate visits.'

'Shall I do it, sir?'

'No, leave it to me. I would like to see if she can muster an apology at the very least.'

'I would consider that very unlikely, sir. She is quite vicious.'

'Yes, I believe I've had a glimpse of that already.' And here Mr Crabback laughed nervously.

'That was a most unfortunate incident, sir. I regret you had to experience such a thing,' said Mrs Baird, and then added, quite unnecessarily, with a pointed look at Mrs Hopkins: 'Things go from bad to worse here lately.'

But Mr Crabback did not notice the hostility directed at Mrs Hopkins, as he was too busy going through his keys. 'Now, which one was it again?'

'That big one, sir. The rusty one,' said Mrs Baird. 'I'll get dinner served at once, Mr Crabback. We'll have the place spick and span for our visitor.'

And off she bustled towards the kitchen.

Mrs Hopkins had listened to all this in silent bewilderment. What on earth were they talking about? And who was this Burke girl, about whom she had heard not a single word in the entire four days she had been at Biloela. (Was it really only four days she had been here? And now that she thought of it, had she not seen the name 'Amelia Burke' listed amongst the older girls in the school roll?) She dared not ask any questions however, and instead meekly followed Mr Crabback. He was marching through the empty mess-hall and out through the far door to a barren promontory, where stood the old guardhouse, a relic of the convict days.

To the left of this guardhouse, positioned right at the very edge of the cliff, stood another structure built of the same crudely hewn blocks of sandstone, outside of which sat a handful of girls, including Annie Laughton, the sullen, freckled girl who had insulted Catherine's mother in class the previous day, and Bridget, the young Socialist. They jumped up at once when they saw Mr Crabback approaching with the keys.

'Are you letting her out, Mr Crabback?' asked Annie, her face lighting up with hope.

'I may do. We shall see,' said Mr Crabback, and he proceeded to unlock the door of this building, revealing a space dark and empty, its floor marked by what appeared to be a series of trapdoors: square frames of solid wood, with cross bars of iron and padlocks. At once, Annie pushed past him and dropped to her knees atop one of these trapdoors.

'Amelia!' shouted Annie as loud as she could. 'Be good! He's going to let you out!'

'Be good, Amelia!' cried little Bridget, who had rushed in right behind her. 'Please be good!'

From deep down below, Mrs Hopkins heard something hoarse and indistinct, a sound that had she not known better she might not have recognised as human. A ghastly chill went through her.

'Girls, get out of here,' said Mr Crabback. 'You are not aiding your friend's cause. You are only potentially making matters worse. Go on, get out!'

And anxious not to harm their friend's chances, they moved to a position just outside the building, where they could hover near the doorway and still see what was happening.

'Well, we shall see how this goes,' said Mr Crabback to Mrs Hopkins, and he sank to his haunches and busied himself with the key to the padlock of the trapdoor.

'Are you saying there is a girl down there?' asked Mrs Hopkins, and she realised that her voice was shaking.

'Yes, she has been placed in close and separate confinement, as per the regulations,' said Mr Crabback briskly, as he struggled with the key in the padlock.

'For how long?'

'Well, that is at all times up to the discretion of the Superintendent, but in this instance, given the nature of the offence she committed, and the general depravity of her behaviour, a week down the cells on bread and water seemed sufficient. But who knows? Given the circumstances, if she plays her cards right and apologises nicely, I may consider letting her out.'

By now, Mr Crabback had finally succeeded in unlocking the ancient padlock and, with effort, he heaved the heavy trapdoor open. At once, the foul and sickly smell of urine and faeces pervaded the atmosphere. Mr Crabback proceeded to lower down a rope ladder.

'All right then, Burke. Come up. Let's hear what you have to say for yourself,' he called.

Leaning forward, Mrs Hopkins peered down and her stomach lurched in horror. The ladder disappeared into a deep black hole, carved into the raw stone of the cliff. From the darkness below emanated the sound of faint scuffling.

Mr Crabback waited a moment or two, then bellowed, 'Well, are you coming up or not!'

'I'm trying!' came the pitiful response from deep below.

Minutes passed: they could hear the sounds of whimpering and panting as the girl tried to pull her way up the ladder.

Frequently it seemed she had to stop in a bid to regain her strength; at one point she must have almost fallen for she cried out in fright. Finally, as she neared the top, Mr Crabback reached down and, with great effort, pulled the girl up roughly onto the stone floor. There she stayed for several moments on all fours, swaying slightly, her head hanging limply. A more pitiful sight could scarcely be imagined.

'Stand up now, Burke. Stop carrying on,' said Mr Crabback.

The girl struggled to get to her feet. Her friends stood in the doorway, stricken with anxiety, their hands clasped over their mouths. Once upright, the girl stood there, blinking and dazed in the shaft of weak sunlight that came in through the doorway. She was about sixteen years of age, thin and pale, with long black tangled curls. She wore only a tattered chemise and was shivering violently.

'What do you have to say for yourself?' said Mr Crabback.

The girl frowned and put a hand to her eyes to shield them from the sunlight which seemed to bother her.

'Will you give me the apology I am owed?' demanded Mr Crabback.

The girl muttered something in a voice so faint that Mrs Hopkins could not make out what she had said.

'It was only a *what?*' asked Mr Crabback, apparently incensed by what he had heard. 'Speak up!'

'It was only a lark,' said the girl.

'A *lark?*'

'I didn't mean anything by it!' cried the girl.

And now she began to sway so wildly it seemed for a horrifying moment that she might plunge backwards down the hole again.

Mrs Hopkins could bear it no longer. She rushed forward and caught the girl in her arms. 'Leave her be!' she said to Mr Crabback, her voice thick with fury. 'I am taking this child to the infirmary.'

And supporting the meagre weight of the girl, she led her out of the grim building and into the sunshine, whereupon the other girls swooped upon her.

'Amelia! I've missed you so much!' cried Annie, and she hugged and kissed her.

'Me too!' cried little Bridget, and she wrapped her arms devotedly around the older girl.

A flurry of other girls, big and little, came rushing out of the mess-hall in excitement. 'Amelia's out!' they cried, and they gathered around her joyfully.

'Girls,' said Mrs Hopkins, 'I know that you are very glad to see your friend again. But just at this moment, we need to get Amelia to the infirmary. Annie, you can help by going at once to the mess-hall and fetching a plate of food for her. Just bread and vegetables, mind, no meat! And Bessie, bring me some sugar if you can find any, and we will make her a good strong cup of tea.'

And although some of these girls had thrown stones and chanted 'Witch!' at Mrs Hopkins only hours before, it was as if the entire episode was forgotten, so grateful were they that she was caring for their beloved Amelia.

Mr Crabback, meanwhile, was left standing there, the padlock still in his hand. Once again, Mrs Hopkins' behaviour had left him gripped with uncertainty and shame. Of course, it looked bad, a young girl stuck in a black hole for so many days on bread and water. But he had been under strict instructions to deal with these girls with an iron hand—from all reports, Mr Baker-Hunt had been too kindly, too lenient, too ineffectual; the girls had ridden roughshod over him. And of course, Mrs Hopkins had no idea of the nature of the offence the girl had committed to earn such a punishment; Mr Crabback had frankly been too embarrassed to tell her. Amelia was in the habit of sharing her bed with the girl Annie Laughton, and frankly this had seemed innocent enough to Mr Crabback, considering how cold and damp were the dormitories and how meagre the blankets provided them. But the Colonial Secretary had hinted that he must guard against certain acts of depravity known to take place amongst the older girls. Uncertain what these acts might be, he nonetheless felt it best to separate Amelia and her friend, which resulted in the Burke girl flying into a rage, picking up the slop pail and throwing it at him. There was not much in it admittedly, just a small amount of urine, but still the episode had been humiliating, and Mr Crabback had of necessity to soak his trousers in Borax overnight. Further, and again Mrs Hopkins was unaware of this, the girl was very much the ringleader of the inmates—if Amelia Burke thought it only a 'lark' to throw a slop pail over the Superintendent, then the other girls would undoubtedly follow her lead. Strict measures must be brought to bear. Such incidents must be dealt with decisively, in a manner that made it clear that this sort of behaviour would not be tolerated.

A blast of horn sounded. The one o'clock steamer ferry was approaching the wharf. Standing at the bow of the vessel, idly surveying the grim aspect of the island before them, stood not only Mr Henry Noyes, Esq., the Water Police Magistrate, highly regarded by all who knew him, but also the impressively bearded figure of Mr John Massie, the Colonial Secretary himself.

It was unfortunate that, just as Mr Crabback was unlocking the gate to allow entry to the visiting dignitaries, they were assailed by the sight of one of the girls, Hannah, bent over in the quadrangle, vomiting up her lunch. Mr Noyes at once proceeded over to her, though Mr Massie apparently felt it wiser to keep his distance.

'What is the matter with you?' asked Mr Noyes.

'I'm sick, sir. The meat was off,' said the girl.

'The meat was off?' he asked, turning to Mr Crabback with an expression of incredulity on his face.

'This is news to me,' said Mr Crabback, attempting to adopt a similar expression.

'Get yourself to the infirmary and ask Nurse for some water with a little baking soda,' he instructed the girl. 'Be sure to drink it while foaming.'

'Yes, Mr Noyes, sir,' said the girl.

'Your name is Hannah Eddington, if I recall?'

'Yes, Mr Noyes, sir.' Even in her wretched state, the girl seemed pleased that he remembered her. He had committed her to Biloela some twelve months ago when she was found wandering the streets in the company of prostitutes.

'Off you go then, child.'

She stumbled off towards the infirmary.

Mr Noyes turned to Mr Massie. 'Her mother is a very great drunkard and is most of the time in gaol,' he explained.

His attention drawn to the din coming from the mess-hall, Mr Noyes then indicated that they proceed in that direction. The dinner meal was its usual scene of chaos. The girls sat on the tables and picked at their meal with their fingers; the little ones stuffed bits of bread into the pockets of their pinafores and wandered outside. Many of the older girls recognised Mr Noyes as the Magistrate who had committed them to Biloela, and their interest was piqued by his sudden appearance. Mr Noyes turned to a girl of about twelve seated nearby and asked if he might be allowed to inspect her plate of food; he sniffed the meat and put the bowl down at once.

'Have you eaten any of this meat?' he asked the girl. 'No, sir. It stinks.'

'Indeed it does.' Then he turned to the hall at large. 'Silence!' he thundered.

The girls stopped talking and stared at him.

'If you have meat on your plate, do not eat it. If you have already eaten the meat and you are feeling unwell, I give you permission to take yourself to the infirmary and ask Nurse for some bicarbonate of soda.'

At once, several girls rose up and made their way out of the mess-hall. Others, even some who had not partaken of the meat, followed at short intervals, a few clutching at their stomachs and groaning rather theatrically.

Mr Crabback was by now feeling quite incensed. Mr Noyes was turning out to be the most appalling busybody—surely the question of what food was dished out to the girls was not part of his remit as Water Police Magistrate? His taking charge in this manner, in front of the Colonial Secretary no less, only served to undermine Mr Crabback's own authority. And who was this fictional Nurse he kept referring to? Did he imagine that their shabby infirmary was presided over by a Florence Nightingale in a lace bonnet and crisp white apron? The reality was they had no Nurse, and the infirmary was little more than a storeroom with two narrow beds, and a cupboard containing some meagre and ancient medical supplies. Meanwhile, Mr Massie stood about smiling genially at some of the older girls as they made their way past him, many of them in their short dresses torn off at the gathers, exposing their bare ankles and an inch or two of their calves.

Just at this moment, Mrs Baird wandered in from the kitchen, chewing on a crust of bread and butter. She took fright at the sight of the two dignitaries and attempted to duck out before they saw her. Too late, alas!

Mr Noyes called her over. 'What is your name?'

'Mrs Baird, sir.'

'What is your position here, Mrs Baird?'

'I am the new House Matron, sir, after what happened to Mrs Dunstable.'

'Are you responsible for the serving of this meal to the inmates?' asked Mr Noyes.

Mrs Baird hesitated and glanced at Mr Crabback. 'Only in that Mr Crabback asked me to, sir. Normally the House Matron has nothing to do with the kitchen; we are more concerned with our other responsibilities—'

'Are you responsible for the serving of this meal to the inmates?' Mr Noyes spoke rather forcefully over the top of her.

'Yes, sir. I did serve it up, sir. Mr Crabback asked me to do so.'

'Did you not notice that the meat was rancid?'

Mrs Baird seemed momentarily paralysed. She peered at the two gentlemen through her thick spectacles. 'I hoped it might be just on the turn, sir,' she said at last. 'We often get meat a bit on the turn. The girls don't seem to mind, sir. It does them no harm most of the time.'

'We have just observed Hannah Eddington vomiting in the quadrangle.'

Mrs Baird heaved a sigh. What with one thing and another, she was quite at the end of her tether, and unusually for her (she was normally deferential to the point of obsequiousness when confronted by any person of authority), she found herself suddenly speaking out in defiance. 'I was just doing as I was told, sir. Mr Crabback asked me to serve dinner as quickly as possible and have it all cleaned up before you got here,' she said.

'That is true,' said Mr Crabback. 'However, I was not aware of the state of the meat.'

'I mean no disrespect to you, sir,' said Mrs Baird, turning to Mr Crabback. 'As Superintendent, you shouldn't need to be bothered with such trifles. By rights, it's the Matron's duty to oversee these things. It should not be left for me and Miss Foy to do everything.'

'Why was not your Acting Matron overseeing the serving of dinner?' asked Mr Noyes of Mr Crabback.

'I cannot say, sir.' What an appalling coward he was! He was shocked sometimes at his own spinelessness. 'It's all been so busy, utter pandemonium, as you can imagine. Let me think. Oh, now I recall. Yes, I had asked her instead to accompany me on a tour of inspection. Of the institution, sir.'

'You asked her to accompany you on a tour of inspection? For what purpose?'

'Well, to have the place shipshape, sir. In readiness for your visit.'

'I am the Police Magistrate, here to investigate the death of Mrs Dunstable,' said Mr Noyes, frowning as if in puzzlement. 'I am not the Inspector of Public Charities. I do not require the place to be "shipshape", as you put it. Do you understand me?'

'Yes, sir.' How he hated Mr Noyes.

'Where is your Acting Matron at this moment?'

'I believe she is in the infirmary, sir.'

'Is she unwell?'

'No, sir. I believe she is tending to one of the inmates.'

'Why does she not leave such duties to the Nurse?'

'Well, we have no Nurse, sir. Hence my confusion when you kept mentioning her.'

Here he gave a small chuckle. It was ill-advised for Mr Noyes did not seem at all amused by this information.

'The institution has no Nurse?'

'No, sir.'

'We haven't had a Nurse the whole time I've been here,' offered Mrs Baird. 'Which is coming up to three years in November.'

'Nor a Cook either. She left in February,' said Miss Foy, who had been hovering nearby. 'She couldn't stand the flies. The kitchen being right near the earth-closets.'

'Nor do we have a Laundress,' said Mrs Baird. 'It is up to me and Miss Foy to do everything. And poor Mrs Dunstable, of course. Is it any wonder she felt . . . unappreciated . . . well, she was at the end of her rope, I suppose.'

Mr Noyes' expression drew grave for he saw that, behind her spectacles, Mrs Baird's eyes were glistening with tears.

'Let us leave any speculation about Mrs Dunstable aside,' he said gently. 'But I thank you both for speaking openly and honestly.'

This comment galled Mr Crabback further. Had he not spoken openly and honestly of the lack of a Nurse? Why were the two Assistant Matrons singled out for praise and he not? He was beginning to get the feeling that Mr Noyes had it in for him and was deliberately embarrassing him before the Colonial Secretary. Fortunately for him, Mr Massie did not seem as exercised as Mr Noyes by the state of affairs at Biloela. In fact, when Mr Noyes had called upon him unexpectedly that morning, requesting that he accompany him to the island on account of the sudden demise of Mrs Dunstable, he had thought it would be a pleasant opportunity to get out of the office. In his time as Colonial Secretary, he had never actually visited the island, but the stories of the various unspeakable depravities these girls were known to engage in rather intrigued him.

One thing the infirmary did have was a nice little potbelly stove, which Mrs Hopkins was able to get going in short order, warming the room and also boiling the kettle. The poor Burke girl was still shivering, despite being wrapped in as many blankets as they could find in the infirmary. Annie Laughton produced from the pocket of her apron several portions of Sunday's suet pudding which she had been saving specially for her friend. Bridget proudly produced a large knob of butter, purloined from Miss Foy's quarters. (Miss Foy was known to be partial to butter, and her personal stockpile, kept tucked away in her quarters, was a reliable source when the girls felt themselves in need.) Bridget spread it thickly over a hunk of bread and presented it to Amelia. The girl gobbled it down ravenously, and then set upon the suet pudding, shovelling the soggy pieces into her mouth. Mrs Hopkins poured her a pannikin of hot tea with two large spoonfuls of sugar, and this the girl sipped gratefully. Bolstered by this nourishment and the obvious adoration and affection of her friends, the colour began to return to her cheeks.

'Amelia, you'll never believe it,' said Annie, who had cuddled up next to her friend on the bed, 'Dunnekin is dead!'

'What!' cried Amelia, her mouth full of suet pudding.

'Oh, girls, please don't call her that,' implored Mrs Hopkins, as she tended the teapot.

'Yes, she was all in a tizz because Mrs Hopkins here clocked her one.'

Amelia turned to look at Mrs Hopkins, her eyes widening in amazement. 'This skinny bint here clocked Dunnekin?'

'Please let's not call her Dunnekin—' said Mrs Hopkins.

'Punched her with a closed fist. I saw it myself,' confirmed Bridget, beaming with self-importance. 'Knocked her to the ground and everything.'

And here, to everyone's surprise, Amelia let out a big chortle of glee. 'Oh my word, I wish I'd seen that!' she cried. 'She had it coming, the old bitch. Oh, the misery that cow has put me through, you wouldn't believe. I could kiss you, I could!'

And here she reached out and grasped Mrs Hopkins' hand and leaned her head against her in such a disarming display of affection that Mrs Hopkins (who was somewhat shocked at the girl's callous attitude to Mrs Dunstable's passing) found herself nonetheless blushing with pleasure. Although she was far from being a pretty girl, there was something rather striking about Amelia with her tangled dark hair and her big green eyes. When she smiled, Mrs Hopkins saw that she was missing a front tooth, and yet somehow it added to her charm.

'What, and now Dunnekin's dead?' continued Amelia, slurping her tea.

'Yes,' said Annie. 'She jumped off the steamer.'

'Ha!' laughed Amelia. 'That would be typical. Anything for attention, that one. Probably thought some handsome sailor would jump in and save her!'

And here the girls all joined in the laughter, even Bridget.

'Who are you anyway?' asked Amelia of Mrs Hopkins.

'I am the new School-Mistress. And also, for the moment at least, the new Matron.'

'Oh, you're Crabback's missus?'

'No! No, Mrs Crabback . . . has been detained on other business. So I am filling in for her.'

'She's really nice!' This from Eliza.

'Well, I can see that, stupid! I'm not blind!' said Amelia. 'Can you imagine Dunnekin making me a nice hot cup of tea? Not likely!'

'Oh, and guess what, Amelia! She's going to have a special day where everyone's mother visits!'

And the girls went on to describe in some detail the games and the afternoon tea with sponge cakes and the concert that all the mothers would enjoy.

'That's nice,' said Amelia, and she seemed rather subdued for a moment. 'Wish I had a mother.'

'Well, do you have a father?' enquired Mrs Hopkins carefully. 'Or a grandmother? Or an auntie, perhaps, who could come along?'

'No one at all,' said Amelia, quite matter of fact now. 'I was found as a newborn wrapped up in a bit of brown paper at Redfern Station. In the water closets in the Ladies' Waiting Room, would you believe? I read all about it in my notes. There was a newspaper cutting and everything, and me just a baby!'

'She's been in the newspaper lots of times,' said Annie proudly.

'Not really. Just when I tried to burn the place down,' said Amelia, with an air of modesty. 'That was the main time.'

'She got up in front of all the beaks and told them what she'd suffered here,' said Annie. 'The jury was crying their eyes out.'

'They still stuck me in Darlo for a month, the bastards.'

'What about when you dressed up in Miss Day's old hat and ulster and got all the way to Parramatta on the steamer before anyone even noticed you were missing!'

'Oh, that was funny, that was! Right under Glassington's nose, the silly prick!'

'What was the headline that time, 'Melie?'

'"*Virago Hides in Cargo*". Which is bullshit, because I went in the main saloon and nobody batted an eyelid!'

The atmosphere in the infirmary was cosy and convivial. There had been enough tea in the pot for several pannikins, and the girls passed them around between them, even offering some to Mrs Hopkins. In former times she might have declined, but she had not had any tea all day and her head was aching. It was hot and sweet and she felt it doing her good.

'Thank you,' she said after taking her sip, passing the pannikin back to one of the smaller girls, one of Bridget's friends. It was at that point that Hannah came in, having been sent there by Mr Noyes. She did not look at all well. She seemed dismayed at the sight of Amelia and her cronies gathered together, and even more so at the sight of her younger sister about to drink from the same pannikin from which Mrs Hopkins had sipped.

'Don't drink that, Clara!' she cried, knocking the pannikin from her sister's hands and causing the tea to spill to the ground.

'What did you do that for?' cried the girl in dismay.

'She will poison you, like she poisoned me.'

'Take no notice of this one,' said Amelia to Mrs Hopkins. 'She is as mad as a cut snake.'

'It's true, I tell you!' cried Hannah. 'She turned the meat bad and ever since I've been chucking my guts up!'

'The meat was already bad, Hannah,' said Mrs Hopkins. 'I did not turn it so.'

'You see?' said Amelia to Hannah.

'She is a witch,' declared Hannah. 'And that's why Mrs Dunstable is dead, and now I am poisoned!'

'Take that back!' ordered Amelia.

'I will not!'

'Take that back or I will rip your tongue out and shove it down your throat and then you will know what it's like to be poisoned!' cried Amelia, and she rose up from the bed like a Fury and grabbed hold of her by the arm. Hannah screamed and, in her panicked state, vomited all over the floor. Amelia reeled back and struck her hard across the face. The poor girl fell to the floor in a puddle of her own vomit; other girls swooped down upon her and dragged her roughly from the room.

'Pay no attention to her, Hopkins,' said Amelia. 'She makes our lives misery—her and the other two—always spying on us and telling tales.'

'Nonetheless, she is ill and I must go to her,' said Mrs Hopkins and she hurried out of the infirmary after Hannah.

The girl was lurching wildly across the quadrangle; as Mrs Hopkins tried to approach her, she backed away fearfully.

'Hannah,' cried Mrs Hopkins, trying to modify her approach so as not to appear too terrifying, 'let me get you something for your biliousness!'

'Get away from me!' screamed the girl. In her panic, she ran to the gate of the institution and realising that it was locked, backed up against it, issuing shrill staccato screams as Mrs Hopkins approached her. There was nothing to be done to placate her; the girl was quite hysterical. Other girls, leaving the mess-hall, stopped and stared. Disturbed by all the commotion, Mr Noyes and Mr Massie emerged also. It was altogether an unfortunate scene for them to witness.

'We have called upon you, Mrs Hopkins, as our first witness,' said Mr Noyes, 'because in amongst the few possessions Mrs Dunstable left aboard the *Emu*, we found this.'

He stared for a moment at the sizeable lump on the School-Mistress's forehead but made no comment. Perhaps staff incurring such injuries was commonplace upon the island. The Superintendent himself was also sporting an injury over his eye, he had noticed.

Now he passed a scrap of paper across the table to Mrs Hopkins. They were seated for the interview in Mr Crabback's front parlour, the only place in the institution deemed sufficiently private. Mrs Hopkins felt some measure of discomfort, for the room was alive with memories for her. It was the room in which, on her first night, by the fireside, Mr Crabback had wiped away her tears with his handkerchief smelling faintly of turnip soup. And only the previous evening, before the horrors began to unfold, he had clasped her hands and pledged that together they would 'find a way'.

Mrs Dunstable's note was written in pencil on a torn scrap from an exercise book. It read:

WARNING school-mistress now unfarely MATRON not to be trusted believe her to be SORCERESS leading girls into Vice and Wickedness Mister Crabback under her Spell she has done for me Goodbuye Ernestine G. Dunstable

Mrs Hopkins read it once through, then passed it back to Mr Noyes without comment.

'Why would she write such a thing?' asked Mr Noyes.

'I do not know,' said Mrs Hopkins. 'I cannot warrant it. It is very hurtful.'

'You must know something of her reasoning?'

'There was no reasoning to speak of. She was upset and entitled to be. Mr Crabback had, quite unexpectedly, elevated me to the position of Acting Matron. Had I known of the efforts that Mrs Dunstable had gone to on behalf of the girls, I would not have accepted the position so readily.' Her voice trembled a little and a blotchy colour rose to her cheeks. The lump on her forehead seemed almost to throb a little.

'Mrs Hopkins,' said Mr Noyes gently, 'nobody blames you for Mrs Dunstable's actions. The unsteadiness of her writing alone indicates the state she was in. She had become unhinged; it is plain to see. I simply ask if you can shed any light on why she would accuse you of sorcery.'

'I can only think—' And here Mrs Hopkins hesitated.

'Yes?'

'I can only think that sometimes my appearance causes people to think such things. And yet I cannot help the way I look.'

'People have accused you of such things before?'

'Not in as many words. But I am aware that sometimes people—strangers, generally—seem uneasy in my presence. I think it is a combination of the mourning garb and the particular cast of my features. It is a great pity, but as I say, it cannot be helped.'

She offered this so simply, sitting there with her hands clasped together on her lap, that Mr Noyes was at a loss to know what to say. Perhaps he should offer her some mollifying compliment? And yet she did not seem to require one. Nor could he actually think of one at the present moment that would seem entirely sincere.

'I understand that Mr Crabback gave Mrs Dunstable immediate notice and bade her depart on the one o'clock steamer.'

'I believe so. Although I was not present when he did so.'

'For what reason did he do this?'

'In her anger at being overlooked as Matron, she told falsehoods—in front of the girls and the matrons, I might add—regarding the Superintendent and myself.'

'What were these falsehoods?'

'I would prefer not to repeat them. Suffice it to say, that, should anyone choose to believe them, it would render it impossible for myself or the Superintendent to exert any moral authority whatsoever over the girls.'

'She was suggesting that Mr Crabback was giving you the glad eye in some way?' asked Mr Massie, the Colonial Secretary, barely bothering to hide his incredulity. Given the number of comely girls here wandering around in their short dresses, it seemed highly unlikely that Mr Crabback would be under the homely School-Mistress's spell, as the dead House Matron's note had stated.

'Mr Crabback is a married man, and I am a widow still in mourning. I have been at the institution all of three days. I have already mentioned my appearance. It was an outrage to suggest such things as she did. The Superintendent would not stand for it and gave her notice, effective immediately.'

'I understand she was a drinker?' asked Mr Noyes.

'I cannot say. There was talk of her carousing with the officers of the *Blanche,* performing "Ta-ra-ra-boom-de-ay" and suchlike. Certainly, she appeared to be under the influence of liquor when she came to my schoolroom to ask for my forgiveness.'

'She came to your schoolroom?'

'Yes.' And here Mrs Hopkins turned to address Mr Massie. 'May I take this opportunity, sir, to state that the schoolroom windows are still broken from the recent riots, and the stench from the earth-closets intolerable.'

'I am well aware of the state of the windows. It is not the first or even the second or third time they have been smashed by the girls. It will do them no harm to suffer a stiff breeze for a while. That way they will "learn their lesson", as it were, as they are learning their lessons.' And here he gave a light chuckle.

Mrs Hopkins said nothing but seethed quietly. She found she did not care for his attitude.

'Mrs Dunstable asked for your forgiveness, you say?' continued Mr Noyes.

'Yes, and I did not give it to her, a fact which I regret bitterly. "*Judge not and ye shall not be judged; condemn not, and ye shall not be condemned; forgive and ye shall be forgiven.*"'

Mr Noyes could not help but be impressed by her. Her composure and dignity, given the recent events at Biloela, including the startling scene he had just witnessed with the screaming, vomiting Eddington girl, were something to be marvelled at.

'There is also the question of the letter I received from Mrs Crabback,' said Mr Massie, who was considerably less impressed and found her pious attitude rather tiresome, 'in which she states that you permitted the girls to romp about on the beach while scantily clad in their under-things, in full view of every dinghy, skiff and pleasure craft in the harbour.'

A tremor of shock ran through Mrs Hopkins. She had forgotten all about Mrs Crabback's threat to report her to the Colonial Secretary. Had Mr Crabback not assured her, that evening on her doorstep, that his wife would present no further difficulties?

'It is true that some of the girls were bathing in their petticoats,' said Mrs Hopkins. She was certainly not going to mention the water-sprites jumping about in all their nakedness, for clearly Mr Massie found it all rather titillating. 'I exhorted them to come out of the water at once; they would not listen to me. I realised I would need to resort to unusual measures in order to gain their compliance, so I had the idea of teaching them a new song. The girls delight in singing; it is one of the few pleasures they are afforded in this place.'

'Surely it is possible for them to engage in this "pleasure" while fully clothed and out of view of the public gaze,' said Mr Massie. 'If I might suggest, radical as it may seem, the schoolroom perhaps?'

'As I stated earlier,' said Mrs Hopkins, 'the windowpanes in the schoolroom are broken and the proximity to the earth-closets, not to mention the pigsties and the cow shed, render the atmosphere injurious to the young ones' health. To have our music lesson upon the beach seemed to me a harmless enough activity. One can hardly blame the girls for enjoying the sunshine and fresh air when they are confined to the bleakest prison imaginable, through no fault of their own.'

She had never in her life been so outspoken, but suddenly she found that she could not stop herself. It all seemed so unfair. What innocent, harmless fun the girls had had that afternoon, romping about in the sunshine. And yet these men would not abide it.

'Are you mistaking Biloela for the Crystal Palace Gardens?' said Mr Massie. 'Should we install a skating rink and a bowling green? I am telling you now, Mrs Hopkins, you will get nowhere by being so lenient. The girls will detect your weakness and ride roughshod over you.'

'In the short time I have been here, I have found the girls respond readily to the smallest amount of kindness and sympathy.'

'Kindness or no, it is harder to reclaim a fallen woman than to bottle a sunbeam,' intoned Mr Massie. '*The sow that is washed returneth again to wallowing in the mire.*'

'I will tell you this much—' started Mrs Hopkins, her voice catching. Why must tears always come when she was angry? 'Yes, the girls have been brought up amidst vice and depravity, but they are good girls at heart, and many of them show great promise. Why, Catherine reads so well, she could be a School-Mistress herself one day, and Rosabella in her gentleness would make a fine Nurse. And as for Mary-Ann, with her pretty face, she could surely be on the stage! You call them sows? Not a one of them! Yes, they can be provoking—on the night of my arrival, a child spat upon me. That girl is now my class monitor, and I could not ask for a better one.'

And now poor Josephine, her class monitor, doing cartwheels in the quadrangle only yesterday, was fading upon her sickbed.

'You have an unnaturally high opinion of them,' said Mr Massie, absently combing some pipe tobacco from his beard. 'Might I remind you that it is scarcely possible to open a newspaper these days without reading about some poor fellow, thinking he has met a good sort, being plied with liquor and robbed of all his possessions! That is why Mr Noyes here is forever packing them off to Biloela. They are crowding up his courtrooms.'

Mr Noyes nodded in agreement. 'That is so,' he said.

'They steal because they are hungry and destitute,' said Mrs Hopkins. 'And then, in the guise of welfare, they are detained in barracks that were deemed unsuitable for the most hardened convicts. Why, only an hour ago, I witnessed a girl dragged up from a hole in the ground where she has spent four days in utter darkness and isolation.'

'Yes, of course, that was Amelia Burke,' said Mr Massie. 'Mr Crabback wrote to me about it.'

'What did she do this time?' asked Mr Noyes.

'She threw the slop pail, full of excrement, over Mr Crabback's head.'

'Good heavens,' said Mr Noyes, with a grin. 'That's a new one.'

Mrs Hopkins stared at them. A slop pail, full of excrement, thrown over Mr Crabback's head? Was Amelia truly capable of such an action?

'What do you say about that, Mrs Hopkins?' asked Mr Massie.

'I can only wonder what caused her to act in such a way,' murmured Mrs Hopkins.

'I'll tell you what caused her to act in such a way. Mr Crabback was attempting to stop her from engaging in—'

here he hesitated and glanced at Mr Noyes '—in practices that are frankly too repulsive for me to reveal to you, Mrs Hopkins.'

'But to place her in a dark pit—'

'In cases of gross indecency, the offender will be kept in close and separate confinement for such a period as may be directed by the Superintendent.'

'Surely there are other means of correcting a child,' began Mrs Hopkins, though she had lost some of her previous conviction.

'Other means! Such as?' persisted Mr Massie. He seemed to have taken over the interview completely, while Mr Noyes wrote a great many notes in his notebook. Every now and then, he would lift his head and gaze at her curiously through his spectacles.

'Well, if it were left to me, I would try to talk to the girl, reason with her, if you will,' said Mrs Hopkins. She was aware of how futile this seemed, especially if one were covered in excrement at the time. In truth, she was not at all sure what she would do had she had a slop pail tipped over her. If the incident with Josephine was any indication, she would spend the night weeping and berating herself.

'I would endeavour to make her understand the error of her ways, and to encourage any feelings of remorse she might be experiencing,' she continued. And what else? She cast about in her mind for some worthy-sounding notion. 'And pray, of course! We would pray. I would ask the child to pray with me, and then after we had prayed, I would urge the child to apologise—'

At this the two men laughed out loud.

'I wish you good luck with that!' chortled Mr Noyes.

'Clearly you have had little contact with the Burke girl to even entertain such notions,' said Mr Massie. He was not chuckling now, but instead glowering at her over his spectacles. 'Perhaps you are not aware, Mrs Hopkins, that when a new girl is received into this institution, she must submit to a filthy and disgraceful practice as a process of initiation, and that your Miss Burke is the ringleader!'

Mrs Hopkins stared at him. An initiation practice? What on earth was he alluding to? She remembered with a stab of shame the thrill of pleasure she had felt when Amelia had grasped her hand and leaned her tousled head against her. She had felt at the time that the girl was expressing her gratitude, and yet, was it possible that Amelia was instead initiating some sordid rites, the nature of which Mrs Hopkins could not even imagine? It would be advisable to be more cautious in her dealings with this young woman. This brief time she had been on the island revealed just how hopelessly susceptible she was to any overtures of interest or affection. She had been starved of attention for too long, that was the problem.

'I was not aware, no,' said Mrs Hopkins. 'But I have only been here three days.'

'And in those three short days, you seem to have formed a great many opinions about the running of this institution,' said Mr Massie. 'I would wish to remind you that we have some considerable experience in these matters. Perhaps you will do us the courtesy of gaining more experience yourself before you impose upon us your notions of reform.'

'I do apologise, sir,' said Mrs Hopkins, and now a sense of panic overtook her. What had she been thinking to speak out in such a manner, and to the Colonial Secretary, the highest official in the land? She was exhausted, that was the problem, she had barely any idea of what she was doing. She was simply stumbling along blindly and ignorantly, lurching from one crisis to the next. 'I apologise most sincerely if I have spoken out of order,' she continued desperately. She plucked from her sleeve her black lace-edged pocket handkerchief and dabbed at her eyes in the hope that they might take pity upon her. 'I was distressed by seeing the girl come up out of the pit and I've not yet recovered from the shock. And of course, this whole business with Mrs Dunstable, well, it has shaken me up terribly—'

But at this point the Colonial Secretary simply dismissed her with a wave of his hand, not even allowing her to finish her sentence.

Once out of the parlour, Mrs Hopkins hurried along the path back to the institution. It was time for the older girls' class, of course, for which she was entirely unprepared. But first she must see how all the sick girls were going, for even amidst Hannah's hysterics, she had been aware of a procession of bilious looking girls heading to the infirmary.

'Mrs Hopkins!' cried a voice. It was Catherine, breathless and distraught, grabbing hold of the gate post for support. 'Come quick! It's Josephine! She's sinking! She's sinking fast!'

Mrs Hopkins took off at once, picking up her skirts and running as fast as she could towards her quarters, with Catherine struggling to keep up with her.

The sight that greeted her as she flung open the door and entered her quarters caused her to drop to her knees.

'No!' she cried. 'No, dear God, please, no!'

For there on the bed lay Josephine, deathly pale, her eyes sunken. Standing in the middle of the room was Rosabella, weeping. The smell of urine hung heavily in the air, for poor Josephine had wet the bed.

'Oh, Mrs Hopkins,' cried Rosabella. 'We tried! We tried our best, truly we did!'

At that moment, Josephine emitted a strange gasping breath. Mrs Hopkins lurched to her feet and rushed to her side. She was alive, but barely so. Her skin was cold to the touch, and she appeared to be unconscious. Her skin was beginning to mottle just as Eugenie's had, her lips quite colourless, and her eyes—those dear mismatched eyes, now glassy and unseeing—those had been Eugenie's eyes in the hours before her death. A sob rose up from the very pit of her belly.

'Oh no, darling girl,' she cried. 'Stay with us! I cannot lose you a second time!'

She pulled the girl into a seated position, propping her limp body against her own. Taking a jug of water, she held it to the girl's parched lips, attempting to tip some into her mouth. Water spilled down the front of the girl's nightshirt, but this did not deter Mrs Hopkins. She stuck her fingers into Josephine's mouth, prising it open wider; then, pulling her head back by the hair, emptied the jug of water directly into her mouth. Immediately Josephine began to splutter and choke, the water spilling out of her mouth. She gasped for air, flapping her hands desperately, her eyes wide with panic.

'Come on, girl,' she cried. 'Drink! Drink, for God's sake.'

Rosabella and Catherine stared. Mrs Hopkins was being awfully rough with the sick girl.

'Maybe if you try a flannel soaked in water,' suggested Catherine. 'She could maybe suck on that. It might be easier for her.'

'Yes!' cried Mrs Hopkins, and she pulled out her handkerchief and dipped it in the jug of water and held it to Josephine's lips. And after a moment, Josephine made a little sucking sound, and then she sucked a little harder. Mrs Hopkins dipped the handkerchief in the water again and held it to the girl's lips. She gave a small tentative suck but then her head lolled back on her neck and she fell quite limp.

'Oh God! Oh dear God!' cried Mrs Hopkins. 'Save this little soul, I beseech you!'

She laid the girl back against the pillow and gazed at her in despair. Then she began to weep. Catherine and Rosabella looked on in dismay. They did not know what to do. All they knew was that they very much wanted to get out of there.

'Mrs Hopkins, we haven't had any dinner,' ventured Catherine. 'Could we go and have something to eat?'

'Yes! Yes, of course. You have been such good girls. I thank you, I thank you!' cried Mrs Hopkins. 'You must think my grief extreme,' she continued, as she followed the girls to the door. 'It's just that I had a daughter once just the same! The same eyes and everything!'

Again, the girls did not know what to say. Their School-Mistress seemed practically insane.

'Do you want us to come back after we've had something to eat?' asked Catherine, desperately hoping that she wouldn't.

'No. No, I will stay with her now. Tell the girls I am indisposed and unable to teach this afternoon. They are all in the infirmary anyway. Don't eat the meat! Whatever you do. It is rancid. I tried to tell them, but they would not heed me!'

And here she began to weep afresh, so Catherine and Rosabella took the opportunity to open the door.

'Oh, and girls!' Mrs Hopkins cried. 'They will try to tell you I am a witch. I implore you, don't listen to them. I am not a witch. It's just unfortunate the way I . . . the way things have—'

The minute they got out of there, Catherine and Rosabella began to run, so great was their relief at escaping. The dreadful convict barracks seemed a far happier alternative in that moment to those grim quarters of Mrs Hopkins, with the dying girl and the smell of urine and Mrs Hopkins acting so deranged. They stopped by the kitchen and spooned some treacle onto a couple of stale crusts left over from the dinner meal and then they retreated to their dormitory, where they found their friend Hannah lying wanly on her bed. The first thing she told them was that Mrs Hopkins was a witch: Mrs Dunstable had told Mrs Baird so, and then Mrs Dunstable was drowned because Mrs Hopkins had cast a spell on her.

When Catherine and Rosabella offered a feeble defence of their School-Mistress, Hannah pointed out that Mrs Hopkins had made the meat turn rancid, and all the girls were vomiting, and if Catherine and Rosabella didn't believe her then go and see if the cows will milk, because if they don't, then it is absolute proof for it is just like a witch to cast a spell on a milking cow.

And the second bit of news she had for her friends, not good news at all, was that Amelia Burke was out of solitary confinement.

Catherine and Rosabella did not tell anyone—neither Mrs Hopkins, nor Hannah, nor any of the other girls—of the shocking and terrifying episode they had experienced in Mrs Hopkins' quarters.

For most of the morning and afternoon that they had spent with her, Josephine had dozed fitfully, whimpering at times and refusing anything by way of water or nourishment. But suddenly, around two in the afternoon, she had opened her eyes and sat up quite straight in bed. Her eyes were fixed on something unseen at the end of her bed. 'Go away!' she had said, quite firmly and clearly. 'I do not like you. Take your doll with you! I don't want to play with it—it's ugly! Go away!'

She became increasingly agitated as she spoke and then she backed right up against the bars of the bedhead, drawing her knees up as if in defence.

'Josephine,' ventured Catherine, 'there is no one here but me and Rosabella.'

At which Josephine jerked her head towards her, seeing her for the first time. She clutched on to Catherine's arm, digging her nails into her skin. 'Tell the little girl to go away. I do not like her!'

'There's no little girl, Josephine. There's just me and Rosabella, here to look after you.'

But Josephine's gaze was again fixed upon this unseen presence at the end of the bed. 'No!' she cried furiously. 'I told you I don't want to play with your fecking doll! Go away! You too, you ugly old bats!'

And then she suddenly emitted a scream as she was thrown violently out of bed and onto the floor, like she had been seized by unseen hands. For a moment, she lay there in shock; Catherine and Rosabella stared at her in disbelief. What had just happened? Then, emitting a shriek of panic, Josephine scuttled on her hands and knees towards the door. Catherine and Rosabella ran to grab hold of her for she was now trying to force the door open. The older girls tried to prise her fingers from the doorknob, but the small child had a fierce grip and seemed determined to escape. And yet, as she pulled at the door, other forces seemed to pull it shut. Taking an arm each, Catherine and Rosabella dragged her back across the floor to the bed. She wrestled with them furiously all the way, tossing her little body about violently and yelling the most obscene epithets as she did so. Finally, they managed to heave her up on the bed and there she fell into convulsions, her thin body jerking violently, urine staining the sheets an ominous dark yellow. Then her little body fell limp, her eyes open and unseeing. Catherine and Rosabella stared at her in horror.

'We've killed her!' whispered Rosabella.

'We haven't killed her! She's breathing,' said Catherine. 'I think,' she added doubtfully.

They listened carefully. Was she breathing? If so, it was barely discernible. Her lips were grey-blue; she looked dead.

'What will we do?' cried Rosabella.

'I will run and get Mrs Hopkins,' said Catherine.

'Don't leave me here alone with her!'

'I will be quick! Try to clean her up. Oh, this is terrible!' And Catherine fled out the door to find Mrs Hopkins.

Left alone with the girl, Rosabella wiped the trail of saliva that had dripped down Josephine's chin and neck. She used the black lace-edged handkerchief that Mrs Hopkins had given her the day before when she had wept over her lost little brothers. She was sorry to soil it, but something had to be done, for the girl looked a wreck after her ordeal and Rosabella feared it might reflect badly on her and Catherine. She looked about to try to find some clean bedding. Mrs Hopkins had few possessions, but there was a chest with a heavy pot sitting upon it. Would it be too much of a liberty to look inside for a fresh sheet or a blanket? Better surely than Mrs Hopkins finding her in this state. So she lifted the pot and opened the chest and reached in; the very first thing she saw was the doll, Miss Minnie, and at once the lid of the chest slammed down upon her hand.

For a long moment, Rosabella stood uncertainly in the middle of the room, rubbing her hand ruefully and staring at the prone form of Josephine, lying in her own urine. They had likely killed her. They would probably get an awful telling-off, perhaps even a stint down the cells. And so Rosabella, who had tried so hard to do her best for Mrs Hopkins, commenced to weep.

Mrs Baird was the next person to be called by Mr Noyes and Mr Massie. She was quite prepared for the interview and knew what she wanted to tell them: this whole catastrophe had been brought about because Mrs Hopkins was a witch. Quite simply, she had cast Mr Crabback under her spell in order to become Matron. Mrs Dunstable had recognised this at once, and so was cast to her death from the steamer by means of Mrs Hopkins' sorcery. If this wasn't sufficient proof, Mrs Hopkins had offered to say a prayer for Mrs Dunstable at muster, and yet was *unable to complete any prayers*, and had forced the girls, quite against their will, to sing an obscene song instead, with the lewdest lyrics imaginable that would curl your hair if you heard them. Also, she had turned the meat rancid and stopped the cows from producing any milk. Oh, and this might be hearsay, but there was talk that on the night of Mrs Hopkins' arrival at the institution, she had circled several times over the island on her broomstick; one of the girls swore black and blue that she had seen this with her own eyes. Yes, certainly the inmates were known to tell tales, but this information came from some of the more trustworthy girls (Hannah Eddington), who had never been known to tell a lie.

Mrs Baird's rambling testimony and the excitable manner in which she delivered it caused Mr Noyes and Mr Massie to discount much of what she said. In fact, they were just about to terminate the interview altogether when Mrs Baird remembered another point which had slipped her mind.

'Oh, and when poor Mrs Dunstable came to Mrs Hopkins to ask forgiveness for speaking out of turn, Mrs Hopkins punched her smack in the face. Can you believe it? In front of all the little girls in the schoolroom.'

This information gave Mr Noyes pause. He had earlier that morning visited the dead house in Circular Quay to view the corpse. It was true that she sported a black eye, a real bruiser such as he had seen on those who had died in street brawls or boxing rings.

'How do you know this?' he asked.

'Bridget Murphy told me only this morning. She was terribly upset about it for she witnessed the whole thing.'

So Bridget Murphy, much to her surprise, was called as the next witness. She sat upright and defiant in her chair, for she well remembered the stern admonishment Mr Noyes had given her widowed father in court. If he had spent less time in hotels drunkenly reciting 'The Song of the Shirt', intoned Mr Noyes from the bench, and more time instead looking after his daughter, she would not have been found wandering the streets at night in the company of other wayward youngsters, stealing the lead off people's rooftops. Mr Murphy pled tearfully for another chance, for his girl was all he had in the world since her mother took off. His entreaty was dismissed by Mr Noyes for this was Bridget's third appearance on larceny charges in the Water Police Courts, and she was only eight years of age at the time. The little girl was duly packed off to Biloela.

'What do you know of Mrs Hopkins punching Mrs Dunstable?' asked Mr Noyes of the little girl.

'What? Nothing. Who told you that?'

'Mrs Baird told us you witnessed Mrs Hopkins punching Mrs Dunstable. Is that so?'

'Good grief, the lies that woman tells!'

'Are you saying that you didn't see this?'

'I am indeed. And I'll tell you something else for free: Mrs Baird has a regular down on Mrs Hopkins and tells us all she's a witch and everything. She wants her given the boot because she wants to be Matron, that's the God's honest truth of the matter. And I'll tell you this also, if Mrs Hopkins gets given the boot, we won't stand for it. Not for one minute. We will burn the place to the ground, for Mrs Hopkins is the only one who has ever been the slightest bit kind to us. May God strike me stiff if I tell a lie.'

'That is quite enough of that sort of talk, young lady,' said Mr Noyes, and that was the end of Bridget's interview.

Miss Foy was called in next. She did not impress the two gentlemen, for she kept changing her mind about things. Yes, she believed that Mrs Hopkins had cast a spell and turned the meat rancid, but then again the meat was often not as fresh as it could be; on various occasions in her experience, they had had to give it to the pigs and the girls had had to fill up as best they could on bread and boiled turnips. She knew nothing about Mrs Dunstable performing 'Ta-ra-ra-boom-de-ay' for the benefit of the sailors on the *Blanche*, although, yes, the Assistant Matrons were on quite cordial terms with some of the officers of the ship and had occasionally spoken humorously with them at the wharf if they were venturing into town for the evening. As for Mrs Dunstable being drunk on the morning of her departure, well, yes, that was possible for she had witnessed Mrs Dunstable swigging from a bottle, although Miss Foy could not say for sure what was in the bottle, for as far as she knew, Mrs Dunstable was a teetotaller, although she had certainly smelt of liquor on that occasion and seemed unsteady on her feet. As for Mrs Hopkins, she had to admit that she would make a very good Matron, in spite of the possibility of her being a sorceress, for she seemed to have great control over the girls and had them all on their knees saying their prayers last night, just as meek and docile as you like.

Meanwhile, as all these interviews were being conducted, Mr Crabback paced the path that led from his house to the institution. He had been quite startled to see Bridget Murphy being led in; what on earth did she have to do with anything? Not much apparently, for she came out very shortly afterwards, looking well pleased with herself.

'They're a couple of old gudgeons, Crabapple,' she told him cheerfully. 'Don't take any shite from them.' And then she skipped gaily back into the institution, eager to convey to Amelia and the rest of them the substance of her interview.

Mr Crabback watched her go, stroking his side-whiskers thoughtfully. It was timely advice from the young girl; here he had been bowing and scraping and apologising, and why should he? What had he to apologise for? He had done nothing wrong. He was entirely within his rights to dismiss Mrs Dunstable, and the fact that she had then thrown herself off the steamer, while unfortunate certainly, was really none of his concern. Furthermore, he would take this opportunity to make it plain just how impossible it was to improve the lot of these impoverished waifs without some financial support from the Governors. He was quite capable, he knew, of moving an audience to tears with his oratory, and as he paced impatiently while Miss Foy had her interview, he began to rehearse what he might say.

On entering the room, Mr Crabback began his declamation straight away. 'They are the hardest, most depraved and wanton vagabonds you could ever chance to meet, rendered that way by a life cast out upon the streets, yet last night I witnessed something of a miracle; these same girls, their heads bowed in prayer as they knelt upon the cold flagstones of this bleak prison in which they have been incarcerated for the entirety of their girlhood. So moving was the sight that I was reminded of that marvellous poem: *HUSH! 'tis a holy hour—the quiet room Seems like a temple, while yon soft lamp sheds A faint and starry radiance, through the gloom—'*

'That's quite enough of that, thank you, Mr Crabback,' said Mr Massie, for he felt he ought to nip this sort of carry-on in the bud. 'You are here to explain the reasons for Mrs Dunstable's abrupt dismissal, not to wax poetical upon us.'

And so ensued more questions, and from Mr Crabback, a repeat of Mrs Dunstable's horrifying and wholly unfounded allegations at muster; her ongoing drunkenness ('often quite helpless and incapable by lunchtime'); her lifting her skirts for a rendition of 'Ta-ra-ra-boom-de-ay' in front of the entire assembly of officers and sailors of the *Blanche* ('Go down and talk to them, by all means; I have the information on good authority'); her notorious short temper, as evidenced by her striking his little dog Tippet for no reason whatsoever; and on top of all this, her bizarre notion that Mrs Hopkins was a witch, when a more perfect example of female piety could scarcely be imagined.

'When will your wife be returning to fill her position as Matron?' enquired Mr Massie, gazing at the very letter Mrs Hopkins had penned the evening before.

'Shortly. Very shortly. There have been problems—you may well be aware of them—at the Haven of Hope.'

Mr Noyes was certainly aware of them, if the Colonial Secretary was not. The Haven of Hope, though ostensibly a lying-in home for fallen and destitute women, had been of recent times discreetly offering its services in the back pages of certain newspapers for 'medical surgery and midwifery, guaranteed results in all cases'. Recently, Elizabeth Andrews, a young woman from up in the country somewhere, had come to the Haven seeking these 'guaranteed results' and was dead within the week of septic peritonitis. The newspapers claimed that the lass had died as a result of a 'certain event'. Mrs Crabback declared the girl had simply suffered a miscarriage and that they had done all they could to save her. The jury delivered an open verdict and yet a cloud still hung over the place. The advertisements continued in the newspapers.

It was for this reason that Mr Noyes did not regard the Crabbacks entirely favourably; in fact, he had been surprised and dismayed that Mr Massie had chosen to appoint them as the new Superintendent and Matron of such a troubled place as Biloela. And yet, he considered, perhaps it was in one way a good thing, for installed upon the island, Mrs Crabback would at least be forced to discontinue her sideline as an abortionist.

'She is engaged in the task of securing a new Midwife, of course, to take her place,' continued Mr Crabback. 'Finding one with the necessary skills and qualifications is proving more difficult than she anticipated.'

Mr Noyes' heart sunk at this news; the necessary skills and qualifications no doubt included the use of the flushing curette, at sixteen shillings a go.

'It is made quite clear in the regulations, Mr Crabback, that any staffing decisions are to be made by myself,' said Mr Massie. 'In future, you will write to me to advise me of any problems and allow me to take the necessary course of action. That way we might avoid some of the bad press we will no doubt be in for in the *Evening News*.'

'Yes, sir,' said Mr Crabback. The *Evening News*! That scandal rag. The same newspaper that had covered every sordid detail of the Elizabeth Andrews trial. The very newspaper that had cast doubt on Mr Crabback's book-keeping and spread the story about the Crabbacks making off with the fine-quality tea and biscuits intended for the women. (It had only been a tin or two and most of them were broken.) The same newspaper that had published an unflattering caricature of Mr Crabback as a fat koala in a gum tree stuffing himself with biscuits. What a feast they would make of this story! A copy was delivered daily on the four o'clock steamer; it was imperative that he get to it before anyone else did.

'In the meantime, I will go along with your suggestion of Mrs Baird taking on the role of House Matron, although she seems a very strange woman,' said Mr Massie. 'But certainly, the cost-cutting measures are welcome. And Mrs Hopkins may stand in as Acting Matron until your wife returns; I am assuming that is imminent?'

'Yes, of course, undoubtedly. I'm sure my wife will present herself in the next few days. As I say, it is only the difficulty she has had in securing a new—'

But as was his way, Mr Massie dismissed him with a wave of his hand before he could complete his sentence.

As Mr Noyes and Mr Massie were making their way down to the wharf, their preliminary investigation complete, Amelia Burke came tearing down the hill after them.

'Mr Noyes, Mr Noyes!' she called out, and the two men stopped and looked back.

'Good grief,' said the Colonial Secretary. 'What on earth does she want?'

'You go ahead,' said Mr Noyes, for he knew that Mr Massie was anxious not to miss the four o'clock steamer which was ploughing towards the island, billowing smoke. The Colonial Secretary had mentioned several times between interrogations (and even during interrogations, when he felt Mr Noyes' questioning was dragging on) that he was anxious to be at the Australian Club, ensconced in a leather armchair and enjoying a whisky, by half past four. In truth, Mr Massie felt that the Police Magistrate was making rather a meal of it all, when it seemed perfectly obvious that the woman Dunstable was drunk or unhinged or both and had plainly committed suicide by jumping off the steamer. So Mr Massie proceeded to the wharf, waving his umbrella furiously at the onslaught of screaming seagulls, while Mr Noyes waited for Amelia to catch up with him.

'What are you doing outside the school gate?' he asked with an affectation of sternness, for in truth he had a soft spot for Amelia Burke.

She had presented in his court several times over the years, always memorably, once giving an impassioned speech in her own defence after wilfully and maliciously attempting to burn the school down. She had turned to the jury and told her life story, from being abandoned as a newborn in the Ladies Waiting Room at Redfern Railway Station to the long and loveless years at Biloela. 'You may judge me harshly for my actions, gentlemen, but I beg of you to bear in mind that I have never known the deep abiding love of a mother, nor have I had any guiding moral influence in my life. My entire life has been spent behind the cold stone walls of a prison. My only crime? Being abandoned by my own mother. Many nights, too many to count, I have wept bitter tears with no gentle voice to comfort me. I often ask myself, what hope is there for me in this life? Will no one give me a chance to better myself?'

This had been the general gist of her statement, as embellished by the newspapers, along with the comment that her speech had reduced several jury members to tears. Mr Noyes, who had already been impressed by her deft cross-examination of the witnesses, was himself profoundly moved by the girl. The jury had no choice but to find her guilty, albeit of the lesser crime of damaging government property; however, the foreman appealed to Mr Noyes, on behalf of the jury, that mercy be shown in her sentencing. He even went so far as to offer Amelia a situation in his own home once she had served her time in gaol. Nothing had come of this, however; it seemed that the foreman or perhaps the foreman's wife had begun to entertain doubts as to the wisdom of inviting this young arsonist, too clever for her own good, into the peaceful sanctum of their family home. Thus, upon her release after a month of picking oakum at Darlinghurst Gaol, Amelia was sent straight back to Biloela.

Now, as she caught up with him, a little flushed in the cheeks from running, she seemed quite recovered from her spell down in the dark cell. She had a clean dress on and had arranged her tangled mane of curls with a pretty green ribbon which brought out the colour of her eyes.

'I wanted to ask you, sir, if you could find me a situation. In service. Remember in court that day when the juryman offered me a job? And you said how I would benefit from getting out of this place and earning a living?'

'But Amelia, you have just tipped a slop pail over the Superintendent. That does not indicate to me that you have gained control of your temper, as you promised me you would.'

'It was just a little bit of wee on his trousers,' said Amelia.

'Do you not like Mr Crabback?'

'I think the world of him,' said the girl, rolling her eyes. 'He just stuck me down the cells for four days on bread and water! And then he goes and expects me to apologise. He is as bad as the last one.'

'I see. And tell me, what is your opinion of this Mrs Hopkins?' asked Mr Noyes, for he was curious as to what this observant girl made of the Acting Matron.

'Oh, she is wonderful. No, I mean it this time. We love her to bits. She is the kindest, sweetest, gentlest soul you ever met in your entire life,' said Amelia.

'You are not fearful that she is a witch come to eat you?' teased Mr Noyes. He was enjoying their chat and wanted to engage the girl a little longer.

'Oh, that is stuff and nonsense,' said Amelia, slapping him lightly on the arm. 'Surely you don't believe it, a fine brainy fellow such as yourself? Betty Four-Eyes has had some kind of conniption, that's all, and Dunnekin before her.'

He smiled, although he knew he shouldn't indulge that sort of talk about the Assistant Matrons. There was something about the lass, with her big green eyes and her missing tooth, that appealed to him. Several of the other girls came running down the hill to join them. Mr Noyes felt a twinge of irritation; he had rather hoped to have Amelia to himself. Besides, weren't they all supposed to be confined to the grounds of the institution, for God's sake?

'What are you two gasbagging about then?' asked Annie Laughton, slinging an arm around Amelia's neck.

'Noysy asked me what I thought of Mrs Hopkins.'

'Mrs Hopkins? Oh, she is lovely,' said Annie.

'Though she looks like a fright, especially if you catch her in the dark,' added Eliza, who had joined them along with the others.

'She can't help what she looks like, any more than you can,' Amelia retorted, poking her friend in the ribs. 'At least she's not a ginger.'

'She should do something different with her hair, that's all I meant. Just try and look less like a vampire bat.'

'You know what, Mr Noyes?' said Sarah, tugging at his jacket to get his attention. 'Mrs Hopkins said if we say our prayers and do our chores and stuff, she's going to organise a special day where all our mothers and fathers and brothers and sisters come to visit us. And we'll have cakes and play rounders and hoops and have a concert and everything!'

'Is that so?' And here Mr Noyes' expression began to grow grave.

'Yes, but only if we behave ourselves. We have to be on our very best behaviour, to show Mr Crabback and Mr Massie that we deserve such a privilege.'

'But some of us don't have a mother or a brother or a sister,' said Amelia crossly, punching Eliza on the arm. 'Anyway, we weren't talking about that, we were discussing me getting a situation. So what about it, Noysy? Will you find me one? Please?'

'Me too! Me too!' cried the other girls. 'Will you, Mr Noyes? Please!'

'I'm very good at laundry. Just ask Miss Foy!'

'I'm a better ironer than she is. She always leaves black marks on everything.'

'You can talk! You scorched Mrs Dunstable's blouse!'

'Also, I'm very good at looking after children, Mr Noyes. I don't hit them or nothing, not unless I have to.'

'I can sew good,' offered young Bridget. 'Mrs Baird said my apron was better than anyone's.'

'Now you are just telling fibs, Bridget Murphy,' said Sarah. 'You did the whole thing with the wrong-coloured cotton and had to pull it all out and start again, and Jesus Christ, did you raise a stink about it!'

'I have a strong urge to punch your bloody head in, Sarah Gilbert,' said Bridget, clenching her little fists.

'I'd like to see you try,' laughed Sarah.

This only enraged Bridget further, and she was just winding back her arm in preparation for the haymaker her father had assiduously coached her in when Amelia grabbed her arm and stopped her.

'Calm yourself, Bridget Murphy!' she said. 'Is Noysy ever going to find you a position if you're forever walloping folk? I should say not! He needs us all to control our tempers, especially me.' And here she turned and smiled sweetly at the magistrate. 'Isn't that right, Mr Noyes?'

'It is, Amelia. Well said,' said Mr Noyes. 'And I'm sorry to say, Bridget, that you are too young for a situation. You must be at least twelve years of age before we can send you out to service. And how old are you now?'

'Nine. Almost ten.'

'Two more years, and I promise you, I will look into it. As for the rest of you, if we were fortunate enough to find you situations, you must realise they would be as far removed from Sydney as possible. You will be sent out into the country, away from all those bad influences that have caused you to be sent here in the first place.'

'You can send me to Timbuktu, I don't care, I just want to get out of this rathole, and the sooner the better,' said Amelia.

And at this point her friend Annie began to fret. 'But if you go, what will become of me?' she lamented.

'You can come too, Annie! Could you find a situation for the two of us?' asked Amelia, turning back to Mr Noyes. 'She is a good little laundress, that one, and I'm not bad either.'

'I very much doubt that that would be possible,' said Mr Noyes, for he knew well the stories about Amelia and Annie and their insistence on sharing a bed. But seeing Annie's eyes fill with tears, he added, 'Initially, at least. Let us worry about the fine details later. In the meantime, Amelia, you must demonstrate to me that you can behave yourself for at least three months before I could even begin to contemplate sending you out to service.'

'Three months!' cried Amelia, and she stamped her foot in a petulant manner. 'Why not say three years and have done with it? And you sit there in court and wonder why I want to burn this place down, by Jesus! I swear to God, I will too if you let me rot here any longer.'

'Now, now, that's exactly the sort of behaviour I'm talking about. You must curb this temper of yours, Amelia. No more lashing out and tipping slop pails over people and trying to strangle School-Mistresses with their own neckties. And stay away from safety matches. Do you promise me that?'

'All right, all right,' conceded Amelia, folding her arms somewhat sulkily.

'And promise me you haven't hidden any more axes up in the rafters.'

A sly grin crept over Amelia's face. In court, it had been revealed that she had gone at the dormitory door with an axe before giving up and setting fire to it. An axe was a useful piece of equipment to stow away.

'Promise me,' said Mr Noyes sternly.

'Promise you what?'

'That you haven't got an axe tucked up in the rafters.'

'Oh, for God's sake, how would I have had the chance? I've been stuck down a hole for a week!'

At this point, the four o' clock steamer sounded its warning horn.

Mr Noyes glanced towards it. 'I must go now, or I will miss my ferry,' he said. He was rather sorry to leave on this note, with Amelia annoyed with him. 'Be good,' he said to her, 'and I will see what I can do about a situation for you.' He patted her lightly on the shoulder.

She shook his hand off crossly and turned her back on him.

Somewhat abashed at receiving this brush-off, he bid the other girls goodbye and set off down to the wharf.

'Oh, Mr Noyes!' called Amelia after he had walked some little distance. He stopped and turned around, whereupon she hurtled into his arms and kissed him full on the lips. 'Thank you, Mr Noyes,' she whispered, her breath soft upon his cheek.

The girls whooped appreciatively. Mr Noyes reddened. It was a rare treat to have a young girl pressing her firm little breasts against him. His hands, quite unconsciously, found their way to her waist and were in danger of wandering further. She kissed him again, longer this time, and only then did he realise that Amelia's hands were doing some wandering of their own. He backed out of her embrace sharply, patting down his pockets as he did so.

'What's the matter? Do you not like me kissing you?' asked Amelia, gazing at him with her big green eyes.

'Hand it over.'

'Hand what over?'

'You know very well. And I am surprised at you, Amelia, for trying it on, when I had just assured you that I would find you a situation.'

'I'm sorry, I couldn't help myself. You're a handsome bastard after all.'

And, quite cheerfully, she produced from her sleeve a small roll of bills which she had just plucked from his trouser pocket.

'And the watch.'

'What watch?'

'Don't toy with me, Amelia, I warn you—'

'Why? What will you do to me?'

'I have no time for this nonsense, Amelia.' The steamer sounded its horn a second time. 'Give it back at once, I tell you!'

With a great show of reluctance, she dug into her pocket and handed him back his fine gold watch. 'There was no need to fuss, I would have given it back to you. I was just practising my dipping skills, that's all. And let's face it , you enjoyed the smooching.'

The other girls chortled merrily.

Mr Noyes' face darkened. He felt he had been humiliated, deliberately; the girl had detected his fondness for her and played upon his weakness. 'You make a grave mistake, I warn you, Amelia, if you take me for a fool,' he said. 'I can lock you up quite happily for a long stretch if I choose to, and by golly, I will if you push me. And that means the lot of you!' He cast his arm out towards the rest of the girls. 'In solitary confinement at Darlinghurst Gaol. How would you like that? Would you find that so amusing? '

The girls turned mute and cast their eyes downward. Bridget snorted as she tried to stifle a giggle and got herself slapped by Eliza. Even Amelia looked contrite, alarmed at the shift in Mr Noyes' mood.

'I'm sorry, Mr Noyes, I just did it as a lark,' she said. 'I'll try to be good from now on, I promise you.'

'That's what you always say, Amelia.'

'I know I do but I mean it this time. I swear! You've always been good to me, Mr Noyes. I never meant to upset you, not for a minute. I'm a damned fool and I could kick myself. I always mess things up, all the time. What was that thing you said to me in court once?'

'Which time?'

'The last time. After I tried to burn the place down.'

'Was it about learning to curb your impulses?'

'Yes, that. That's what I need. I need to curb my bloody impulses.' Her eyes now were welling with tears.

He could hardly bear it. 'There, there, wipe your tears now, girl. I'll accept your apology, and we will forget the incident, and you will try harder to be a good girl from now on, as you promised.'

'On my mother's grave, sir!'

Some of her friends smirked at this: they knew this was her little joke which she would cackle about later in the dormitory ('I don't have a fecking mother, you stupid idiot!'). But on this occasion, she looked so sorry and forlorn that they gazed at her uncertainly.

'Prove to me you are trustworthy, and I will find you a situation,' said Mr Noyes gently. He tried patting her on the shoulder again, and this time she allowed it. She even permitted him to stroke her wild curls, just for a moment. He hoped it would be perceived as a gesture of comfort and not in any way lustful or predatory.

'You've gone and missed your ferry, Mr Noyes,' said Eliza. He glanced down at the wharf. The gangplank had been pulled up and the *Emu* was steaming away.

'I will wait for the next one,' said Mr Noyes. If only it were possible that Amelia could wait with him, sitting on his lap perhaps, playing with the buttons of his shirt, poking her naughty little fingers where they oughtn't be. How gladly he would offer up all the contents of his pockets for such simple, wondrous pleasure as that!

'Back inside now, all of you!' he barked, for he felt he needed to reassert his authority. 'At once! You are out of bounds. And make sure the padlock of the gate is locked behind you.'

The girls headed back up the hill, arm in arm. Now they were out of Mr Noyes' earshot, they could laugh and chatter freely amongst themselves.

'Oh, look!' said Amelia, producing from the sleeve of her dress a gold coin and gazing at it in wonderment. 'A nice little sovereign! Now where did that come from?' The girls squealed in delight. 'Why, I think it might belong to Mr Noyes. Do you know, I truly meant to give it back to him, but when he kept jawing on and on about how I must curb my temper, it somehow slipped my mind.'

Noticing that her friend Annie still looked troubled, she pressed the sovereign into her palm and gave her a kiss.

'Don't be jealous, Annie Laughton,' she said. 'I only smooched him for a lark.'

Mr Noyes did not really mind that he had missed the steamer for he felt he might appreciate a moment of quiet to sit on the wharf and watch the river boats go by. In truth, the incident with Amelia had completely undone him. He needed to compose himself, for he was well aware that his feelings for her were entirely inappropriate.

'She's a colt,' he said to himself out loud. 'A wild little colt who cannot be broken.'

So many times Amelia had absconded from the school, singing lewd uproarious songs all the way back to Biloela in the Water Police boat; so many times she had stood before him in the docks pleading her innocence and then grinning at him and winking if he showed her any lenience. Nothing, it seemed, could tame this extraordinary girl.

'Mr Noyes! Mr Noyes!'

He turned instantly in the hope that it was Amelia coming after him again, but instead it was Mrs Hopkins hitching her skirts up as she ran, revealing her thin grey-stockinged calves.

'Oh, Mr Noyes,' she cried as she reached him. 'Would you summon a Doctor for me as a matter of urgency? I have a child who is not well, not well at all!'

'From the meat?

'What?'

'Did she eat the spoiled meat?'

'No, no! It is nothing to do with the meat! Just fetch me a Doctor, I beg of you!'

'I can do nothing till the next ferry comes—'

'Surely, it will arrive at any moment?'

'It departed not five minutes ago.'

'Then when is the next ferry due?'

He pulled out his watch and gazed at it solemnly. 'Another fifty-five minutes. If it is on time. Which experience has taught me is unlikely.'

And here Mrs Hopkins let out a wail of fury and despair. Mr Noyes stared at her in alarm. Then she turned and bolted up the hill towards the institution.

'Mrs Hopkins!' called Mr Noyes, but she paid no heed. He set off after her. 'Mrs Hopkins, I say! I will send a Doctor as soon as I land in Sydney. In the meantime, let me see the girl—'

'What good would that do?'

'I may be able to assist.'

'Oh, all right, if you must!' She took off again up the hill, waving her arms furiously at the onslaught of nesting seagulls impeding her path.

Mr Noyes hurried after her. Her imperious manner galled him: impudence was so much more appealing when it came from a saucy sixteen-year-old with a missing tooth.

As soon as he laid eyes upon the girl, pale and sunken eyed, Mr Noyes feared the worst. He touched her forehead and took her pulse then he turned to Mrs Hopkins. 'I'm afraid she is not long for this world. We must get her mother here at once.'

'She has no mother,' said Mrs Hopkins. 'The poor child was found wrapped in a bit of brown paper at Redfern Railway Station.'

'Oh no, you are quite mistaken. You are thinking of Amelia Burke. This girl's mother is the notorious prostitute Bessie Briars.'

Mrs Hopkins' mouth tightened.

'I've known this one since she was a babe in arms,' Mr Noyes continued. 'Bessie always drags her into court with her in the hope it will encourage us to go soft on her. You should see the theatrics they put on, the pair of them.'

'In that case, with respect, sir, perhaps it is best that we do not notify her,' said Mrs Hopkins. The idea of the notorious prostitute tending the deathbed of this poor neglected angel filled her with a simmering resentment.

'Why, Mrs Hopkins, I'm surprised at you. Surely it's the least we can do for a dying child.'

'Of course,' said Mrs Hopkins, flushing violently. 'My only concern was that her presence might perhaps agitate the child, and hasten her—' But she could not bring herself to utter the word.

'I doubt the child will be much aware of her, though it's possible she may derive some comfort from her presence. No, I am thinking mainly of the child's mother; she has been petitioning me almost daily for the girl's release. The least I can do is allow her to keep vigil by her death bed.'

But that is what I am doing—I am keeping vigil! Mrs Hopkins thought angrily, though she dared not say it aloud. Instead, she went to her chest, removing the pot that sat atop it, and pulled out the battered cloth doll. This she placed under the sheets, next to the girl.

'Rest, Josephine, rest,' she said softly, stroking the girl's brow. 'You must rest in order to get well again. Then we will play and sing and read stories . . . Oh, I cannot lose her, Mr Noyes—not again, not again! Once was enough! I could not bear it a second time!'

Mr Noyes stood by, lowering his head a little in a manner he hoped looked sympathetic. *Once was enough?* What on earth was this woman going on about? It seemed to him she might be losing her marbles.

'Pray—we must pray for her!' cried Mrs Hopkins. Then she dropped to her knees and gestured furiously that Mr Noyes do the same.

He lowered himself to his knees beside her and closed his eyes. Her prayer was rambling and repetitious: chiefly she seemed to be begging the Lord for mercy and asking for His forgiveness. It was as if the Lord needed these requests drummed into him over and over again, thought Mr Noyes wearily. It was as if the Lord were slow on the uptake.

Opening his eyes, he surveyed the sick child. Personally, he found her an unappealing little ragamuffin. He had once had to have her removed from the court when she unleashed the foulest stream of vitriol imaginable, just because he'd packed her mother off to gaol for three months. Three months! She was fortunate not to get six. The girl was dragged out, kicking and spitting and flailing about; meanwhile Bessie wept crocodile tears and begged Mr Noyes for mercy. It was all a big show, of course, devised by the pair to garner sympathy.

'The girls told me you are planning a visiting day for mothers and families,' ventured Mr Noyes, once she had finally finished exhorting the Lord for mercy and they had both clambered to their feet. 'And I am not entirely unsympathetic to what you are endeavouring to do. But may I take the liberty of cautioning you in the strongest possible terms against taking this action?'

'You may caution me all you wish,' said Mrs Hopkins. 'But I would like to hear a valid reason.'

'Very well. I will give you valid reason. The parents of these girls are thoroughly irredeemable, and any contact with them only makes the girls restless and unmanageable. The parents get into their ear, you see, thinking of the income the girls might provide for them. And the girls, mistaking their parents' interest for genuine love and concern, agitate to be released. If we give in to their pleas and let them go home, we soon find that they are drinking beer and wearing jewellery and hanging about in dancing saloons. Come Monday morning, they're standing before me in the dock—'

Knock-knock! A furtive rapping upon the door. Mrs Hopkins swept across the room to open it. There she found Mr Crabback, all red in the face and sweating. He thrust a copy of the *Evening Star* at her.

'Read it. I have mislaid my spectacles. Read it for me at once, would you?'

The headline *'Mysterious Drowning of Matron at Biloela'* was all Mrs Hopkins had time to glimpse before Mr Noyes came up behind her.

Mr Crabback withdrew the newspaper at once, tucking it behind his back.

'Good evening, Mr Crabback,' said Mr Noyes. 'What is that you say about the *Evening Star*?'

'Just an article about Mrs Dunstable, that's all. I thought Mrs Hopkins might be interested in reading.'

'I am not the slightest bit interested in what the *Evening Star* has to say,' said Mrs Hopkins in a firm voice.

'Quite right. It is a gutter-rag,' said Mr Noyes. 'Nevertheless, they are often able to get their hands on the most interesting titbits of information. May I see?' And here he reached out for the newspaper, which Mr Crabback reluctantly handed over.

Mysterious Drowning of Matron at Biloela

'Biloela', that Paradise of Port Jackson, home to as fine a collection of female vagabondage as you could ever hope never to meet, finds itself in the news once again. This time in the mysterious passing of House Matron Mrs Ernestine Dunstable, whose body was found, quite naked, in the early hours of this morning, washed up on the shores of that infamous island from which, hours earlier, she had vainly attempted to escape. The body was conveyed to the dead house at Circular Quay; it is believed to have been in the water for twelve hours or more. Although there were some marks of violence upon the body, it presented the usual appearance of death having resulted from suffocation by drowning.

It is believed that Mrs Dunstable leapt from the steamer, having been summarily discharged from her duties by the new Superintendent, Mr Charles Crabback, formerly of the Haven of Hope for Fallen Women, who has himself presented within these pages on other matters. The circumstances behind the House Matron's dismissal remain mysterious. However, it is understood that a note was found amongst her few belongings, the contents of which hinted at unnatural practices, including sorcery, taking hold at the

> institution under the auspices of a new staff member whom the Superintendent holds in high regard. The matter is being investigated by Mr Henry Noyes, Esq., Water Police Magistrate, who is himself known for his great interest in the welfare of certain young inmates of the institution.

Mr Noyes read all this in silence. When he had finished, he made a sort of 'harrumph' noise, and folded the newspaper briskly under his arm. 'I will be off then,' he said. 'I have much to do back in the city.'

'I too have a great much to do,' said Mr Crabback, glaring at his newspaper, now nestled in the crook of Mr Noyes' arm. In truth, he was somewhat rattled at having found Mrs Hopkins to be entertaining the Magistrate alone in her quarters. He had assumed Mr Noyes had departed with Mr Massie on the four o'clock steamer—instead here he was hanging about idly, enjoying the company of Mrs Hopkins!

'Are you—will you do what I asked you to do?' asked Mrs Hopkins of the Police Magistrate.

For a moment, Mr Noyes looked at her blankly. What was it again that Mrs Hopkins had asked him to do? Ah yes, the Doctor. And Bessie, of course; he needed to pop around to Bessie's. 'Yes, yes, without delay; as soon as I get back to Sydney,' replied Mr Noyes.

'Thank you,' said Mrs Hopkins. And she shut the door somewhat abruptly on the pair of them.

The two men looked at each other.

'I see she has you doing errands,' said Mr Crabback, his voice shaking. 'I advise you to take caution. She seems the very model of Christian piety but I believe she may be a hysteric.'

'Not a witch, then?'

'That I could not say. Certainly I believe that she is capable of—' and here he paused a moment '—of casting spells upon people.'

'Mr Crabback, I have but one word of advice for you,' said Mr Noyes, not unkindly, for he could see that Mr Crabback had formed an unwholesome interest in the School-Mistress. 'Get your wife back here as soon as possible.' And he tipped his hat and sauntered off down the hill, leaving Mr Crabback to stand there, brimming with resentment.

'That is rich, coming from you!' he cried out.

'Oh yes? And what do you mean by that?' said Mr Noyes, turning.

'I saw what I saw,' said Mr Crabback. A small smile played upon his lips.

Having closed the door upon the two gentlemen, Mrs Hopkins was surprised to see that Miss Minnie had been tossed clear across the room. Stooping to pick the doll up, she heard a feeble, muttering sound. Josephine was struggling to sit up.

'Josephine!' cried Mrs Hopkins, hurrying to help her. 'Are you feeling better?'

'Get that thing away from me!' said Josephine.

'Why, Josephine, Miss Minnie has been watching over you while you lay sick. She has been your little nurse. Haven't you, Miss Minnie?'

Then she adopted her 'Miss Minnie' voice. 'Yes, I have, Mrs Hopkins—'

At which Josephine let out such a full-throated scream that Mrs Hopkins immediately hastened to her chest and shoved Miss Minnie back in it, placing the heavy pot on top. She had vainly hoped that the girl might derive some comfort from the doll, just as her daughter had. Eugenie had crossed into the hereafter with one little hand clutching tightly onto Miss Minnie's woollen hair, as if desperate not to leave her behind; in fact, Mrs Hopkins had had to cut away some wool in order to release the doll from Eugenie's rigor mortis grip. She had wondered if she ought not bury Miss Minnie with Eugenie, if the girl had sought such comfort from the doll, but in her selfishness, she had found that she could not bring herself to do it.

But now she wondered if she had not made a grave mistake. In the first week or so after Eugenie's death, she was stricken with the fear that Eugenie might suddenly awaken in her dank, dark coffin and feel about for her beloved doll. Unable to find her, she would fret and cry for her mother and, her mother not responding, would commence to scream and beat upon the lid of her coffin till her little fists bled and she expired all over again from exhaustion and, eventually, asphyxiation. Oh, it was too unbearable to contemplate.

'There, there—she is gone now, Josephine,' said Mrs Hopkins. She felt the child's forehead; it seemed cooler. Perhaps the fever had at last broken. 'Are you hungry?'

'A bit.'

'That is wonderful news! What do you feel like eating?'

Some rancid mutton perhaps? Some elderly turnips, boiled and cold? There was no seed cake left, nothing at all to entice an invalid. If only she could offer the child a nourishing soup, such as Mr Crabback's pea and bacon hock soup which Mrs Hopkins had found so restorative the evening before. That was impossible, of course, for any request for pea soup would warrant a visit to Mr Crabback's quarters, and the less she had to do with him the better.

So she made the girl a cup of sweet tea, and shredded some stale bread and soaked it in what little milk she had left in her jug, and there stirred in a spoonful of sugar. It was the best she could do for the moment. But Josephine sat up and sipped her hot tea and sucked the sweet milk from the bread scraps with evident enjoyment.

'Why, I swear you are looking better every moment,' said Mrs Hopkins, for the roses were returning to the girl's cheeks. 'Oh, let us say a prayer of thanks for your recovery!'

'Let us not,' said Josephine, in that blunt way of hers.

And with that, a sudden thought struck Mrs Hopkins, and she rose at once from the kneeling position she had assumed. 'I will be back in a minute,' she said hoarsely.

'No!' cried the girl. 'Don't leave me. Don't leave me alone!'

'I will not be long.'

'There's bad people! Two bad ladies! They don't like me!'

Mrs Hopkins stared at the girl. Who could she possibly be referring to? The paupers?

'I will be very quick. No one can hurt you. But I must do what I have to do.'

And she hurried out of her quarters, not even stopping to put on her ulster. Once outside, she commenced running as fast as she could down to the wharf, not caring one whit about the angry seagulls rushing out of their nests, beaks wide open and beating their wings. The five o'clock steamer was in, the passengers had all boarded and the gangplank was in the process of being raised.

'Stop! Stop!' she cried.

For there was now no need for Mr Noyes to summon the Doctor: more importantly, *there was no need to summon Josephine's mother.* What was the point, dragging her over here when Josephine would probably be skipping about tomorrow, full of beans? It was altogether best that the woman stay away—well away—especially given the alarming things Mr Noyes had just told her about the girls' families. And Bessie Briars sounded worse than the lot of them!

With a blast of its horn, the *Emu* pulled away from the wharf. There was no sign of Mr Noyes; he was probably already ensconced in the saloon. Only the ticket collector remained on deck; he looked towards the woman tearing down the hill, screaming at them to stop. Well, well, he thought, for he recognised her as the pious do-gooder they had dropped off here less than a week ago. Already desperate to get off the island, he thought to himself. That was hardly surprising. She would have to wait for the next ferry, as the *Emu* was behind schedule; they would get a bollocking from the timekeeper when they returned to Sydney.

'Tell Mr Noyes we don't need the Doctor! Or the mother! Josephine is better now!' Mrs Hopkins cried out to him.

The ticket collector shook his head and shrugged his shoulders: he could see she was shouting something but what exactly he could not make out. He proceeded into the saloon and closed the door behind him.

Mrs Hopkins stamped her foot in frustration. What a blessed nuisance. Now she would have to deal with the child's mother!

''As the Josephine girl got a sickness?' asked Henry, who had been hanging about the wharf, pestering people for money. (Mr Noyes, rummaging through his pockets, found he was missing some change, but nonetheless gave him a penny, for which Henry had seemed, he thought, insufficiently grateful.)

'She had a sickness but she is better now,' replied Mrs Hopkins.

Henry produced from inside his coat a clump of milk toffees, half-melted and all stuck together, scarcely recognisable as confectionary. He had found it on the beach that morning, washed ashore along with a shilling or two.

'Give her this,' he said.

Mrs Hopkins peered at the sandy clump in his grimy hand uncertainly. 'What is it?'

'Lollies.'

Why, they are my milk toffees, thought Mrs Hopkins. What was Henry doing with them and why were they all covered in sand and clumped together like this? Still, she took the proffered lump, partly because she did not wish to anger him by refusing, and partly because, if washed and melted down over the fire, they might perhaps be salvageable enough to cheer the children.

'Thank you. That is kind of you. I will pass them on to Josephine,' said Mrs Hopkins.

'Is it true you're a witch?'

'No. It is not true. It is a story made up to spite me. There is no such thing as witches.'

'Oh no, there is such a thing. That place is full of 'em.' He gazed up at the institution. 'Sometimes about the new moon—you wait and see—there comes upon them a wild fit. Only the big ones, mind, never the little ones. Oh yes, you'll see, there's witches all right.'

Mrs Hopkins did not reply, for what was the point with an imbecile like Henry? And what did it matter, even if they were? For she had glimpsed, in some of them anyway, that certain sign—the cast of the eye, a pointed tongue, a mole on the cheek, a missing incisor. But it did them no good. They were still stuck behind stone walls, their girlhood perishing, helpless as ducklings. So Mrs Hopkins turned and hurried back up the hill, but she did not return to her own quarters; instead she proceeded towards Mr Crabback's house to avail herself of some of his pea and bacon hock soup.

Mr Crabback was not in his quarters when Mrs Hopkins knocked upon the door; he was in the mess-hall, helping to clean up after tea. The encounter with Mr Massie had frightened him; he was determined to prove himself. In fact, for all his apparent failings in the role—his laziness, his tendency to become distracted by matters other than the welfare of the inmates—Mr Crabback had one great redeeming quality: he liked the girls. He enjoyed their cruel wit and their fighting spirit; he didn't mind at all their slovenly ways or their general unruliness. Left to his own devices, he would probably have kept as amenable a group of girls as you could hope for in the circumstances. It was only when he felt the pressure from his superiors that he acted in a manner out of character: the terrible business with Amelia Burke was a case in point. For Mr Crabback had been told in no uncertain terms upon taking up the position of Superintendent (barely a month ago now) that he must assert his authority from the outset and 'nip bad behaviour in the bud'. Amelia Burke, ringleader of the recent riot, was singled out as one to be kept on as short a leash as possible.

'The one thing we cannot tolerate is another riot,' said Mr Massie. 'Every time the girls riot, there is a public outcry, and people start agitating for an enquiry.' Why an enquiry was a bad thing, to be avoided at all costs, he did not explain. 'Send them down the cells at the first sign of trouble, and they will understand that you mean business.'

The knock upon Mr Crabback's front door had set Tippet off barking. Mrs Hopkins hesitated, waiting to hear Mr Crabback's customary jovial admonishment for the dog to be quiet. However, no such admonishment ensued and Tippet continued barking, unchecked. 'Hush now, Tippet, it is only me,' she said through the door, and the dog quieted at the sound of a familiar voice. She tested the door handle: it turned. Mr Crabback had left the place unlocked. She opened the door and stepped inside: the little dog rushed towards her, wagging its tail, glad of the company. Mrs Hopkins stooped to pet it. It followed her into the kitchen where she found the pot of pea soup sitting on the table. She lifted the lid; there was not much left, barely enough for Mr Crabback's meal tonight. Still, it might fill a little girl's stomach. She scraped every last morsel into a tin dish and left by the back door.

When she arrived back at her quarters, Mrs Hopkins was surprised to find Josephine sitting up in bed, holding court with the three little Tunks sisters. They had sadly missed their friend that day, and upon learning that she was sick and being cared for in Mrs Hopkins' quarters, had hobbled out of the school gate to find her.

Mrs Hopkins was somewhat dismayed to find the visitors for there was only soup enough for one. And yet as she was warming it up upon the stove, she could see by the look in their big wistful eyes that the visitors were hungry, too.

'Did you girls have your tea?' asked Mrs Hopkins.

The older girl, Emma, nodded, but Martha and Janie shook their heads.

'That's all right, they can share mine!' declared Josephine.

'Are you sure, Josephine? After all, you need the nourishment after your illness.'

But Josephine was adamant. Mrs Hopkins could hardly refuse her, for the Tunks girls were more emaciated than Josephine. Whatever other failings she possessed, Josephine's mother had fed her up as best she could. So Mrs Hopkins gave them the bowl and a spoon, and the girls passed it around between them, taking a spoonful each. The soup did not last long; each child had barely a few spoonfuls. Nevertheless, they declared it the nicest soup they had ever tasted.

'Is there more?' asked Josephine hopefully.

'No, I'm afraid not. But I will make a big pot of it, perhaps tomorrow,' said Mrs Hopkins, wondering where she would obtain the ingredients. Although they were allocated a weekly allowance of meat, bread, sugar and tea, it was up to the staff to order in their additional requirements. Mrs Hopkins had not received any wages yet; nor was she entirely sure when she could expect them.

The girls set up a plea that Josephine might be able to join the Tunks girls in Dormitory One tonight, as promised a lifetime ago by Mrs Hopkins. Certainly, Josephine seemed to have staged an astonishing recovery; there was colour in her cheeks again and her spirits seemed high. And although Mrs Hopkins wished to keep the little girl to herself, she also longed for a decent night's sleep. So she found a clean chemise to dress Josephine in (she was still wearing Mr Crabback's nightshirt, soaked in urine) and led them all back to the institution. It was just after six, but the girls had already been locked into their dormitories. There was no sign of Mr Crabback nor Mrs Baird nor Miss Foy; they had all gone to their separate quarters for their tea, grateful to put their feet up after a long and harrowing day.

Mrs Hopkins unlocked the door to Dormitory One, where the younger children were playing leapfrog. Some of them squealed and hid under their beds at the sight of her, but Bridget climbed up upon her bed and made a short speech: 'Friends, do not be frightened. Come out from under your beds. It is true that she clocked Mrs Dunstable a doozy, but she did it with just cause. She is a friend to us, Amelia says so. And all that witch talk is sheer bunkum. Mrs Baird had one of her conniptions.'

With that encouragement, the little ones crept out from under their beds. Some managed even to approach

Mrs Hopkins and smile shyly up at her or stroke the fabric of her mourning skirts.

'Now children, you have a new roommate tonight,' said Mrs Hopkins.

Josephine tugged at her sleeve. 'Tell them if they feel sad or lonely, they can come to me and I will comfort them,' she said.

'And should you feel sad and lonely, you can go to Eugenie and she will comfort you.'

Josephine stared up at her, angrily. 'I am not Eugenie!' she declared. 'I am Josephine.'

'Yes, yes,' cried Mrs Hopkins, turning to the other children. 'I'm sorry. Josephine will look after you. Now where is a spare bed?'

It turned out there wasn't a spare bed, so Josephine would have to sleep top and tail with Emma. Both girls were perfectly happy with that arrangement; Emma jumped up and down excitedly and Martha and Janie commenced to cry because they wanted Josephine to sleep in their beds. So Mrs Hopkins moved their beds alongside Josephine and Emma's bed, and then all the other children wanted their beds joined up too. There were twenty children in the dormitory, so Mrs Hopkins had a lot of beds to move, but the little ones were keen to help and an air of merriment pervaded.

'Have you said your prayers?' asked Mrs Hopkins when all the furniture moving was done, and the beds made up as best they could.

The little girls shook their heads.

'Then sit up on your beds and hold your hands together like so. Now close your eyes.' And she commenced to pray.

Dear God, kind Gardener of my heart,
Plant seeds of goodness there.
Protect that Spring-time Garden
By Your loving thought and care.
O plant good thoughts in my heart
Each known by name to show
That there is left no room at all
For evil weeds to grow.
Amen.

And then she left them in the darkness.

Walking back into the quadrangle, Mrs Hopkins was struck by how quiet the institution was that evening. No doubt the dramas of the day had affected them all, even those not struck down by food poisoning. An enormous sense of fatigue descended upon her; not just physical fatigue but a mental and emotional exhaustion. The day she had just lived through had seemed interminable: Mrs Dunstable's corpse washing up on the beach; Josephine falling ill; the terrible scene at morning muster where Mrs Baird accused her of being a witch. The awful drawing on the blackboard (who had done that?); the rancid meat; the girls vomiting everywhere. And perhaps worst of all, Mr Crabback bringing Amelia out of the dark pit where he had left her for four days and nights! What a place this was. Mrs Hopkins longed to run away as it was all too much: her constitution was not strong enough to withstand it.

Under the light of the waning moon, she stood in the empty quadrangle and closed her eyes. 'Be strong and of good courage,' she told herself.

And as she stood there, she heard a voice singing, slightly hoarse but nonetheless soft and warm and lilting. It was coming from within Dormitory Four. The hoarseness and huskiness, the slight lisp caused by a missing tooth: it was Amelia singing, and the song was 'Annie Laurie'.

Her brow is like the snowdrift,
Her throat is like a swan,
Her face it is the freckliest
That e'er the sun shone on.
That e'er the sun shone on,
And hazel is her eye,
And for bonnie Annie Laurie
I would lay me down and die.

She was by no means an exceptional singer: her voice cracked on the higher notes and wobbled in the lower register. And yet, there was something about the gentle conviction with which she sang that pulled Mrs Hopkins in, as a sailor is lured by the siren's song. I will teach her the correct lyrics, she thought as she crept down the passage towards the dormitory. No doubt the girl had picked it up as best she could from listening to others.

Like birds in the air a-flying
As soft as a fairy's feet,
And like winds in the summer sighing
Her voice is low and sweet.

Taking care as best she could not to reveal herself, Mrs Hopkins peered through the grate. The girls lay in their beds or sat together in small groups. They had managed to procure a few candles, which made the dismal stone-walled barrack seem less forbidding. No one spoke; they all listened to Amelia as if bewitched. She was sitting up in her bed, singing softly, her bonnie be-freckled friend Annie reclining in her arms.

Her voice is low and sweet,
And soft as a baby's sigh,
And for bonnie Annie Laughton,
I would lay me down and die.

The first glimmerings of a grimy grey dawn crept over the island. Mrs Hopkins awoke with a groan: a vague dream, a figure in a tattered shawl aboard a ferry, had turned into a sudden conviction. Bessie Briars was on her way to Biloela. It was imperative that Mrs Hopkins fend her off somehow. She must meet her at the wharf and send her back to Sydney.

She realised with dismay that she had fallen asleep, fully clothed, upon the urine-soaked bed. Still it spared her the minutes it took to dress. She got up, pulled her awful ulster from its hook and threw open the front door. Then she stopped. She heard voices, murmuring. A long silence, then a stifled giggle.

Peering around her doorway, she saw, a short distance away, leaning against the outer wall of the institution, the comely water-sprite Mary-Ann in the arms of a brawny sailor. He was trying to pull up her skirts: she was slapping his hands away, and all the time they were kissing each other like they would swallow each other up. Mrs Hopkins stared at them in fascination. How tall he was, and how handsome, with his dark hair and his thick arms, and how irresistible the lovely Mary-Ann, so round and plump and bountiful. The approaching steamer sounded its horn and this seemed to startle them; a short, whispered conversation ensued. Mary-Ann seemed to be doing most of the whispering, earnest and insistent, as if trying to extract from her lover a promise. He mumbled something into her neck; she slapped him hard across the cheek, and to Mrs Hopkins' horror, he slapped her back again. There followed giggling and more kissing; a tight embrace, whispered declarations. Then the sailor formed a step of sorts by linking his two hands together, onto which Mary-Ann sprung lightly, one hand gripping his shoulder. He hoisted her up now high above his head, staggering back and forth until she was able to just grab hold of the top of the great stone wall. 'Higher!' she hissed, and with a grunt of effort and Gallic cursing, he straightened his arms over his head so that she was able to swing one leg over the wall. Her skirt rode up to reveal her bare white bottom. Why is she not wearing her drawers? thought Mrs Hopkins, shocked. The sailor whistled. The girl blew her sweetheart a kiss and disappeared over the wall. The handsome sailor sauntered off, hands in pockets, in the direction of the dry dock.

This cannot be allowed to continue, thought Mrs Hopkins. I will talk to Mrs Baird and ensure that the girls have enough underwear. They cannot be permitted to get about without their drawers on; it is unhygienic. But she did not have time to dwell upon the matter, because the first ferry of the day was at this moment pulling in.

She hurried down to the wharf (the seagulls were sound asleep in their nests, so for once she made her way there without harassment) and watched as the gangplank was lowered. Several workmen sidled off, clutching their lunchboxes.

'Hurry up then, love!' cried the ticket collector, and a small pretty lady appeared from within the saloon, one hand clutching her shawl tightly against the cold wind, the other hand gripping a battered old carpet bag. The ticket collector seemed concerned about her: he took her elbow and helped her carefully down the greasy gangplank. Sighting Mrs Hopkins, he called out, 'Oi! Aren't you one of the Matrons from the school then?'

'Yes, I am,' responded Mrs Hopkins, stepping forward. She could feel her heart beating hard in her chest.

'This lady's come to see her sick lass!'

'Yes,' nodded Mrs Hopkins. Her bun was falling out from having slept in it, and now the wind was pulling it apart.

The pretty lady looked at her hopefully. 'I've come to see Josephine,' she said.

'Josephine who?'

'Josephine Briars.'

'In that case, you are too late,' said Mrs Hopkins.

A pause, laden with dread.

'Too late?'

'She is dead.'

She could scarcely believe that she had said it. Oh, she had imagined herself saying it, certainly, when Mr Noyes had first advised that he would summon the woman. But then she had quickly dismissed the idea as preposterous and cruel and too difficult to get away with. And yet now the words sprung out of her mouth, unheeded! It was extraordinary.

'She is dead,' Mrs Hopkins repeated, bowing her head gravely. Since it was done, she might as well carry it through with conviction.

The woman stared at her. Then she doubled over and dropped to her knees. She let out a terrible wail as if her very insides were being ripped out of her.

'No!' she cried. 'Not my baby!'

'It is a great pity you could not have got here sooner,' said Mrs Hopkins. She felt a rush of self-righteousness: had she a sick child, she would surely not have waited till the next morning to visit her.

'I tried! I tried!' the woman sobbed. She was rocking backwards and forwards on her knees and making a great spectacle of herself.

Presumably, this was part of the courtroom theatrics that Mr Noyes had mentioned; all this flailing about a bid for sympathy. Passengers on the deck of the ferry were staring.

'You had best take her back to Sydney,' Mrs Hopkins said to the ticket collector. 'There is nothing we can do for her here.'

'Couldn't you give her a cup of tea or something?' he said. 'She just found out her daughter's dead, for Christ's sake.'

'Could I see her?' asked the mother suddenly, clutching onto Mrs Hopkins' skirt.

'No. I'm afraid that's not possible.'

'Just to hold her for a moment—' And then, she opened the battered carpet bag and began pulling out old toys, some ribbons, a little bag of broken biscuits. 'I brought her some things, you see. I could put these ribbons in her hair—'

'She is buried.'

'What? Already?'

'Oh yes. There was a great danger of contagion. It would tear through the whole school. We could not hang about and wait for you, I'm afraid. You should have notified us. We had no idea when you would turn up.'

The poor woman moaned and doubled over again, her shoulders heaving with sorrow.

'Give her a cup of tea!' insisted the ticket collector. 'Have a heart, for fuck's sake.'

'There is too great a danger of contagion,' repeated Mrs Hopkins. 'You must take this lady back to Sydney.'

The man leaned down and helped poor Bessie to her feet. She could hardly stand. She was like a broken doll.

'Was someone with her?' she asked feebly. 'When she passed?'

'Of course. I sat with her the whole time, right to the very end.'

'Did you hold her hand?'

'Oh yes. I held her hand. I stroked her brow. I prayed for her.'

'Did she ask for me?'

'Yes, repeatedly.'

'What did she say?'

'"When is Mother coming?" That sort of thing. "Will my mother be here soon?" She became quite fretful, of course, wondering why you did not come.'

'Did you tell her I was on my way?' cried Bessie Briars, a note of hysteria rising in her voice.

'Oh yes. Every time we heard a steamer horn, I would tell her, this is Mother, Mother will be on this ferry, just you wait and see. And then, when you didn't come, I told her, never mind, Josephine, the next ferry, Mother will be on the next ferry. And yet I knew full well there were no more steamers for the night.'

'I didn't have the fare, you see, for the John Hops have shut me down,' cried the poor mother. 'So I went round to Bill's but he was skint, so I tried my luck down at the Man O' War steps but it was so bitter cold last night, there was nothing doing. So I got my coat and I took it to the pawn shop, and by then—by then—by the time I got down to King Street, there were no more ferries—'

Great hacking sobs, like her heart would rip out of her chest.

The ticket collector stared at Mrs Hopkins as if in disbelief. 'A cup of fucking tea,' he said. 'You could bring one down for her; it wouldn't kill you.'

'If you would like, Mrs Briars, I will say a short prayer,' said Mrs Hopkins, ignoring the man.

Amidst her sobbing, the woman nodded gratefully. 'Yes!' she managed to say. 'Please, Miss!'

'It is sort of a prayer, anyway. Perhaps it is more of a poem. It is told from the point of view of the dead child, which is rather interesting.'

The words 'dead child' caused the poor woman to moan afresh, shaking her head in despair.

'If I am to say this prayer, I will need you to not carry on so,' said Mrs Hopkins.

Bessie Briars nodded, ashamed of herself. She gathered her thin shawl around her and bowed her head. Mrs Hopkins commenced to recite what she could remember of the poem.

Mother! If I should ever go,
Where the angels are singing so—

Here Mrs Hopkins broke off for the woman was sobbing again.

'I must ask you to make an effort to compose yourself,' she said. 'I cannot say the prayer if you are carrying on like this.'

'Yes,' said Bessie. 'I'm sorry.' And she clamped her hand across her mouth to muffle her sobs, for she could not seem to stop them rising up from within her.

Mother! If I should ever go,
Where the angels are singing so,
I'll sing so loud that the winds shall bear,
My voice on their wings to my mother's ear—

Here a cry erupted from poor Bessie. Mrs Hopkins paused and waited.

'I'm sorry,' cried Bessie. 'I can't stop!' And she balled up a section of her shawl and stuffed it into her mouth.

Mrs Hopkins continued.

I'll sing so loud that the winds shall bear,
My voice on their wings to my mother's ear
And I'll tell you not to weep for me,
For I am as happy as I can be.

There was more to the poem, but Mrs Hopkins could not remember it. There was something about the mother joining her child in heaven, not right away but eventually, when she was old and weary.

The ticket collector opened one eye and looked at her.

'*Amen*,' she added, for it seemed to need some sort of conclusion.

Bessie opened her eyes. 'Is that it?'

'Yes. It is only a short prayer.'

Bessie nodded. Tears streamed down her cheeks. She wiped them away with a corner of her shawl. 'Thank you,' she said in a broken whisper.

'That's all right,' said Mrs Hopkins. 'I have lost a child myself, you see.'

Bessie held up three fingers. 'I have lost three,' she said. 'Two as babies. Josie was the only one that grew.'

The ticket collector led the woman back onto the ferry. The seagulls were awake now and wheeling in the sky. The wind blew; the gangplank went up; the steamer blasted its horn.

And as it pulled away from the wharf, Mrs Hopkins realised what a terrible thing it was that she had done.

In the weeks and months following Eugenie's death, the child had frequently visited upon her mother, often when Mrs Hopkins was sleeping, but sometimes when she was quite awake. The little girl wore her death shroud, which she fingered disconsolately, and her general demeanour seemed to be one of confusion and unhappiness. She seemed not to understand what had become of her and this was causing her some distress. She would sit in the corner and weep and sniffle, and this had begun to fray upon Mrs Hopkins' nerves. Finally, she had found it necessary to explain to the child that she was no longer part of the living world. She had to speak quite plainly for it never seemed to quite sink in. 'You are dead,' she would say, over and over. The little girl would stare at her, bewildered.

Eventually, after a year or so, the visits stopped, and it was then that Mrs Hopkins felt her loss most heavily. She was filled with remorse that she had dealt with the little lost soul so brusquely. The child had come to her mother seeking comfort and reassurance and instead had been cast back into the wilderness. What would have been the harm in letting the girl dally, just for a little while? Why had she not sat the child upon her lap and sung her songs and wound her hair around her finger to make corkscrews? The answer to this question she scarcely dared admit: the child gave her the horrors.

It was the deadness, the stench of decay, the maggots, the ghastly mouldering of the ears and nose and fingertips. Her shroud was filthy as if she'd been dragging it through the greasy muck of the graveyard; she was a careless child, and this was entirely typical of her. There were holes in it also where her feet had become entangled and she had rent them free in frustration. No, this endless wandering and moping and sulking could not be encouraged; Mrs Hopkins had had no choice but to speak plainly, although it grieved her to think of it now.

Occasionally the two paupers accompanied the small child, the old crone humming her strange lullaby to the small child, who snuggled against her, oblivious to the old woman's bony breast. The younger ginhead poked playfully at the little girl's sunken belly; horrifyingly, her finger became stuck in the girl's ghastly entrails—there was a disgusting squelching sound and a terrible smell as she pulled it out, which only made them all giggle.

No doubt these were dreams, but nonetheless they greatly disturbed Mrs Hopkins. Yes, in a way it was comforting: they were taking care of her little girl as she had sometimes hoped they would, but they were coarse and foul. They reeked of decay, and she was repulsed by them. Also, or so it seemed to Mrs Hopkins, they seemed to manifest a strong element of judgement, evident in the scornful way in which they gazed upon her. What kind of mother would not sit her own little child upon her lap, the rotting old crone seemed to say? What kind of mother would not even know in which unmarked grave her child was buried? Mrs Hopkins could only be thankful that their visits were infrequent.

And yet now, in the dawn light, as the steamer carrying Bessie Briars away, there they were, quite unmistakably, standing upon the wharf in their rotting rags. They said nothing but their meaning seemed to be evident.

'Josephine is not your child,' they seemed to say as they glowered at her. 'Eugenie is your child.'

'No!' cried Mrs Hopkins. 'Josephine is Eugenie brought back to me! That's why—that's why—I had to do what I did!'

Holding onto each other for support (for they were quite frail in their decomposed state), they began to move towards her. She had never noticed before the ghastly rictus on the ginhead's face; it was a grimace, a horror. A shudder of fear overwhelmed Mrs Hopkins. She lifted her skirts and tore off in a run up the hill back to the school, where she flung herself gasping against the front gate, which was locked, of course. She clenched her eyes shut and braced herself. This was it: there was no salvation; she was to receive what she was due. The two wretched ghouls had come for her, and after the terrible deed she had just committed, she deserved her fate.

The hairs on her arms horripilated. She wrenched her keys from her pocket and fumbled furiously with the padlock. It was safer inside those grim sandstone walls where surely the two dreadful phantoms could not reach her—where, oh where was the key to the gate?

'Mrs Hopkins!' A male voice, right behind her. It was Mr Crabback, come to open up. 'What is it? Are you all right?'

She fell at once into his arms, sobbing. He held her tightly, smoothing her wild windswept hair. He could not get any sense from her, except that she had been wicked, terribly wicked, though how she had been wicked she would not say.

'There, there, do not fret, I forgive you,' he murmured. In his vanity, he imagined that Mrs Hopkins' remorse was due to the anger she had displayed towards him when Amelia was brought up from the cell. 'I understand why you were angry: indeed, I feel angry, too. The governors do not care about the girls, that much is plain to see. Nevertheless, we will find a solution, together, the two of us, Mrs Hopkins, you and I.'

He passed his hand down her thin back, feeling each knobbly vertebrae. How frail she was, yet how brave and strong. Overcome with tenderness, he pressed his lips against her forehead. Her face, wet with tears, turned up to his as a flower would to the sun, her lips seeking his.

And in that embrace, the two were bound, their only witness a small spaniel cowering behind a shrub, the hackles on its back raised in a ridge, growling low and long as it gazed down towards the wharf.

Love changes everything. The day that had started so dreadfully seemed suddenly full of miraculous possibilities.

'Oh, Mrs Hopkins!' cried Miss Foy, galloping across the quadrangle towards her. 'Come see what they've sent us! You'll scarcely believe your eyes!' And gaily taking Mrs Hopkins by the arm, she led her down the steps to the store area, where Henry was dragging up the last of the provisions from the previous steamer. Instead of the usual dismal selection of stale bread, aged vegetables and a side or two of mutton on the turn, there was a cornucopia of delights. Sacks of fresh carrots and potatoes and swedes; crates of little pink apples; baskets of eggs; hessian sacks groaning with oats and flour and sugar; great jars of jam and marmalade and honey; tins of molasses; crusty white loaves of bread; the dearest little fruit buns; great square lumps of butter wrapped in linen cloth; giant tins of Arnott's biscuits. There was even, in a cage, a half-dozen fat chickens, doted upon immediately by the little ones. After yesterday's fiasco with the rancid mutton, it seemed someone might have had stern words with the providore.

'Wake me up, I must be dreaming!' cried Miss Foy, lashing some butter on a fruit bun. Mrs Hopkins carried the box of apples into the mess-hall, where the girls were finishing their porridge, and announced that they if they formed an orderly queue, they might each have one. Some of the girls had never even tasted an apple before. Josephine had to show the Tunks sisters how to take lots of little bites, round and round, till you got to the core. 'Don't swallow the pips,' she told them. 'Or an apple tree will grow out of your ears.'

'My plan is this: since the "powers-that-be" are so disinterested as to the welfare of our inmates, I am going into town to talk to some gentlewomen of my acquaintance, seeking donations for the institution,' said Mr Crabback. 'I would like to take some of our more presentable girls to aid the cause. Whom do you recommend?'

'Why, let me think. There's Catherine, of course. She is a good girl, and I will plait her hair nicely for the occasion. And Mary-Ann is very appealing.'

Even as she said that, she remembered the flash of bare buttocks as Mary-Ann had summited the fence early that morning. I will make sure that she has some drawers on before she goes, she thought.

'And perhaps the poor little Tunks girls, for they are very pathetic,' Mr Crabback suggested, gazing down at the little rickety-legged waifs, who were nibbling away at their apples. 'They will tug at the necessary heart-strings.'

'Yes,' said Mrs Hopkins, eyeing them doubtfully. Perhaps the gentlewomen of Mr Crabback's acquaintance would overlook the fact that the Tunks sisters were all to some degree quite addled in the head. 'In which case, it might be a good idea to take Josephine also, for the Tunks sisters will do nothing without her.'

'Josephine?'

Mrs Hopkins pointed her out.

'Ah yes, the girl who does cartwheels. That could be useful. Might you have the girls prepare a short song or poem that they could perform for the ladies?'

'Why, certainly. In which case, may I suggest Amelia go as well? She has a lovely voice; I heard her singing only last night.'

'It wasn't one of her riot songs, I hope?'

'No indeed, it was "Annie Laurie", and she sung it very movingly.'

'And yet she is probably the wickedest child in the institution: ought she be permitted to go on an excursion?'

'I believe if she is given an opportunity such as this, she will do her utmost to prove herself worthy of the faith that we invest in her.'

Mr Crabback beamed at her. His hand sought hers; he gave it a little squeeze, right there in the middle of the mess-hall. 'Might I visit you this evening after lock-up?' he murmured.

Mrs Hopkins nodded, her cheeks pinkening.

It was extraordinary how almost attractive she could appear sometimes, he thought. And yet at other times, she looked like she had risen freshly from the grave.

'Girls, I have asked you to come here during your dinner meal because Mr Crabback and I have selected you specially to help us in our bid to raise funds for the school. We are going into town to visit some gentlewomen of Mr Crabback's acquaintance, and we are going to put on a little concert for them. It is our hope that in so doing, we will be able to raise sufficient funds for our Special Visiting Day for Mothers.'

'I can understand you choosing me and Mary-Ann. I mean, we can sing at least,' said Amelia, who seemed to be in quite a grumpy mood that day. 'But why the others?' Here she pointed to Catherine. 'She's so ugly she'll put them right off. And the little ones are short of a few shingles, anyone can see that.'

The Tunks sisters commenced to cry. They had never heard themselves described in that way before, and it hurt their feelings.

'You shut your fat gob!' said Josephine to Amelia.

Whereupon Amelia clouted the younger girl swiftly over the head, knocking her sideways into the desk. 'Don't you ever talk that way to me again,' she said. 'You're new here so I'll let you off with a warning. Learn to respect your elders and betters, or I'll sort you out quick-smart.'

Now Josephine commenced to cry.

'And don't be a bloody cry-baby,' added Amelia.

'Pick on your own size, why don't you?' said Catherine.

'All right, here we go. You want to fucking take me on, do you? Me locked in a pit four days for you telling tales.'

'I never told tales—'

'Oh, sure you did, about me and Annie.'

'All I said was you share a bed—'

'That's what I mean, you stupid bitch.'

'Everyone knows you share a bed! You don't exactly keep it secret!'

'Girls! Stop it!' cried Mrs Hopkins. She had caught Amelia's arm just in time, for she was about to knock Catherine sideways.

Mrs Hopkins sighed. This was not a good beginning.

'I don't think you understand,' she said, 'that this is a special privilege, an honour that has been bestowed upon you on behalf of all the girls, to improve conditions in the school. Why, if this goes well, we might be able to purchase lamps for the dormitories, and books to read and nice silks for fancy work; perhaps we might even be able to make you all new dresses! Wouldn't that be wonderful? But I cannot take you into town if you're all fighting one another. Do you understand? We need to make a good impression.'

Amelia strummed her lower lip with her finger. 'Into town, you say?'

'Yes, on the ferry, and then who knows? Possibly even a tram ride!'

Mary-Ann clapped her hands together in joy.

But Amelia still seemed dubious. She looked at the weeping little ones, and looked at Catherine, and then she looked back at Mrs Hopkins. 'Oh, all right!' she said suddenly. And she dropped to her knees and pulled Josephine and the three Tunks sisters into her arms. 'I'm a grumpy old cow, so I am. Don't you take any nonsense from me. If I do that again, you say to me, "Amelia, don't be a grumpy old cow."' And she gave each girl a tickle in the ribs to make them giggle. 'Now give your Auntie Amelia a kiss and tell her she's forgiven.'

And to Mrs Hopkins' surprise, Josephine and the three Tunks sisters kissed her on the cheek and giggled and snuggled up to her.

'But I'm not forgiving that one,' said Amelia, pointing to Catherine. 'So you can forget trying to make us friends.'

And now it was Catherine's turn to burst into tears, a flood of them.

These girls are so emotional, thought Mrs Hopkins in despair. Had she been like that when she was their age? She couldn't remember.

'You've always had a down on me,' sobbed Catherine. 'Ever since I came here! You pick on me and pick on me!'

'That's because you keep telling tales about me.'

'I don't—I swear I don't—it's just Mr Crabback asked me and I didn't realise what he meant. I didn't mean to send you down the cell—I didn't realise—I would gladly have gone down in your stead!'

'Oh, sure you would, you mealy-faced wombat! I never saw you offer to at the time.'

'That's because I was scared!' wailed Catherine. 'I didn't want the rats to eat me!'

'Can you believe this girl's nerve?' said Amelia, turning to Mrs Hopkins who was watching it all helplessly. 'And yet it's all very well for the rats to eat me, is it? That's rich, my girl—I can show you their tooth marks! I had to stash my dress and my shimmy in the holes to try to stop them but still they came—hundreds of them in the darkness—and me all alone.'

And now it was Amelia who stood and wept, terrible retching broken sobs, her fists clenched in fury. In a heart-beat, Catherine flew across the room and embraced her, to which Amelia responded by casting the little ones rudely out of the way that she and Catherine might clutch hold of each other more tightly, kissing each other and wiping away each other's tears.

'I'm sorry,' wept Catherine. 'I'm so sorry, Amelia.'

'I know you are, my love,' said Amelia.

'Are we going to learn a song or what?' asked Mary-Ann.

'Yes, let's,' said Mrs Hopkins, who had been watching the girls in fascination: was this something to do with the initiation rites referred to by the Colonial Secretary perhaps?

In any case, now all that was out of the way, she had the happiest little troupe of performers she could have hoped for.

Her plan was this: the girls would begin the concert by together singing a hymn entitled 'The Prodigal', by Charles

Edward Pollock, one of Mrs Hopkins' favourites. She thought the lyrics rather apt.

Wayward child, whose footsteps stray
From the Father's house away
Where the path seems bright and fair
But whose sinful pleasures snare
And whose false, deceiving glare
Leads to deserts bleak and bare
Oh! return, deluded child
Seek thy Father reconciled.

This would be followed by a series of 'Questions and Answers', which Mrs Hopkins had stumbled across in the old crone's stinking book of private devotions. She thought it could be a good way to bring the pathetic Tunks sisters into the concert. Mary-Ann would sit on a stool, with the little girls clustered around her. She would ask the 'questions' and the children would chorus the 'answers'.

Flowers, wherefore do ye bloom?
—We strew the pathway to thy tomb.
Stars, wherefore do ye rise?
—To light thy spirit to the skies.

On and on in that vein it went. It was ambitious certainly to expect so much of the little ones and it took a good deal of rehearsal. Mary-Ann of course was delightful, her voice ringing out like a bell, her face a study of puzzlement and consternation as she posited each question to the waifs. What a little actress she was! Josephine, quick as a whip, led the struggling sisters gamely in their responses, and yet even as they mumbled and stumbled along with her, the overall effect of these poor fragile foundlings offering up such words of wisdom was undeniably pitiful and touching.

Amelia would then sing 'Annie Laurie' (Mrs Hopkins ensured that she learned the correct words), and Catherine would close the concert with this short prayer.

Should Poverty's consuming blow
Lay all my worldly comforts low
And neither help nor hope appear
My steps to guide, my heart to cheer; Lord!
Pity and supply my need
For Thou on Earth was poor indeed.

To cap off the entertainment, Josephine would then perform a cartwheel, followed by a backflip.

Weeks had passed and the girl had regained her full health. As for Mrs Hopkins, she had succeeded in putting the episode with Bessie Briars out of her mind almost completely. There had been no ramifications; it was for the best, painful though it must have been for the mother. Mrs Hopkins could now take responsibility for the little girl, for if Josephine was Eugenie brought back to her in this fashion, then it was clear that she had been given a second chance as her mother. Far better Mrs Hopkins than the brothel-keeper.

These were the happy days. The news spread rapidly throughout the institution that a select group of girls were to be taken into town to conduct an entertainment for the Ladies of the Benevolent Society. At first, there was resentment amongst some of the other girls, of course, for who had been on a trip to town, unless they were being taken straitjacketed and gagged to Darlinghurst Gaol to cool off after a riot? But once Mrs Hopkins explained that it was for the good of all the girls, that they might be able to buy all the things that the school needed, and then ultimately, as a reward for everyone, have their Special Visiting Day for Mothers, everyone did their very best to contribute in some way.

Great thought was given to what the performers might wear for their concert. They had only their dungaree dresses, of course, but the girls on laundry duty rummaged through till they found the dresses that were least torn and mended. Some of the older girls adept at fancy work crocheted pretty trimmings in white cotton for the hems and cuffs and collars of the dresses, and this brightened them up considerably.

Rosabella (who as well as being the only girl in the school who could milk a cow, demonstrated a great talent for needlework) embroidered a string of forget-me-nots around the neckline of Catherine's dress. Of course, then the others all wanted forget-me-nots, too, so Rosabella was permitted a candle by her bedside in the evening that she might finish the embroidery in time for the concert.

'Who taught you to embroider so nicely?' Mrs Hopkins asked her one evening.

'My nan,' said Rosabella. She had her head down, concentrating on her work. She gave a great sniff, then wiped away a tear with the back of her hand, lest it fall upon her work.

One morning at muster, Mrs Hopkins felt her skirt being tugged. It was Bridget.

'I can juggle, you know,' she said. 'I'm only telling you because it might be what you need for the concert and all.' And she produced from behind her back, four small cloth bundles she has tied up tightly with string to resemble balls, and these she proceeded to juggle quite expertly, only dropping a ball occasionally. 'Shit!' she would say every time she dropped one. 'Aw, fuck it!'

'My goodness,' said Mrs Hopkins. 'Whoever taught you to juggle?'

'My dad,' she replied. 'He's way better than me—he can juggle anything. But he liked me to do it because folks find me appealing and that way we'd get more spondulicks—the ladies especially. They'd say, "Oh, isn't she just a little lamb!" and they'd throw any amount of boodle at me. I'm only mentioning this 'cause it might be good for your show.'

Mrs Hopkins noticed that she had torn the bottom of her skirt off at the gathers to make her juggling balls.

'Yes, you're quite right, Bridget,' she said. 'It is just what we need for our show. But in the meantime, you must practise your juggling at every opportunity. For I cannot have you using that language in front of the Ladies of the Benevolent Society.'

'No, Miss,' said Bridget. 'I won't drop any on the day, I promise you.'

'But even if you were to drop one, you must not swear, do you understand? So you must also practise not swearing when you drop one.'

'Yes, Miss,' said Bridget, though she seemed a little doubtful.

'Now fall into line for me, please. And after muster, you are to apologise to Mrs Baird for tearing off your skirt and promise her you will repair it yourself in your own time, if she would be kind enough to allow you the fabric.'

'Yes, Mrs Hopkins,' said the girl. 'Thank you!'

And she galloped off in high glee, shouting her news to her friends.

Rehearsals occurred every day at dinner break, the other girls peering in through the windows of the schoolroom and applauding boisterously. 'Aw, stop it,' said Amelia bashfully after a rendition of 'Annie Laurie'. 'You're putting me off!' But you could tell she was delighted.

The poor little rickety-legged Tunks girls were now the pets of the whole school, pulled onto laps in the mess-hall and fussed with at every opportunity. They blossomed with the unexpected attention. Their sallow cheeks grew pinker, and little dimples appeared when they smiled or laughed.

These were the happy days, too, between Mr Crabback and Mrs Hopkins. They had formed a little custom, now, of spending the three hours between lock-up and lights out together, mostly in Mr Crabback's quarters, but occasionally in Mrs Hopkins', for she took pleasure in preparing him a nice little supper when she had the means. They would spend these hours composing letters on behalf of the institution to those of a philanthropic bent, stating the good work that was done on behalf of these neglected waifs and the need for support from civic-minded citizens. Lists were compiled of everything that the school required. Mrs Hopkins loved to work on these lists, arranging items in terms of priority and adding fresh items on a whim with Mr Crabback's encouragement.

'Might not a small harmonium be nice to encourage the girls with their singing?' she would ask dreamily. 'We could gather around it of an evening and sing the hymns of Ira D. Sankey.'

'Why not?' said Mr Crabback, beaming at her across the table. She looked her best in the candlelight. Occasionally, he would reach across and squeeze her hand. If they were in Mrs Hopkins' quarters, they would sit side by side on her narrow bed, their knees touching. He had asked if she might undress for him one night, and after a moment of hesitation, she had obliged.

'Here, let me,' he murmured, as she fumbled with her buttons.

She pulled down her dress to reveal her chemise, her stays, and her dowdy old drawers, drooping below her knees.

'It's all right, you may put your dress back on,' he said, for he saw her discomfort. 'Thank you,' he added, 'for obliging me.'

She pulled her dress back up and returned to the table to resume her list-making. *Fine French linen,* she added in her spidery hand, *for the making of drawers and other sundries.*

Another time he had undone the buttons of his fly and permitted her to stroke his member. It roused slightly from its slumber, and she sighed in wonderment.

'Do you think you might kiss it?' he had asked her, and she stared at him in astonishment. But then she had lowered her head dutifully and pressed her lips briefly upon it. He held her head down there for several moments in the hope of encouraging her to go further, but to no avail.

'I might put it away now,' he said finally. 'But thank you for obliging me.'

Another night he had lain on top of her, fully clothed, making small sporadic thrusting movements with his groin. Eventually he had fallen asleep, and she laid there beneath him, not wishing to disturb him but thinking about Mary-Ann and her lover and all the slapping and kissing and groping they carried on with. Those early morning scenes at the fence had become a regular event, always culminating in the acrobatic feat of getting Mary-Ann over the wall. Mrs Hopkins liked to watch them from behind her curtains. 'Oh, to be young,' she often said to herself, for she envied them in a way. One day, having tossed Mary-Ann back into the school grounds, the handsome sailor had come and urinated against the wall of her quarters, not realising that she was hidden behind the curtain. She watched in fascination, her heart beating hard in her chest. On and on he pissed, for eternity, like a horse. She wondered if she ought to reveal herself, for a small part of her felt indignant at the violation he was committing against her property. In the end, however, she did nothing, for she did not wish to startle him.

The night before the visit to the Ladies of the Benevolent Society, a full dress rehearsal was staged in the mess-hall for the benefit of Mr Crabback, and indeed the whole school. The artistes wore their dungaree dresses with the carefully crocheted trims and the lovingly embroidered forget-me-nots; their stockings were clean and mended; their boots polished to the brightest shine imaginable.

Miss Foy had taken on the task of arranging their hair. There was not a lot could be done for the Tunks sisters, of course, whose hair had been shaven off upon induction at the institution and was only just now growing back into wispy curls. Nonetheless, pretty ribbons were tied around their heads and bows pinned into place on top; the effect, though somewhat odd, was also undeniably rather charming. A looking glass was produced so that the little ones might survey the effect. They appeared quite stunned; it was perhaps the first time in their short lives that they had laid eyes upon their own reflections. And what did they see? Sunken eyes, cheeks pale and drawn, tiny teeth a-tangled, and atop all this, a giant incongruous bow. And yet Josephine and the other girls exclaimed to such an extent about how pretty they looked that they flushed with pleasure and smiled shyly back at themselves (with the exception of the contrary middle Tunks, Martha, who tore out her bow and refused to wear it).

Josephine and Bridget were content to have their hair braided fishbone-style in two long plaits, so long as they were tied with red ribbons (of this last point Bridget was adamant). Since Josephine was to perform her cartwheel and backflip, she wore a special pair of new bloomers fashioned by Mrs Baird for the occasion. For even Mrs Baird had warmed to the excitement of the project, and although still cool with Mrs Hopkins, complied quietly with any request made of her. Nor was there any further talk of the School-Mistress being a witch. It was as if Amelia, pulled from the pit, decreed it thus.

The older girls, Mary-Ann and Amelia and Catherine, had studied closely several illustrations of popular hairstyles, which Miss Foy had torn from the newspapers. Conscious of their more senior years, they felt they needed to wear their hair up to convey an aura of sophistication, and with the help of Miss Foy, hair pins tucked tightly between her lips, they attempted as best they could to emulate the styles in the pictorials. No accompanying instructions were supplied with the illustrations, however; nor had Miss Foy any of the necessary accoutrements beyond hairpins; and yet, with the aid of these and lengths of rag with which to fashion rag curls, their unruly locks were wrestled into a reasonable semblance of the illustrations.

'Why, girls, you look beautiful,' cried Mrs Hopkins, clasping her hands together.

The girls blushed and lowered their heads in a display of modesty. They then proceeded to spend a considerable time gazing (somewhat less modestly) at their reflections in the looking glass from every angle. They had never seen themselves look such a picture! The other girls, who must have longed for the same treatment, gazed wistfully at them and showered them with compliments.

Privately, Mrs Hopkins thought it rather a shame that the girl's long tresses were all dolled up in these fanciful hairstyles. To her mind, they looked their loveliest with their hair streaming down their backs, particularly Amelia, with those wild dark curls. These same curls had now been tortured into an elaborate construction upon her head, resembling nothing so much as a small bristling animal, poised to leap off and attack. But of course, Mrs Hopkins would never give voice to her true thoughts, for she understood the girls' longing to appear fashionable. 'You have done a fine job,' she said to Miss Foy.

'They scrub up all right, don't they!' Miss Foy beamed in return.

After tea, under the supervision of Mrs Baird and Miss Foy, the mess-hall tables were pushed against the wall and the benches arranged in a semi-circle to create an open area for the stage.

The smaller children were instructed to sit cross-legged on the floor, with the older girls on the benches behind them.

Outside in the darkness, Mrs Hopkins gathered her small troupe of artistes. It was time to talk to them about the seriousness of this undertaking.

'Girls, the funds we are hoping to raise in presenting this concert will make a profound difference to every child in the institution. Everything now depends upon your performance. But do not fear: I have every confidence in your success for no one could have possibly worked harder than you girls have worked in this past week. You are a credit to Biloela.'

'Oh, damn and blast,' cried Bridget, who had been diligently practising her juggling. 'Sorry, Miss. I'm so nervous, I keep fucking dropping them!'

'Now, Bridget,' said Mrs Hopkins, for she was starting to feel that Bridget had not grasped the point about the importance of not swearing. 'It does not matter if you drop a ball. But it does matter if you say bad words, do you understand? For if you say bad words tonight, I must make the painful decision of striking you from the performance for the Ladies of the Benevolent Society tomorrow. Can you see my difficulty? If you were to say bad words in front of the Ladies of the Benevolent Society, they might become very upset, do you understand, for they are not used to such talk, and then they might no longer feel inclined to give us the funds we require.'

'Might they faint?'

'They might faint, for they are very delicate. It is entirely possible. But my point is, Bridget, that if you say bad words tonight, I would not be able to risk including you in the performance tomorrow.'

'But my juggling is the best thing in the whole darn show, Miss!'

'Stop swearing, Bridget, for fuck's sake!' screamed Josephine, whose nerves were on edge. While executing a last-minute practice backflip, she had fallen and incurred a grass stain on her beautiful new bloomers.

'We would not be able to include you in the concert, and you would have to miss out.'

'What if I swear tonight, but promise not to swear tomorrow?'

'I could not take that risk, do you see?'

'Then could I at least come on the ferry trip?'

'No, Bridget. That would not be fair on all the other girls.'

'Miss, can I talk to you?' It was Amelia, suddenly materialising out of the shadows.

'Yes, certainly, Amelia. What is it?'

'In private, Miss. I need to talk to you in private.'

And taking Mrs Hopkins forcefully by the arm, she led her away from the other girls to a high point overlooking the dry docks. The giant spars of the man o' war *Blanche* loomed up at them.

'I can't do it, Miss.'

'What?'

'I can't do it. I can't go on.'

Mrs Hopkins stared at her. Her eyes were glassy, her skin pale, her face stricken. She looked worse than when she had been pulled out of the dark cell that dreadful day, on the verge of collapse.

'Oh, don't be silly!' cried Mrs Hopkins gaily, considering it best to make light of things. 'You've got the collywobbles, that's all. They will disappear the instant you step onstage.'

'You don't understand, Miss,' said Amelia, and she seemed suddenly furious, as if she might reach out and wrench Mrs Hopkins' head off. '*I can't do it and I won't do it and you can't fucking make me!*' Her voice rang out shrill as a banshee in the darkness. Her fellow performers, huddled together in the shadows, watched anxiously.

'You can and you will do it, Amelia,' said Mrs Hopkins quietly. 'For without "Annie Laurie", we do not have a concert.'

'Get someone else to sing it then! Get Catherine. She's got a nice voice.'

'She has indeed a lovely voice, but she could not sing it as you sing it.'

'Anyone can sing it, what difference does it make?'

'It makes a great deal of difference,' said Mrs Hopkins, and she took a deep breath. It was one of those moments, she realised, when she must reach out and pluck from some distant portal the exact right words with which to forestall the impending calamity. It felt almost as if she must run onto the street, waving her arms in front of runaway horses. For she could no sooner force Amelia to do anything than stop the bolting horses, she recognised that. 'The girls look up to you, Amelia. You are their leader, their guide and their inspiration,' she began hopefully.

'I don't give a fuck—I'm not doing it.'

'It is not a role that you have chosen for yourself, I grant you, and you may well wish it otherwise. But the girls have placed this mantle upon you, and thus you must wear it. It comes with a great many obligations attached—can you picture it?—like so many ribbons. Foremost amongst them is the ribbon of Hope—do you understand me, Amelia? You give the girls Hope, and without Hope, they have nothing—all is lost for them, do you see?'

Amelia made no response. She stood scowling down at the dry dock.

Down below, some sailors had spotted the two women and were calling out to them. '*Mademoiselles!*'

Amelia raised her middle finger at them.

'And second to Hope comes the ribbon of Courage,' said Mrs Hopkins, and she reached out suddenly and grasped hold of the girl's hand. 'You give the girls Courage, Amelia; you give us all Courage! And oh, how we need Courage in this place, Amelia, we need it desperately! I saw you pulled out of that dark pit; you were faint as who wouldn't be, but five minutes later, you were laughing, Amelia! *Laughing!*'

Still, Amelia said nothing, but gazed down at the sailors below. Several had gathered now and were shouting out ribald phrases in French. Some were thrusting their groins and simulating fornication. It reminded Mrs Hopkins briefly of Mr Crabback, but she quickly put the thought out of her mind.

'I don't say that it is easy for you, Amelia,' said Mrs Hopkins softly, and she took the liberty now of stroking the girl's hand. 'This mantle you must wear is both an honour and a burden, and I know you feel greatly your responsibility. But remember this one thing, Amelia: you may have been left with nothing as a baby, but one thing you were blessed with was Courage—yes, Courage in abundance. In fact, you have so much Courage, you can afford to share a little around with the rest of us.'

The back door opened, and Miss Foy stuck her head out. 'They're all ready for you, Mrs Hopkins!' In her excitement, there was a slightly hysterical tone to her voice.

'Thank you, Miss Foy,' Mrs Hopkins called back, making sure to keep her voice as steady as possible in contrast. She turned back to Amelia. 'Will you sing for us this evening, Amelia?'

In the darkness it was impossible to read the girl's expression. But there! She saw it (or at least she thought she saw it)—the tiniest of nods, barely perceptible.

'Good girl,' whispered Mrs Hopkins. And realising that she was still clutching onto the girl's hand, she gave it a little pat and let it go.

'Ladies and gentlemen,' commenced Mr Crabback, and a thrilled sort of hush fell over the assembly in the mess-hall. 'Well, of course, I am the only gentleman present, am I not?' He chuckled.

A murmur of amusement passed through the crowd; they were feeling generous towards their Superintendent this evening.

'Let me say instead: welcome ladies of Biloela, young and old, big and small, to our very special concert this evening. As you know, we are endeavouring to raise funds for the institution that you might all enjoy more in the way of reading materials and drawing tools and games to play such as rounders and hoops and so forth. Also, we hope to make the institution feel more homely by hanging inspirational scenes from the Bible, such as baby Moses in his basket and what have you—'

'What about blankets?' interrupted Mrs Baird. 'Never mind baby Moses, we need new blankets. We hardly have a single one that has not been ripped to shreds by the girls to start fires with.'

'Yes, new blankets certainly. They are foremost upon our list.'

'And some decent pots and pans,' offered Miss Foy. 'The handle of the frypan came right off in my hand the other day. I found myself knee-deep in chicken giblets.'

A wave of mirth broke out amongst the girls in the darker recesses of the hall.

'It wasn't funny at the time, let me tell you,' Miss Foy said, scowling into the shadows.

'No, indeed, I daresay it could have been quite serious, for a braised giblet carries a quantity of heat,' said Mr Crabback.

This only evoked more hilarity from the back rows. He wished the Assistant Matrons would stop interjecting for he could not get a decent flow going.

Seeing his predicament, Mrs Hopkins—who had just entered by the side door—felt bound to speak up. 'We have listed new pots and pans as foremost amongst our requirements,' she said. (In fact, the idea of replacing the institution's cookware had not occurred to her, and now that it had been brought to her attention, it all seemed rather dreary and costly. Wasn't that Henry's job, to patch these things? And surely the handle to the frypan could be screwed back on again? Mrs Hopkins had a mind to have a go at it herself.)

'And what else—pray remind me, Mrs Hopkins—what else is upon our list?' asked Mr Crabback.

Since she had jumped in, she might as well continue, he considered. This whole list business had been her idea and, as usual, he was the one being 'hung out to dry' for it.

'Oh, well, a great many things really for the school is sadly in want. Musical instruments, for example—a harmonium perhaps—and for the little ones, some tambourines and triangles.' Here she mimed the action of striking a triangle, seeming to think it called for elucidation in this way. 'Oh, and the girls must have proper crockery to eat from instead of those awful tin pannikins—nice Delftware bowls, for example—'

'Delftware bowls? They will not last two minutes before they are taken down to the rocks and smashed!'

'Well, there I must disagree with you, Mrs Baird. I believe that, given the opportunity to have nice things, the girls will learn to appreciate their value and look after them—'

Now Mr Crabback felt it necessary to intervene, for he could see by the colour rising from her collar that Mrs Hopkins was beginning to grow somewhat overheated. 'Yes, indeed, I am sure there is a great deal in the way of minutia to discuss, but there is one thing we can all agree upon, and that is that there is much to accomplish in our time together at Biloela.'

That felt better! He was back in control. He saw Mrs Baird settle into her seat, arms folded, pleased to have said her piece and only slightly disgruntled.

'For it is my firm belief,' he continued, 'that, by pulling together as a team, just as we have done in the preparation of this concert, we can achieve most. For, I tell you now, it is my fervently held dream that with care and attention, this rundown, decrepit old barracks in which we daily toil might one day, like the great French reformatory Mettray, become a shining example to other industrial schools the world over. And our first step in this direction is to petition by means of this short entertainment the good Ladies of the Benevolent Society—several of whom I consider to be dear friends of many years standing.'

Mrs Hopkins felt a small lurch in her belly. *Dear friends of many years standing?* This was the first time she had heard him refer to the Ladies of the Benevolent Society as such. Up to this point, he had conveyed the impression that he only knew them vaguely as acquaintances from years past. How dear exactly were these friends? Did they permit him to lie atop of them in the evening, as she did? Had they disrobed for his pleasure or performed other unspeakable acts?

'And now,' cried Mr Crabback, 'without further ado, let the concert commence!'

Jolted thusly from her thoughts, Mrs Hopkins flung open the door and the performers made their entrance. A cry of collective awe and delight rung out. Mrs Hopkins had appropriated as many lanterns she could lay her hands upon and arranged them in in such a manner that, as they took their positions on the makeshift stage, the youthful artistes appeared to acquire a kind of lustre, a magical luminosity about them. The little Tunks sisters with their giant bows (Martha had been finally coerced into wearing hers) hobbled to the foremost position, while Josephine and Bridget stood to the side of and slightly behind them. Amelia, Mary-Ann and Catherine took up the rear, with Amelia, being the tallest, in the centre. There they stood, in this miraculous pool of light, for one long moment of stillness. Their eyes were trained upon Mrs Hopkins, awaiting their cue. She raised her hand, and on its downward stroke, like horses at a country racecourse, they launched haphazardly from the gate and into the opening hymn.

Richly blest, are those who share
In an earthly father's care
Share his gentle heart, that bides
Firm and true, whate'er betides
Though the path be sin defiled
Still the father loves his child
And his patient spirit yearns
Till the prodigal returns.

At once, the great surprise to everybody was little Emma, at six years old, the eldest of the Tunks sisters. Normally desperately shy to the point of muteness, on this occasion her sweet, piping voice could be heard ringing clearly above the others. She did not always hit the correct note—in fact, there were moments when it appeared that she might be improvising another melody altogether. But given the stark fact that the 'earthly father' of the three little Tunks sisters had abandoned them in a derelict, rat-infested warehouse, with no food or water and only filthy straw for bedding, the earnest plaintive hope with which she sang of him now was almost unbearable to hear. It was as if the bow-legged waif was trying to summon him, if only in spirit, to convey to him somehow her forgiveness for the terrible deed he had committed of having left them utterly for dead. The youthful audience grew silent and sorrowful, their thoughts dwelling upon their own earthly fathers, or mothers, wherever they were; and the circumstances which had led to them being interred for their entire girlhoods in this dreadful sandstone prison.

When the song reached its conclusion, and Mrs Baird and Miss Foy had dabbed away their tears, Mary-Ann stepped forward, smiling merrily at her audience. She sat herself upon a small milking stool, arranging her skirts that she might reveal a glimpse of comely stockinged ankle, and at once Josephine and the Tunks sisters assumed their positions at her knee, gazing up at her adoringly.

'Now, girls,' she addressed them, bright and confident, 'I have some questions that have been puzzling me. Will you try to answer them for them for me please?'

She then proceeded with her questions in a sprightly, sing-song voice, to which the little ones made their stilted and stumbling responses.

Mary-Ann: *Nature, whence sprang thy glorious flame?*
Girls: *My Master called me, and I came.*
Mary-Ann: *Winds, whence and whither do ye blow?*
Girls: *Thou must be born again to know.*

On and on it went, with the audience struggling to make sense of it. Even Mrs Hopkins, watching from the wings, began to grow doubtful as to its merit. Mary-Ann pressed gamely on; a forefinger placed upon her chin in mock-puzzlement.

Mary-Ann: *Flowers, wherefore do ye bloom?*
Girls: *We strew thy pathway to the tomb.*
Mary-Ann: *And tell me Death, how ends thy strife?*

A pause here, then after much whispering and prodding from the others, Janie, the youngest of the Tunks sisters, a scrap of a thing at three years old, lisped in a tiny voice:

It endth in everlathting Life.

It was too adorable! In those few lisping words, mouthed by a bandy-legged foundling, the whole piece seemed suddenly a tremendous joke. Life was filled with puzzles, like bubbles and wind and flowers; it was baffling but deliberately so and it didn't matter because it ended in Death, which *endth in everlathting Life*!

The audience erupted into wild applause while Mrs Hopkins beamed. The idea of having the child lisp the last line unaccompanied had come to her only hours earlier, when she had realised, after subjecting the child to extensive and exhaustive drills, that the poor thing with her hare lip was never going to be able to enunciate her sibilants. And in that same moment, she saw that the little one's speech impediment, far from diminishing the piece, might actually add to it a certain heart-rending pathos. And so it had, if the audience response was anything to judge from! Clapping was too meagre a means of conveying their enthusiasm; they began to stomp their feet upon the floorboards, which startled little Janie such that she burst into tears. Josephine immediately hoisted her up on her hip and spoke to her earnestly, and soon a shy, sweet smile came over the little one's face when she realised that all the commotion was for her. Overcome, she buried her face into Josephine's shoulder, and the audience whooped and stomped their feet all the harder.

Now it was time for 'Annie Laurie'. Mary-Ann and the little ones fell back into the shadows, and for a long moment, the stage stood empty. Mrs Hopkins' hand flew to her mouth in breathless horror. Had her speech (of which she had been quite inordinately proud) with its depiction of mantles and ribbons not succeeded in emboldening the girl after all? The audience sat tense and silent, for somehow they seemed to sense the underlying drama. And then—yes!—a happy murmur, a collective sigh of relief, as Amelia stepped forward into the light, smoothing down her dress with trembling hands. Brave girl, thought Mrs Hopkins, inhaling again, her hand fluttering upon her chest. *Brave, courageous girl!*

A moment as the girl just stood there, a frail and solitary figure in her preposterous hairdo, trying valiantly to summon her courage.

The audience stared up at her, silent and fearful. Fearless Amelia, champion of foundlings; their ringleader, their hope, their inspiration—sing forth!

Amelia opened her mouth. Nothing came out. She swallowed and tried again. And now, so thin as to be barely audible at first and wobbling precariously, the sombre opening lines of the Scottish ballad began to rise.

Maxwellton braes are bonnie
Where early falls the dew
And it's there that Annie Laurie
Gave me her promise true—

A tremor of nerves or emotion caused her voice to crack on 'promise true' but this seemed only to heighten the poignancy of that line. It seemed also to strengthen her resolve for she lifted her chin defiantly, and her voice grew stronger now, more certain.

Like dew on the gowan lying
Is the fall o' her fairy feet
And like wind in the summer sighing
Her voice is low and sweet.
Her voice is low and sweet
She's a' the world tae me
And for bonnie Annie Laurie
I'd lay me doon and dee.

Such a lovely, mellifluous, sorrowful voice! And with what sadness and regret and longing she imbued each single word. The girls leaned forward, gazing up at her with wide unblinking eyes, just as if she had cast a spell upon them. And yet from the dark shadows of the back rows, Mrs Hopkins began to grow aware of a disturbance. Sullen, befreckled Annie Laughton appeared to be working herself into a state. Her friends were attempting to hush her, but to no avail; the keening was turning into a wail.

Mrs Hopkins felt herself grow rigid with anger. It was distracting and disruptive and attention-seeking, and although Amelia seemed oblivious, this sort of carry-on could not be tolerated.

Moving swiftly around to the back of the hall in the darkness, unseen in the blackness of her mourning garb, she came up behind the girl and grabbed her fiercely by the arm. 'Out!' she hissed. Annie shrank back in fear. '*Out!*' repeated Mrs Hopkins, and with a violent jerk, she pulled the weeping girl to her feet and swept her out of the mess-hall, closing the door upon her.

All of this caused her to miss the last verse of the song, for by the time she had got rid of the girl (there had been an unseemly tussle over the doorknob, with Annie trying to force her way back in), the song was over and the audience erupting into ecstatic applause.

With a small bow of acknowledgement, Amelia turned and resumed her position in the group of performers. As she did so, Catherine's hand sought hers and gave it a squeeze, her eyes shining up at her.

Bridget was now stepping forward to the front of the stage, clutching her juggling balls. 'I would now like to surprise and delight you with my juggling prowess,' she announced. Then she turned and gave the girls behind her a nod. They launched into a jaunty accompaniment, whistling 'Blue-Tail Fly' and clapping along lightly in time. Bridget commenced to juggle with three balls, and after succeeding without dropping any for several runs, she caught the last ball in triumph. This prompted a round of applause, but she shook her head briskly to indicate that she had not finished. She motioned to Josephine, who stepped forward and passed her another ball. (Mrs Baird had gone to the trouble of making her a new set out of fabric scraps, each of a different colour.)

'I will now juggle four balls,' she announced and, taking a deep breath to prepare herself, she launched into it. Her little face screwed up in concentration, gazing upwards at each flying ball. 'Up!' she ordered them through clenched teeth. 'Up! Up! Up!' The whistling of 'Blue Tail Fly' grew faster now, as Bridget's juggling grew more confident. The audience began to clap in time: some even began to sing along with the chorus:

Jimmy Crack Corn, and I don't care Jimmy Crack Corn, and I don't care Jimmy Crack Corn, and I don't care, My Master's gone away!

Fffft! A ball fell to the floor. Here was the moment of truth!

'Don't swear, little Bridget, don't swear!' whispered Mrs Hopkins in a panic.

The danger passed quickly, however; Bridget swooped down to pick the ball up, and stood, red-faced and erect, before her audience. 'I will now attempt to juggle five balls,' she announced. 'Five balls is very difficult, much more difficult than four balls, anyone will tell you that. Therefore, I must ask the audience for complete silence.'

A few moments of frenzied shushing amongst the audience members and then silence. Mad little Martha, the middle of the Tunks sisters, stepped forward with the fifth ball extended in her hand.

'Don't fuck it up, Bridget, whatever you do,' she said earnestly.

A gasp of shock, then a wave of laughter rippled through the hall.

Bridget glanced up at the audience, and, skilled at improvising as she was, seized the moment and wagged her finger at the little girl. 'Excuse me, Miss Martha,' she exclaimed. 'If anyone is going to swear around here, I think it oughta be the juggler!'

Now the laughter could not be restrained. Mr Crabback had to pull his spectacles off to wipe his eyes; even Mrs Baird was seen to be giggling hopelessly behind her hand. Not caring one whit about silence anymore, Bridget commenced juggling the five balls. She dropped a couple almost immediately, flung the rest of them in the air, bowed with a great flourish, and then Josephine, getting her cue wrong, cartwheeled, high-kicked and backflipped across the stage.

It was a triumph. The applause was so loud that the sailors down at the dry docks turned their heads and gazed up at the dreary old cooler in amazement.

Finally, it was Catherine's turn. She stepped forward and waited with quiet dignity for the merriment to subside.

'I would like to close our entertainment with a short prayer,' she said and duly placed her hands together and closed her eyes. The girls, eyeing her reverently, did the same, and so then did the Assistant Matrons, Mr Crabback and Mrs Hopkins.

Catherine commenced.

Dear Lord,
Should Poverty's consuming blow
Lay all my worldly comforts low
And neither help nor hope appear
My steps to guide, my heart to cheer; Lord!
Pity and supply my need
For Thou on Earth was poor indeed.
Amen.

The evening was undoubtedly a tremendous success. Spilling out into the quadrangle, the girls embraced the performers rapturously.

How glamorous they seemed, what stars! Cartwheels were attempted in the quadrangle by the light of the moon, and juggling lessons freely dispensed by Bridget. The little Tunks girls were carried about and generally doted upon until Janie, the little one, became over-tired and began to bite people. Josephine carried her off to bed.

Mr Crabback, Mrs Hopkins, Mrs Baird and Miss Foy stood watching from the doorway of the mess-hall.

'We will let them stay out and play a little longer,' said Mr Crabback. 'I feel they deserve a reward for good behaviour.'

'Yes, indeed,' agreed Mrs Baird. 'Their behaviour has been excellent.'

'Oh, it was a wonderful show,' cried Miss Foy. 'I loved every minute of it.'

'It was just long enough and not so long that it got on your nerves,' said Mrs Baird. She had evidently endured some tiresome entertainments in her time.

'Well, I could not have done it without your efforts,' said Mrs Hopkins. 'Let us hope that the Ladies of the Benevolent Society enjoy it as much as our girls did!'

'They'd be mad if they didn't!' cried Miss Foy.

When the inmates were finally locked up for the evening, nobody noticed that Annie Laughton was not in her bed. Nor for that matter was Amelia. Taking advantage of the Matrons' inattention that evening, she had slipped into Catherine's dormitory for the night.

A furtive knock at the door, just as Mrs Hopkins expected. A thrill of excitement ran through her. The performance had been such a triumph, everything had gone off so perfectly, that she knew—she *sensed* somehow—that there was enchantment in the air and further wonders yet awaiting her.

Mr Crabback had given her a certain look as he bid them all good evening before returning to his quarters. It was a look laden with meaning. Perhaps roused by her success, the calm and accomplished manner in which she had conducted events, he saw her now, not just as loyal helpmeet but in a wholly different light. *Tonight I mean to have you, fully and completely.* That is what the look said. It was a look of admiration, tinged with stark desire.

In readiness, she had taken down her bun and unplaited her hair, teasing it out from her scalp and running her fingers through the long tresses that they might ripple out in a voluminous cloud. She wore only her chemise and bloomers, for she hoped to convey the illusion that Mr Crabback had interrupted her just as she was preparing for bed. She had an idea that she might slap him, in the playful way that Mary-Ann enjoyed slapping her lover.

'May I come in?' said Mr Crabback.

She had opened the door just an inch or two and peeked out at him.

'Would you allow me a moment or two? You have caught me half-undressed—'

Just as she had hoped, he pushed the door open and forced his way in, taking her in his arms and sweeping her onto her narrow cot. He pulled off her bloomers in one swift action, and as he began to fumble with her chemise, she seized the opportunity to slap him, though in her excitement somewhat harder than she had intended.

He stared at her in shock, an angry red mark surfacing on his cheek. 'What did you do that for?' he asked.

'Well, because you were being ver—' She had not really expected to have to justify her actions and had no answer at the ready. 'You were being very brazen,' she concluded.

'Brazen? And yet I thought, from the enthusiasm of your response, that you were enjoying my advances.'

'Oh yes—very much.'

'Then why did you slap me?'

'Well, just—you know—I thought as a bit of fun.'

'*A bit of fun?*' he repeated, as if in disbelief.

'I thought you might slap me back,' she responded dismally.

How she longed for the swarthy French sailor at this point.

Mr Crabback rubbed his red cheek ruefully. He did not quite know what to make of it. It was the hysteric in her perhaps, just as that newspaper article had forewarned. The hysteric was not content with a simple, straightforward coitus—she must add these elements of drama.

'Alas, your "bit of fun" has had the effect of robbing me of my necessary juices,' he said.

'Yes, it has robbed me of mine also,' said Mrs Hopkins sadly. She wished she might pull her bloomers back on; however, Mr Crabback, in his initial enthusiasm, had flung them across the room.

'Then again,' said Mr Crabback, after giving the matter a moment or two of consideration, 'if your womanly instincts desire it, I suppose I might be persuaded to engage in a bit of the old rough play. A touch of the cane, perhaps?'

And here he picked up her cane, which happened to be sitting on her bedside table. Mrs Hopkins heart sank: this was not at all what she had intended. But given that her notion of playful slapping had caused such offence, she felt that she could hardly refuse him. Commencing with a few light strokes across the palms of her hands, he then proceeded to a series of stinging blows across the backs of her thighs. It hurt a great deal more than she anticipated; visions of all the little girls she had caned in her years as School-Mistress passed fleetingly before her, their faces puckering in disbelief, gasping and whimpering. She clenched her jaw and dismissed these images, choosing instead to fix her gaze upon Miss Minnie, who stared upon her in button-eyed dismay from her position at the top of the bed.

Nor was Mr Crabback particularly enjoying the experience. Her thin white spider-veined thighs mottled angrily, and with every blow she emitted a kind of wheezy grunt; a very displeasing sound, not at all arousing if that had been the intention. Perhaps she would prefer to do the caning herself, he wondered. After all, she was the one who had started it all with her slapping. Besides, his arm was getting tired.

'Here,' he said, passing her the cane. 'You have a go.'

He lowered his trousers and, as she seemed uncertain as to how to proceed, he indicated that she might lash him across the backs of his knees. This she did very tentatively, as if not wishing to hurt him.

'Harder,' he urged sportingly. 'As hard as you like!'

Thus encouraged, she pulled her arm back and walloped him with as much might as she could muster. At once, his knees gave way and he toppled face forward onto the bed. She hesitated, gazing down upon his prostate form. His bare buttocks had a light covering of fairish down, and she thought at once of peaches. A barrowman had given her one as a child, whereupon she had dropped it upon the cobblestones, and he had yelled at her for bruising it. When she picked it up and took a bite, the fuzzy texture of its skin had set her teeth on edge. She could not understand what all the fuss was about. She would rather a crunchy pink apple any day.

'Go on then!' urged Mr Crabback, his voice muffled by the pillow.

(Miss Minnie had by now fallen to the floor, out of view, much to Mrs Hopkins' relief.)

Thence she proceeded to cane him across his rear end, quite gently at first, as she could not shake the idea of peaches and their propensity for bruising.

'Harder!' urged Mr Crabback, for he wished to prove to Mrs Hopkins that he was more than willing to partake of her sexual shenanigans.

Mrs Hopkins flogged him harder.

After five or six blows, they found they were both quite enjoying the experience. On the tenth blow, the cane broke. Mr Crabback pulled her down onto the bed and there, their juices thus replenished, the Superintendent and Acting Matron achieved sublime connection.

Afterwards, they had snuggled together happily under the blankets, bestowing small kisses upon each other's faces and whispering endearments. Starved of affection for so many years, their lovemaking, unconventional as it had been, had released all doubts and reservations.

'I love you,' declared Mr Crabback.

'And I love you,' whispered Mrs Hopkins into his side-whiskers.

'What tonight has proved,' said Mr Crabback, 'is that you and I, working together in this fashion, will be unstoppable.'

Was he referring to the concert or the caning? she wondered. Either way, she nodded fervently.

'The concert, as noted, went off very nicely. However, if I could humbly offer a few small criticisms—' he began.

Mrs Hopkins braced herself. She had not expected any criticism at all; had it not been universally declared a triumph? But then again, of course, there had been mishaps: Amelia's nervousness, the dropping of the juggling balls, Martha's use of the 'f' word.

'The entertainment needed a host, a master of ceremonies if you will. As it was, it went from one act to another, with the audience forced to sit through all the necessary shifting of props and bodies. And yet if the spotlight were to fall upon a host at these moments, it might fill the spaces, as it were, providing perhaps a little background material as to the girls, and the pieces they are performing.'

'Oh yes, that is a marvellous idea!' exclaimed Mrs Hopkins.

'Naturally, I could not expect you to fulfil such a role. But with my own meagre oratorical skills, perhaps I might step in with a few well-chosen words, and add context and interest, if you will, to the entertainment provided.'

'I cannot imagine why this did not occur to me earlier! Why, you would be wonderful!' she enthused warmly.

'That is as may be,' Mr Crabback acceded modestly.

'My second point is this, and it is a good deal more serious: the girls were far too well-presented. Why, they looked fetching enough to be promenading along the boulevarde, with their pretty dresses and their hair all dolled up. No, they need to look as drab and pitiful as possible: that is the whole point of the exercise. Certainly, they must be clean and tidy, but their dresses should be torn and mended; the soles of their boots worn through, the toes scuffed out; and as for all those ribbons in their hair, I don't know what you were thinking. "If they can afford luxuries such as ribbons, then they scarcely need our donations." That is what the Ladies of the Benevolent Society will say.'

'I only thought—' began Mrs Hopkins, for she was remembering how thrilled with themselves the girls had been as they gazed at themselves in the looking glass. And how proud the other girls were of their friends, and how nicely they scrubbed up.

'You are quite right,' she said. 'How foolish of me. I will set things to rights first thing in the morning.'

And so she did. Rising before dawn (Mr Crabback had returned to his quarters shortly after giving the above pronouncement), she lit her lantern, hurried to the gate of the institution and set about unlocking it with her usual mounting panic at its stubbornness. Once at last successful, she then flitted over the quadrangle in the darkness, directly to the laundry, where she placed down her lantern and set about combing through racks of dungaree dresses, looking for the most worn and shabby.

'What on earth are you doing?' asked Mrs Baird, who came in to find Mrs Hopkins ironing out the creases as best she could of a particularly tattered specimen.

'The girls' dresses are too pretty,' said Mrs Hopkins. 'They need to look more pitiful.'

'But these dresses we had put aside to use for mending scraps,' cried Mrs Baird. 'The girls will look as if they have been dragged out of the gutter.'

'That is the whole point of the exercise,' said Mrs Hopkins.

'And further, we must take down their hairstyles,' said Mrs Hopkins, as she swept into the dormitories. The girls were just now rising from their beds, carefully pulling the pillowcases from their heads to see how their hairstyles had survived the night. 'They must wear their hair tied back simply, but there are to be no ribbons. And that includes the Tunks sisters. They are not to wear their bows.'

A wail of protest rose up from the girls when they realised how they were to be presented. Mrs Baird and Miss Foy were just as upset, if not more so.

'All the work we have done to scrub them up and make them look respectable! What does it say of us matrons that we let them go out looking like that?'

'We will look like little more than street arabs!' cried Mary-Ann in horror, as she saw the ragged dress she must now attire herself in.

'It has never bothered you before,' said Amelia. 'Why, you're always tearing the gathers off your skirt so your fella gets to see it all.'

'Oh, shut it, Amelia, for once in your life!' cried Mary-Ann, and she burst into tears and threw herself upon her bed.

'Can Josie and me wear our red ribbons?' asked Bridget.

'No, you may not. No one is to wear ribbons, do you understand? "If they can afford luxuries such as ribbons, they will scarcely need our donations." That is what the Ladies will say. It will defeat the whole point of the exercise, don't you see?

So take your hair down and brush it out, girls. Miss Foy, will you help them please?'

'I won't!' cried Mary-Ann, wild-eyed, clutching onto her hairdo.

'You must, Mary-Ann. Please see reason here!' cried Mrs Hopkins. She was feeling a tiny bit hysterical herself.

'Listen, Mary-Ann, it's pretty straightforward: we need to look like we need boodle,' said Amelia. 'All dolled up like we were last night, everyone will say, "Those Biloela girls are doing all right. Look at all those ribbons, and their dresses all crocheted and embroidered nice. Why should we give them any dough?" We need to look like ragamuffins, so they feel sorry for us. We need to pluck at their heartstrings, don't we, Mrs Hopkins?'

'Yes, Amelia, that is exactly right. We need to pluck at their heartstrings,' said Mrs Hopkins, gazing at Amelia in wonderment. 'And believe me, girls, you will still look lovely, each and every one of you, because you *are* lovely, through and through—'

'All right, that's enough. You are laying it on a bit thick now, Mrs Hopkins,' said Amelia, and she began to pull the pins from her hairdo and set her wild dark curls tumbling down the back of her chemise.

'And when you say we need to *look* like ragamuffins, we need not *act* like ragamuffins, of course,' said Mrs Hopkins, feeling that point needed to be clarified, especially for the benefit of the younger ones.

'Oh no, Mrs Hopkins, don't you fret: we will get them bawling, just like we did last night, won't we, little Baby Tunks?' And Amelia scooped up Janie, who had joined in the general crying, and gave her a big fat kiss.

'And all those lovely dresses with the crochet work and the forget-me-nots, we will put them away for special occasions, for our Special Visiting Day for Mothers and suchlike,' announced Mrs Hopkins, for she had noticed that Rosabella and the other girls were looking a little disconsolate now that their own efforts no longer mattered to the success of the day. 'In fact, now that I think of it, we will start a special project where all the girls learn to do the beautiful fancy-work on their own dresses. And Rosabella, you and Winnie and Margie Blackman might perhaps be the teachers? For your embroidery and crochet work is far better than my own!'

By the time Mrs Hopkins hurried back to her quarters for a cup of tea and a bite of breakfast, the girls had got over most of their disappointment, and a feeling of 'let's make the most of it' had taken over, largely thanks to Amelia's cool acceptance of events. There was no doubt that the girls looked to her for guidance, Mrs Hopkins told herself as she opened the front gate. And then she pulled up with a sharp shock.

For there on the great flagstone just outside the gate, crudely depicted in chalk, was a drawing of a woman, her hair out wild like a harpie, or even a witch, standing over a bed where a side-whiskered man lay prone and bare-bottomed. The harpie, smiling gaily, was beating the man with a stick. The man had his mouth open in some kind of rictus of agony.

Her heart thumped hard in her chest. Had anyone else seen it? For it was dark when she had first entered the institution that morning, but what about Mrs Baird and Miss Foy? When had they come? Was the dawn breaking as they unlocked the gate to enter? Had they glanced down and seen it and reeled back in horror and disgust, as she had done just now? And—more terrifying thought yet—*who had drawn it?*

Someone lurking in the darkness outside the boundaries of the institution! And had that same person—people? *unspeakable thought!*—peeked through her windows and witnessed their antics? Were these abominable caricatures at her feet, God forbid, a depiction drawn from life of her and Mr Crabback?

Could it be, she asked herself, that the two ghouls of the paupers' graves had taken this action as a means of revenge?

In a furious manner, she set about scuffing the drawing out with the soles of her boots, back and forth, back and forth, back and forth.

How stubborn it was—it did not seem to want to budge. She looked wildly around in the hope of handy mop and bucket but of course, nothing so useful was at hand, nor did the heavens promise a cleansing shower of rain. The quadrangle behind her was empty for the moment—the girls still occupied with their dressing. Without another thought she squatted to her haunches, reaching beneath her skirts to pull at the opening of her drawers that she might piss the crude figures out of sight.

Given that the ensemble was having such a special outing, Mr Crabback decreed that the rest of the girls, and indeed the Assistant Matrons, should have the morning off, and spend it sitting in the sunshine or playing upon the beach as they wished. But first the whole school was to wave the troupe off at the wharf. (Rosabella alone was excluded from this. Horrified to find that someone had urinated at the front gate, Mrs Baird, who had spotted Rosabella lurking in the near vicinity earlier, duly blamed and punished her. She had a long history of bed-wetting, after all. 'A big girl like you can't hold her bladder!' cried Mrs Baird, before shutting her up in the dormitory.)

How proudly the Biloela ensemble boarded the paddle steamer *Emu*, their heads high even in spite of their dreary attire. They lined the decks and blew kisses to their friends, while the other passengers stared dumbfounded at the rowdy turn-out on the shore. Those inmates staying behind launched into a kind of school song, one that neither Mr Crabback nor Mrs Hopkins had heard before.

Here's for Biloela girls
We're the toughest in the world!
Don't come knocking on our door
For if you do, you'll get what-for!
Don't come climbing o'er our walls
We'll kick you in the effing balls—

Fortunately, at this timely moment, the *Emu* blasted its horn to signal its departure. The girls broke off from their singing and screamed in excitement, many with tears streaming down their cheeks. The brave little troupe of performers on the steamer gave their last ceremonial waves and the steamer heaved away. Mr Crabback turned to Mrs Hopkins with a smile and slipped his arm around her waist.

'Well, my love, we have done it,' he said.

'Yes, indeed,' she responded, removing his hand as soon as she could do so without causing offence (he was taking more and more liberties of this kind of late, she had noticed). 'Or at least part of it, anyway. We have boarded the steamer.'

'Oh, don't be putting the mockers on, Mrs Hopkins! Today is a grand day for Biloela. Put a smile on your face and your best foot forward!'

With some effort, she managed to summon a thin smile; apparently satisfied, Mr Crabback headed off to the bow.

The truth was, Mrs Hopkins was experiencing a kind of queasiness in her belly, which she could best define as misgivings as to what lay ahead. And now, when the steamer moved off, she saw that Henry had materialised amongst those assembled on the shore. The girls were still jumping up and down and waving, but he stood quite still. His gaze was fixed upon Josephine, standing next to Mrs Hopkins on the deck of the steamer. His expression was one of puzzlement at first then a kind of creeping horror, as if he had sighted a ghost.

She was not the only one feeling queasy, for Bridget soon reported that Mary-Ann was vomiting over the side. Mrs Hopkins hurried over to assist her.

'Oh, Mrs Hopkins, these boats, they do make me seasick,' moaned Mary-Ann, wiping her mouth with the back of her hand. Mrs Hopkins led her to a seat within the saloon and instructed that she close her eyes and do her best to think of other more pleasant things such as dancing or roller-skating. This proved a mistake; the girl then vomited over her dress and, after complaints from other passengers, was brought out onto the bow again.

Amelia and Catherine sat together a short distance away, attempting to appear as if they were out on a pleasure trip and not connected to the Biloela party at all. Mr Crabback stood at the most forward point of the bow, hands folded behind his back, gazing out benignly towards the approaching township like a general surveying the lands he would shortly conquer. How smart he looked today, thought Mrs Hopkins with a tingle of pleasure. He was wearing a plaid jacket that she had not seen before, with a high collar and covered buttons.

The ticket collector ventured out of the saloon and at the sight of his uniform, Mrs Hopkins' heart lurched as a sudden fear assailed her. But it was not the same ticket collector who kept insisting she make a cup of tea for Josephine's grieving mother that dreadful morning. He did not look at her accusingly; in fact, he ignored her, and made his way over to Mr Crabback.

'Ah yes,' said Mr Crabback as the man approached him. He reached into his breast pocket, then looked uncertainly at Mrs Hopkins. 'Did you bring the fare money?'

'No, I did not,' she responded firmly, for she felt sure he had promised some days ago that matters of travel and itinerary were to be left to him. She had enough on her plate with the rehearsals, he had assured her, not to mention maintaining her dual roles of School-Mistress (for classes continued throughout) and Acting Matron.

'Did we not discuss this?' said Mr Crabback.

'Yes, we did.'

'Did you not say you would get it from the laundry money?'

'No. For we have no laundry money. We have never had any laundry money.'

'Goodness—do you know, I believe that I have become confused with the Haven of Hope. Well, this is very awkward. Very awkward indeed. Might I assure you, sir,' he said, turning back to the ticket collector, 'that on our return trip, I will be flush with funds and able to pay you in full for all parties both ways. I am the Superintendent of the Biloela Industrial School for Girls, so you'll find that I am a man of my word.'

'None of my beeswax, mister—they won't let you through the turnstiles without a ticket. How many of you are there?'

'There are ten of us, but three of them are babies,' he said, pointing to the smaller Tunks.

'No one goes through without a ticket.'

'As I say, I am the Superintendent of the Biloela Industrial School for Girls—'

'We'll put you off at King Street, and you can have it out with Mr Morgan. Likely as not, he'll send you straight back—he's not a patient man at the best of times. In the meantime, you better get this lot to behave themselves or I'll chuck 'em overboard.'

It was true: Bridget and Josephine were running wildly from port to starboard to port again while the Tunks sisters hurled themselves after them, giggling and falling over and getting oily muck all over their raggedy dresses.

'Josephine!' called Mrs Hopkins.

The girl hurried over dutifully.

'Sit beside me quietly like a young lady and set an example to the others.'

And although she would rather have been attempting a cartwheel on the pitching deck, Josephine sat herself demurely beside Mrs Hopkins. Immediately, the doting little Tunks girls followed suit.

'Good girl,' said Mrs Hopkins, patting Josephine's hand. The girl smiled up at her: the School-Mistress felt her heart thud tenderly.

The party was ushered off the steamer at the King Street Wharf, and Mr Crabback despatched to plead his case with Mr Morgan.

Meanwhile, Mrs Hopkins and the girls must stand about, trying not to get in the way of bustling ferry passengers. They were in anxious need of the W.C.'s, but they were not to be permitted through the turnstiles until the matter of fares was cleared up. The girls huddled together in a tight little cluster, attempting to feign indifference to their surroundings and yet their eyes, wide as saucers, gave them away. It was the ladies of Sydney who drew their attention; never in their lives had the girls seen such finery. Shiny black shoes with double buckles and hats trimmed with roses and ostrich plumes (one lady's hat was even trimmed with a large green parrot, much to the unbridled guffaws of Bridget, thus warranting a hard slap from Amelia). Dresses of Scotch gingham and travelling cloaks of cashmere; striped satin parasols and silver buttons and ruches of Breton lace or cascades of plaited flounces; surreptitiously the girls whispered and pointed, until Mrs Hopkins was forced to remind them that it was ill-mannered to behave in such a fashion (although she was every bit as agog herself, and ashamed of her dismal faded mourning).

Finally, Mr Crabback approached them, rather red in the face and agitated. Mr Morgan opened a side gate and ushered them through, disappointing the younger girls who had hoped to experience the thrill of pushing purposefully through a turnstile. After a longer than anticipated sojourn in the Ladies' Lavatories (Amelia and Catherine had had to be forcibly extricated from a cubicle, where it seems they had been enjoying a cigarette they had fashioned from tea leaves and Bible leaf paper), the small party stood about, blinking and staring at the great sandstone buildings surrounding them.

'By golly, this concert had better go off,' was Mr Crabback's grim aside to Mrs Hopkins. 'Otherwise, we'll have to swim home.'

Mrs Hopkins felt a twinge of irritation. It was his fault they had found themselves in this predicament: he had simply not given a moment's thought to the details. Also, she hated it when he used low expressions like 'by golly'. It cheapened him somehow.

'All right, young ladies!' he declared, clapping his hands together. 'Are we all set? Then what are we waiting for? Let's get going!'

This forced heartiness irritated her, too.

'But how are you proposing we get to Woollahra?' asked Mrs Hopkins. She had never heard of the place, much less had any notion of its location. Also, she had heard him talk of a tram at some point and had invested much hope in this option.

'Shank's pony, of course! The very legs we were blessed with!' he replied. And here, they glanced doubtfully at the Tunks girls with their rickety little limbs.

'We will carry the little ones.'

It was an unseasonably warm day and the journey to Woollahra involved a long, long walk up an ever-steepening hill. Mrs Hopkins and the older girls took turns in carrying the smaller Tunks, but Emma, the eldest, insisted on making her own way, hobbling along at an increasing distance behind them. There was little shade, and the noisy horse-drawn omnibuses trundled blithely past them, throwing up clouds of dust.

'Mrs Hopkins, I think I'm going to faint—' murmured Mary-Ann, before dropping to her knees and spilling to the ground in a swoon.

Almost immediately, she was surrounded by various gentlemen, young and old, rushing to her assistance. As pale as she was, she did look rather comely, with her full bosom glistening with sweat.

'Where are you lot off to then?' called a portly gentleman, leaning out from the door of his handsome brougham carriage. It was painted deep maroon with all sorts of fancy brass trimmings. He had instructed his coachman to pull aside when he saw the girl collapse.

'We are on our way to Woollahra,' responded Mr Crabback stiffly. 'A residence by the name of Trelawney; you may have heard of it.'

'I'm going right past there. Hop in, I can give you all a lift.'

'Are you sure, for there are ten of us,' said Mrs Hopkins. The carriage, in her estimation, looked barely to fit four.

'Well, I can't say as there might have to be some sitting on laps,' he said, eyeing Mary-Ann keenly. 'I'm sure I don't mind if you don't.'

'Oh no, we don't mind!' chorused the little ones, jumping up and down excitedly.

'Either that, or I take the poorly one with me now, and come back for you lot later on.'

'Well, if that wouldn't be too much trouble—' began Mrs Hopkins.

Mr Crabback would have none of it. 'Thank you for your offer but we prefer to walk,' he said firmly.

Mrs Hopkins turned to him quickly. 'Should we not accept?' she pleaded *sotto voce*. 'Mary-Ann is not well at all, and poor little Emma—she just can't manage it.'

'Thank you! Good day!' Mr Crabback called out, indicating with a toss of his hand that the gentleman move along. And so, with a shrug, the gentleman closed his door and the handsome brougham trundled away.

'I did not care for the cut of his jib,' said Mr Crabback to Mrs Hopkins, who was gazing at him despairingly. 'I suspect he had designs upon Mary-Ann. Besides,' he continued, 'can you imagine what the Ladies of the Benevolent Society would think if we arrived in such a salubrious conveyance as that? I hardly think it would aid our cause, do you?'

'No, you are quite right,' she responded dismally.

Meanwhile, the other gentlemen who had come to Mary-Ann's aid were in the process of administering her brandy. It appeared she had enjoyed several snifters already, for some colour had returned to her cheeks and she was able to smile wanly at their various jokes and overtures. Mrs Hopkins shooed the men away and the straggling party proceeded up New South Head Road.

They were forced to take many breaks, waiting for little Emma to catch up, or allowing Mary-Ann a moment of rest if they found a patch of shade. The little ones were complaining loudly of their dry mouths and their thirsty throats, for Mrs Hopkins had not thought to bring water, or indeed any refreshments at all. I had thought we were taking a tram, she told herself furiously. Had I known we were to walk such a distance, I would have prepared accordingly.

Once they reached Woollahra, Mr Crabback became muddled as to the exact location of the fine residence. Up and down the various back streets they tottered. Mary-Ann was looking decidedly unsteady on her feet, and complained that her head was aching now, on top of her biliousness. Little

Emma started to cry for her feet were hurting, so Mrs Hopkins passed Martha to Catherine and lifted the girl into her arms.

But Emma struggled furiously for she would prefer to totter on sore feet than suffer the indignity of being carried by the School-Mistress. An impasse of sorts occurred: the child finally agreed if Amelia would give her a piggy-back ride. Still the grand house eluded them.

'Just ask somebody!' Mrs Hopkins pleaded of Mr Crabback, but for some reason he seemed disinclined to do so.

'I cannot understand where it has got to; I have been there many times,' he said. 'Of course, on those other occasions I arrived by carriage, and one tends to take less notice of one's bearings when travelling by carriage.'

Mrs Hopkins felt that, had it not been for the presence of the children, she might cheerfully have struck him.

At last, after summiting another hillock, there it was, tucked away in secluded gardens behind a long fence of sandstone with cast-iron railings, elaborately curlicued. A gleaming brass nameplate spelled the name '*Trelawney*'.

Mr Crabback pushed the front gate open, and they walked in utter silence down the winding driveway to the beautiful, sprawling house. Fragrant gardenia bushes lined the path, amidst clusters of peach-coloured roses and shrubs of fat pink camellias: in the centre of the drive, a huge jacaranda tree extended its pretty mauve blossoms. For the children, who had at best plucked an angry yellow daisy from the cracked clay at Cockatoo Island, such floral magnificence was overwhelming.

On the rolling lawns, they glimpsed several children frolicking with puppies; when they sighted their visitors, a small boy yelled, 'You're late!' and was hastily shushed by his older sister.

They hesitated at the front door. Mrs Hopkins, who had once for a brief unhappy period worked as a governess, felt strongly that it might be frowned upon for their tattered party to assume an entrance by such a grand and imposing portal.

'Don't be ridiculous,' said Mr Crabback, and with a great show of confidence he likely didn't feel, he bowled right up to it and tugged at the bell-rope. After a moment, a housekeeper opened it, and indicated in a peevish fashion that they proceed to the servants' entrance around the back of the house, before closing the door upon them.

The same housekeeper met them at the servants' entrance and told them to wait in the kitchen and try 'if you can help it' not to get in the way. Their lateness had apparently messed up everything; the refreshments that had been prepared for the occasion were in critical danger of spoiling. Waves of sullen resentment emanated from the Cook and her various assistants; Cook slammed her mixing spoon down at one point and heaved a great sigh as if the burden imposed upon her by their lateness could scarcely be endured. The Biloela girls paid no heed: they were staring at the three little scullery maids. They were roughly of the same age as the girls themselves; one appeared to be barely older than Josephine. They wore starched white aprons over pale blue blouses with snowy linen cuffs and collars and they went about their chores meekly and silently. Every now and then, one of the maids might sneak a glance at the shabby troupe and for a fleeting second, a certain look, almost a shudder of repulsion, would pass over her. *There but for the grace of God go I,* the look seemed to say.

They had been provided no seating, and the kitchen was very warm from the heat of the ovens. Little Emma slumped silently to the floor. It took all of Mrs Hopkins' courage to step forward.

'Might the children have some water, please?'

Oh, it did not go well, it did not go well at all, whichever way you looked at it. Perhaps the most that could be said was that it started off all right—*but really, did it?* Mrs Hopkins wondered, when much, much later that same night she clutched Miss Minnie tightly to her and tried to take stock of the day's proceedings. From the moment that they were ushered into the drawing room by the sneering housekeeper, it was evident that the girls had already lost all their confidence, all their *brio,* that brash and radiant light with which they had shone on the previous night of the Dress Rehearsal. They were awe-struck and overwhelmed by the grandeur and opulence of the house; they were intimidated by the company for whom they were expected to perform; they were ashamed, desperately ashamed, of the torn and tattered dresses that they had been forced to appear in.

There were seven ladies present from the Woollahra Ladies of the Benevolent Society, matrons all, resplendent in silk brocades of lavender and grey with Mrs Elsbury, the lady of the house, magnificent in deep green, embossed in a pattern akin to flower petals or possibly, if it caught a certain light, reptile scales. (One shouldn't pay such attention to superfluous, unimportant matters such as fashion, Mrs Hopkins told herself, but, oh, when confronted by such finery, it was difficult not to stare.) Mrs Elsbury's two daughters (blonde, brunette), and a friend of theirs (auburn-haired) arranged themselves artfully on a loveseat, visions ethereal in organdies of pink and lemon and the palest mint green. Several of the ladies' younger children had been invited also (including the rude little boy who had yelled out, 'You're late!'); this was to be a lesson for them about poverty, its causes and consequences. Present also was the local vicar, Reverend Allcock. It was an unfortunate name, and upon his introduction, Bridget had emitted a loud snort, requiring Mrs Hopkins to slap her. Even then, it seemed she did not slap the girl hard enough to compensate for the offence given, to judge by the disapproving looks she received from the Ladies of the Benevolent Society.

Mrs Hopkins did not care. She found that she hated all of them, immediately and quite irrationally.

Oh, they were kind enough, conspicuously so; Mrs Elsbury, in particular, exuded an air of Christian piety, yet seemed simultaneously dazed and excitable, as (Mrs Hopkins thought uncharitably) one who had secretly imbibed a snifter of laudanum . . . *How kind of them to travel such a distance . . . oh, but they had not realised that the Biloela children had prepared a concert . . . but of course, that would be quite charming . . . the difficulty, of course, being their lateness of the hour, for a luncheon had been planned . . . not for the Biloela children, of course (though what a charming idea! A luncheon for poor children! Jot it in the minutes, Mrs Rutter!) . . . oh, will you look at their dear little faces . . . why do they look so downcast? . . . Surely all is not lost! If the concert were a short one, perhaps it could still proceed? Yes, yes, at once! Let us commence the entertainments!*

And with a fluttery clapping of hands, and a pull of the bell-rope with a message to Cook to hold off for another fifteen minutes, Mrs Elsbury arranged herself on the settee with the Reverend Allcock, and the other ladies settled themselves around her.

Mrs Hopkins turned to the children, who stared at her with expressions of hurt bewilderment, as if she had brought this upon them herself. *And hadn't she?* Forgetting all about Mr Crabback's proposed introduction, she launched them into their opening song, 'The Prodigal', and once again, brave little Emma's voice rang out, sweet and pure, for her father.

Richly blest are those who share
In an earthly father's care
Share his gentle heart that bides
Firm and true whate'er betides . . .

The rude little boy had commenced to titter as Emma's voice wavered freely from the melody: he had been glowered at by Mrs Elsbury and one of the other ladies, and hushed half-heartedly by an older sibling, but still an atmosphere of snide merriment pervaded amongst the Trelawney children.

Mrs Hopkins grew furious; she would have slapped him if she were Mrs Elsbury, and slapped him far harder than she had slapped poor little Bridget. The song drew to a close, and Mr Crabback stepped forward to begin his introductions; however, before he could clear his throat, Mary-Ann and the children, in their heightened state of nervous anxiety, had already launched into 'Questions and Answers'. Mr Crabback reddened and stepped back again, bumping into a side-table and almost upending it in so doing; he threw an irritated glance at Mrs Hopkins, for clearly she had not warned the girls that he would be speaking.

'Questions and Answers' seemed to drag on even more than it had the previous evening, and Mrs Hopkins began to wish that she had cut it, for the children were not doing well. The shyness induced by the grand house and the grand company was crippling them; even Josephine and Bridget were not immune to its effects. Only poor sick Mary-Ann held it together as best she could, though she could not quite seem to remember the order of the questions, and flung them out at random:

'O Sun, what made thy beam so bright?'

(Inaudible mumbling from children.)

'Ye Dead, where can your dwelling be?'

(Silence. Fierce whispered prompting from Mary-Ann, followed by inaudible mumbling.)

'O Grave, Where is Thy Victory?'

(Complete Silence. Nothing whatsoever from the lisping Janie, too paralysed with terror to say her line. A pinch ensued from exasperated Mary-Ann whereupon the little child burst into tears.)

'The end!' cried Mary-Ann, hopelessly, for no one seemed to know if it had finished or not. A desultory round of applause; the Trelawney children were now forced to bury their faces in their hands to stifle their giggles: this was all far more entertaining than they had dared hope. Mr Crabback seized his opportunity and at once stepped forward.

'My dear ladies, and Reverend Allcock. Never has it been more truly said, than *'Out of the mouths of babes and sucklings . . .'* For it is difficult to believe that this sweet-faced young lady before you—' here he indicated Mary-Ann '—was found in a hotel drinking a glass of stout with an I-talian and admitted to having sexual connections with him on three separate occasions. She dreams of being on the stage, yet is altogether too fond of boys. Such are the stories of Biloela.

'The three little ones you see here, the sisters Tunk, were found abandoned in a lowly skillion on George Street, huddled together in abject filth and squalor. Their mother has long been committed to a lunatic asylum; their father abandoned them with nary a thought as to their welfare. When the policemen came to take them away, they fought and scratched like wild animals, frantic in the belief that their father would return and not know what had become of them. Alas, their faith in their father was wholly misplaced; he spent what little money he had and drank himself to death. They found him in the gutter only two blocks away; he had got as far as the nearest hotel. Wherefore, you ask, go thy poor, defenceless children? To Biloela—we will take them in, with arms wide open . . .'

A wail had started up—it was Emma. She was staring at Mr Crabback with her big dark eyes and the terrible keening sound, barely human, would not stop. This was the first she had heard of the fate of her father, and her little heart was breaking; Martha began to wail too, and now Janie. 'Take them out,' whispered Mrs Hopkins to Mary-Ann. 'Take them outside!' It was too awful to bear.

Mary-Ann, her face stricken, humiliated by Mr Crabback's account of her, gathered the little Tunks up and fled from the drawing room.

A moment of uncertainty followed, and then Amelia stepped forward, for now it was her turn.

'And now our dear Amelia, without doubt the worst girl in the school,' continued Mr Crabback. 'She was found left for dead as a newborn in the Ladies Water Closets at Redfern Railway Station—it was thought that her mother was a maid-servant, too ashamed to reveal her condition . . . for when a woman falls, she falls very low indeed . . .'

The awful Trelawney boy was convulsing into his sleeve at the notion of a baby being left in a water closet, and at last Mrs Elsbury banished him from the room. But the damage was done—Amelia must stand in her too-short dress before the lovely girls in their organdies, smirking at her in obvious distaste. Mrs Hopkins could see her jaw tighten as she tried to summon the necessary courage; she opened her mouth and bravely commenced to sing. Her voice wobbled worse than ever to begin with, but as she continued, it gained in strength and Mrs Hopkins felt she had never sung the song more sorrowfully. It was as if 'Annie Laurie' was now an ode to her lost mother. The truth was that Amelia had known nothing of her mother prior to this moment and the information that she was likely a maidservant was a revelation to her.

Her mother—till then a phantom, a nobody—now came to life before her as a girl of her own age in a desperate situation, giving birth to a baby in a crude clapboard cubicle, having somehow managed to hide her condition from her employers this whole time. Bitterly, Amelia regretted the scornful disregard with which she had always spoken of her mother in front of her friends.

And it's there that Annie Laurie
Gaed me her promise true
Gaed me her promise true
That ne'er forgot will be
And for bonnie Annie Laurie
I'd lay me doon and dee.

What promise true had that terrified maidservant left her newborn in the Ladies Water Closets of the Redfern Railway Station? A promise that she would come back one day for her? Yes, and baby Amelia had heard her—she knew that now, even as she sang the words—she had heard her mother's urgent whisperings as she clutched her infant one last time.

—and ne'er forgot would be, would ever be.

Amelia cast her spell upon the room. There was something heart-wrenching about this wild-haired girl in her ill-fitting dress, standing up so straight and tall and dignified and singing of Maxwelton Braes and Redfern Railway Station, and Cockatoo Island where she had been interned her entire life. For a moment there, from the rapt attention of those assembled, it seemed that the concert might even be salvaged until—until—the girls in their fruit-cup organdies began to whisper behind their hands in horror, for a stream of brownish blood was dripping down the inside of Amelia's thin white stockingless calf.

Was she aware of what was happening, that her menses had arrived at this most inopportune of times? It seemed she must have been, and yet steadfastly she continued singing till she reached the end of the song. Amidst the smattering of applause, Mrs Elsbury stood and swept the girl from the room; Mrs Hopkins herself was paralysed and did nothing. There were never enough rags at the school to cope with the girls and their bleeding; it was the bane of Mrs Baird's existence, as she had told Mrs Hopkins on innumerable occasions, and one of the many tasks that the Acting Matron must sort out at once, for it was impossible to keep the girls tidy. Blood stains on sheets and blankets and chemises and petticoats, and always the dark patches seeping through the backs of their dresses. (Mrs Hopkins had her own problems in that regard, and frequently had cause to be grateful for her mourning, for it hid all manner of unhappy accidents.)

The rest of the concert passed for Mrs Hopkins in a daze. Bridget did not swear, but nor did she juggle particularly well, and without Martha to present the fifth ball, there was no triumphant conclusion.

Josephine launched into her cartwheel, but the waxed parquet floor sent her colliding with a side-table artfully arranged with bisque porcelain curios that were now sent smashing to the floor. In the flurry to pick them up, she was spotted by one of the ladies pocketing a tiny porcelain spaniel with a collar of blue flowers. (It had not helped matters that Mr Crabback had introduced her as 'notoriously light fingered.') Asked quite kindly to put it back upon the table, she did so churlishly, seeming to feel that the mishap on the slippery floor had entitled her to some form of compensation.

'Her mother runs one of the lowest bagnios in Burnell Lane,' Mr Crabback added, as if by way of explanation.

After the concert, the young ladies in the organdies and the Trelawney children hastened the Biloela inmates back to the kitchen garden, where a wonderful morning tea had been laid on in their honour. Never in their lives, even at Christmas-time, had the girls seen such a spread. Laid out on the table, dressed with a chequered cloth, were plates of cream cakes and ginger cakes, lemon creams and chocolate macaroons. There were delicate little sandwiches made with peach jam; sandwiches of minced ham and mustard and finely chopped chicken with celery; others filled with grated cheese, then gently browned in the oven. Most coveted by the Biloela girls were strawberries sliced and sprinkled with sifted sugar. All of this was washed down with cool glasses of lemon barley cordial.

Amelia, returned now in a hand-me-down print dress and brand-new blue stockings, refused to partake of any of it, but stood off to the side, feigning to be interested in the garden.

'I am not the slightest bit hungry,' she said, when pressed. Even Catherine could not coax her to eat.

The others, however, could not gulp the food down quickly enough. Even Mary-Ann seemed sufficiently recovered to take her fill. They stood about the table, grazing freely and filling their pockets with leftovers for the inmates left behind.

'You don't need to eat so fast, you know,' said the nasty little Trelawney boy to Bridget, who was especially enjoying the warm cheese sandwiches. 'Don't you know it's bad manners to bolt your food?'

To which Bridget clocked him decisively with a well-directed elbow to the jaw—she didn't even stop chewing to do so. He fell to the ground and commenced to bawl—the girls giggled. It was the first laugh they'd had since they'd arrived at the great house; even the poor little tear-stained Tunks sisters broke off from mourning their father and managed a gleeful chortle.

'May God strike you stiff for what you said to me,' said Bridget, as the brunette in the lemon organdie endeavoured to comfort the boy. He wiped his snotty nose on her dress, and now she was angry with him, too.

Meanwhile, back in the drawing room, Mr Crabback and Mrs Hopkins found they were facing something of an interrogation.

'It seems to me a great shame that more care is not taken with their appearance,' said Mrs Bacon, the treasurer, to Mrs Hopkins. 'Are you not the Matron?'

'Acting Matron,' said Mrs Hopkins.

'Teaching the girls to take a wholesome pride in their appearance would surely be a first step in the reformation of their character.'

'Yes,' said Mrs Hopkins unhappily. She was sorry that she had allowed Mr Crabback to persuade her to allow the girls to appear in this slovenly fashion, against her better judgement. I should have stood my ground, she thought angrily.

'Also it strikes me that rather than depending on charity, most of these girls are old enough to go into service,' said Mrs Elsbury. 'Surely, that is the whole principle of the institution: to train girls for service?'

'We are desperately short of servants here in Sydney,' added the Secretary, with feeling.

'Some of these girls are not fit for service,' said Mr Crabback. 'That Amelia girl, for example: she was sent to service in the country—all goes well, so the family asks for another Biloela girl—next thing you know the two of them get together, steal some money and make off with one of the ponies. They thought it a great lark! Even when they were caught, they frolicked and leap-frogged all the way to the police station!'

By the enjoyment with which he told the story, it was evident that Mr Crabback thought it something of a lark himself. The ladies, however, did not seem amused at all.

'Unfortunately, we have numerous cases of distress continually pressing upon us, and very limited means at our disposal,' said Mrs Elsbury. 'Mrs Rutter, would you kindly read for

Mr Crabback and Mrs Hopkins' benefit the list of cases relieved by our society this previous year alone?'

Mrs Rutter was not best prepared for this, and it took several moments of rifling through papers before she finally produced the required sheet.

'Thirty-six widows, suffering illness and old age. Twenty-three deserted wives. Thirty-five sick and infirm. Fourteen wives whose husbands are in prison. Forty-eight wives whose husbands were unemployed, many of them affected by old age, sandy blight et cetera. Thirty-nine single women, some with young infants . . .'

'So you do see how pressed we are financially,' said Mrs Elsbury.

'Experience has sadly taught us that promiscuous alms-giving does more harm than good,' sighed the Reverend Allcock, his hands clasped contentedly across his belly.

'Even just a few pounds would be helpful,' said Mr Crabback feebly.

Mrs Hopkins stared at him in dismay. She longed to produce her list, the one she had laboured over, pages and pages of necessary requirements for the school. And what had happened to the impassioned speech he was supposed to deliver, reducing the ladies to tears? Could it be that, like the girls, he too was intimidated by these supposed 'dear friends of many years standing'?

'I'm afraid that is out of the question,' replied Mrs Elsbury firmly. The pleasant giddying effects of the laudanum had apparently worn off, and now she was keen to draw proceedings to a close.

Taking his cue, the Reverend Allcock rose to his feet. 'These ladies do their good work with no thought of reward, but gladly and from love of their fellow creatures in distress,' he said. 'And yet it is often the fact that their sympathy and kind words do almost as much to assist the needy as the money itself.'

'Yes, indeed,' said Mr Crabback doubtfully. In the end, he was able to procure just enough to cover the fares home. This was presented to him in the form of special charity tickets so it could not be spent on drink.

To top off a disastrous day, a terrible incident blew up at King Street Wharf, wholly unexpected to everybody and most certainly to Mrs Hopkins. Fortified by the food and cordial, and unaware of the disappointing developments which Mrs Hopkins and Mr Crabback had experienced with the good Ladies of the Benevolent Society, the little troupe of girls made their way in reasonable spirits down the long hill back to the city. Josephine, a sensitive soul, took great care of the poor little Tunks sisters who had learned such sorrowful news of their father, as did Mary-Ann, who, while still recovering from Mr Crabback's humiliating account of her, was at least feeling considerably less queasy.

As they walked, the girls began to revise the story they would soon tell their friends left behind at Biloela: the beautiful house, the delicious food but, oh, what a bunch of unbearable stuck-up snotty-nosed toffs!

Soon the mishaps of the actual performance became a source of merriment, especially Josephine's knocking over of the side-table of the porcelain curios, which was now portrayed as a deliberate and masterfully timed act of vengeance. Bridget's elbow to the jaw of the horrible little boy was of course a great highlight which Bridget was encouraged to re-enact (miming, of course) to much hilarity. Of the girls, only Amelia, stomping moodily on ahead, refrained from joining in the general discussion, refusing to engage even with Catherine, who trotted along anxiously beside her.

At King Street Wharf, all was chaos. By now, all the workers of the city were beginning to head home, and Mr Crabback had to fight his way to the gates, holding his Benevolent Society tickets above his head. 'Let us through! Let us through!' he bellowed.

Mrs Hopkins had her hands full trying to keep her little party from being separated by the crowds, or worse still, trampled upon by the burly workers. At one point, Mrs Hopkins thought she had heard someone call out Amelia's name, and looking around had glimpsed a beggar lady, draped in a shabby cloak, gesturing wildly. Martha at that point had fallen, and Mrs Hopkins was trying to prevent her from being trampled; Mr Crabback was shouting with great urgency that they would miss their ferry if they didn't get a move on.

'Come on, girls!' cried Mrs Hopkins shrilly, somewhat shocked at his language. 'Hold hands and stay together!' She had lifted the struggling Martha in her arms, while Mary-Ann grappled with the biting and scratching Janie; Bridget and Josephine made their own way, elbowing their way furiously through the scrum. Once through the turnstiles, Mrs Hopkins heard another cry of *'Amelia!'*, only this time it was much more piercing and desperate, and it was Catherine, jostled by the crowds, her mouth agape in horror. Amelia and the beggar lady were bolting down King Street as fast as they could, knocking people out of their way in their haste. Within moments, they had disappeared into the crowd.

The five o'clock steamer left for Biloela without them. The constabulary had had to be called in; detailed descriptions of the girls given. It was Catherine (once they could get any sense out of her through her sobs), who pieced together the story: Annie Laughton, herself having slipped away the previous night, completely undetected by the Matrons and possessed of Mr Noyes' gold sovereign, which Amelia had pressed upon her, had been lying in wait for the group's return from the concert. She was determined to get Amelia back, at any cost. Seeing an opening, a chance of escape, desperate now after the mortification of her public bleeding, Amelia had seized upon her moment and run.

The bilious rolling motion of the six o'clock steamer back to Cockatoo Island caused Mary-Ann to be sick again. Mrs Hopkins stood beside her at the deck railing, holding back her hair as the poor girl vomited over the side.

'Oh, Mrs Hopkins,' she said, wiping her mouth roughly on one of Mrs Hopkins' lace-edged mourning handkerchiefs, 'I'm in trouble. I'm in terrible trouble.'

'Whatever do you mean?' asked Mrs Hopkins.

For a moment, the girl was quite unable to speak. She simply stood there and wiped away her tears hopelessly with the back of her hand. She could not have looked more forlorn, more filled with despair. 'If I tell you, you mustn't tell anyone,' the girl insisted finally. 'Will you promise me?'

'I promise you,' said Mrs Hopkins.

'You must promise!'

'I do promise!'

'I'm up the duff!' whispered Mary-Ann, and she fell against Mrs Hopkins' narrow chest, sobbing.

Extraordinarily, it had not occurred to Mrs Hopkins for a moment that this could be the problem. In her innocent, romantic way, she had thought that perhaps the girl had had a tiff with her handsome French lover. She had imagined that the pair of them simply billed and cooed away their time together, kissing and slapping and teasing each other the way young people liked to do. The thought that these moonlight assignations had most likely consisted of rutting away in the cold sand shocked her deeply. Had she been aware that they were up to such antics, Mrs Hopkins felt that she would have surely brought a stop to it. Did the poor deluded girl not understand that such things were to be preserved for the sanctity of marriage? (It did not appear to occur to Mrs Hopkins that she had herself engaged in sexual connection outside of the sanctity of marriage only the night before.)

Meanwhile, everybody was staring at them. From the expression on Mr Crabback's face, it seemed that he strongly disapproved of the scene that the girl was making, and yet Mrs Hopkins found she had almost no choice but to hold the crying girl and pat her limply on the shoulder. The girl seemed to expect it of her, some measure of comfort. And yet Mrs Hopkins was feeling rather cross with her. This was a problem that Mary-Ann had brought upon herself with her well-documented fondness for fellows, and it was a big problem, almost more than Mrs Hopkins felt that she was capable of dealing with. And yet, as Acting Matron, she had no choice. Deal with it she must.

She stopped patting the girl and instead took hold of her arm rather forcefully. 'How long since you had your last courses?' she asked in a low voice. Could it be the foolish girl might have it all wrong?

But Mary-Ann simply shrugged her shoulders hopelessly. 'I don't know! Ages!' she cried out.

'Pull yourself together,' hissed Mrs Hopkins. 'You are making a spectacle of yourself.'

At once the girl gave a great sniff and blew her nose upon Mrs Hopkins' vomit-stained handkerchief.

'I'm sorry,' she said.

'People are staring, and you will raise suspicions,' said Mrs Hopkins. 'You must carry on exactly as normal. Tell nobody. This evening after lock-up, you and I will have a private word together. And we must talk to the fellow involved also.'

'Talk to—? Oh no, he mustn't know! He will be angry with me!'

'Angry or not, he must do the right thing by you, and sooner rather than later.'

'He can't, Mrs Hopkins! That's the whole problem!'

'Why can't he?'

Mary-Ann cast her eyes about wildly, lest someone hear what she was about to say. 'He's already married!' It was half-hiss, half-sob. 'That's what he says, anyway,' she added doubtfully.

Well, this was altogether too much. Mrs Hopkins felt a great wave of impatience for the child, too caught up in the romance and the nonsense to think anything of the consequences. (And once again, it failed to occur to Mrs Hopkins that she had herself been comporting with a married man. Or if it did occur to her, the fact that Mr Crabback was entrapped in a loveless marriage involving ink-stand projectiles hurled at the head made it seem somehow acceptable.)

There was yet more drama, if such a thing was imaginable after such a day, awaiting the party as the ferry pulled into Cockatoo Island. It was dark by now, of course, and the girls left behind were locked up for the evening. As the gangplank was lowered, the sound of riotous singing emanated from the barracks high up on the hill; it was hard to catch the words, but not at all difficult to feel the spirit of uprising and mutiny.

'Dear, oh dear!' cried Mr Crabback fretfully. 'This is not a good sign, not a good sign at all. What on earth could have happened? How could the Matrons have lost control? I'd believed that we had taken all the worst girls with us.'

As the little party disembarked from the steamer, Henry, of all people, materialised before them, blocking their way. He raised a trembling finger towards Josephine.

'Are you a ghost?' he asked in a tremulous voice.

'What?' said Josephine.

Mrs Hopkins clutched her hand tightly. She had not realised how big a man Henry was, for he loomed over them threateningly.

'Go away, Henry!' she said, for her heart was starting to thump wildly in her chest. An imminent riot was quite bad enough; she did not need any such wild assertions from an imbecile.

'I thought you was dead,' said Henry to Josephine.

'Well, I'm not, I'm alive,' said Josephine, quite cheerfully.

'You are alive! You are alive, too!' cried Henry joyfully.

Then he swung angrily upon Mrs Hopkins. 'Why did you tell her poor little ma that she was dead?' he said.

'I did no such thing!'

'You did too! I seen you! You told her the girly was dead and you made her cry and then you said a prayer over her!'

A wave of shock passed over the little group.

Josephine gave a little cry. She turned and stared at Mrs Hopkins. 'Did you—?' she began, her thin little voice surprisingly sharp.

'No! No! Of course not! Why would I do such a thing? And when was I supposed to have done it? As far as I know, your mother has never even visited—'

'You lie! You lie!' cried Henry. He was blocking the path before them, his trembling hand pointing accusingly at her. 'You told her the girl had died in the night! You broke her poor ma's heart, and for what? She is alive this whole time!'

Whereupon Mrs Hopkins did the only thing she could think of to do—she gave a little moan and fainted. Or at least, she pretended to faint. In imitation of Mary-Ann that morning, she dropped to her knees then spilled to the ground in a dead swoon. At once, Mr Crabback rushed to her aid, propping her up in his arms and fanning her with a copy of the *Telegraph*.

Josephine also rushed to her side and crouched beside her. 'Now look what you've done!' she cried angrily at Henry.

Mrs Hopkins kept her eyes firmly closed, for it would not do to recover too quickly.

And yet, unfortunately, Henry would not desist. He kept repeating his accusations and now that Mrs Hopkins was busy pretending to have fainted, she had no way of refuting him.

'Stop it, Henry!' cried Josephine. 'Leave her alone! She would never do such a thing!'

Henry stared at her in bewilderment.

'She did, I swear!' asserted Henry. 'I was there. I saw the whole thing!'

'I don't believe you,' cried Josephine, covering her ears with her hands. 'Stop talking!' Now she started to cry. Mrs Hopkins at once came out of her faint.

'You see how you have upset the child,' she said to Henry. 'You ought to be ashamed of yourself. Come now, Josephine, take yourself up to your dormitory. Pay no attention to Henry. He is a simpleton and is quite liable to say anything to stir up trouble.'

With Bridget and the Tunks sisters by her side, Josephine took herself up to the school. She was still crying, and yet she did not seem to believe what Henry was saying. Her loyalty lay with Mrs Hopkins.

'Might I pay you a visit later this evening?' asked Mr Crabback as he helped the School-Mistress to her feet. But this was more than Mrs Hopkins could bear. She longed for her bed and Miss Minnie; she longed for the horrors of the day to evaporate.

Mr Crabback took her by the arm, and they commenced to trudge up to the institution, and yet all the while Henry was still shouting, 'You lie, you lie! The poor little ma!'

'The man is a half-wit,' said Mr Crabback quietly. 'He has no idea what he is talking about.'

Mrs Hopkins felt her eyes prick with tears. Henry told the truth, and she knew it and Henry knew it, and now her best hope was that Josephine would not believe it, would never believe it. After all, Mrs Hopkins told herself, was Josephine not better off away from the terrible influence of her degenerate mother? Even locked indefinitely within the grim confines of Biloela, was Josephine not better to have the guiding moral influence of Mrs Hopkins? Yes, she was clearly attached to her mother in some way, and yet (since the spitting incident of the first night) she had never spoken of her. Why eventually, when the girl was able to be released, Mrs Hopkins had hopes that they might live together as mother and daughter.

And yet, Mrs Hopkins knew she had done a terrible thing—the wickedest possible thing you could ever do. Worse still, she had quite callously put it out of her mind completely in the intervening weeks, with all the excitement of the concert.

She of all people knew what it was to lose a child, but in her desire to claim the girl as her own, an incarnation of her lost daughter Eugenie, she had inflicted upon this poor woman this brutal untruth. What kind of person was she? In the darkness, Mr Crabback heard her stifle a sob.

'You mustn't fret so,' he said with concern. 'You are a good woman, a very good woman if I may say so, and I see that you have taken the disappointments of the day to heart. I urge you not to. It was perhaps not the unqualified success we had hoped for, and indeed had toiled so hard for. And yet, with the exception of one or two mishaps, I think it all went off really rather well, don't you? Certainly, the ladies gave the impression of having enjoyed themselves.'

A wave of impotent fury overwhelmed her and she seized upon it, for it had the effect of pushing aside her dreadful guilt about Josephine. So much of the failure of the day was his fault! It was Mr Crabback who had made the girls dress so shabbily; it was Mr Crabback who had humiliated them with his stories of their lurid pasts; it was Mr Crabback who had been so ill-prepared as to not have the money for the fares.

And now they returned to Biloela with nothing! What was she to tell the girls, so filled with hope for a brighter future, or at least the chance of a Special Visiting Day for Mothers?

A figure now came running down towards them in the darkness; it was Miss Foy, all in a flap. 'Mr Crabback, there you are, there's been such a rumpus! Mrs Crabback turned up on the one o'clock ferry and saw all the girls on the beach—you told us we could all have a holiday—and she said it was disgraceful and locked them all up in the dormitories without bread or water, and they've been singing their riot songs ever since, and Rosabella found the axe in the rafters where Amelia had hidden it, and she's been trying to break the door down and, Lord, we managed to get the matches off her otherwise she would have set fire to it! And oh, Mrs Crabback is blaming me and Mrs Baird for everything, and we tried to explain all about the concert and how good it would be for the school, but she said it was all typical of your claptrap!'

'Oh, she did, did she,' said Mr Crabback, his face growing grave, and involuntarily he drew his hand to the faded bruise where Mrs Crabback's ink-stand had so deftly clocked him.

The incarcerated girls had taken position in the window openings and, with the assistance of Josephine and Bridget and the Tunks sisters, who since they were not locked up were free to gather supplies of stones and rocks and pass them up to the inmates, were pelting anyone who ventured within their range of sight within the quadrangle. Miss Foy had the good sense and experience to stick close to the walls where the girls' munitions could not reach her, and she urged the other two to follow her. Having been clobbered on the head by a sizeable rock, Mrs Crabback had apparently long since retreated to her quarters.

'Came up like a boiled egg,' chortled Miss Foy gleefully.

In spite of her earlier misgivings as to the young woman's propensity for foolishness, Mrs Hopkins found all of a sudden that she rather approved of her spirit.

Mr Crabback strode forcefully into the centre of the quadrangle, keen to assert his position as Superintendent of the institution. 'Give it up, girls!' cried Mr Crabback. 'You will only make things worse for yourselves!'

'Aww, fuck off!' was the girls' response, and for his efforts he was pelted with a fresh barrage of small stones. He rushed to hide behind Miss Foy, where Mrs Hopkins was already cowering.

'It's the injustice,' cried Miss Foy. 'That's what they're so angry about. It's not fair that she locks them up for no reason, even the little ones, without having nothing to drink so much as to eat. And them supposed to have a holiday today!'

And in fact, the kind-hearted girls who had been on the excursion were at this moment passing up the cakes and sandwiches they had saved for their friends. Bridget was standing on Catherine's shoulders, feeding squashed morsels through the window openings. Of course, there was not much to feed so many hungry mouths.

At that moment Mrs Baird staggered out from the kitchen, dragging with some effort a wooden crate filled with whatever she had been able to scrounge from the stores. Seeing Mr Crabback and Mrs Hopkins, she waved her arms quite threateningly at them.

'I don't care what you say, I will not see those girls go to bed without their tea!' she cried furiously. 'Sack me, if you please, Mr Crabback, but I will not stand for it!'

Mrs Hopkins stared at her in astonishment. The stone pelting had desisted from the windows. Someone tried to raise a cheer but they were abruptly shushed. The moment was apparently too critical to interrupt.

'Why, Mrs Baird,' said Mr Crabback, venturing out from between Miss Foy and Mrs Hopkins. 'I have no intention of sacking you. The girls must be fed, and I applaud your initiative in so doing.'

'That's as may be,' said Mrs Baird gruffly, for she had not expected this response, and although it was welcome, it had knocked the wind out of her sails somewhat. She had rather been enjoying her moment of high dudgeon. 'I'm just doing what I feel I ought, and I hope you don't mind me saying, Mr Crabback, sir, never in my life have I been spoken to so rudely than what your wife spoke to me, not half an hour ago. She said I had better go back to keeping a public house like I did before! Yes, my late husband Mr Baird kept the Lord Nelson at one time, but I have had the great pleasure of serving Mr Noyes himself there—'

And here, unable to continue, she burst into tears. Miss Foy ran forward to comfort her.

'Give us the food then!' cried someone from within the windows, apparently unmoved by the scene.

'My dear Mrs Baird,' said Mr Crabback, and here he lowered his voice discreetly, 'I am well acquainted with my wife's views on such matters. I can only apologise on her behalf, for unfortunately I fear you will never hear her utter such an apology herself.'

Mrs Baird nodded and sniffed.

'She's a right cow, your wife,' said Miss Foy, seizing her moment. 'She called me a jumped-up little trollop. And other stuff I won't repeat.'

Mr Crabback turned to her wearily. 'She is a very difficult woman; however, Miss Foy, I would appreciate if you do not refer to her in that manner.'

'A cow? A cow's not half as bad as a jumped-up little trollop,' said Miss Foy, taking umbrage. 'Why, there's some perfectly nice cows about, so I believe, not that I've ever met one.' And here she giggled into her shawl. Even Mrs Baird smiled. The milking cows at Biloela had always been of the difficult variety, very much inclined to kick.

'Stop with the blathering and bring on the food!' The voices from within the barracks were beginning to grow restless.

'Mrs Baird, you have done quite enough for the day. Take yourself off to bed now. You too, Miss Foy. Mrs Hopkins and I will feed the children. No, I will hear no objections! Why, we have had a day of fine food and luxuries, have we not, Mrs Hopkins?'

Mrs Hopkins watched the scene with a sense of dismay. She felt tired, immensely tired, and filled with fury that Mr Crabback somehow saw the humiliating and exhausting expedition as a day of unbridled pampering and indulgence. And yet also—was there not a stab of guilt, of self-loathing even, for not having herself acted in the forthright and compassionate manner of Mrs Baird? Why, feeding the children had not even occurred to her! She had simply wished that they would stop with the stone-throwing and go to sleep. Silently and furiously, she chastised herself. Why was she always too preoccupied with her own woes to think of others?

'Yes, indeed,' she responded limply, for Mr Crabback was looking at her expectantly. 'It would be my honour to feed the children.'

The next morning, Amelia and Annie Laughton were apprehended and brought back to the school by none other than Mr Noyes himself. It had apparently not been a difficult matter to find them: they had gone straight to Annie Laughton's grandmother in Surry Hills and were found tucking into a bowl of tripe stew. Far from being contrite, or even disappointed at having been so promptly re-captured, the two girls seemed positively exuberant about it all. It had been a grand lark! They sang ribald songs all the way back to the institution on the police boat.

'Well, Mr Crabback,' said Mr Noyes, as he hauled the girls before him. He had had quite enough of them: their impertinence towards him on the boat had been sorely testing. 'As Superintendent, it is your duty to set the punishment. What is it to be?'

They were standing for the moment in the empty mess-hall, its flagstones still wet from a scrubbing after breakfast. Amelia and Annie slouched together, arms behind backs. They did not seem to understand the seriousness of their predicament, or if they did, they were deliberately making matters worse for themselves by giggling and snorting at anything anybody said. And yet as the sun spilled through the open back door of the mess-hall, it was plain to see the guardhouse in which the dreadful dark cells loomed.

'Girls,' said Mrs Hopkins crossly, for if they were not aware of the dangers that lay before them, she certainly was. 'Stand up straight and behave yourselves.'

There had been no sign of Mrs Crabback, so Mrs Hopkins, as Acting Matron, was there in her stead. Mrs Crabback was apparently still nursing her injury and did not wish to be seen with the lump on her forehead. Furthermore (although Mrs Hopkins knew nothing of this), there were few fond feelings between Mr Noyes and Mrs Crabback since the death of the young girl from Orange, for which Mrs Crabback, in her capacity as Nurse, had narrowly escaped charges. Mrs Crabback's intention apparently was to lay low until such time as Mr Noyes' departure.

'Well,' said Mr Crabback, shuffling nervously, 'I have not yet had time to give it much thought. Of course, the only power given me by the Act is to, uh, confine them for fourteen days on bread and water.'

'Whereabouts?'

'I beg your pardon?'

'Whereabouts do you intend to confine them?'

'Well, if we had a separate dormitory, we could confine them in there. However, we simply do not have the space.'

'If you haven't the dormitory space, then obviously you must confine them in the cells,' said Mr Noyes.

But at this, Mr Crabback said nothing.

The silence was filled by Amelia, whose bravado was now failing her. 'No!' she cried. 'Please, not the cells.'

'Be quiet!' snapped Mr Noyes, for he was annoyed with her. She had ridiculed him on the boat by calling him a goo-goo-eyed old masher. 'You have forfeited your right for any say in the matter by running away in the first place.'

It was a ridiculous thing to say, of course, for there was never any question of the runaways having 'a say in the matter'.

'There has been some general concern about the cells,' said Mr Crabback.

'Such as?'

'Such as being injurious to the girls' health. Rats and so forth.'

'Whose concern is this?'

'Well, myself and the Acting Matron. We have spoken about it at length. It is something we would wish to bring an end to.'

Mrs Hopkins looked at him in surprise, for although she had made her feelings known to him at the time, they had had no further discussion about it. It had been as if it were too contentious a subject to venture into if they were to keep relations in any way harmonious between them.

Mr Noyes frowned. Although he avoided looking at her, he could hear Amelia whimpering. It served her right. She got away with much too much as it was.

'As I understand it,' continued Mr Crabback, gaining conviction as he continued, 'no correction which may affect the health of the offender may be imposed. And of course, Mr Noyes, I appreciate that you have a longstanding interest in young Amelia's welfare.'

It was a bold move, and Mr Noyes blanched. He had forgotten that Mr Crabback had witnessed Amelia's canoodling and carrying-on that day.

'In that case, what do you suggest by way of correction?' snapped the Water Police Magistrate. 'For you surely can't be proposing they go unpunished?'

'No, indeed not. The punishment must meet the severity of the crime. It must have a long and lasting impact, so that should they ever find themselves contemplating a repeat of the offence, they will think twice.'

Mrs Hopkins gazed at him in admiration, for the coolness of his composure as much as the content of his proposal. She had been bracing herself to make an impassioned speech to keep the girls out of the dark cells, and now perhaps it would no longer be necessary.

'Yes, but what exactly do you propose?' barked Mr Noyes impatiently.

'Quite simply, I would do this—' And here Mr Crabback gave a pause for effect. 'I would cut off all their hair.'

There was an audible intake of breath from the girls. 'No!' cried Amelia.

'No!' cried Annie. And yet Mr Crabback looked well-pleased with himself. He turned to them in surprise.

'It is surely preferable to being locked in the cells!'

At once Mr Noyes, glancing at Amelia, was beset with the inadvisability of this punishment. She had burst into tears—authentic tears by all appearances—and was gazing at Mr Noyes beseechingly with her big green eyes.

'For goodness' sake, girls,' said Mrs Hopkins, for she felt that she must support Mr Crabback, and the hacking off of hair did not seem such a bad punishment as being plunged into a dark pit for days on end. Certainly, she was not sure that she would mind it so terribly, but then she could always resort to a bonnet. 'It is only hair! The wonderful thing about hair is that it always grows back!'

'You don't understand!' cried Amelia furiously.

'How dare you speak to me like that!' said Mrs Hopkins.

'In my experience in the courts,' said Mr Noyes quietly, and here he drew Mr Crabback and Mrs Hopkins aside in the hope that the girls would not hear what he was about to say, 'the cutting off of hair as a form of punishment has had the most inadvisable effects. It may seem to you a foolish vanity, but the girls' hair is all that they possess. Cut it off and she has nothing. I have seen the unhappy results time and again in my courts: once a girl's head is shorn, it becomes impossible to elevate the child, or to restore her spirit of self-respect. She becomes to all intents and purposes a lost cause.'

And glancing across at Amelia's mane of tousled curls, even Annie's wispy braid, Mrs Hopkins began dimly to understand.

However, Mr Crabback seemed determined to dig his heels in on the matter. 'Then they should have thought of that before they took it into their heads to run away,' he said briskly. 'It will be the matter of a few short minutes, over and done with before they know it.'

'It is not the act I speak of; it is the consequences,' said Mr Noyes. 'I urge you, Mr Crabback, to reconsider. If the cells are deemed unsafe, then lock them in a dormitory on bread and water for fourteen days.'

'Fourteen days and they will dance and skip as they like. It is nothing but a spree for them. Why, they will be better fed within than they are without—their little friends soon see to that.'

'Then board up the windows.'

'Sir, with the greatest respect,' said Mr Crabback, drawing himself up to his full height (which was still a good deal less than Mr Noyes), 'your jurisdiction is within the Police Courts: mine is within this institution. Please allow me to do as I deem best. I think I have some insight into the thinking of these particular truants, if you can call it thinking. Personally, I suspect there was scant thought involved. It was an impulse, a spur of the moment whim, and that is exactly the sort of behaviour which we must do our best to quash. Do you think the girls will wish to abscond again looking like a pair of badly shorn sheep?'

And here, Mr Crabback allowed himself a small chuckle.

'Hardly,' he continued, and seeing that his attempt at humour had not been received well by his listeners, he withdrew his smile and grew stern. 'They will stay hidden within these walls quite thankfully till such time as their hair grows back, years possibly. In the meantime, their shame, their folly, is manifest in their appearance—and it serves dual purpose as a visual reminder to the other girls of the consequences of foolish impulse.'

'I would urge you to reconsider,' repeated Mr Noyes, more forcefully this time, and he turned to Mrs Hopkins with a look of silent appeal. 'It is easier to raise the devil than to lay him.'

And with these words he took his leave, quite unable to bring himself to look at the two girls who were both awash with tears.

'Right,' said Mr Crabback. 'Let's get this over and done with.' He passed swiftly to the doors of the mess-hall, front and back, and pulled the bolts across.

'Scissors,' he said, holding out his hand to Mrs Hopkins.

'Scissors,' repeated Mrs Hopkins, in a vague tone, as if uncertain for the moment where they might be found. She felt an impulse to delay the proceedings somehow: perhaps Mr Crabback may yet be convinced to implement another punishment. 'The only scissors we have are the sewing scissors, and I fear they will all be too blunt to do the job properly.'

Mr Crabback made a gesture of exasperation and looked at her in dismay. 'The scissors, Mrs Hopkins!' he repeated, in a forceful manner.

She at once propelled herself to the cupboard and pulled out a large pair of dressmaking shears. The handles were small and black and melded into a tortuous shape supposed to be better for gripping; the blades were long and curved and rusted.

At the sight of these fiendish shears, the girls commenced to wail.

'I wonder,' said Mrs Hopkins, and her speech came out rapidly for she was beginning to feel quite desperate, 'if Mr Noyes did not have a point about the effects of this punishment, the difficulty in reclaiming the girls afterwards and so forth. I suppose I am only wondering if we are doing the right thing—'

Annie was now howling loudly, her hands clutching onto her head as a feeble means of protection. It was difficult to hear above the din she was making.

'You see what you have started now with your prevarication?' cried Mr Crabback. 'Let us try to have some order here. Annie, quieten down at once and step towards Mrs Hopkins.'

But Annie refused to move. She stared wild-eyed at Amelia for guidance. Amelia shook her head to indicate that she should stay where she was.

'Very well,' said Mr Crabback. 'If Muhammad will not come to the mountain . . .'

And with a nod of his head, he indicated that Mrs Hopkins must proceed to where Annie stood. Keeping the shears by her side in a bid to minimise their fearfulness, Mrs Hopkins approached as calmly as she could, though she could feel her knees quaking at the task before her. At least Annie's hair was tied in a simple braid: if she could only grasp hold of it, it would be the work of several seconds to hack it off, even in spite of the bluntness of the shears.

Seeing the School-Mistress's intent, Annie commenced to shake violently.

'Never mind, Annie, dear,' said Mrs Hopkins, and she noted with distaste how hollow and insincere she sounded. 'It will all be over soon if you simply stand still and allow me to do it. It will not be so bad, wait and see. In fact, with these warmer months approaching—'

'Leave her alone!' said Amelia, and her voice was dark with threat.

'Steady now,' said Mr Crabback warningly. And yet he made no move to back Mrs Hopkins up and stayed where he was. The cutting of hair was apparently a woman's job, not that of the Superintendent.

Mrs Hopkins took several more cautious steps towards the girl, fearful that she might alarm her with any abrupt movement. 'I will do as nice a job as I can,' she said. 'Wait and see.'

'No!' whispered Annie desperately. 'Please not, Mrs Hopkins. I beg of you. Please not—'

And seizing her moment, Mrs Hopkins grabbed the girl's braid with her free hand. Caught now, Annie fought desperately, pulling and bucking and slapping wildly at her captor, making it impossible for Mrs Hopkins to utilise the shears. She was forced to wave them wildly in the air with her free hand, scissoring the blades open and closed in the hope that, in spite of the onslaught she was experiencing, she might somehow make contact with the girl's braid and rend it off. What a dreadful hoarse sawing sound the shears produced!

'Hold still, hold still and it will soon be over!' she cried.

At which Amelia picked up a bench seat and threw it at her. 'I said leave her alone!' she cried.

The bench seat knocked Mrs Hopkins to the floor, and within an instant, Amelia was straddled on top of her and had wrenched the shears from her grip. She held them high over her head, demented with rage. It appeared for one terrible moment that she might stab Mrs Hopkins with them.

'Amelia!' cried Mrs Hopkins in horror. 'Have sense, child! If you kill me, you will go to gaol for the rest of your life!'

'I don't care!' cried the girl. 'I might as well be hung for a sheep as a lamb!'

And now, galvanised at last into action, Mr Crabback threw himself into the fray, knocking the girl sideways with his entire bodyweight, freeing Mrs Hopkins and sending the dressmaking shears skidding across the flagstones.

'Get them, Annie!' cried Amelia, for Mr Crabback had her pinned to the floor.

For a long moment, Annie seemed paralysed and stood as one dazed and bewildered.

Seeing her opportunity, Mrs Hopkins scrabbled to her feet, but at once slipped upon the damp flagstones and fell in an ungainly heap.

'Get them, Annie!' screamed Amelia, and now Annie awoke from her trance and looked about wildly. Spying the shears under a nearby table, she dived under it and grabbed them.

Undeterred, Mrs Hopkins crawled at full speed after her, and using strength she did not know she possessed, seized hold of the girl's hands in a bid to force the shears from her grasp. A fierce grunting tussle of several moments ensued during which Annie, though caught by the hands, contrived through use of her shoulders to knock Mrs Hopkins' head rhythmically against the underside of the table. Bump! Bump! Bump!

Enraged, Mrs Hopkins wrestled all the harder for possession of the shears, twisting Annie's hand so that her thumb and forefinger became painfully contorted within the narrow handles. The girl let out a howl of pain, and in that instant, Mrs Hopkins tore the shears violently from the young girl's grip.

There was a moment then where nothing happened.

Caught under the table as they were, the dressmaking shears in her grasp and Annie spent from her efforts, it would have been a relatively simple action for Mrs Hopkins to reach across and cut off the girl's matted braid. In fact, it dangled conveniently over the shoulder closest to Mrs Hopkins. Why, the child did not even make a move to push the braid out of reach. It was as if she had given up.

'Please, Miss,' Annie whispered feebly. 'Please not.'

Mrs Hopkins sighed. 'It is only hair,' she said, for she could still not quite understand what all the fuss was about. Her own hair had been shaken free from its restraints with all the banging and struggling. It was a nuisance, that was all. She felt like reaching up with the scissors and hacking her own greying mane off, perhaps as an example to the girls. And yet, was she not homely enough, even with her full head of hair? Besides, people would think she had head lice if she cut it off. Which reminded her: she must treat Josephine's hair with a dousing of kerosene.

Mrs Hopkins turned and crawled out from under the table. She rose shakily to her feet and looked about.

It was all so unseemly. Mr Crabback lay spread-eagled across Amelia, pinning her wrists to the floor. He could scarcely breathe with all her dark curls in his face. He twisted his face from one side to the other, but the curls seemed always in his mouth. Meanwhile, Amelia kicked stubbornly against him. It seemed she had been doing it for some time and was running out of puff. Annie crawled out from under the table, rubbing her hand ruefully where it had become caught so painfully within the handles. Mrs Hopkins could see a nasty bruise coming up already on the girl's pale skin: she had caused that. What on earth had possessed her? And yet, putting a hand to her mottled cheeks, she could feel her own set of bruises emerging from all the slapping.

Nobody spoke. Nobody dared to say anything. But at least the girls still had their hair.

Giving up entirely on the idea of cutting the girls' hair, Mr Crabback placed Amelia and Annie in Dormitory Three, its usual inhabitants moved temporarily to Dormitory Two. They were given no bedding except a blanket each, and the windows were boarded up to prevent any passing in of food. This meant that the small space was plunged into abject darkness. A bucket of water was placed within, along with a slop pail. Here the girls were to stay confined for fourteen days, the maximum time permitted according to the rules of the establishment. And yet this punishment was preferable to the dark cells or the cutting off of hair.

'Mrs Hopkins?' said Mary-Ann, when she saw the School-Mistress emerging from the dormitory and locking its heavy door. 'Did you not want to talk to me?'

Mrs Hopkins gazed at her blankly. After the dramas of the mess-hall that morning, it was as if she had forgotten the various other problems that still beset her. Then she remembered.

'I tried to find you last night,' said Mary-Ann, 'but you disappeared.'

It was true: after the feeding of the locked-up children, Mrs Hopkins had gone directly to her quarters without a backwards glance. Once inside, she had changed into her nightgown and taken Miss Minnie to bed with her. So often, over the years, holding the doll tightly to her breast had brought her comfort and solace, and most importantly, sleep. Sometimes she even spoke to the doll for guidance, though she suspected the doll only told her what she wanted to hear. There were times, however, when Miss Minnie would berate her in her shrill voice, and yet perhaps even that was what Mrs Hopkins had needed at the time.

But that evening, she drew no comfort from the doll. Although stuffed with rags, she felt hard and knobbly against Mrs Hopkins' breast. She tried kicking the doll to the end of the bed, and yet even there the doll chafed against her chilblained feet. Finally, she got up and placed Miss Minnie in the chest, with the heavy pot on top. Perhaps she had hung onto the doll too long. Perhaps it would have been best to let Eugenie have her after all.

'I have not forgotten about you,' said Mrs Hopkins to Mary-Ann. 'I am only trying to consider which is the most practicable course to follow, given the circumstances . . . given the circumstances in which we—you—find yourself.'

She gazed doubtfully down at Mary-Ann's figure. Fortunately, there did not yet seem to be any noticeable bulge—the shapeless dress she wore helped conceal it. Could they possibly hide the girl's condition until such time as she gave birth, and then feign surprise at the unexpected arrival? Was that a practicable course to follow? Surely, it was the only course to follow, for what else could be done?

'In the meantime, it is imperative that we treat this matter with the utmost secrecy,' said Mrs Hopkins. 'Nobody must know of your condition. Do you understand me?'

'Yes, Mrs Hopkins,' said Mary-Ann, nodding her head vehemently.

And yet, had Mrs Hopkins been less preoccupied with her other woes, she might well have detected from the guilty manner in which the girl cast her eyes downward that perhaps that horse had already bolted.

'We have a very serious problem on our hands,' said Mr Crabback. 'May I come in?'

He was standing on her doorstep, his colour quite grey. It was by now teatime, and Mrs Hopkins had retired to her quarters for a slice of bread and butter before muster and lock-up. It had been a busy day.

There was as yet no sign of Mrs Crabback, and Mrs Hopkins was still endeavouring to fill her dual roles as School-Mistress and Acting Matron.

'By all means,' she said, opening the door for him.

Entering, he hesitated, uncertain as to whether it was best to sit or stand to relay his news. He glanced uneasily at her bed, the scene of their recent dalliance.

Finally, he threw himself down on her one hardwood chair in such a way as to indicate his extreme consternation. The chair creaked beneath him as if it might give way. Then he cleared his throat.

'When lovely woman stoops to folly,' he intoned. *'And finds too late that men betray What charm can soothe her melancholy What art can wash her guilt away?'*

Mrs Hopkins stared at him in alarm. Was he referring to their horseplay of the other evening? Had she 'stooped to folly'? Had he come to condemn her for such?

'What are you alluding to?' she cried out.

'There is no point in beating about the bush,' he said. 'I am sorry to report that we have a girl in the family way.'

'No!' said Mrs Hopkins. But she felt a wave of relief. It was only Mary-Ann. He had not come to condemn her after all.

'Who is the unhappy child?' she asked. She had decided the best course was to feign ignorance entirely.

'It is Mary-Ann,' said Mr Crabback, eyeing her suspiciously. 'Did you know about this?'

'Mary-Ann!' cried Mrs Hopkins. 'Are you sure?'

'Yes, quite sure. Mrs Baird told me not ten minutes ago, and she has it directly from Miss Foy who heard it from the girls in the laundry. Was she not crying with you on the boat yesterday?'

'Yes,' said Mrs Hopkins. 'But I understood that she was disappointed with the day's proceedings. Also, being unaccustomed to such heavy food upset her belly.'

'Well, we are in quite the predicament,' he said.

It felt useless to stand about. She flopped herself down on the bed, but after a moment stood up again. She would have like to have finished her slice of bread and butter, half-eaten on a plate next to where Mr Crabback sat, but it would seem impolite to eat in front of her visitor. She might offer him some, of course, but she felt she had little enough to share. He would be well supplied in his own quarters, she felt sure.

'The fact that she has fallen into this condition is a grave mark against the discipline of the school,' continued Mr Crabback. 'It will reflect very badly on us all. I imagine we will be removed from our positions without ceremony.'

'Me also?' said Mrs Hopkins. Why did he always include her in everything? 'But I am only the School-Mistress.'

'You were . . . *are* the Acting Matron at time of the . . . event.' He sighed heavily. 'How on earth she came to find herself in this fix is beyond me.'

Mrs Hopkins thought at once of the handsome Frenchman, and the slapping and whispering and the tossing over the fence. 'It is very mysterious,' she said. 'Have you spoken to her?'

'No!' cried Mr Crabback, apparently horrified at the thought. 'The less I have to do with the girl, the better. As the only man in the institution, you understand, and new to the position, I shall find myself subject to some suspicion. My wife being away for such time will not help matters, of course.'

'How is your wife?' asked Mrs Hopkins, unable to resist the question. The thought that Mrs Crabback was on the island, liable to loom into view at any moment, lump or no lump, greatly unsettled her.

'She is recovering steadily. It will be the matter of a day or two, and she will resume her duties as Matron.'

'I see.'

'She is a tremendous organiser and will soon drive a broom through this place. Yes, her manner can be plain-spoken, brusque even, but yet in an institution such as this, there is surely no place for molly-coddling.'

'As I recall, she threw an ink-stand at your head,' said Mrs Hopkins. A wave of fury overwhelmed her. Mr Crabback had had some kind of rapprochement with his wife. Where did that leave Mrs Hopkins, especially after the business of the other evening?

'Ah yes, but perhaps that was not entirely unwarranted,' said Mr Crabback. He would not look at her, but instead gazed at his hands, one on each knee. 'It was a private matter. Of course, Mrs Crabback's return means you will be free to resume your role as School-Mistress, untrammelled by other duties,' he continued. 'This must surely come as a relief for you. Looking back, I feel I may have expected too much of you.'

'And yet I felt I was making some headway,' said Mrs Hopkins. 'In terms of the girls' behaviour and so forth. It would be a great pity if there was a setback.'

Again, Mr Crabback sighed. 'I do not know, after this morning's business with the scissors, if it can be claimed that we have made much progress. At one point, I greatly feared for your life.'

'Back to the question of the girl,' said Mrs Hopkins, for she did not wish to linger on the incidents of the morning. The glazed, demented look in Amelia's eyes had been frightening enough. She had imagined she had a rapport of some kind with the girl, but clearly it did not amount to much. 'Might we not simply let nature take its course? We might keep the girl out of view, should there be visitors. That could be achieved by locking her within a dormitory for the duration.'

'How do we explain the sudden arrival of a newborn baby within the institution?' demanded Mr Crabback impatiently. 'What you are proposing is simply deferring our problem to a later date. No, we must take action of some sort . . . and quickly. To do otherwise will land us in serious trouble.'

'But what sort of action are you proposing?' asked Mrs Hopkins, quite mystified. She knew so little about these things. Was it to do with those pills that 'restore regularity', which she had seen advertised in the back pages of the *Sydney Morning Herald*? For a small amount, you could send away for a pamphlet. It seemed doubtful, but one never knew. Surely such things would not be advertised in such a reputable newspaper as the *Herald* if they were ineffective?

'It is a very delicate subject; one that I scarcely feel equal to discussing with you,' said Mr Crabback. 'I had hoped that you might have some experience in the matter. But perhaps I have overestimated you in this regard. I do not say that as a slight: it simply reflects upon your virtue.'

Happy to be perceived as virtuous, Mrs Hopkins felt she might now seat herself down upon the bed.

'In many ways I have led a sheltered life,' she said quietly, her hands clasped demurely on her lap.

'Yes,' said Mr Crabback. There was a long silence. Finally, he rose to his feet. His manner was of one who had made his mind up. 'Fortunately, my wife, being a trained Nurse, has had some little experience in dealing with these matters,' he said. 'I will talk to her. She will not be happy that she be forced to "mop up", as it were, the misdeeds of a foolish girl. But when I explain to her the potential ramifications of our *not* acting, I believe she will see that we have no other option.'

Since the failure of the school expedition to the Ladies of the Benevolent Society, the institution had plunged into abject gloom. Such hopes had been pinned on the success of the enterprise, most especially the prospect of the Special Visiting Day for Mothers, any prospect of which now seemed to have evaporated entirely. No one spoke of it, certainly not Mrs Hopkins. The older girls gazed at her resentfully in class: she had raised their hopes unfairly and she had let them down. And now, to make matters worse, as far as Mrs Hopkins was concerned anyway, Miss Minnie appeared to have been abducted.

'Girls, I have an announcement to make,' she said at muster. 'I have had a small rag doll removed from my quarters. It is nothing of any value, of course, but nonetheless it is of great sentimental value to me and I would appreciate it if it was returned at the soonest possible convenience. If the doll is returned undamaged, the person or persons responsible will not be punished for their actions.'

Mrs Hopkins had discovered the doll missing the evening before. It had spent several nights in the chest; unusually for the School-Mistress, she had slept without Miss Minnie since beginning to sense that the doll had feelings of stern reproval towards her. She might consult the doll for guidance as she had done many times in the past when in need of a differing perspective on matters, but the thought of what Miss Minnie might say to her in her 'suffer-no-fools-gladly' manner filled her with a sickening apprehension. She did not wish to be censured by the doll, and she knew in her heart that she would be and deserved to be.

Of course, she had assumed the doll was in the chest those few nights, but she had not bothered to check on her. In fact, for all she knew Miss Minnie had been missing for several days. A sense of shock, almost of panic, overtook her when she opened the chest and realised that the doll was missing. She rummaged desperately amongst the few articles of clothing and linen, hoping that Miss Minnie might be entangled somehow in the folds of her shabby old skirts and nightgowns, but to no avail. In disbelief, she threw the lid of the chest down and proceeded to ransack her own quarters. In her madness to get rid of the doll, could she possibly have placed it elsewhere? She stripped her bed of its blankets, she crawled underneath amidst the drifts of dust and spider webs; she pulled out the kerosene boxes that served as storage under the kitchen table. There was no doll: the doll had gone. Someone had taken it.

Her thoughts turned to the older girls, who were entirely capable of ransacking and pillaging—had Sarah and Eliza not pilfered ribbons from her chest on the very first night of her arrival? But when she tackled the senior girls on the subject, they clearly knew nothing, nor did they care. And the more Mrs Hopkins brooded upon it, the more she began to wonder if the doll's disappearance might not have been the result of a visitation from Eugenie's companions of the grave, the old lady and the ginhead girl, meddling again.

A night or so ago, they had come to Mrs Hopkins, once again in a dream. Their visits were always preceded by the smell of pipe tobacco and the School-Mistress awoke to see the wizened old hag sitting on the end of the bed smoking her clay pipe and crooning quietly to herself. She paid no attention to Mrs Hopkins. Eugenie sat on the ginhead girl's lap. The little girl was scowling and plucking at the blanket in a doleful fashion.

'Well, what is it, Eugenie?' asked Mrs Hopkins. 'Will you stop plucking at the blanket? You will put holes in it.'

Eugenie's little chin quivered and her mouldering mouth turned downward in dismay. Mrs Hopkins felt immediately ashamed. Why would she greet her long-lost daughter like this? And yet the three visitors smelt so strongly of decay; mixed with the pipe tobacco, it made Mrs Hopkins feel quite ill.

'It is nice to see you,' she said to Eugenie, attempting to make amends. She intended to ignore the other two as she did not at all enjoy the way they seemed to judge her. The young girl seemed particularly scornful of her. Propping herself up on her elbows, Mrs Hopkins realised for the first time that the girl was wearing what looked like the rotting remains of a Biloela dungaree.

'Tell me, do you know what has become of Miss Minnie? She has disappeared. If you wish to have her, you are very welcome to her. After all, she is your doll. I feel that by rights she should have stayed with you. It was selfish of me to hang onto her. I would just like to know where she is, that's all.'

Eugenie folded her arms across her chest. A petulant look crossed her face. 'You did a bad thing,' the little ghost girl said.

'What bad thing?' said Mrs Hopkins. There were so many bad things she felt she had done in recent times. Which one was Eugenie alluding to in particular?

'Is it what I said to Josephine's mother?' asked Mrs Hopkins.

'Josephine is not your little girl,' said the ginhead angrily.

'No,' said Mrs Hopkins sadly. 'I realise that now.'

'You have done other bad things,' said the little girl.

A stab of fear pierced Mrs Hopkins' breast. What was Eugenie alluding to now? Was it Mrs Hopkins' dalliance with Mr Crabback? Did ghost children see everything? Was there anything they didn't see? How mortifying if that was the case!

'I intend to make things right,' she said. 'I shall go and see the mother and explain everything and apologise for my terrible action. Of course, in my defence it has to be said that the mother runs a notorious bawdy-house, and this was partly my reason for wishing to keep the child from possible harm in the first place.'

And here, to Mrs Hopkins' horror, Eugenie hoiked her head back and spat at her mother, just as Josephine had on that very first night at Biloela. The gob of spit landed on Mrs Hopkins nose, and then dropped onto her nightgown. She wiped it away as best she could, while the little ghost child cackled gleefully.

The ginhead girl hooted in delight. It seemed that she had taught the little girl how to spit, and she was well-pleased with the results.

'Well, Eugenie, I see that you have learned some very bad manners in the afterlife,' said Mrs Hopkins. Of course, there was no spittle; the whole thing was just a bad dream, but it was all very disquieting.

It took Mary-Ann just over a week to die from the septic peritonitis brought on by Mrs Crabback's abortion. Some kind of curette had been used to scrape out her innards; when the first time 'failed to take', Mrs Crabback had simply tried again. The poor girl sank quickly.

Once it became clear that the girl was gravely ill and unlikely to recover, Mrs Crabback again took leave of the island. Mrs Hopkins had not sighted her in the few days that she had been there.

'You will have to nurse the girl as best you can,' said Mr Crabback to Mrs Hopkins. They gazed upon the girl in the infirmary. She lay pale and weak, wracked with fever.

'But what of your wife?' demanded Mrs Hopkins. 'Should she not be taking care of her? She is a Nurse, after all.'

'Her business calls her back to Sydney,' said Mr Crabback.

'Then we must call Doctor Owens in at once. The girl needs to go to hospital or there is no hope for her,' said Mrs Hopkins.

'No!' cried Mr Crabback, for the presence of the school's resident physician, who apparently visited only occasionally (although Mrs Hopkins had never personally sighted him), seemed to greatly disturb him. 'She will rally! She is young and hearty. To bring in the Doctor will only create for us enormous difficulties; I believe he is great troublemaker. Almost certainly, we will lose our positions. And for what? For the sake of this foolish girl's inability to control her appetites.'

So Mrs Hopkins took on most of the nursing, although she had no skills in this area. The best she could do was hold the girl's hand and cool her feverish brow with a damp cloth. This seemed to bring the girl a small measure of relief. Every so often, Mrs Hopkins managed to get her to take a sip of sweet tea.

The pleasure this gave Mary-Ann was poignant to see, and she smiled feebly as she lowered herself down on the bed again. 'That's nice,' she whispered.

It occurred to Mrs Hopkins that Mary-Ann had not often been treated with kindness.

'Mrs Hopkins,' the girl asked weakly, just a day or two before she died, 'is it true what those ladies said, that I'm just a lowly gutter girl?'

'A gutter girl? Who called you a gutter girl?'

'Those young ladies at the house. The big house. Because I don't consider myself a gutter girl at all, and they made me feel very ashamed.'

'Why, of course you are not a gutter girl,' said Mrs Hopkins angrily. 'They are very ignorant. They do not know what they are talking about. You are the prettiest, sweetest, cleverest girl in the entire school.' She squeezed Mary-Ann's hand.

The girl smiled. It was the nicest thing that anyone had ever said to her.

The news of Mary-Ann's condition had plunged the girls into grief and despair. Her closest friends, the water sprites, gathered at the door of the infirmary to gaze upon her. They would not stop weeping, and sometimes Mrs Hopkins had to ask them to go away.

'She will know that she is dying,' she whispered to them. 'We must make her feel that she has a chance. The best you can do is go to your dormitories and pray for her.'

The girls at once did as they were bid, hoping that with their bowed heads and fervent prayers they might somehow make a difference.

Mrs Hopkins knew of course that if Mary-Ann did have a chance, it was a very slight one and depended entirely on getting a Doctor. They would not tell Mr Crabback, who seemed determined to prevent such an intervention. But perhaps she could be taken to hospital—could an operation of some sort save the girl?

'Mrs Baird,' she said, calling the House Matron over, 'take the next ferry and tell the Doctor he must come at once—that a girl is dying and we greatly fear for her life.'

At this, Mrs Baird burst into tears, but she pulled herself together within a few moments, wiping her eyes briskly. 'Shall I tell him . . . shall I tell him what it is?'

'What it is?'

'What it is that has made her so sick.'

'Yes. There is no point in concealing anything at this point. But he must hurry. Press upon him the urgency.'

Between the two women, and with a few coins from Miss Foy, they managed to scrape together the fare to the city. From there, Mrs Baird would have to find the Doctor's surgery. She had some idea that it was in Castlereagh Street, she had heard it mentioned.

'I will knock up all the Doctors' rooms until I find him,' she vowed.

'Yes,' cried Mrs Hopkins. 'And if you cannot find Doctor Owens, any Doctor will do. But he must hurry—that is the main thing!'

'Mrs Hopkins,' said Mary-Ann, 'will you ask my mother to come and see me?'

'Your mother! Why, of course,' exclaimed Mrs Hopkins. For some reason, she felt a wave of surprise that Mary-Ann even had a mother. These girls seemed so neglected and alone. 'Where would I find her? Do you have her address?'

'Oh, she can be found at the Theatre Royal most any night,' said Mary-Ann. 'She is on the stage.'

'How wonderful! Nor does it surprise me. Obviously you take after her.'

Even in her weakened state, the dying girl smiled proudly. 'Her stage name is Madame de La Forge. She is a singer and a dancer.'

'Then I'm sure I will have no difficulty in finding her. The Theatre Royal, you say. I will take the one o'clock steamer.'

'She may not be there so early,' said Mary-Ann. 'She works in the evening. On the stage.' This was explained carefully, though feebly, to Mrs Hopkins who obviously had no understanding of the glamour of such a place as the Theatre Royal.

'I see,' said Mrs Hopkins. 'Then I will go this evening. It is for the best as we are expecting the Doctor to arrive very shortly.'

In fact, Mrs Baird had returned after several hours. As a result of much pounding of the streets, she had succeeded in finding Doctor Owens' rooms, and had tried her best to impress upon him the urgency of the situation. He had claimed to be very busy but would 'do his best' to visit the island. And yet, Mrs Baird did not seem entirely confident that he would come, and conveyed her doubts to Mrs Hopkins.

'You told him that she is dying?' demanded the School-Mistress, and it came out rather more harshly than she intended.

'Yes!' cried Mrs Baird, and once again she burst into tears. 'Of course I did! He said since when was I a Doctor, so what would I know?'

'But he is coming, Mrs Baird?'

'I don't know! I think so!'

'But he must come!' cried Mrs Hopkins. 'We have nothing to give her for her pain. He must bring morphine; he must bring something!'

Mrs Hopkins felt a wave of despair; after all, the Doctor had failed to make an appearance when Josephine had been so ill and she had begged Mr Noyes to fetch him. But in that instance, the child had recovered of her own course; this situation was entirely different. She could not help feeling that an attitude prevailed that Mary-Ann had brought her plight upon herself, and thus deserved the consequences.

Nonetheless, she thanked Mrs Baird for her great efforts and told her of her plan to go to the Theatre Royal that very evening and have Mary-Ann's mother come to visit the girl.

Here, Mrs Baird bit her lip and shook her head sadly. 'Her mother is not on the stage,' she said. 'She is in the Maitland Gaol.'

'Are you sure?'

'Oh yes. She has been there for many years.'

'Many years?' Mrs Hopkins almost dared not ask what crime Mary-Ann's mother had committed to warrant such a sentence. And yet a great curiosity overwhelmed her. She knew so little, she realised, about the girls in their charge. 'What—what did she do?'

'She poisoned two husbands,' said Mrs Baird. 'Rat poison.'

Mary-Ann continued to sink. She had barely any pulse; she was pale and feverish and groaning in pain. There was still no sign of any Doctor, though Mrs Hopkins sent a girl to run down to the wharf at the arrival of every steamer.

'Why, Mary-Ann,' Mrs Hopkins whispered to the girl, 'I have just this moment come from seeing your mother! Oh, what a beauty she is—I see where you get your good looks! She was performing a wonderful dance on the stage, with feathers and suchlike, and the audience were standing up and clapping and cheering. Oh, it was wonderful!'

Mrs Baird and Miss Foy stared at Mrs Hopkins in a moment of incredulity.

'Oh yes,' said Mrs Baird, after a moment. 'She was wonderful!'

'Such a lovely voice,' added Miss Foy.

But by now, it was no longer clear that Mary-Ann could even hear them. She appeared to be unconscious. The older girls sat at the door of the infirmary weeping; even Amelia and Annie, now released from their confinement.

'She is coming,' whispered Mrs Hopkins, leaning close to Mary-Ann in the hope that she might hear her. 'Your mother is coming. She is catching the very next ferry, just as soon as she can get off the stage.'

Shortly thereafter, following days of suffering, Mary-Ann haemorrhaged violently and died.

Possessed of a great fury upon the death of the poor blighted girl, Mrs Hopkins marched directly to the Superintendent's house, and knocked smartly upon the door. Where was he? Why did he always seem to be cowering out of view, leaving the running of the institution to the three beleaguered women?

'She is dead,' she told him when he finally opened the door.

To her surprise, his eyes filled with tears and he commenced to cry. For a moment, she wondered if it was genuine grief and compassion at the loss of such a young life.

'This is dreadful news,' he said. 'It is the worst possible outcome, one I hoped we might be able to avoid.'

A wave of scorn overtook her. He was concerned about his own position: that's all it amounted to.

'Had we been able to procure the Doctor, she may have been saved,' said Mrs Hopkins. 'As it was, the girl had no chance.'

'*When lovely woman stoops to folly,*' sniffled Mr Crabback.

'She was a child and knew no better.'

The truth was, Mrs Hopkins felt, that the handsome Frenchman gave the girl some moments of affection, even tenderness—qualities in short supply at the institution.

Mr Crabback made a scoffing noise. 'She knew plenty well,' he said.

Mrs Hopkins bristled. 'I am going to gather the girls in the quadrangle. Will you speak to them and offer a prayer?'

'Oh no,' said Mr Crabback, and he was already beginning to close the door upon her. 'It is simply too delicate a matter for a man in my position to discuss. Surely, you must see that. No, as Acting Matron, I will leave the matter entirely to you.' Mr Crabback closed the door.

She stared at it in disbelief for a long moment, and then turned with great weariness and trudged back up to the school. In the last few days, nursing the dying girl, she had barely slept. Now what needed to be done? The girls comforted; Mr Noyes advised; Mary-Ann's mother must be written to.

Mrs Hopkins returned to her quarters and went through her prayer books. What could possibly offer these girls any solace upon the loss of their friend? And yet she must give them something. So she gathered them all in the quadrangle and spoke of Mary-Ann's lovely nature, and how surely she would be in heaven at this moment, out of pain and in the arms of Jesus, and they must all take comfort in that fact.

'Shall we sing the hymn?' she asked, turning to Mrs Baird doubtfully.

'Hymn?'

'"Shall We Meet Beyond the River"?'

The last time they had attempted it, on Mrs Dunstable's death, it had ended disastrously in lewd verse. But it was the only hymn that the girls knew. They sang it sadly and respectfully, and it seemed to help.

While the two Assistant Matrons bathed the girl and wound her in the least-patched sheet they could find, Mrs Hopkins took the Entrance Book into the schoolroom and wrote to Mary-Ann's mother.

Mrs Fenella Garbutt
Maitland Gaol Maitland

My dear Mrs Garbutt,
I regret that I must write to you with the gravest possible news. Your daughter, Mary-Ann, passed into the Hereafter this morning, as a result of—(here Mrs Hopkins hesitated—a miscarriage? 'a certain event'?)—*a certain event. Every possible comfort was made to alleviate her suffering.* (And yet, was it? A damp cloth, whispered lies; nothing, no morphine, no Doctor in attendance.) *She was dearly loved amongst the girls and indeed the matrons.*

She spoke of you throughout her ordeal with the greatest fondness.

I pray that our heavenly Father assuage the anguish of your bereavement, and leave you only her cherished memory.

I do indeed know what it is to lose a child and feel for you with all my heart.

Yours sincerely,
Constance Hopkins, School-Mistress
Biloela Industrial School for Girls

She gazed for a long moment at that last sentence:

I do indeed know what it is to lose a child and feel for you with all my heart.

Turning the pages now of the Entrance Book, she saw that Josephine had been the most recent arrival, only months ago now. She had arrived before the departure of the Baker-Hunts; hence her notes were quite clear. She had been removed from her mother, owing to her mother running a bagnio of ill-repute. There had been instances of stealing money from drunken customers, an occupation at which the child had been quite nimble; further, the girl had been exposed to sights of which, at her tender age, she should remain quite ignorant. The mother, noted Mr Baker-Hunt, while by all accounts attached to her daughter, seemed little concerned about the moral effects of such an environment. Mr Noyes himself had removed Josephine and placed her in Biloela.

Mrs Hopkins gazed at these notes for some time. It seemed to her almost to vindicate the great crime of what she had done. By assuming responsibility for Josephine's welfare by allowing the girl's mother to believe she had died, was she not giving the child a better hope for the future? She would ensure that the girl learned all the skills that would enable her to work in the future as a servant. In fact, all the girls must learn these skills; the school was remarkably remiss in such matters.

It was not, Mrs Hopkins told herself firmly, that Josephine was Eugenie brought back to her. The coincidence of the mismatched eyes meant nothing. She saw that now. If anything, Eugenie's two wretched companions from the paupers' grave had made that clear to her.

And yet, Josephine's attachment to Mrs Hopkins seemed to be daily strengthening. Quite often, she hung off Mrs Hopkins' skirts, and her manners were steadily improving. The girl never mentioned Henry's account of what had transpired on the wharf that morning with Bessie Briars—and after all, who could believe Henry, and as if Mrs Hopkins would ever do such a thing?

I do indeed know what it is to lose a child and feel for you with all my heart.

The address of Bessie Briars' bawdy-house was in Burnell Lane, Darlinghurst. Mrs Hopkins left the two Assistant Matrons to attend to the dinner meal (much to their irritation, because, not unlike the behaviour of Mr Crabback who was still apparently skulking in his quarters, afraid of the ramifications of the girl's death, Mrs Hopkins herself appeared to be doing a lot of skiving off.) She made no explanation, however, but simply caught the next available ferry to the city.

It took some little time to find the laneway in question, and Mrs Hopkins was immediately assailed with doubts. It was a muddy right-of-way, lined with shabby two-room shacks. Piles of stinking rubbish lay in the street; barefoot raggedy children clambered over them looking for food scraps. Rats scampered everywhere. Pickets had been pulled from fences, possibly for use as weapons.

Her heart pounded in her chest. She did not belong here, and to continue on down this laneway might lead perhaps to a mugging, a robbery. Rough sorts sitting in gutters made unpleasant jibes at her.

But finally, pressing a few paltry coins on a small child who had been following her down the laneway demanding money, Mrs Hopkins asked for directions and was given them to Bessie Briars' bawdy-house. She gazed at it in dismay. It was a shabby two-room hovel. Poor little Josephine, she thought to herself, to have grown up in such dissolute and unhygienic surroundings. Once again, she wondered fleetingly, had she not in fact done the right thing that morning on the wharf by telling Bessie Briars that the girl was dead?

She knocked on the door several times. A small commotion seemed to unfold within.

'Who is it?' called a female voice, after a moment.

'My name is Mrs Hopkins,' she responded through the closed door. 'I am the School-Mistress from Biloela. I have come with news of your daughter.'

Again, a few moments passed. Bessie Briars opened the door. She was wearing a grubby chemise, and had pulled a shawl around her against the cold.

Mrs Hopkins felt a wave of guilt and shock; the little woman looked even more fragile than she had as she fell to her knees on the wharf that dreadful morning.

'May I come in?' asked Mrs Hopkins. With a display of reluctance, Bessie opened the door just enough to allow her entry. She seemed somewhat ashamed at the circumstances in which the School-Mistress found her.

'What do you want?' Bessie asked.

Mrs Hopkins had in fact rehearsed what she might say on the ferry over, and now, taking a breath, she launched into it. 'Mrs Briars, I have come to you as the bearer of good news, and to beg of you your forgiveness for the terrible misdeed I have committed against you.'

How pompous and priggish she sounded. There was no doubt that she lacked the common touch.

Bessie Briars stared at her in bewilderment.

'Josephine is not dead,' continued Mrs Hopkins. 'She was poorly, certainly, and it was true that I feared for her life. But she is not dead; in fact, she is very much alive and well.'

Bessie Briars continued to stare at her a long moment. Then, belying her frail state and diminutive size, she reached out and slapped Mrs Hopkins hard across the face, knocking her to the ground and bloodying her lip.

'Why would you do such a thing?' the woman wailed, standing over the fallen School-Mistress. 'I have wept and wept for weeks on end.'

And then she kicked Mrs Hopkins hard in the ribs, once, twice, three times, causing the School-Mistress to groan in agony. What could she say to stop this onslaught, to somehow make amends? She was so winded by the attack she could barely speak.

'I lost my own daughter, you see,' she gasped. She began to fear that her ribs had been broken, for it hurt to breathe. 'Josephine was so like her. It is no excuse, of course. And yet I was quite unhinged at the time, I believe.'

Bessie stared down at her a long time, occasionally offering another kick should Mrs Hopkins make any attempt to get up. The realisation that her daughter was in fact alive, after these long weeks of grief and misery, seemed to be slowly dawning on her, and the deep lines between her brow seemed to soften.

'Will you buy me a jug of beer?' she asked. 'By way of making up for things?'

'Why, of course,' said Mrs Hopkins.

And with her few remaining coins, the same neighbouring child was sent out for the beverage.

Bessie hoisted Mrs Hopkins roughly off the floor and onto her bed. Once the beer was delivered, she drank it down and a sweet smile spread across her face, her spirits rising with it. When she had finished, she wiped her lips and politely requested another jug.

Although Mrs Hopkins had little money, she felt she could scarcely refuse her.

'I can barely believe it,' Bessie kept repeating, shaking her head. 'Oh, it is glorious news. My own little girl, still alive!'

'May I see her?' she asked eventually in a tentative voice. 'I would give anything just to touch her little face.'

And in fact, Mrs Hopkins had begun to form a plan on the steamer trip over. Christmas was only weeks away. Might not Biloela have a Christmas party, to which family members (suitable ones, of course) could be invited? Surely even Mr Noyes could not wish to deprive the girls of such a simple pleasure on the Holy Day? And perhaps his wealthy benefactor friends, of whom he had occasionally alluded, could be prevailed upon to contribute to the costs in some way?

'Oh yes,' announced Mrs Hopkins happily. 'For of course, we are to have a grand Christmas party! Mothers and fathers and brothers and sisters will all be invited. There will be a big Christmas tree, which the girls will decorate, and under the tree, a present for each of them: inspirational books such as those of Ester Reid; ribbons and fancy-work threads; and musical instruments and pretty lace-edged handkerchiefs. And we will sing carols around the harmonium! And our dinner—roast beef with potatoes fried in goose fat; plum puddings with custard and cream! Cakes and fruit and lollies! And then after the dinner meal, the girls can play rounders with their friends and brothers and sisters until it's time to go home!'

Bessie clasped her hands together in delight; tears sprang to her eyes.

'Why, you mustn't cry!' exclaimed Mrs Hopkins, patting her arm.

'It's just the thought of seeing her again!' cried Bessie through her tears.

The two women took leave of each other in the friendliest possible terms. Bessie even apologised for the kicks, and wiped Mrs Hopkins' cut and bloody lip with the cleanest handkerchief she could find.

Mrs Hopkins caught the four o'clock steamer back to Biloela, and just as she had on the day of her arrival, she eschewed the saloon in favour of a hard wooden bench on the front deck. She felt a great buoyancy in her heart from having made things right with Josephine's mother, having not realised up to that point what a great burden it had placed upon her. And looming large within that burden had been the feeling that in so doing she had betrayed the memory of her own little girl, her dear little Eugenie with the mismatched eyes. She wished fervently that she could make it up to the girl. She felt badly that the old crone and the ginhead took better care of her little one in the paupers' grave than she did.

But of course, Mrs Hopkins told herself, what could she do in reality?

The child was dead and buried.

Sitting on the hard bench, shielding her small notebook as best she could from the spray, she began to compose a list of requirements for the Christmas party. Firstly, she must prevail upon Mr Noyes and his wealthy associates; he had not seemed entirely unsympathetic to the idea of the girls having some relief from their prison-like conditions, and surely he could see how, even if just for one day, the Holy Day, they might be reunited with their loved ones. And no doubt, appealing to their Christian spirit, his friends and associates could be prevailed upon to provide the tree and the presents and the food. Why (it suddenly occurred to her joyfully), she could write to the Randwick Asylum for Destitute Children, and ask that Rosabella's brothers, the boy bushrangers, be released for the day! Imagine how delighted Rosabella would be at the sight of her brothers, spruced up for the day as best they could manage, alighting from the steamer and joining the festivities!

And of course, all the girls—she must go through the Entrance Book and find out all their details and write to their families, inviting them to the party. She thought back to the day of the brawl in the classroom, and poor Catherine's misery at missing her mother. And what about poor Amelia, completely without a family? How to not make her feel excluded? Well, it would just be up to Mrs Hopkins to take care of her throughout the day.

The ticket collector ventured out onto the deck now and eyed her dubiously. Clearly, he recognised her from the day that Bessie Briars had come to visit, and Mrs Hopkins had refused the stricken woman so much as a cup of tea. She paid for her ticket and ignored him. She would not allow him to dampen her mood.

The paddle steamer pulled into the wharf and Mrs Hopkins alighted. She would be just in time to assist with the girls' evening chores, and then it would be time for tea. She must take some of the burden from the two Assistant Matrons as she had been relying too heavily upon them.

Glancing down into the shallows lapping around the pylons of the wharf, something caught her eye drifting in the water. She let out a cry: it was Miss Minnie! How had the doll ever found its way into the water? No matter; Mrs Hopkins heart thumped joyfully. The reappearance of the doll seemed to be the fitting end to the day. She would rescue the doll, clean her up (even from this short distance she could see that the rag doll seemed steeped in mud), and then at last reunite her with Eugenie on one of her nocturnal visits. They would play one of their 'Miss Minnie' games, and the little girl would chortle merrily with laughter.

Tugging off her boots and scooping up her skirts, Mrs Hopkins hurried down to the shallows to scoop the doll from the water. The steamer blasted its horn and began to pull away from the wharf; the great wash that this created collected the doll from the shallows and pushed it out to sea. A surge of alarm overtook Mrs Hopkins. Having found the doll, she could not possibly lose it now. She lunged after it and made a desperate scoop for the doll. Maddeningly, she missed; the churning wash pulled Miss Minnie further away; the turbulence knocked the School-Mistress from her feet. Under the water she went, then with great effort, she pulled herself to her feet, gasping. The kicking she had endured to the ribs from Bessie Briars was not helping; she could not seem to get a proper breath of air. Mrs Hopkins looked about in a panic. Her little notebook, with all of its careful Christmas planning, fell from her pocket into the water. The ink washed away almost at once. She tried to grasp hold of it, but the notebook slipped away from her. And yet, as she became aware of her mounting predicament, it seemed imperative that these plans for the Christmas party be preserved. The girls must surely have something to look forward to.

Miss Minnie seemed yet further out of reach now, but Mrs Hopkins would not give up; she was determined to reach the doll for the sake of her daughter. Under the water she fell once more, her sodden mourning skirts pulling her under. With great effort, she pulled herself to her feet, gasping for breath. The steamer had pulled away now; there was no one about to witness her plight. And yet gazing across the water to the opposite shore, her heart thumped with a sudden joy.

She realised, as had happened that day of the waking vision, that she was being summoned to continue onwards. A small girl with golden curls was beckoning, calling her across to the fair, celestial shore; to the Bright Forever.

Author's note

The true story of Biloela Industrial School on Cockatoo Island is so desperately sad and horrifying, that I feel a good deal of guilt for having concocted my little fiction against such a bleak and terrible backdrop.

So my meagre way of making amends is to try to give some kind of account of what transpired there, lest the horrors be forgotten.

In 1866, in response to public concern about the problem of child destitution and delinquency, the Act for the Relief of Destitute Children (also known as the Industrial Schools Act) was passed by the Government of New South Wales under the guidance of Henry Parkes, with the intention of providing care, education and training of neglected and abandoned children. The idea of Industrial Schools was that these children would be trained with the necessary domestic skills, that they might go out to service. There was a desperate shortage of servants in Sydney at the time.

The Newcastle Industrial School was established on 6 August 1867 in the former Military Barracks on the Newcastle Government Domain. The Newcastle site was open to public view—and the inmates, almost all used to wandering freely and not having to follow rules—protested their confinement with wild rioting, obscene language, lewd behaviour and frequent escapes.

> Latterly, the girls confined in the institution have been encouraged in their outrageous conduct by a number of vagabonds who are in the habit of congregating outside the walls and inciting them to revolt.
>
> Riots ensued.

> The girls barricaded the doors, broke up the bedsteads, smashed the crockery, and using the broken bedsteads broke every window and window frame in the Industrial School wing. Nine more girls were placed in the cells where they set up the most unearthly yells and foul language, which continued throughout the night. (From the Newcastle Industrial School for Girls website.)

It became apparent that the situation could not continue. In 1871, the girls were moved to the abandoned convict barracks of Cockatoo Island, safely out of public view. The institution was re-named 'Biloela' (an Aboriginal word meaning 'white cockatoo') in an apparent bid to remove any association with its convict past. That appears to be the only attempt to soften the environment into which the girls were interred. A bleaker, more prison-like environment could scarcely be imagined. (It can still be visited on Cockatoo Island.) And yet the girls, aged from three years to the age of eighteen when they were cast out once again upon the streets, having committed no crime except to be destitute, spent their entire girlhoods locked up like prisoners. To make matters worse, a new Superintendent, George Lucas, was installed, along with his bad-tempered wife as Matron. He was illiterate and incompetent, and prone to rages.

There seems to have been remarkably little compassion for their plight; in fact, on the whole, girls were despised and vilified by the public. This from *Sydney Punch* (26 July 1871) is typical:

> They are Arabians of the most untameable breed, and the Government having caught and caged them at Cockatoo Island, is through its officials, abused, slanged, pelted and clawed by them daily. They have no respect for King, Kaiser, Constitution, Colonial Secretary or Constable. They shriek and blaspheme in defiance of their pastors and masters and the classic shades of Cockatoo—now called 'Biloela' out of compliment to its fair occupants—are desecrated by the revels of nymphs whose goings on are really awful.

Certainly, the girls rioted, smashing windows and setting fire to bedding. For this, they were punished by extended periods of being locked up in darkened dormitories for extended periods on bread and water. Sometimes they were interred in solitary confinement (again, for days on end) in underground cells, remnants of the convict days, carved into the rock.

Horrifyingly, as evidenced in the Commission witness testimonies, there seems to be almost no compunction about locking girls in these underground solitary confinement cells—one of which can be viewed to this day on Cockatoo Island. In the Commission testimonies, only Sister Mary Benedict, who would bring religious instruction to the Catholic girls on Sundays, expressed any protest:

> *Commission:* You think that shutting them in the dormitories would be better than putting them in the cells?
>
> *Sister Mary Benedict:* I would not put them down that hole at all—I would not allow it; it is cruel in the extreme. I would not put them there myself; it would put a woman out of her mind. If I were put down there, I know I could not be put down the second time. I would die.

Scant attention appears to have been paid to her. In fact, Dr Evans, the school's Medical Officer, offered this:

> Believe that when insubordinate, the girls should be put into the cells, and then if they choose to tear their clothes, their hands should be fastened behind them until they were quite quiet.

In 1873, a Commission was conducted into Public Charities. Members of the Commission visited the island and were shocked by what they discovered:

> On arriving at the Industrial School, it was found that a number of windows had been broken in a riotous disturbance which had

taken place some few days before, and a number of the girls engaged in the disturbance were still locked up in two of the dormitories.

One of the girls requested permission to make a statement to the Commission was called in and examined. She complained of ill treatment on the part of Mr and Mrs Lucas, stating that both these officers had beaten her, and other girls named, by knocking them down, striking them with the fist, a cane and a broomstick; and by knocking their heads against a wall on which some caricatures of Mr and Mrs Lucas had been drawn. She exhibited the marks of blows recently inflicted in support of her statement. The other girls named by her were called in and examined. Every one of these girls bore marks of violence and corroborated the account given by the first witness of the ill-usage to which they had been subjected.

One girl was found with discoloured bruises on her arms, shoulders and bosom, and asserted, as did the other girls, that they were the effects of blows inflicted by Mr Lucas.

They complained of having been beaten, kicked, dragged by the hair, caught by the throat, and having had their heads struck and rubbed against a wall, apparently in a rough effort to make them rub out a caricature on the wall with their hair.

The former witnesses having complained of being locked up in a dark room, which was so oppressive and foul from its closeness that they were unable to sleep, the Commission repaired to No. 3 dormitory, the room spoken of. On opening the door of this dormitory, eight girls, from fourteen to seventeen years of age, were found in a half-naked condition, and all without shoes and stockings. The room had a stone floor, was without a chimney, had every window boarded up, was without an article of furniture, and had a foul and sickly smell, every call of nature being there answered by its inmates. On the door being closed upon the Members of the Commission, it was impossible to see each other until accustomed to the darkness. Into this room, when still damp from a recent scrubbing, it appeared the eight girls had been put, and kept in the dark from Friday morning till the visit of the Commission on Tuesday night, in the semi-nude condition in which they were found. Fed on bread and water, they drank, as they said, like dogs, from a bucket placed in the room, no utensil being allowed. They were so hoarse from the effects of the confinement in the closed up room and sleeping on the flags, no bedding being allowed them but blankets, that they were almost unable to speak, and the Commission deemed it advisable to recommend their immediate release from confinement, as well as a supply of clothing and mattresses to those still locked up.

The Commission regretted to witness a most unseemly display of temper on the part of Mr and Mrs Lucas in the presence of the girls, on a suggestion being made to them by the Commission as to the advisability of opening one of the windows for the admission of light and air, and of adopting some more judicious method of dealing with the girls incarcerated in the darkened dormitory.

The Commission, to their credit, conducted an exhaustive enquiry, interviewing in detail everyone from the Lucases to the girls themselves. (This extraordinary document can be viewed in the State Library of New South Wales). Among their findings, they found that Biloela was unsuited as an Industrial School, owing to its prison associations and inaccessibility from Sydney, and should be moved as soon as possible to some situation more accessible to Sydney; that the management of Mr and Mrs Lucas was defective (they were removed from their positions, much to their outrage); that corporal punishment was too frequently resorted to; that the institution be placed entirely under the control of a woman; that in the new institution, 'care should be taken that the older and more vicious girls be isolated from the younger and more innocent'; that it was highly important that some provision be made for their supervision after they have left the Industrial School.

And yet Biloela remained at the Cockatoo Island site until 1887, some fourteen years after the Commission's findings. It was then moved to Parramatta, to become the Parramatta Industrial School, which has its own bleak history. In 1888, Biloela became a women's prison; its offenders chiefly 'vagrants, drunkards and prostitutes'. It is dispiriting to think how many Biloela girls may have returned there.

The Sad Story of Sarah Bourke

In the Commission testimonies, one particular girl stands out. Her name was Sarah Bourke; at the age of fifteen, in 1871, she was brought before the Central Police Court, charged with habitually wandering about in the company of prostitutes. Her mother instituted the proceedings, and Sarah was sent to Biloela.

Sarah Bourke's name features quite prominently within the pages of the Commission. She seems to have been something of a ringleader among the girls; on the whole, many of them seemed to have had a great respect and fondness for her, if for some laced perhaps with a tinge of fear.

> **Sarah Littlewood (another inmate)**
> We sat there talking till at last the candle went out. We were a good while before we could find the matches, and at last Sarah Bourke said, 'I can find the matches'; then she went to some place and she found them. Then she said, 'What do you say if we have a fire and we burn the door down?' And I said, 'O don't Sarah—don't let us burn the door.' They would not mind me, but got all the matting together and set it on fire . . .

In October 1871, only months after her admission, eight girls, including Sarah, were charged with damaging and destroying government property on Cockatoo Island. Thirty panes of glass were broken.

Sarah Bourke and her friend Jane Murphy received an extra two months for damaging a door, four months at Darlinghurst Gaol in total. One of the girls said they had provocation, as there were six girls placed in a dormitory with nothing but the bare flags to lie on. They were ordered to pay 1.3s each, in default to go to gaol for two months with hard labour (*The Empire*, 19 October 1871). Once placed in the water police boat, the girls apparently commenced singing all the way to Circular Quay.

In March 1872, Mrs Kelly, the School-Mistress, by all accounts a kindly and concerned woman, much loathed by Mr Lucas, the Superintendent, selected Sarah Bourke to be a School Monitor in her schoolroom. Whether this was a case of keeping the troublesome ones close by or allowing them an opportunity to redeem themselves is not entirely clear. By June 1872, it had come to an end. Sarah and three other girls were confined to the No. 3 dormitory for ten days on bread and water for riotous behaviour.

> *Commission:* When you were leaving No. 3 dormitory, to go over to No. 5 at our request, I believe that some of the girls you were leaving cried when they wished you goodbye.
>
> *Sarah Bourke:* Yes.
>
> *Commission:* What was it Mr Lucas said about their 'blubbering'?
>
> *Sarah Bourke:* He said they were a pack of babies to be blubbering and I was gammoning all this to get away.
>
> *Commission:* We know that you have a good deal of influence over the girls, and you have promised us to use that influence with them to prevent them from rioting in the future?
>
> *Sarah Bourke:* Yes, I have.
>
> *Commission:* And will you do so?

Sarah Bourke: Yes.

Commission: When you come out, you will use your influence with them to keep them quiet?

Sarah Bourke: Yes, but we do not care too much about coming out just yet, for we know our lives will be made a misery to us by Mr Lucas after what we have said here.

At one point, Mr and Mrs Lucas (the Superintendent and Matron) were using her as a servant in their quarters. Girls were often given the role of 'servant' for the matrons, to assist them in the privacy of their quarters. It is not clear from the Commission notes whether this was in order to teach the girls some skills in service (there does not seem to be much of this at Biloela) or give them a break from the drudgery of their day-to-day lives.

Mrs Connell (Gate-keeper): It is not an easy matter for anyone to manage those girls. It is very difficult, for there are two or three of them set to watch a person while the rest are doing mischief.

Commission: How do you mean?

Mrs Connell: I mean if one of the matrons is occupied with anything and requires a couple of girls and they want to scheme away, they will watch their opportunity and scheme until they have their wishes fulfilled.

Commission: They will do that?

Mrs Connell: Yes.

Commission: How well that girl Sarah Bourke got away the morning before yesterday. How did she do it?

Mrs Connell: It was by the half past 7 boat, she went up the river. I cannot tell how she managed to get the clothes, but she got on board the steamer and escaped.

Commission: Had she a hat on?

Mrs Connell: Yes, some kind of bonnet on. She got up the river as far as Gladesville.

Commission: How did she get through the gate?

Mrs Connell: She did not get out at the gate, but she got through a hole in the fence—a large hole that was made for the occasion.

Commission: Has she been brought back?

Mrs Connell: Yes, she was brought back by half past 9 o'clock. The police found her.

Commission: Do you know what duty she was performing in the institution?

Mrs Connell: She was on Mrs Lucas's place.

Commission: Is she usually a well-behaved girl?

Mrs Connell: Well, I cannot say much for her. She is one of those who ran away before—one of those that were in gaol.

Commission: And you mean to say that this girl got away from the institution and from the island, dressed up in clothes not belonging to the institution, and without any person on the place knowing about it.

Mrs Connell: She did; she got on the boat and went away . . .

Commission: She was acting as a servant to Mr and Mrs Lucas?

> *Mrs Connell:* Yes, and Mrs Lucas said that the policeman came and told them she was on the boat. The policeman saw her on the boat and he said, 'You belong to the institution?' She said, 'Yes, I was there but I have a place on the river, and I came down and slept at Mrs Connell's place last night.' So the policeman took it to be the truth and let her go. Then he came up to me, and said, 'Is Sarah Bourke in the institution?' I said, 'She ought to be.' He said, 'Is she out at service?' I said, 'No, she should be here.' He said, 'She has gone off in the boat, and she told me that she slept last night at your place.' So I said, 'No, she did not sleep at my place—she ought to be in the institution.' He then went down and reported it, and they went up the river and brought her back.

In May 1874, Sarah Bourke turned eighteen and was released from Biloela. Horrifyingly, it appears that the girls were offered no support at all upon their release, but simply cast out upon the streets to fend for themselves as best they could. Almost immediately, Sarah fell upon hard times. In August 1874, only a couple of months after her release, she was brought up for protection, supposed to be of unsound mind. She was remanded to gaol for medical treatment.

From there, following her progress as best I could from police and court reports, she was in and out of gaol on a regular basis:

> 9 October 1877. Darlinghurst Gaol Entrance Book. Sarah is charged with 'threatening'. Gets 1 month.
> 20 November 1877. SB sent to Lunatic Reception House, 'positively mad from effects of drink'.
> 18 February 1877. Darlinghurst Gaol. 'Unsound mind.'
> 11 September 1879. Darlinghurst Gaol. 'Drunk.' 4 days.
> 10 October 1879. Darlinghurst Gaol. 'Drunk.' 4 days.
> 23 January 1880. Darlinghurst Gaol. 'Drunk.' 4 days.
> 2 March 1880. Darlinghurst Gaol. 'Drunk.' 7 days.
> 17 March 1880. Darlinghurst Gaol. 'Assault.' One month.

9 June 1880. Darlinghurst Gaol. 'Drunk.' 4 days.
14 June 1880. Darlinghurst Gaol. 'Drunk.' 4 days.
4 April 1881. Darlinghurst Gaol. 'Drunk.' 7 days.
28 April 1881. Darlinghurst Gaol. 'Drunk.' 7 days.
13 May 1881. Darlinghurst Gaol. 'Insulting words.' One month.
28 June 1881. Darlinghurst Gaol. 'Drunk.' 7 days.
19 August 1881. Darlinghurst Gaol. 'Drunk.' 7 days.
27 August 1881. Darlinghurst Gaol. 'Drunk.' 4 days.
4 March 1882. Darlinghurst Gaol. 'Drunk.' 7 days.
28 April 1882. 'Stealing.' 48 hours.
10 November 1882. 'Indecent language.' One month.
14 March 1884. 'Obscene language.' One month.
29 October 1884. Darlinghurst Gaol. 'Drunk.' 4 days.
19 September 1885. 'Riotous.' 7 days.
24 December 1885. Darlinghurst Gaol. 'Drunk.' 7 days.
13 February 1891. 'Drunk and obscene language.' 7 days.
13 March 1891. Biloela Gaol. 'Drunk and dis.'
23 May 1891. Biloela Gaol. 'Drunk.' 7 days.

It is dismaying to think she ended up back at Biloela. How must that have felt for her? These are the last references that I could find for Sarah Bourke within the court reports of the newspapers, when she disappears from view. She would have been thirty-five years of age.

Of course, when one looks at the horrors of the Don Dale Youth Detention Centre in the Northern Territory, with its use of tear gas, restraint chairs, cable ties and solitary confinement, one feels that over a hundred years later, nothing has changed and that abject cruelty towards children in these conditions continues.